The Conclave

Michael Bracewell was born in 1958. He has published two novellas, *The Crypto-Amnesia Club* (1988) and *Missing Margate* (1988), and one novel, *Divine Concepts of Physical Beauty* (1989). He lives and works in Surrey.

Michael Bracewell

The Conclave

Minerva

A Minerva Paperback
THE CONCLAVE

First published in Great Britain 1992
by Martin Secker & Warburg Ltd
This Minerva edition published 1993
by Mandarin Paperbacks
an imprint of Reed Consumer Books Ltd
Michelin House, 81 Fulham Road, London SW3 6RB
and Auckland, Melbourne, Singapore and Toronto

Copyright © 1992 by Michael Bracewell
The author has asserted his moral rights

AUTHOR'S NOTE
Some readers might assume that *The Conclave*
is thinly veiled autobiography. It isn't. – M.B.

The lines on pp. 78, 128 and 165 are from *Collected Poems*
by T.S. Eliot, quoted by permission of Faber & Faber Ltd;
those on p. 183 from 'Letter to Lord Byron' by W.H. Auden
in *The English Auden*, ed. Edward Mendelson, quoted by
permission of Faber & Faber Ltd; those on p. 246 from
Swann in Love by Marcel Proust, trs. Terence Kilmartin,
quoted by permission of Chatto & Windus; those on p. 289
from 'I am the Fly', quoted by permission of
Carlin Music Corporation, Iron Bridge House,
3 Bridge Approach, London NW1 8BD; those on p. 310
from 'Getting away with it', published by
Warner Chappell, quoted by permission
of International Music Publications,
Southend Road, Woodford Green, Essex IG8 8HN

A CIP catalogue record for this title
is available from the British Library
ISBN 0 7493 9167 7

Printed and bound in Great Britain
by Cox and Wyman Ltd, Reading, Berks

For Andrew Renton

With thanks to my parents

Some shooting stars suddenly slid past, describing a course in the sky like the parabola of a monstrous rocket.

'My word,' said Bouvard, 'look at those worlds disappearing.'

Pecuchet replied:

'If our world in its turn danced about, the citizens of the stars would be no more impressed than we are now. Ideas like that are rather humbling.'

'What is the point of it all?'

'Perhaps there isn't a point.'

'Yet . . .' and Pecuchet repeated the word two or three times, without finding anything more to say.

Gustave Flaubert, *Bouvard and Pecuchet*, 1881

One: *An Aesthetic Education*

It was the 12th of June, 1987. The evening was warm, despite an earlier shower. The french windows, which gave the dining room its character, were open. Outside, the damp garden was fragrant, and dim. Some white blossom, which overhung the wall, was luminous in the dusk. In the dining room, six young people were conversing. On the table before them were dessert dishes, wine bottles, cheese and fruit. Four thick white candles shed a soft light.

At one end of the table, seated slightly apart, a young man with dark, short hair and a satisfied expression was studying his reflection in the bright silver blade of an unused knife.

'At thirty,' he said, slowly, 'you've got the face that you deserve.'

His neighbour nodded.

To the young man's left, sitting with her back to him, a young woman was gesticulating with her right hand, as she corrected herself in mid-sentence.

'No, I know what it was,' she said, 'they're not Chinese, they're Japanese . . . Or is it the other way round?' She laughed, and shook her head. 'Anyway, I used to know this place where you could get them . . .'

The young man smiled, and then continued to scrutinise his features. I wonder if I'll remember this evening when I'm thirty? he thought.

Three years later, when he was thirty, he didn't.

The young man's name was Martin Graham Crispin Knight. He was born on the 12th of July 1960. Years later, when he acknowledged that the subject which interested him most was himself, he liked to believe that his place of birth – on the extreme southern edge of London – had installed an argument within him, and a sense of contradiction, the source of which lay in the fact that he was brought up between the city and the country. His family home was located upon a peninsula of dwellings which seemed only to exist as a point between two views: to the north, the London skyline; to the south, the colourless grass and the sparse, melancholy trees of the North Downs. He believed that these two views, the urban and the pastoral, had tugged at his spirit with equal force. He also liked to think that his proximity during childhood to these two opposed prospects, both of them almost within reach but neither of them actually possessed, had been his introduction to the erotic. Such theories, verging upon the superstitious, were typical of him.

His childhood was as complex or as dull as he was. Complexity and dullness, in fact, lived side by side within him. He had a sister, Anne, who was two years his senior, and he grew up afraid of her ability to crush him with a word or a glance. As he was quick to respond to either flattery or criticism, Anne's wounding comments made him painfully aware of his heightened sensitivity. Worst of all, his sister knew how to make him look ridiculous in his own eyes, and she would puncture his pretensions and his enthusiasms in such a manner that he quickly learnt the short distance between self-satisfaction and self-hatred.

His earliest memories (he thought) were of sunlight. A colour snapshot of Martin, taken when he was two years old, seemed to qualify this. The photograph showed a bewildered child, with blond hair and serious eyes, gesticulating towards the camera as he sat, encircled by a moat of brightness, upon the lawn on a summer day. Behind him, out of focus, pink and yellow roses stood out against the grey fence.

As Martin ceased to be a baby and became a little boy, two fundamental aspects of his personality took their place within him. The first of these was an inclination towards sentimentality. Torrents of pity, laced with an intoxicating sadness, would unbalance the small boy at the slightest provocation. But Martin was aware, even then, that the basis of his sadness was self-indulgent: he was crying for himself because he was crying. His sister, on these occasions, showed him no mercy.

The second important strand to emerge so early in the pattern of Martin's personality was his virtually morbid relationship with the weather: each change in light or temperature would bring about exaggerated shifts in his sense of hope, despair, or contentment.

Taken in isolation, neither of these traits was remarkable; but mixed together, to create a concentrate of sensitivity, they began to dominate Martin, and to shape the manner in which he lived.

Martin Knight interpreted himself through his surroundings. Beyond puberty, he would enrich this process by interpreting himself through other people, as well as through his surroundings. In this manner he studied himself, and developed himself, and tried to live with beauty. He wanted beauty more than anything else. Frequently troubled, and prone to despair, he regarded beauty as the eye of the hurricane.

A further photograph in the Knights' family album showed Martin at eleven years old. By now he was a pretty child, with dark brown hair parted at the side, a small, freckled nose and thin lips which seemed too red. His expression remained serious. His brown eyes were flecked with gold, and they seemed to glare at the photographer from beneath long, black lashes. He was dressed in a white shirt and a pair of grey trousers. He looked neither weak nor athletic. But he did look vulnerable.

Martin's father was a stern, forceful man. He was the manager of an office in Holborn, where technical drawings were made. As a child, Martin imagined this office to be like a huge schoolroom, with tall, Gothic windows and with his father, all-powerful, seated upon a dais at one end. This schoolroom would be high up. Slanting, dust-filled sunbeams would fall across the desks and the drawings. Far below there would be a busy, old-fashioned city street.

On rare occasions, Mr Knight would bring his children some big sheets of paper home from the office. Anne would trace horses and Martin would begin vast, fantastic landscapes. There was often a quarrel over crayons. Both the children were afraid of their father. He was tall, and brisk, and his hair was silver before its time. Nobody in the family dared to contradict him, but they all sought his praise.

Martin's mother was petite and pretty. She was cheerful and energetic, and before she married she was going to be an actress. While she did housework she sang, in a jazz soprano. 'I Could Have Danced All Night' was her favourite song. She seemed to have two, quite separate lives. One was her daily routine with her children; the other, invisible, was her relationship with her husband. When she was dressed for special occasions, in a dark blue dress and high-heeled evening shoes, Martin thought she looked beautiful. He always knew when his parents were going out for the evening because he could smell the strong, citric scent of his mother's hairspray.

Anne, pursuing her robust and independent path, was popular, out-going and contemptuous of everything save her immediate enthusiasms. Between the ages of eight and sixteen these enthusiasms were: horses, Jesus and boys.

From the beginning, Martin regarded his home as a collage of atmospheres. Its position, standing in an isolated road which was called Thornby Avenue, was more important to the young boy than its box-like shape or modest size. Thornby Avenue seemed to lead nowhere. It terminated at the edge of an expanse of open country which the residents called the Heath. Martin's home seemed to cling to the Heath, and from his bedroom window, which was at the back of the house, he could look out over the acres of long, windswept grass and see, at a distance which his youth exaggerated, the overgrown wood of mournful silver-birch trees that surrounded a derelict asylum. The Heath was as big as a sea to Martin, and he would survey its vastness from his room as though he lived upon a high cliff.

The Heath installed a further sense of paradox in Martin. His niche of middle-class comfort, it seemed, stood side by side with a tract of romantic wilderness. The old asylum, and a shallow quarry which lay to one side of it, increased the mystery of this wilderness. Neither the quarry – which contained some charred branches and an old iron cistern, crimson with rust – nor the decaying asylum attracted many of the local people who strolled with their dogs in the evening. But for Martin, both of these melancholy sites were a source for games and reverie. Sometimes, he shared his explorations with his best friend, a pretty, fair-haired girl called Christine.

Christine was the same age as Martin, and she too lived in Thornby Avenue. Their parents were friends, and the children had played together since they were babies. By the time that Christine and Martin were eleven years old their friendship was as strong as ever. Christine was the more reckless of the two, but it was Martin's imagination which inspired their pastimes. In particular they loved to play in the wood which lay before the asylum.

At dusk, during the late spring, Martin and Christine would make their way to the secret camp which they had established deep amongst the trees, and there, within the tangled under-growth, they would dig, ceaselessly, an enormous hole. Martin, as the light began to fade, would beseech Christine to join him in spending the night away from home, seated before a crackling fire. 'I can't,' she would say, 'and neither can you.'

The purpose of the children's excavations was never clear. Grave, tunnel, or bunker – it didn't matter. Soon they became too old for the game, and spent their time instead throwing stones at the rusted cistern, or searching for interesting rubbish.

In the summer of 1973, just before he was sent off to be a boarding pupil at Tiles, a public school in Kent, Martin became aware of art. The sense of his discovery could be expressed thus: to be able to do one thing well is to engage with beauty.

Martin Knight was thirteen years and two months old when he entered Withers House at Tiles. This fact was recorded on the house list: M. G. C. Knight (W) 13.2. Seeing himself denoted so baldly, Martin feared for the safety of his complex and extraordinary character. He was homesick, and wept for the first three weeks.

And yet Tiles was more beautiful, as a place, than anywhere else that Martin had ever been connected with. At least, he thought that it was. The main school buildings were grey, and covered with copper-coloured ivy. Vast, flawless lawns, separated by leafy avenues and shadowed in their corners by spreading cedar trees, ran down to the acres of playing fields. The seven boarding houses seemed imposing to the youngest boys who arrived at them, and the complexities of their geography were mirrored in the traditions and codes of conduct upon which they were run. Amongst the older boys, a counter-culture of pop music and politics was rife and controversial. During his first term, in both the weekly Big School assembly and in the dim, soaring school chapel, Martin witnessed demonstrations: a refusal to stand when the Head Boy entered, a stamping of feet during the Chaplain's sermon. The Upper School, the Headmaster said, was the worst that Tiles had ever known. Martin found this rebellion romantic, and regarded its leaders as gods.

Tiles, however, was a fake. It posed as an ancient seat of learning, informed by centuries of scholarship and achievement, and yet, in truth, it was a middle-class invention of the late Victorian period. Even its buildings were hastily constructed copies of more venerable structures. One block of classrooms would mimic the shape of a West Sussex convent; another would resemble a London barracks. Behind the ivy-clad façades of the boarding houses there were ugly red-brick extensions which dated from the 1930s and which had been added in a summer to accommodate the growing number of boys from Kent and Surrey whose parents had decided that Tiles offered 'breeding' at reasonable rates. Thus, superficially, the school could pass for a mellowed haven of antiquity and grace; within, it was mediocre.

As the dread of being a new boy passed, Martin looked to Tiles as a further source of beauty. He found isolated corners of the school, where the lime trees overhung the wall, or the afternoon sun touched the leather bindings of old books, and tried to write poems about them. Full of confidence, he delivered his efforts to the glamorous editor of the school's literary magazine. None of them was published.

After this, when he was fifteen years old, Martin attempted to learn the piano. His senses had been stirred, in the Musical Appreciation classes, by the delicate works of Satie and Ravel. The pieces that Martin most wanted to master were the ones which brought a tear to his eye, and would bring tears to the eyes of others. For Martin, tears and beauty were inextricably linked. The Music master started him off with 'Fun On The Piano'. To his credit, Martin soldiered on. He wanted to do just one thing well, and triumph over dullness.

When he returned home for the summer holidays in July 1976, Martin was tall and well built, and looked older than his sixteen years. He was also, perversely, top of his class in Maths. His mouth had lost its childish redness, and his face had lost its puppy fat. His eyes, however, remained serious, and now they seemed alert. Tiles had opened up Martin's sense of ambition. But by offering an imitation of grandeur, combined with elusive glimpses of loveliness, the school had caused him to make a serious error: it had made him mistake luxury for beauty, and extravagance for art. In some people this wouldn't have mattered, but for Martin, with his weakness for aesthetics and poetic states of mind, it had turned him into a snob. Also, it had forged a new aspect of his personality: he could absorb (later, this would be called 'consuming'), but he could not create. Spiritually, therefore, he was in harness.

Emotionally and romantically, Martin had awoken much earlier than most. Sexually, he had dozed. By the time that he was top in Maths, his body, too, had become responsive.

The summer of 1976 was important for Martin because it filled him with hope. For two months the sun beat down, scorching the Heath and wilting the roses. Indoors seemed cool and dark. The sunsets were protracted. Martin looked at the blue sky and imagined Rome.

Christine, who was still the boy's closest friend, had moved with her parents to a bigger house a mile away from Thornby Avenue. This new house had large, high-ceilinged rooms, and it seemed magnificent to Martin. He loved to go there and, as Christine was 'doing' her new bedroom, the two young people became inseparable once more. Martin became Christine's artistic adviser – and her confidant.

First, in the hot mornings, they painted the room the palest of lemon yellows. This made the bay window seem bigger. While they painted they listened to records: sophisticated disco and glamorous rock. They also studied one another. Christine, like

Martin, looked older than her sixteen years. She had put blond streaks in her long fair hair, and she now had breasts that (she freely admitted) 'some girls would die for'. Martin, despite himself, imagined a literal interpretation of this comment. Christine wore make-up while she decorated, and her old white shirt was drenched in a perfume called 'Charlie'. She was falling in love (she said) with a man of twenty-two, called Jonathan, who lived in London. Jonathan became a frequent topic of conversation.

As they moved on to the window frames and woodwork, which required two careful coats of white gloss, Christine realised that Martin had become effeminate. This was fashionable at the time, and so she didn't mind. Rather, she was intrigued. As the cloudless weeks went by, and as an extravagant bouquet of peacock feathers was assembled by Martin to take pride of place in an otherwise barren corner of the big bedroom, Christine began to understand that her oldest friend was in love. This pleased, her, for it meant that they could talk more about Jonathan.

During that summer, as he encouraged Christine to decorate her walls with posters of illustrations by Aubrey Beardsley and to mingle the sultry culture of modern boutiques with the luxurious and sensual sadness of art nouveau, Martin believed that he was homosexual. He wasn't. He was, as ever, seeking beauty, and beauty had been communicated to him through the face and body of a pretty boy at school. At last, it seemed, love had created a fourth dimension to Martin's life. All the music, and the pictures, and the loveliness of nature and architecture, were now summed up and empowered by the appearance of another person. Life, in short, had been given a point.

As the summer wore on, and began to wane, and as the first hints of autumn made their subtle arrival, Martin and Christine got ready to accept that they must part company once more. The two months they had shared in the big, airy bedroom were now coming to an end. Vase upon vase of wide-petalled roses had stood upon Christine's dressing table; confession after confession had been exchanged; a billowing canopy of patterned Indian cotton had been tacked to the ceiling above Christine's bed; an exquisite, temporary intimacy had been created.

The summer had seen an intensity of mood of the kind that could never be forced. Martin had returned home each night to read the obvious classics of his condition: *The Picture of Dorian Gray*, *Death In Venice*, and the poems of Theocritus in translation. The two young people had lived through music as well, mixing Mahler and Fauré with the latest records by sexually ambiguous pop stars. In choosing the posters for Christine's room, they had studied lush impressionists and decadent symbolists, not knowing whether Monet's water garden or Khnopff's leopard woman was best for the wall by the window. Martin's favourite painting at this time had been 'Chatterton', by Wallis, which depicted the poet lying on his deathbed, wearing blue satin knee-breeches and an open, frill-cuffed shirt. Later on, Martin would recognise all these first loves as being little more than clichés, but as first loves they were pure loves, and thus they left their mark. Besides, these clichés were to be amongst the artistic informants of an epoch.

Living upon, and through, their respective unrequited loves, Martin and Christine had spent their summer in gaining an aesthetic education. Christine, a month after Martin returned to Tiles, finally got her man.

The autumn of 1976 was bright and blustery – a roaring season of blue and gold. At Tiles, the year's leaves bowled and scattered across the immaculate lawns, but despite the wind the sun remained warm. Those who played rugby in the afternoons trudged back to their houses amidst lengthening shadows. Martin had to play rugby. His house and his build demanded it. He derived some pleasure out of running and kicking, but he hated to tackle and was afraid of physical pain. It was ironic, therefore, that his presence on the rugby pitch won him the approval of the authorities.

Academically, Martin was at odds with his instinct. He was in the sixth form now, and just beginning the vast quantity of work which would have to be done in order for him to sit A levels in Maths, Economics and Biology. Martin had hoped to study English, or Art History, but his mind was not right for those subjects. Whilst poems or paintings might move him far more deeply than they did those who went on to study Chaucer or the history of the Renaissance, he was quite incapable of writing anything other than the most leaden and facile of essays about them. Also, he made stupid mistakes. The year before, while studying for his English Literature O level, he had earned the scorn of his teacher by suggesting that a passage in Shakespeare had been inspired by the fear of nuclear weapons. Mathematics and statistics, on the other hand, he could master quite easily. He was one of the first pupils to be allowed to work on the school computer – primitive though it was. The theory of business and accounting seemed quite simple to him, and he enjoyed finding short cuts through the complexities of calculus. Other boys, mystified by basic economics, begged him to lend them his graphs. Martin still had to work hard, but he didn't derive any real pleasure from it.

In Biology, however, Martin did detect some areas of beauty. The processes of natural history, he found, and the scientific terms that were used to describe them, could be seen as metaphors for the workings – as he regarded them – of his own soul. Thus, when he studied the reproductive cycles of plants or the internal organs of mammals, Martin could see, beneath the microscope or upon the dissection board, various analogues of his emotional states. He revelled in this. Also, in the school museum, Martin loved to study the moths and butterflies which were pinned to oblongs of yellowing card, and to scrutinise the obscenely shaped fungi in their jars of Sauterne-coloured formaldehyde. The school museum, which was old and remote, seemed to Martin to be a romantic place. Moreover, he felt excluded from the school library, and from the authorised study of literature and art, so that sanctum held a sadness for him. Drawing his graphs, or tapping digits into his calculator, Martin would sometimes wonder at the manner in which the things he desired contrived to elude him. He saw beauty so clearly, and yet still he could not possess it. He was free, at any rate, of his love for another boy; indeed, he had suddenly become disgusted by it. He did not know why this should be, nor had any new love come to replace it.

That winter, Martin's father died. He suffered a heart attack whilst walking out of Moorgate tube station on a bright, frosty morning during the first week of January. He had been hurrying to get to a meeting.

Mrs Knight cried as she knelt in the hall, alone in her house at Thornby Avenue, after being telephoned with the news of the tragedy. The hall was dim, despite the light which came in through the glass in the front door. Everywhere was quiet. A car passed by. For a long time Mrs Knight did not move, but rocked herself gently to and fro. Her husband had not been old. He had always seemed strong. Finally, as the telephone rang once more and she heard Anne's scared voice on the line, she fell into a seemingly bottomless pit of grief. Outside, the frost on the other side of the road began to melt.

The funeral took place in north London. Martin did not know why. Summoned from school, he had found himself to be incapable of either tears or meditation. He became practical, and begged his mother and sister to let him look after them. He could not admit the reality of the event to himself, and at night he gave way to panic. Secretly, he longed to return to school. Christine did not telephone, fearing that she might be intruding.

12

One of Mr Knight's colleagues had received a first-hand account of the death. A newspaper had been placed over the dead man's face. His briefcase was still in his hand when the ambulance arrived. The crowds of commuters who had been disgorged from each arriving train had parted to pass around the corpse like a river flowing around either side of a rocky outcrop. Some had stared and others had averted their eyes. A member of the station staff had done his best to move on the curious. An hour after Mr Knight died, one of the men whom he had been due to meet telephoned the office, and said that he didn't like being kept waiting. Later, he sent a brief letter of apology and condolence.

By the time that Martin sat his mock A levels, in June 1977, he was aware of a distance between himself and his mother and sister. With the death of Mr Knight, a quiet, self-policing liberalism had entered the family home, but also an immovable sadness. Rules had become less strict and quarrels less frequent, but a deep melancholy, a staleness even, now seemed to replace the vague sense of tension which had previously reigned. Martin felt stifled and repelled by such an atmosphere. For his mother, however, who was showing such courage, Martin cried. Working late into the evening in his study at Tiles, the boy would think of his mother sitting alone in her favourite chair, reading a magazine while the television murmured quietly in its corner. Rushing to the house telephone, he would call her, and she would tell him not to worry, but still he would feel far away from her.

Anne was now engaged, and living her own life.

Martin passed his exams with distinction, and his teachers had high hopes for his success the following year. Oxford was mentioned. But he returned home for the summer holidays filled with a sense of dread. His sentimentality, he later realised, had been stronger, at this time, than his compassion. His sensitivity – he was also forced to admit – had remained shamefully stronger, throughout the bereavement, than any other quality that he might possess or learn.

That summer, Martin discovered that Christine had altered. Her life was now filled with Jonathan, and she no longer needed either an intimate friend or a confidant. Martin, however, was drawn to the past, and he yearned for the long afternoons which had been spent in Christine's pale room, when the smell of fresh paint had mingled with the scent of warm roses. This pure place had now become a boudoir, and Martin's new role within it was to chat with his friend while she dried her hair and put on her make-up and got changed, prior to seeing Jonathan. Martin felt wounded by this, and knew that now he was little more than an accessory to romance.

'What's Jonathan's flat like?' he asked Christine, early one evening. Christine paused to bend forward, in order to 'shake out' her hair. 'Oh, it's lovely,' she replied, vigorously running her fingers through her knotted tresses. 'You'll have to come round one evening. You'd really like Jonathan, and he always asks about you.' Martin nodded, and smiled appreciatively – a soundless expression of gratitude.

Christine had her back to her friend. She was quite unconcerned about getting dressed in front of Martin, and on this particular evening she had received him while wearing nothing more than a cream-coloured satin petticoat. Her body was brown beneath this, and Martin, despite himself, was disturbed by the call of her nakedness. He sat down upon the little chair in front of the dressing table, on the other side of the room, and lit a cigarette. Smoking was a new pleasure for him, and one in which he indulged his taste for opulence. Whilst Christine – when she smoked at all – preferred American cigarettes, Martin, following the example of a fellow aesthete at Tiles, smoked expensive, untipped, Virginia No. 2 brand, which were made by Freiburg & Treyer, in the Haymarket. A box of these cigarettes cost him half his week's allowance. He had discovered, however, that tobacco

14

deadens lust, as well as providing an excuse for idleness, and it was for this former reason that he smoked while watching Christine get dressed. She seemed to think that he had no desires.

'Don't you think these are pretty?' she said, holding up an extravagant article of lingerie. Her tone was that of one woman speaking to another. Martin made a careful reply, as though she had just consulted him about curtain material.

'Oh, they're lovely,' he said, and gently fingered the translucent fabric.

Was Christine becoming stupid? Martin sometimes thought so. In this he was wrong. Had her place been taken by a girl he hardly knew, but whose appearance stirred him equally (or more so, for the erotic thrives upon the obscure), he would have willingly excused her platitudes. As it was, Martin existed between two states, alert to the sensual as the summit of his youthful philosophy, but with nowhere to take his capacity for love. Christine, now, was gently painting her eyelids mauve. She squinted while she did this, and peered into the mirror with a concentration unparalleled within her daily activities. Martin looked out of the window, and thought about the walk back to Thornby Avenue, alone in the fragrant dusk. He wished that he, too, was going to meet a lover. How rich, then, would the sunset seem, and how many strange and beautiful things (he thought) would he have to impart to –

'Do cats eat chocolate?' asked Christine, suddenly.

Martin wasn't sure. Jonathan, however, had a kitten.

In a manner which the ruling spirit of his character seemed to belie, Martin was oddly incapable of gauging his own appearance. He had become handsome, but he spoilt his looks with affected gestures. That summer, as the nation celebrated the Royal Jubilee and as fashionable pop music became fast and aggressive, Martin thought a great deal about his image.

This process was dominated by his meeting with Fenella, a girl who attended the same sixth-form college as Christine. Born in Scotland, but brought up and educated in Hawaii prior to her father's relocation to a London office, Fenella, to Martin, was a brunette Marilyn Monroe. She had the same alluring dark eyes (he thought), the same gentle mouth, the same arched eyebrows, the same bobbing fringe – she even (he inwardly enthused) had an accent that was informed by the American south. She also had a boyfriend.

Martin met Fenella one hot afternoon at the beginning of August. It happened at Christine's house. Arriving for tea, Martin noticed that a car which he had not seen before was carefully parked in a shady part of the semi-circular drive. It was a smart new 'runabout', with scarlet paintwork. Peering in through the rear window, Martin saw, thrown carelessly on the back seat, a fashion magazine, a box of tangerine-coloured boutique tissues and a bottle of Chanel nail polish. Clearly, the little car was no stranger to sophistication. Excited, Martin rang the doorbell. He was admitted by Christine, who was wearing her 'second-best' bikini. 'Thank God it's you,' she said, 'I suddenly had a terrible thought that it might have been anyone . . .' Martin followed his friend through the large drawing room towards the french windows, which were open onto the garden. Then, just as his eyes were adjusting to the light, he heard a girl's voice, low and lilting.

'She's just got no shame . . .' said the voice. The last two words of this statement were playfully emphasised. Martin turned and there, seated upon the side of a white reclining garden chair, he saw Fenella. She was, he thought, the most beautiful thing he had ever seen. Her dark, lustrous hair showed strands of copper where it was touched by the sun; her skin seemed naturally and evenly brown, unlike a forced English tan. She was wearing a black cotton T-shirt, cut low above her breast. Her skirt, too, was black, and pleated, and seemed to be made of a fine, cool material. It reached to just below her knees. On her

16

bare feet she was wearing elegant low-heeled sandals. Martin, looking at her for the first time, felt childish and uncouth. Here was a woman – and yet she was only three months older than himself. He recovered his manners and, smiling, shook her hand. Her nail varnish was the colour of red wine, and applied with such precision that it made the girl's slender fingers look quite perfectly defined. Fenella's face was slightly round, but it was an adult roundness which seemed to compliment her broad shoulders and her strong neck. Above all, the girl looked lazily sophisticated. She appeared to know a great deal about Martin already.

'So you're the boy who likes poetry?' she said, playing, as ever, with the last word in her sentence. Martin tried to look both poetic and indifferent.

'I like poetry,' she continued, 'I like . . . oh God, who is that man . . .' Martin suggested some poets. 'The last one you said,' cried Fenella at last, 'that's the guy.' Martin racked his brain for a suitable quotation, but then simply nodded. Christine went to fetch tea. Martin lit a cigarette. 'Hey, what a beautiful box.' Fenella leant forward and gazed at the airforce-blue packet with its black and gold crest which Martin had placed beside him.

'Would you like one?'

'I don't. But I'd love to keep the box. It's such a great box . . .'

Martin hurriedly emptied the remaining cigarettes out of their container, not pausing to think where he would now put them. 'Here,' he said, 'please – it's just a box.'

'Well, thank you.' Fenella held the cigarette box up to her dark eyes, and scrutinised it as though it was a piece of rare Chinese pottery.

But Martin felt uncomfortable. He was desperate somehow to become Fenella's friend, and yet he was wholly embarrassed about making the most timid of conversation while Christine was present. He was aware, also, that his clothes looked awful. A pair of old jeans and a white school shirt. On his feet were ancient plimsolls. He wished he was wearing something fashionable and impressive. He did not realise that such finery, in the afternoon, would strike both the girls as being little more than ridiculous.

When Christine returned, and began to talk about college work (which merely exasperated her) and about the personnel department of an office (where she hoped to work) and about Jonathan (whom she was seeing later), Martin took advantage of the conversation – which didn't really include him – in order to study Fenella. Her movements were either emphatic, and expansive, or wholly restrained. When she was listening to Christine's complaints about a particular teacher, she folded her arms very tightly across her chest and looked down at her feet. At one point, when Martin ventured a joke, she laughed out loud in a way which pierced his heart.

Martin could scarcely believe his disappointment when Fenella announced that she had to go. Already, he was jealous of whatever appointment was summoning her. He knew so little about her, but she seemed to have taken control of his being. This, he realised, was courtly love.

Then, just as he was standing awkwardly on the hot patio, Fenella touched his arm.

'Call me,' she said. 'Christine's got my number.'

Martin said that he would.

In one way, at least, Martin had succeeded in realising his early ambition: Fenella found him interesting. Also, for his part, Martin – as purveyor of the interesting – now had a single peg upon which to hang all his aesthetic enthusiasms. This peg was made all the more robust for being both new and untested. On the evening after he first met Fenella, Martin returned home to his room drunk with excitement. The dusk made the trees and the gardens appear romantically verdant, and the pale sky, streaked with charcoal and amber, seemed to imply a world of extravagant loveliness, the goddess of which was Fenella. Fenella!

Those three syllables, to Martin, unleashed a torrent of pleasurable emotions. With her, he was sure, he would discover 'the wisdom poets crave'. What else he might discover, on a more amorous level, was too potent to dwell upon lightly. That night, Martin was so restless with happiness that he reached the dawn awake.

Life, for once, did not seem to lag so very far behind imagination. The following week, having first constructed an invitation that seemed to combine good humour with the potential for romance, Martin telephoned the deity of his new religion. He was so afraid that Fenella would not wish to see him that he had half convinced himself of her refusal. He was wrong. From the moment when he heard her voice (despite himself he had failed to recreate, in his mind, the American playfulness of her accent) on the other end of the line, he knew that she was pleased to hear from him. He could hear her smiling. At this, his confidence was renewed, and he became witty. He played up his slight reputation for eccentricity, in order to make her laugh.

'I thought we could go for a walk on the Heath perhaps – and maybe take a dog . . .' he said, cheerfully.

'You got a dog?'

'Well, not as such, but I could borrow one probably.'

'God . . .' Fenella laughed.

'How about Saturday?'

'I can't on Saturday.'

At this Martin faltered, and with a stab of jealousy he realised once more that Fenella had a life in which he played no part. 'Sunday?' he volunteered.

'OK, Sunday. And you get a dog . . .'

Feeling hugely pleased with himself, Martin gently replaced the telephone on its cradle.

On Saturday evening the telephone rang. Hearing Fenella's voice, Martin's heart immediately sank.

'You want to go into town?' she asked.

'I'm sorry? I mean, yes. Which town?' Martin felt confused, and slightly alarmed.

'London.' The word was said quite casually.

'Now?'

'Sure.' Here Fenella laughed.

'I'd love to; but are you sure that . . .'

'Pick you up in half an hour.'

And then Fenella was gone. Martin hurried off to tell his mother that he was going out, and to change his clothes. His fingers were trembling as he buttoned up his shirt.

That drive to London, through the violet summer evening, was to stay with Martin for the rest of his life. Thornby Avenue, by road, stood twelve miles from the Thames at Chelsea, and the route consisted mostly of dual carriageways and long, grey flyovers which, in the August dusk, were lit by tall, peach-coloured lights as they swept between endless rows of dim, small houses and over vast grey recreation-grounds. The sky was the colour of rich blue satin, sprinkled with bright stars, and to the west, shedding a crimson glow, the declining sun made a romantic theatre of the approaching city. As Fenella presided over this magic, Martin was cautiously aware that the pastoral and the urban were merging, giving strength to his spirit on the one hand, and urging him, on the other, to enter an unknown that seemed only to promise miracles. Up until this drive, Martin had only known London as a few theatres and one or two carefully planned visits. That Fenella, who was only a little older than himself, should be so casual about the great city filled him with awe. It was she, not he, who was purveying the interesting.

Parking in Onslow Square, where the trees hung over the black railings and where the tall white houses, with urns of geraniums, and palms, upon their balconies, appeared like calm signifiers of an undreamt-of sophistication, Fenella said: 'You eat Japanese? It's fun. There's a place near here which is quite cheap.

Or we could walk around and look.' Martin felt as though the pavement was sparkling. He glanced at Fenella as she was locking her car. She was wearing a black V-necked jersey, which seemed to have strands of glistening bronze thread woven into it, and a black skirt. A pair of suede evening shoes completed the ensemble. Her earrings looked like big plum-coloured rubies.

She dazzled him. 'I'm afraid I don't have much money,' he said. 'Would it be all right if I just watched you eat? I'll have a coffee or something.' Fenella smiled. 'You spend all your money on those fancy cigarettes. I'll treat you.' She rummaged in her bag. 'Thank God I brought my chequebook. Dad gives us an allowance, and with the allowance . . .' (she found her cheque-book) 'comes a bank account. God though, I spend too much.' To Martin this was all quite new. He still received pocket money during the holidays. At Tiles he had to leave his term's allowance with his house master. The couple began to stroll towards the Kings Road.

Beyond the quiet terraces of private houses, some of which one could see into, glimpsing for a moment the trappings of calm, domestic opulence (a low burgundy-and-silver-striped sofa with faded blue cushions strewn upon it; real paintings, illuminated upon silk-covered walls; shelves of well-read, interesting books; vases of exotic cut flowers — evidence of gracious, prosperous lives), the fashionable shops began. It was a time of change, and the goods on sale reflected this. The clothes shops appeared like art galleries, their stark window displays bathed in ultra-violet light; elsewhere, beneath signs which were covered with bitumen and shards of broken mirror, or behind doors which had been carefully made to look as though a fire had taken place, gawdy, obscene T-shirts mingled with garments that appeared to be held together with chains and straps. A large Union Jack, with SEX PISTOLS scrawled across it, took pride of place in one of the shops.

'Do you like punk rock?' asked Fenella, pausing outside one of the boutiques.

21

'Oh yes,' lied Martin. He didn't really know anything about it. 'I just think it's ugly.'

'But it's quite funny.' Martin said this knowingly, and suddenly felt pleased that he was wearing one of the grey winter suits which were insisted upon at Tiles. With a white shirt, and without a tie, it looked quite smart.

'Punks put razor blades through their ears,' remarked Fenella. 'How do you suppose they do that?' The couple were now walking past a showroom filled with bathroom equipment. A big silver fish was painted on the turquoise rear wall. 'Love that bath,' said Fenella, 'and look at those amazing taps. Wow . . .'

And so they made their way towards the Japanese restaurant, window-shopping all the while. This walk was crucial to Martin's development. It instilled in him, for the first time, the realisation that he would approach the end of the decade aware of three things: money, aesthetics and romance. These qualities were equally important; they existed in crystalline harmony.

A month later, Martin and Fenella were firm friends – but that (as Martin wrote to a friend from school) 'was all'. At the Japanese restaurant, where Martin had tasted sashimi for the first time, Fenella had told him about Charlie. Charlie, a man impossible for Martin to visualise as anything other than a kind of comic lumberjack, was Fenella's boyfriend, who lived in Vancouver. 'We used to camp out on the beach,' she said. And so Martin had accepted Charlie. But how, he wondered, was such a relationship to survive the width of the Atlantic? Fenella, too, seemed troubled by this. 'He's coming over at Christmas,' she said, brightly, 'and you'll have to meet him. You'd really like Charlie.' Martin knew instinctively that he wouldn't.

In the mean time, Tiles, the school routine and the horrors of examinations (Martin had scarcely looked at his holiday-work schedule) were approaching. Fenella, whose ambition it was 'to go into retail management – y'know, have a store', seemed coolly untroubled by the vulgar demands of her college work. The two friends, observed all the while by Christine and by Martin's mother, who monitored the relationship from afar, had spent the summer strolling around the Heath, and sitting in Martin's room late into the night, and making occasional trips to London. And still Martin had not declared his passion. He was afraid of putting limits on the idyll, or of being placed in a position where Fenella would say, 'But I don't like you in that way.' In short, Martin was experiencing an intensity of feeling which an older, or more cynical, person might well have regarded as a dead end.

'You want to watch out,' said Christine to Martin one day; 'girls never fancy their friends.' It was an understanding between Martin and Christine that the latter would not betray the former's confidences to Fenella.

'But what can I do?' said Martin, hopelessly. 'I can't just pounce on her . . .'

'Why not?'

'Because she'd hate it, and she trusts me . . .' Martin had just finished inscribing a card to Fenella with a quotation from Brooke:

> And I shall find some girl perhaps,
>   And a better one than you,
>   With eyes as wise, but kindlier,
>   And lips as soft, but true.
>   And I daresay she will do.

He was now trying to work out, in his own mind, whether or not these lines seemed too ambiguous. 'Anyway,' he went on, 'it's too late now – I go back to school at the end of next week.' Christine regarded her friend for a moment with maternal fondness. 'Listen,' she said, in her 'special' voice, 'just tell her how you feel; she'll probably be thrilled! She can't throw herself at *you*, you know. Tell her.'

*

'But I don't like you in that way,' Fenella was saying, with bright tears standing in her soft dark eyes; 'I mean, I do like you – so much – but . . . Oh God.'

The couple were sitting in the quiet wood which stood before the old asylum. It was evening, a few days after Martin's conversation with Christine. The problem had begun with Martin's melodramatic farewell gift for Fenella. That morning, extremely early, he had gone to the post office and drawn out a considerable portion of his Christmas money. Then, deep in thought yet thrilled by the manner in which he was about to declare himself, he had gone to a perfumers in Bond Street to buy Fenella a bottle of scent. He had been taken aback at how much the scents purveyed in Bond Street cost, but retreat in the face of extravagance, however wanton, was wholly antithetical to his nature. In the end, and uncertain as to whether or not the grand lady who served him was, in fact, suppressing a smirk, he had bought a bottle of English Fern toilet water.

'And shall I have that gift-wrapped for you?' asked the lady, sweetly.

'Oh, yes. Please,' replied Martin, with the air of a man who had expensive perfume gift-wrapped every day, and who found the notion of not having it gift-wrapped wholly eccentric.

'And that will be . . . Twenty-seven pounds and fifty-five pence please.'

At this, a cold, sinking sensation occurred in the stomach of the young consumer. He had enough money, just, to pay for the gift, but such expenditure would leave him severely hard up for some weeks. This sensation was one that Martin was to come to know well over the years, and the impact of its chill never lessened.

Thanking the lady 'very much indeed', he hurried off with his parcel. He was due to see Fenella that afternoon, and he already had a speech prepared.

At home he studied the rich, glossy bag in which his gift

24

resided. Amidst the familiar muted tones of Thornby Avenue it looked like a thing from another planet. The black tissue paper in which the gift-wrapped perfume was wrapped in its turn had the same heavy scent as the shop. Curls of monogrammed silver ribbon protruded from the tissue like the fronds of an exotic plant. This reminded Martin of his A levels. Guilt took its place beside his excitement. He was terrified that his mother or sister might find the gift, and demand to know why he was spending so much money. He hid the package in his wardrobe.

Finally, a little while before Fenella was due to call for him, he took out a small ivory-coloured card and carefully wrote *I love you* upon it. He slipped this message between the folds of tissue paper, and then lit a cigarette. He was afraid that he had made a terrible mistake, but now he was driven to see out his plan.

'What have you got there?' said Fenella, as they strolled across the Heath. 'Have you been shopping again?' This was said in a tone of mock disapproval. Martin smiled, and then changed the subject. It would soon be autumn, and school . . . Fenella did not respond to this. Soon they reached the little wood.

Once at the cool grove (it seemed much smaller now) where years before Martin and Christine had dug their enormous hole, the couple sat down. The scent of the leaves and brambles mixed with the smell of dry soil; beyond the furthest undergrowth, its red brick caught by the sun, the wall of the asylum could be seen. Martin sat at the feet of his beloved, and tried to look both dignified and soulful. Fenella knew that something was wrong, and questioned him about it. 'You seem fed up' (she lowered her lovely face to look at him), 'are you thinking about school?' Fenella, for once, was wearing old jeans and a white man's shirt. Her clothes smelt freshly laundered, and her throat and neck looked soft and tanned against the crisp cotton. As Martin gave a meaningful shrug, the girl picked up three long stalks of dry grass and began to plait them. She had never looked, thought Martin, so beautiful. Oh God, if I lose her now, he thought. He pulled the bag which contained his gift closer to him, and then, as though inspired, said, 'Let's walk a bit more.'

'OK.' Fenella got up, still holding the twisted stalks of grass.

Pushing through the dense interior of the wood, beyond the place where the little muddy path stopped, the couple soon found themselves facing the old side door of the asylum. 'You wanna go in?' said Fenella. 'God, I don't think I've ever actually been in . . .' Curious, she pushed the rotten door ajar, and then slid through the gap. Martin followed. He had been through the door before; he knew that there was nothing much inside – an overgrown courtyard, an ugly building with metal, bolted doors, a few lengths of rusted piping. The sun was cutting across the middle of the courtyard, leaving one half of it in deep shadow and the other filled with a golden, drowsy light. Fenella paused, and took Martin's hand. 'Kind of spooky,' she laughed.

'It's just quiet; there's nothing much to see,' he replied. Vaguely, he wondered what manner of unhappiness and horror had taken place within these walls, and what bleak lives had reached confused or terrified endings. Fenella was still holding his hand.

'I . . .' he said.

'Yes?'

But his speech had deserted him. Thrusting the glossy bag into Fenella's hand, Martin blurted out, 'I love you so much,' and then walked away a few paces. Confused, but still responding in the traditional manner to an unexpected present, Fenella began, slowly, to unwrap the bottle of perfume. Turning to watch her, Martin suddenly realised that his expensive gift seemed wholly useless; it was as though he had just given her a pan-scrub, or a cricket stump. The language of the present would not become articulate.

'Oh, Martin . . .' The perfume was the colour of heavily diluted lime juice. Its exquisite bottle had a ribbon of moss-coloured velvet about its neck. The little card which Martin had inserted fluttered down onto the dirty courtyard. Fenella stooped to pick it up and then, having read it, began to walk back towards the door. She was crying. Martin followed.

He knew that there was no hope. Sitting upon a fallen tree, back in the little grove, Fenella was saying, 'But I don't like you in that way; I mean, I do like you – so much – but . . . Oh God . . .' The sun was beginning to go down. In four days' time, Martin dumbly realised, he would be back in his study at Tiles. But surely Fenella would have to say something? She didn't. She simply sat quietly, deep in thought, and then gave Martin the twisted blades of grass. 'I've got to go,' she said, rising, 'I'm really sorry –' Martin, vague with misery, kissed her once on the cheek; was aware, briefly, of warm skin covered in soft down; and then they had parted. He thought of rushing off after her, but then, his mind filled with incoherent images, he blundered instead towards the old quarry, and sat down beside it. Fenella would be a dot of white and blue soon, hurrying towards her car. Her car always smelt of her perfume. Would it smell of English Fern as it conveyed happy Charlie through the blue Christmas streets? How was it possible to live without Fenella?

Bland as the drama might seem to an adult, Martin had just received the hardest blow of his young life. He had offered his love, and been rejected. More than this, he had submitted his personality, as a kind of emotional dowry, and found it wanting. The only thing that remained, he felt, was his sense of intellectual superiority; in that respect – however wrong his assumption might have been – he believed himself to be intact. The battle now, he knew, would be between his memories and his desires. Each day, he would have to make the past matter less. Suddenly, with cruel timing, the picture of Fenella's thighs, perfectly formed beneath her black skirt, came into Martin's mind. Lust, for a second, overpowered his sadness.

The sun was low and a breeze had picked up as Martin sat

beside the old quarry. For more than an hour he had been flicking stones at the ancient cistern which still stood, surrounded by a narrow moat of muddy water, in the shallow basin of that place. The cistern had become quite rotten. The stones, when they hit it, made a dull, echoing boom. As Martin's mind wandered, he began to compose a curious image, a mental conundrum that was difficult to hold in his mind and follow through to its conclusion: a man was sitting on an island in the middle of a lake; this lake, in its turn, was in the middle of a larger island, and that island, in its turn, was in the centre of a larger lake – and so on, to a hazy infinity. There was a dreadful hopelessness about this specu-lation. It seemed like years since he had gone to Bond Street and bought the bottle of perfume. And then warm thoughts of Fenella swept over him, and he was wretched.

Returning to Tiles for his final academic year, Martin, as a consequence of the summer, had a sudden reversion to male company and to the cloistered, panelled, dusty atmosphere of school. He was in the Upper School now, and it was his privilege – ridiculous or otherwise – to wear a coloured waistcoat and silk socks, and to tap his umbrella on the ground as he walked across the quadrangle. He was made a house prefect, and became a martinet. His booming voice and his excessive punishments, which he meted out quite regularly, made him despised by the younger boys. To his more mature contemporaries, he simply seemed like a caricature. At night, when he was supposed to be catching up on his lapsed work, he brooded instead over Fenella, and wrote page after page of dreadful poetry, all of which he threw away.

The winter term was damp and misty. It seemed barely to be October before the nights were drawing in with hardly a pause for twilight, and in the freezing classrooms the lights were on by four. Martin's smoking had become a problem. He was now addicted to cigarettes, and his rugby, in consequence, had suffered. One evening he was found by the House Tutor, skulking in the senior boxroom where the prefects changed for games, with a cigarette between his lips. The stench of sweat and dust did nothing to mask the smell of Freiburg & Treyer Virginia No. 2.

'Off the team, Knight,' said the House Tutor briskly. 'Organising the junior cross-country ought to improve your health.'

And so Martin organised the junior cross-country, and had to stand for hours in the rain, jogging on the spot as he did so, while the House Master watched him checking off the participants. His vanity was wounded by this, and both his work and his self-confidence began to suffer.

'Tenth out of the eleven boys in your set, Knight,' said the House Master, when the results of the Christmas examinations were posted. Martin shifted in the study armchair, and wondered whether or not to tell the House Master about Fenella.

'I . . .' he began; but the House Master stopped him.

'I've no sympathy, Knight,' he said; 'you're perfectly capable of doing the work, and of keeping a strong position in the house; now you're smoking, and swanning about all day instead of making use of your spare time. You're not even training. I'm disgusted with you, boy, disgusted.' At a better school, the House Master might have mingled his complaints with some carefully worded enquiries about the boy's general condition. This, however, was not the Tiles way. A bastardised version of 'playing the game' was the credo at Tiles, and the weak or difficult boy had little chance of redemption. Martin was set extra work for the holidays, and from that point on Oxford was no longer mentioned.

Christmas was miserable. Thoughts of Fenella still haunted Martin, but the girl had made it quite clear that she was no longer available. What made it worse was the fact that Charlie, so Christine had heard, no longer figured in Fenella's life. Instead,

Fenella had become furiously ambitious, and was spending the winter break engaged upon a Business Studies work placement at a London department store.

Christine herself was living beyond her years. She had moved in, despite parental protest, with Jonathan, abandoning her academic studies and working as a junior in a fashionable hairdressing salon. She was, she told Martin on the telephone, about to become a 'stylist'. Martin felt scared by such a display of bravery. Christine's parents were unhappy about Jonathan, and had even got the impression that he lived, just slightly, on the wrong side of the law. He seemed to be an entrepreneur of some kind, and he hung around in pubs with men who wore sheepskin coats and who frequently ended up spending the night on his sofa, drunk. Jonathan's flat, where Christine now lived, was in New Cross. There was never any talk, now, of Martin 'going round for the evening'. Rather, Christine had become somewhat hard, and appeared (according to her mother) like some kind of moll. Martin's mother was unsurprised by this turn of events. She had always felt that Christine was spoilt, and said as much to Anne. Anne, of course, was deeply unimpressed by the conduct of her brother's generation. For Anne, it seemed, maturity was all, and any course that deviated from the sane and comprehensible was nothing more than affectation. 'They're all the same,' she said, on Boxing Day, 'they just think that they're important. It's because they haven't got enough to do.' And then she went to greet her fiancé, with whom she was saving up to buy a house. At this, Martin picked up his Biology file and took it upstairs.

Time, now, began to accelerate; not much, at first, but gradually building momentum.

During the Easter term, in 1978, a Tiles athlete hanged himself in his study. His name was Richard Alson, and he had always seemed both popular and cheerful. Having reacted to the news of this tragedy, the main body of the school marched on.

Cricket started. The great trees were in full leaf once more. The season of exams was upon the school.

By the time that Martin sat his A levels, during a fortnight of scorching, airless heat, he was amazed at how present the memory of Fenella still seemed. He took his exams in a kind of dream, as though they had nothing whatever to do with him; and after each paper, instead of congregating with his fellows at the school shop to perform a *post mortem* upon the questions, he took himself off to the grassy bank beside the athletics track, and thought of love. He knew that his grades would be poor.

So soon, it seemed, his bags and trunk were packed, and he was standing in his place in the school chapel, about to quit Tiles for ever. It was late afternoon; he officially 'left' that evening. The great stained-glass window above the altar had the declining sun directly behind it, and a pattern of scarlet and blue was falling upon the surplices of the Chaplain and choristers. Pompous to the last, it was a tradition at Tiles that the departing pupils were dismissed with religious ceremony. Gazing up at the window, which he had studied so many times during the previous five years, Martin suddenly felt quite overcome with emotion. He was not regretting Tiles exactly, but more his own sense of failure. He had intended, in the pursuit of beauty, to do one thing well – to become, in short, both rare and extraordinary, like Piers Harding, for instance, who was in the pew behind him, and who was certain to get an open scholarship to Oxford – unless he went to the Sorbonne.

The school had now risen to sing 'To Be A Pilgrim', and as the familiar chords began to fill the chapel Martin felt his throat tighten, and hot tears pricking his eyelids. By the time that he reached the lines

> Then, fancies, fly away:
> He'll fear not what men say;
> He'll labour night and day
> To be a pilgrim

31

he was quite overcome, and found himself forced to stop singing. Would he, he wondered, 'fear not what men say'; and would he, ever, prove capable of labour? He wished that he had worked hard, as opposed to simply encouraging his emotions. He wished that he had brought early honour to both himself and, if he was honest, his school. It was as a consequence of this regret that he could never, throughout the course of his life, wear his crested old-school cuff-links without feeling fraudulent, and somehow cheap.

Returned to Thornby Avenue, and with little to do save wait for his A-level results, Martin was aware that he was standing at a crossroads in his life. Other boys, contemporaries of his in Upper School, were forging ahead already; some, adventurers in the making, had departed for distant and exotic corners of the globe, there to help Third World farmers, or to make their way down lost trails, or towards forgotten cities; others, fully confident of resuming their studies at a tertiary level in the autumn, were taking advantage of family connections to 'get a bit of experience' and 'earn a bit of money'. Reviewing his form, it seemed to Martin that he was the only one who had nothing to do. The empty summer stretched ahead of him, like a sunlit but ugly beach. It was so long since he had heard from Fenella that any shred of intimacy that might have remained between them would have long since crumbled away. Thus the girl took her place in Martin's emotional lexicon, there to stand for something that was rather more than just herself and that, poetically, became an accretion of meanings and images, none of which was wholly true, but none of which was entirely false. Martin retained, however, a snapshot of his love, and the three stalks of grass which she had plaited. He put these in an envelope, and placed it at the bottom of a drawer.

He saw Christine once, and did not know whether to be appalled or impressed. She was hurrying towards her parents' house. Her hair was neon-white, and she was wearing pink trousers. Her eyes were hidden by black plastic glasses. Her make-up was thick and extreme. Martin crossed the road to speak with her.

'I hardly recognised you!' he exclaimed.

Christine seemed embarrassed. 'God, Martin, how are you? I've been meaning to get in touch, you know, but we're really busy and I'm only down here to pick up some stuff –' Martin felt as though all entrances to conversation were being blocked. There was a quality of desperation about his former friend, as though she was trying to persuade him to be enthusiastic about her vague plans.

'I'm starting a business, doing fashion for bands and stuff. It's going great.' Martin wondered why none of this seemed to ring true.

'Would you like to come back for a coffee?' he asked, hopefully.

'Oh, I'm really sorry but I'm just down here to pick some stuff up. And Jon's expecting me back –' she glanced at her watch '– soon, and so I'm really in a hurry; I'll call you though, we must get together . . .'

And thus she clattered off, leaving Martin feeling dismissed. In his vague anger he told himself that she had seemed pathetic and common. 'Just a slave girlfriend,' he said out loud as he continued on his dull way, 'just tied to some man who won't let her out of his sight . . .' He began to feel seriously irritated: 'So long as she's got *him* she'll do whatever he says. Business! That'll simply mean going along with something that one of his friends has said.' Brooding in this manner, Martin reached his home. He did not realise that he was beginning to feel jealous of sex; he thought he was being perceptive.

Girls, it seemed to Martin, were a schizophrenic race: there was the aspect of femininity which he adored (typified in his own experience by Fenella) and this was the aspect which was wise and beautiful and witty and elegant; and then there was the other side: shrill, opinionated, stupid, coarse and incapable of romance. Such was the basic recipe for the misogyny which lurked beneath Martin's sensitivity. Like all aesthetes, he knew only extremes. Between those extremes there lay a mire of anxieties.

He blundered on, studying sunsets.

In August, Martin received his A-level results. He had done badly. He failed his Biology completely (thus making a life-long enemy of his Biology master) and only achieved pass marks in his Maths and Economics. His house master, telephoning the former pupil, suggested resits.

'It's either that or polytechnic' (he spoke the word 'poly-technic' as though it was the punchline to a tasteless joke). 'I hope you understand that?'

Martin said that he did.

'I think it's a great shame, Martin.' He used the boy's Christian name for the first time, as if speaking to one who has just received news of an accident.

'I think I'd rather have studied English, sir,' said Martin sadly.

'The arts, too, require hard work,' replied the House Master. 'You, I am afraid, simply did-not-work. But now, to hard facts: what are you going to do?'

Martin fiddled with the telephone cord. 'I suppose I'll get a job, sir.'

'What manner of job?'

'I'm not sure, sir . . .'

It was then decided that Martin should take a diploma in Accounting and Business Studies at a 'good' polytechnic. The House Master said:

'Your grades are still sufficient to gain late entry; I shall speak to Mr Gavenell-Jones about getting you placed. The final decision, of course, rests with your mother and yourself . . .' (Mr

Gavenell-Jones was the Careers master at Tiles, an energetic bachelor whose greatest joy was to go out for beers with Old Boys.)

Ten days later Martin accepted a rather grudging offer of a place from Liverpool Polytechnic. He was going to work, it seemed, with figures.

Having now put down their deposit on a small house in Reigate, Anne Knight and her fiancé were ready to get married. The wedding was planned for the first week in September and the couple were approaching the ceremony with an efficient single-mindedness which seemed to drain the occasion quite utterly of whatever joy it might have possessed. Night after night they sat in the drawing room at Thornby Avenue, Anne alert and absorbed by her lists, Tim (her intended) tired beyond words and capable only of murmuring agreements into his beard, the lower strands of which he pinched at continually. The lists were manifold: invitation lists, seating lists, present lists, who-needs-a-lift-from-someone lists. It was endless.

Martin, to his mortification, was to be an usher. This privilege had only been granted him at his mother's intervention: 'Well he's got to do something,' she had said. Moodily, her daughter acquiesced. A fitting was duly arranged at the formal-wear hire shop. Martin's name was entered on the 'formal' list. As the great day grew nearer, Martin wished that there was some way in which he could communicate his sincere best wishes to his sister. He eventually reached the conclusion, metaphysically, that whatever affection he might feel for Anne, it would most probably remain invisible, awaiting a constellation of benign circumstances before it would reveal itself. In the mean time he bought her a toaster.

Soon, it seemed, the honeymoon to the Greek Islands was booked, the reception at the Trout in Gomshall had been confirmed, and the church (without flowers, for Anne and Tim had agreed that they were a wasted expense) was ready to solemnise the union. It would not be a big wedding ('we don't want anything ostentatious') but more than sixty friends and relations would sit down to a poached-salmon lunch directly after the service. How different, thought Martin, grandly, would his own wedding be. And in his imagination he saw a private service in a Florentine chapel, and a quiet reception somewhere ancient, with bowls of ice-cold cherries and a simple but delightful buffet . . . For some reason, he could never envisage his wedding without picturing Italy, which he had never even visited. Also, he could not, somehow, envisage anyone he knew at the event. The bride, of course, would be beautiful.

Unfortunately, Martin did not perform his duties as an usher particularly well. There were even complaints about his vagueness from the groom's family. The other usher (a colleague of Tim's from the office) had rushed the boy through his responsibilities at the last minute, and thus there were mistakes. In the end, Martin simply let the guests get on with it. They were a curious congregation, comprised mostly of people who didn't really know one another. This was due to the fact that neither family was in particularly close contact with their relatives, and the relatives, in their turn, only knew one another as names on Christmas cards. Men and women so stooped with age that they could barely walk exchanged ferocious glances across the pews; and here and there, to compound the confusion even further, schoolfriends of both the bride and groom were attempting to recognise one another after years of separation. Some had brought young children with them, who screamed; others, looking out of breath and still clutching road maps and car keys, arrived at the last minute and simply looked shifty. Eventually, after an organ crescendo which seemed to have been played with one finger, Anne, stately in off-white taffeta and attended by three cross-looking girls sheathed in peach organdie, began her walk down the aisle. Martin, despite himself, was reminded of a tanker docking. Outside, it began to rain.

The Trout, where the reception was held, was popular for weddings. It comprised of two bars and a restaurant, and it was housed in 'the old mill'. Its beamed ceilings were hung with the kitchen utensils of three centuries, and its long, dim rooms smelt of furniture polish and smoke. Above the bar, a stuffed and varnished trout gaped mournfully from the dusty prison of an old glass case. The landlord wore a striped shirt and a bow-tie, and spoke briskly to his staff, who were circulating with trays of sherry.

Martin, too, attempted to circulate, but he swiftly grew bored. The conversation appeared to consist entirely of agreements, or of affected gratitude for little blessings. Finally, he found one of the bridesmaids – a young cousin of the groom. Her name was Franny, and she was about Martin's age. She was sitting alone beside one of the blackened chimney-pieces, toying with a glass of gin and orange. Martin thought that she was attractive.

'Hello,' he sighed, 'may I join you?' The girl looked up quickly, as though her train of thought had been interrupted. She had bobbed, chestnut-coloured hair, and extremely dark eyebrows. Her skin was very pale and her eyes were blue. Standing, she was tall and slender. At Martin's approach, however, she had remained seated, and simply pulled off her floral tiara of woven blossoms.

'I feel really stupid,' she said. 'Do you have a cigarette?' Delighted, Martin offered her one.

'What on earth are these? Don't they have filters?' She began to puff away on the Virginia No. 2. 'What strong cigarettes,' she continued, 'I've never had one of these before. Who are you anyway?'

'I'm Martin – Anne's brother.'

'Oh yes, I saw you ushing, and you got it all wrong.' She laughed.

'I've never ushed before. It's a bit of a shambles isn't it?'
Martin was beginning to like this humorous, exasperated girl.
'You're Franny aren't you?'

'Francesca; I prefer Francesca. At least you don't have to wear
this stuff – God, these *are* strong aren't they? I think I'm going to
be sick . . .'

'Wait till you see the vol-au-vents.'

'Chicken?'

'Right first time – creamed . . .'

'How perfectly foul.'

Martin began to study Francesca's face more closely. She really
was very pretty. Her mouth, in particular, delighted him.
Whereas Fenella's lips had seemed soft and voluptuous, Francesca had a broad smile, with only the faintest trace of flesh-
coloured lipstick.

'Are we sitting together at the do?' said Martin.

'I hope so. I hardly know anyone . . .'

But Martin and Francesca were seated at separate tables.
Seeing the girl take her place on the other side of the dining
room, and watching her introduce herself to her male neighbour
with the same friendliness that she had shown to him, Martin was
consumed with bitterness and jealousy once more. As he left his
soup untasted, and merely picked at his salmon, and yearned to
light a cigarette, he continued to glance at his new acquaintance.
As he did this, the lady on his right kept saying, 'But you're not
eating! You've got to eat!' The room was now filled with the
clattering of cutlery upon crockery, and the growing din of
conversation and laughter. Windows were opened.

Immediately after the speeches, which Martin could only
describe in his head as purgatorial, he went outside to have a
cigarette. It was late afternoon, and the sun was trying to come
out, sending amber beams across the little river which flanked
'the old mill'. Beyond the opposite bank, stretching away
towards a low, distant line of woods, there were golden fields. It

was pleasant to be out in the cool air, and to think clearly once more. Liverpool took its place in Martin's mind. He had no desire to go there. He had received, the previous morning, a set of papers relating to his forthcoming registration: course information, 'welfare' information, residential details, 'socs.', 'The City of Liverpool – A Guide'.

'Oh Christ,' he said, out loud. He wished that he was going to some country retreat, a place that mingled the study of interesting things with the ambience of a National Trust property.

And yet he had done nothing to resist the conveyor belt of his class. Despite his strong belief in his own originality, he had merely drifted along, dreaming and élitist, thinking about girls and money. Also, he was afraid of being homesick again. With unexpected brilliance the September sun burst through the remaining clouds. Looking behind himself, Martin could see a purple, stormy sky; ahead, the countryside seemed to have opened up beneath a fan of light. It was a moment of stillness, charged with mystery.

Just then, Francesca came running up. She was slightly drunk.

'I've just seen the salad cart!' she shouted, breathlessly.

'The whatter?' smiled Martin.

'The salad cart, stupid. They've got this old painted wagon in the other restaurant, where you get your salad – it's priceless . . .' She was leaning against him now, and swaying slightly. 'Oops,' she laughed. Martin suddenly felt awkward and uncomfortable.

'So what are you thinking about, all alone out here?' Francesca went on. 'Anyway, I've been hearing all about you.'

Martin grinned, sheepishly. 'I was thinking about Liverpool.'

'That's where you're going, isn't it? Do you know anyone there?'

Martin realised that he didn't. Not a soul.

'What about friends from school? I knew some boys from Tiles once,' she laughed again: 'they were awful. They were all going off to be captains in the Navy or something, and most of them could hardly tie their shoelaces. Incredibly stuck-up . . .'

'Oh, I know,' said Martin, hoping that he didn't seem stuck-up. 'But what about you? Are you going to college?'

'No way! Absolutely not. I screamed and I kicked and I finally got off the hook.' Francesca more or less sang this. 'My cousin was a student, at Durham, and it put me off for life –'

'So what are you going to do?' Martin felt a sinking sensation in his stomach.

'I'm going to Russia. I'm going to be a nanny to an American family.' Francesca was leaning against the low stone wall as she said this. Martin felt as though she was a thousand miles away. He tried to sound enthusiastic and interested, but he knew, in his heart, that all the ridiculous excitement which he had sensed throughout his talks with Francesca was now being cut down to the demands of reality.

'When do you leave?' he asked.

'At Christmas, well, New Year. I'm working in a shop until then, and trying to learn Russian.'

'Oh, right.' This sounded rather abrupt. Francesca, who had been thinking that Martin was nice, but who had not (as he had) mentally pursued the potential romance into a distant and roseate future, began to have second thoughts. Certainly, she thought that Martin was attractive, and amusing, but was there not, possibly, a streak of self-consciousness and affectation which made him seem slightly ridiculous? Studying him once more as he stood beside her, so obviously forlorn, she generously decided that he was simply shy.

Before the party broke up, they exchanged telephone numbers.

Martin, since his disappointment with Fenella, had given some considerable thought to the fourth dimension of love. He no longer, sadly, required romance to be the mainstay of beauty. He still believed that love was the catalyst of aesthetics, and he still indulged in the practice of forcing emotions to the surface of life, in order to provoke a reaction; but his faith in this process was no longer intact. 'To be interesting', it seemed, must be defended as well as dedicated.

Francesca, were she to hear this reasoning, would have had nothing to do with it. Whilst Martin, when he arranged to see Francesca again, just two days after the wedding, regarded their meeting as another wave to bear him up, rushing towards an unspecified shore, the girl (with both feet, as it were, on the ground) was merely quite pleased. Francesca was an only child, and she was both headstrong and stubborn. She was also capable of tremendous charm, and possessed a rare quality which made the recipients of her attention feel flattered. She had never been known to bore anyone. Her male admirers, since her fifteenth birthday, had been legion; some were attracted to her striking looks, others to her wit and energy – one or two had even been attracted to both. And Francesca had been willing to return the interest. She had lost her virginity, and many of her illusions, extremely young. She prided herself upon her autonomy, and once she made a decision she stuck with it. She had decided to see more of Martin.

The first impediment to the blossoming relationship was the fact that Martin would soon be leaving for Liverpool. As the first two weeks of September (Martin left for college on the 17th) were made glorious with a hot, Indian summer, and as the friendship began to deepen, the imminence of tertiary education began daily to recede. It was, in fact, laid to waste in the path of Martin's first experience of requited passion.

Francesca lived nine miles away from Martin, in Wimbledon. She was, therefore, more urban than pastoral. As if to augment this quality, she delighted her new boyfriend by adding surprising touches of punk detail to her otherwise standard wardrobe: a

41

ripped T-shirt, safety-pin cuff-links, an old grey jacket with burnt lapels. Martin began to copy her. Also, Francesca both encouraged and was pleased by Martin's overt romanticism. He was forever sending her little cards, inscribed with meaningful quotations. Their love, he decreed, could be expressed through an entire directory of romantic ciphers.

One day, at the beginning of Martin's 'last week', the couple went to Kew Gardens. It was Francesca's afternoon off from the shop where she worked (the shop was called Originale and it sold posters and postcards, as well as Arthur Rackham mobiles and varnished boxes to keep things in) and the weather was superb. The sky was deep blue and cloudless, and the trees, just beginning to turn, were a mass of green and gold and crimson. Late roses were in bloom behind the Tropical House, and the grass was parched. It being a weekday, the gardens were quiet; and in the great greenhouses the towering palms and extravagant creepers with their exotic fruits and flowers seemed to hang, stately and mysterious, between shafts of sunlight and humid, aromatically scented shadows. 'It feels,' said Martin, 'like a hundred years ago.' The couple walked down the long avenue which stretches towards the bend in the river facing Syon House. There were hardly any other people. Francesca had brought some Persian cigarettes with her, rolled brown leaves tied at one end with pink thread. Sprawling in the sun, the young lovers smoked these exotic intoxicants. A serenity enveloped them.

'Why haven't you got any male friends?' asked Francesca suddenly.

Martin had never given the matter much thought. Being essentially selfish, he was capable of both great love and great indifference.

'But you haven't,' continued the girl, 'you've got Christine – who you hardly ever see – and you had what's-her-face, the American girl, but you never mention any boys. Why is that?'

Martin rolled over and looked at the sky. It was quite true – he shunned male company. There had been, at Tiles, one or two brief intimacies with boys whom he either admired, or found fashionable and enlightened, but none of these friendships had endured.

'There's Piers,' he volunteered, lamely.

'Who's Piers?'

And so Martin went on to give an extravagant eulogy of the Tiles genius whom he had hardly known: part poet, part philosopher – wholly destined for greatness.

'He doesn't sound like a friend exactly,' pronounced Francesca, with worrying perception, 'more of a role model.'

The boy nodded. His interest was only half captured by the conversation. He wanted to continue kissing Francesca's lovely pale face, the eyes so blue and arresting. Also, he had just been introduced to 'serious' kisses. The subject of Martin's male friends drifted away amidst sentimentalities and desire, soon to evaporate in the shadows beneath the trees, where clouds of golden insects hovered.

But Martin was, essentially, friendless. The truth of this statement was derived from the fact that boys – for the time being – had ceased to be of any use to him. There would come a time, fairly soon, when the way to the exceptional would be pointed out to Martin by young men whom he admired, and from whom he realised he could draw strength. For the moment, however, in Kew Gardens with Francesca, there seemed to the young boy to be no interest in anything save the slender girl who was lying beside him. Later, he would regard such devotion as boring.

The golden drowse continued, making a long minor chord of the afternoon. The young lovers, in the manner of youth, snogged.

Two: *Further Education*

When, on the 17th of September 1978, Martin Knight departed for Liverpool, he did so in a lovesick daze. The previous evening, having slipped away from his packed suitcases and the large plastic bag which contained his duvet, he had spent three hours with Francesca, in her romantically candle-lit room in Wimbledon, and there exchanged caresses between impassioned whispered speeches. Francesca and her family lived in a tall Edwardian house which was filled with a bohemian atmosphere. The rooms were crowded with books and pictures and vases of dried flowers; and neither Francesca's father (who was an architect) nor her mother (who was a teacher) would have dreamt of disturbing their daughter's privacy.

Francesca's room was on the top floor of the house, beneath a gable, and it looked out over the long, narrow, but charmingly wild garden, where honeysuckle tangled with the climbing roses, and where the uncut grass at the edge of the lawn seemed to mingle with the trailing branches of an exuberant willow. Halfway down the garden, its uppermost foliage on a level with Francesca's window, there stood a towering lime tree. When the wind picked up, or when it rained, the silence that seemed to surround the top of the house was broken by the soft smack of drops against the leaves and the rustling of branches. Martin had only been to Francesca's house twice before, but already he loved

45

it. In his mind, in fact, he was as entranced by Francesca's house and garden as he was by the girl herself. The lily-of-the-valley perfume which she wore seemed to scent her whole room, and Martin had begged his new girlfriend to drench one of his hankerchiefs with the precious extract, so that he could inhale her in her absence. Delighted, Francesca had done so.

But now it was time to leave for college, and to face the grey chasm of the unknown which would open up between them. As a consequence of this sadness, on his last evening, Martin had felt the tug of Francesca and her sacred room with a force that filled him with melancholy and desire. This feeling had quickly communicated itself to Francesca. Looking at Martin, with his serious eyes and his dark, rather tousled hair, the girl had felt sure that she loved him – and had said so. Outside in the garden, the stately lime tree was black against the deep blue of the evening sky; and on the horizon, high above Fulham (or so it seemed), bright stars were shining.

'Oh, Francesca . . .'

'Yes?' (This encouragingly.)

'Oh, I love you too, you know. I do. I know that we haven't been going out for very long, and that I've got to go off to this stupid college, but . . .'

'Don't go. Stay here with me . . .' Francesca, who had been sitting beside Martin on her wide, old-fashioned bed, now lay back with her head against the wall and looked up at him invitingly. The candle-light made her skin seem brown, and warm; and her blue eyes, gazing with an unerring kindness which seemed scarcely to mask the evidence of a deeper, less chaste, form of affection, appeared darker and more seductive than Martin had ever seen them before. Francesca's shirt was unbuttoned, and Martin, attempting to control himself, traced a line with his finger from her throat to her navel. Encountering no resistance, but, rather, a smile of encouragement, he then leant closer and slipped his hand around the girl's soft waist.

Francesca, who in the past had found herself (at a similarly critical moment) to be suddenly faced with advances that resembled assault, was grateful to Martin for his comparative timidity. For more or less the first time (she dimly realised) she was enjoying a contact which she found sensual, and which made her feel light-hearted, as well as absorbed. Sitting up, and then kneeling, she slipped off her shirt and rested her forearms upon Martin's shoulders. In this position, her head was slightly higher than that of her lover. The moment had made a psychologist of Francesca. The candles were beginning to burn low, and as their light commenced to waver she looked down into Martin's eyes with an imperious, playful smile. She didn't speak, but allowed the boy to contemplate that part of her body which was now only partially clothed. Then, bending forward, she took his head in her hands and kissed him deeply upon the mouth. Martin, feeling her strength, and her warmth, became the passive recipient of these embraces. A fear of disturbing the spell of the evening, as much as anything, caused him to act with restraint. He had virtually no experience of physical love, and thus, as Francesca kissed him, or as she leant back – still kneeling astride his legs – to blow her fringe out of her eyes, an awe of her loveliness made him weak, as opposed to coarse, with desire. He ran his fingers down her neck, and across her perfumed collarbone and breasts. His touch lingered on the soft black fabric of her brassière.

In this manner, Francesca and Martin passed their last hour of freedom together, murmuring endearments to one another until the words had ceased to have any meaning. At one point, aching with desire, Martin attempted to unbutton Francesca's jeans, and to slowly tug down the brass fastening on their zip.

'Don't,' she said quietly. 'We'll do that another time.'

The following morning Martin left for Liverpool. He could think of little save Francesca. Everything else, perilously, was a vague beyond that he wholly and effortlessly denied.

*

It was inevitable, under the circumstances, that Martin should despise his new life as a student. Also, both socially and with regard to his emotional constitution, he was entirely unsuited to the great Mersey city and the world of the polytechnic. For the first two weeks he wandered around in a sullen daze which was taken (with some accuracy) for mere arrogance; but when (realising the impression he was creating) he attempted to make conversation with his neighbours, he found that he simply endorsed their opinion of him. He was known as 'that bloke from public school' and, whilst not provoking actual hostility, his company was shunned. Had he been less obsessed with his relationship with Francesca, he might well have recognised the mistakes he was making, and done something to improve his standing. As it was, initially, he kept himself to himself, and simply snapped on a brief smile when he walked past anyone who looked at him in the corridor. Fairly soon he was ignored.

He was allotted a small study-bedroom in the student hostel that stood half a mile from the Social Sciences building. The hostel had been built in 1968 (its architect was rumoured to have killed himself), and it comprised of little more than four floors of long white corridors, lined with blue doors. At either end of each corridor there was a fire-escape; and as there were no windows that allowed daylight into the corridors themselves, dusty tubes of bright light flickered and hummed throughout the day and night. Many of the blue doors were kicked and scraped; and many more bore stickers and pictures that suggested the temperaments of their owners. All in all it was a dismal, functional place. On the ground floor of the hostel, beyond the echoing entrance hall with its squat and ill-tempered porter who referred to the young male students as 'lads' or 'buggers', depending on their behaviour, there was a shabby, smoke-filled bar, a corridor of small bathrooms and a sparse, savoury-smelling dining hall. 'Tea' was served at six o'clock sharp.

When he arrived in his little room, Martin's first instinct was to turn on his heel and leave it again. Then, lighting a cigarette (the green metal bin was blackened around its inside with the charcoal of many stubbings-out), he realised that he could not, yet, run away, and so he began to survey his new home. There was little to see: a narrow bed took up two-thirds of the space beside the left-hand wall; flush to the head of this bed there was a desk, with two drawers and a broken lamp; in front of the desk a smeared window offered a view towards another wall, which stood beyond the width of a narrow service road. On the right-hand wall there was a baize-covered noticeboard, with three blue-headed drawing pins clustered in its top right-hand corner. A shelf beneath this and a radiator beneath the shelf. Just inside the door there was a wardrobe and a deep cupboard which contained a washbasin and shaving mirror. Peering dully into the basin, Martin saw a white plastic spatula of the kind given away with tubes of hair-removal cream. Girls (he thought vaguely) must sometimes visit this place. And then, as shouts and laughter and strong northern voices sounded loudly along the corridor, the young man flopped down like a sack of wet cement onto his bed and thought about Francesca. Already, he felt as though their love was both threatened and cheapened. Nothing, he thought, could survive or flourish amongst such ugliness and mediocrity.

Martin would recall his first term at college as being, ironically, a time when his senses were almost too alert. Looking back, he seemed to remember that there had always been a smell of frost in the air, and that the sun was very bright in the morning, falling between the tall, grey buildings to flood the busy streets with a white light that forced one to walk with lowered eyes. In truth, the sudden intrusion into Martin's confined and insular life of a bewildering array of new impressions and responsibilities was reduced to three things: the interminable train journey that separated him from Francesca and autumnal Wimbledon; the scratched and exposed pay-phone in the entrance hall of the student hostel from which he telephoned Francesca; and the glass-fronted letter-rack (pigeon-hole 'K') in which, on good, blessed days, he found Francesca's letters to him, with his new address inscribed upon them in her careful, precise handwriting. Her tone in these letters (sometimes they were cards from Originale, which depicted silvery and eerie illustrations from Victorian picturebooks: The Man In The Moon, Rapunzel and 'Mother, Put My Little Shoes Away') was seldom sentimental. He would have preferred them to be more so. Her usual style was to mingle vague suggestiveness with humorous and self-deprecatory accounts of her daily routine, in which she figured as the hapless victim of various comedies of errors. She wrote frequently at first ('I want you to think of me every day'), and Martin responded at length. His letters, however, were always more intense, and filled with a poetic longing, the fervour of which (initially) Francesca found deeply flattering.

'I really think he's the one,' she said to Jane, the other assistant at Originale.

'But you've only known him for a few weeks –'

'Yes, but . . .' Francesca fell silent, and allowed her thoughts to dwell on the distant student. Having indulged her colleague with a brief (and inwardly bored) smile, Jane then shrugged, and continued to polish the Coca-Cola-print mirrors.

Between the beginning of term and the middle of October, Martin travelled down to his home twice – in order to see Francesca. His mother found these visits both irregular and extravagant.

'You can't just keep on rushing down here,' she said, exasperated. Martin, in love, was indurate to common sense.

'It isn't that expensive,' he said.

Unfortunately, these visits were expensive. Coupled with the suppers that Martin liked to buy for Francesca at the little pizza restaurant in Wimbledon, the price of love was dear. Martin considered such issues to be of no importance. His grant, and the moderate allowance that his mother had given him, seemed to the young man to be a fortune. Also, academically, he had discovered that his work at the polytechnic was considerably easier than that which he had crammed for his A levels. Dr Sturridge, his tutor, was pleased with him. Thus Martin's reservoir of optimism was quite full. Finding Liverpool hopelessly ugly, and having neither sought nor made any friends, the young man was living through his intense, yet fragile, first true love. Trusting his desires and his instincts, he marched confidently on down what he assumed to be the path of beauty. By beauty, now, he meant Francesca.

The first weekend of November marked a turning point in Martin's career. That weekend, having saved up the extra money to realise her plan, Francesca came to stay with Martin in Liverpool. She would be greeted by him on the Friday evening, stay with a girlfriend on Friday night, and then, from Saturday lunchtime, spend the whole of the remaining twenty-four hours of her visit in Martin's company. This plan involved some daring, too, for girls (officially) were not supposed to stay in the student hostel. Martin, however, like Lawrence of Arabia in the film of that name, believed himself to be invisible, and thus protected from any detection of his audacity. And he was quite right; nobody, in fact, could care less whether or not a girl stayed in his room. To the outside world, the event was of no significance.

In preparation for the great visit, Martin extracted £30 from his student bank account. This sum represented a considerable portion of his income. He wanted to take Francesca out for dinner on Saturday evening, and do so with the same insouciant nonchalance with which Fenella, once, had treated him to sashimi. Such grand gestures, he believed, had a place on the upper slopes – if not the summit – of romantic achievement. He had already selected a suitable restaurant ('Le Beaujolais') and booked a table. The restaurant, from the street, looked dark and sophisticated, with white candles and a trolley bearing exotic cheeses. He had checked the prices too, in order to avoid embarrassment. This was the first time that the young man had choreographed an evening of adult pleasure, composing the sequence of delightful events by anticipating, erotically, a stylised rehearsal of their procession in his imagination. Anticipation, he already knew, was the greater part of romance.

On Friday evening, shortly before Francesca's train was due to arrive at Lime Street Station, a damp mist descended upon Liverpool. Entering the concourse, where businessmen in beige raincoats were standing with their briefcases beside their feet, and where other travellers were passing the slow moments prior to departure in buying cups of hot chocolate, or nervously watching the quartet of drunks who were shouting their own incoherent logic at one another in a distant corner, Martin was aware of a foreign darkness lapping at the steps behind him. He had no memories, as yet, of the grey, mist-filled city; and without memories the place did not exist for him. Memories, he felt, made a place real. Down the hill up which he had walked, he knew, there were precincts of shops, and the concrete indoor market; taxis were shuddering in the cold at their ranks; along the broad estuary, which others had compared to a vista of Leningrad, there were great rotting warehouses, and the jumble of box-like temporary offices which signified major construction work. And then there were grey roads, bathed in violet light as they swept into bright tunnels before rushing off past the city limits, cutting a path through silent streets of tiny houses, all swathed in white mist. To Martin, warming himself at the centre of his love, the thought of these places was as vague and as remote as the thought of a sweating jungle, tense and battered beneath a monsoon. Fear, as much as anything, closed his mind to the implications of the unknown. He wished, as he lit a cigarette (practicality had forced him to forsake his beloved

Freiburg & Treyer for packets of Marlboro purchased from SuperCigs), that he was meeting Francesca in Oxford. For a moment he remembered the chapel window at Tiles, so aloof and elegant now in his mind; and then he recognised his girlfriend, wrapped up against the damp in an ankle-length white raincoat and hurrying towards him carrying a small travelling bag. Their meeting resembled an advert.

For Francesca, to whom the Soviet Union would soon be calling, love had come as a complete surprise. Unlike Martin, for whom romance was vital, Francesca was concerned primarily with independence, and the pursuit of controlled adventure on her own terms. Prior to meeting Martin, her appointment to be a nanny in Moscow had made the girl sufficient unto herself. Her feelings towards the young man could best be described as infatuation. This infatuation was nearing its peak. Holding hands and talking excitedly, Martin and Francesca made their way to a large, popular pub, where Rosie (Francesca's friend) was waiting for them. Martin – who had not met Rosie before – was over-polite as he sat with the two girls for a little while, prior to 'leaving them in peace'. He was so filled with confidence and happiness that he began, despite himself, to play the part of a busy but loving husband, eager not to intrude on Rosie's share of the visit. Francesca found this irritating, but, being happy herself, said nothing about it. Instead, she arranged to meet Martin the following afternoon. As Martin was leaving the bar, he whispered, too loudly, 'I love you' to his girlfriend. Francesca smiled and patted him on the elbow; Rosie smiled too, but inwardly she was regarding the scene with incredulity. She thought that Martin was silly and affected.

The following day the lovers made a tour of the city. This was difficult, for Martin was none too sure of his bearings. A cold, thin rain was falling, and the slippery streets were crowded with shoppers and cars. It seemed to be growing dark by the middle of the afternoon. Martin and Francesca went to the two big record shops, where they busied themselves (self-consciously) with looking for the latest 'new-wave' releases. Records by strange local punk-rock groups were pinned up behind the counter at one of the record shops, and Martin, in fact, was scared by the local punks who were loitering before them. They wore big black boots and leather jackets covered in studs. Their hair was crudely coloured, and several of them were drunk. One threw an empty lager can across the shop, and was told to leave by the assistant. Martin, whilst attracted to extremes, found this provincial anarchy far less appealing than the fashionable, expensive brand of outrage which was on sale in Chelsea. Francesca thought it was funny. A rumour circulated the shop that a group of skinheads were making their way down the street, and for a moment people stared towards the door. Martin and Francesca left. Martin's heart was still pounding heavily as he took his girlfriend's hand and walked quickly towards the safer, busier end of the street. But he tried to look unconcerned.

To raise their spirits again, Martin suggested that they walk down to the estuary. The rain was pouring down in hard, straight lines now, and so they went for a cup of coffee instead, in a little café located in the basement of a second-hand-clothes shop. Here, amongst tables crowded with soaked young shoppers, the couple found a place in the corner and sat with their hot drinks and slices of home-made flapjack. The furniture in the little café was all mismatched, and around the walls there were elderly glass-fronted cabinets filled with bric-à-brac and 'antiques': old tins that had once held gramophone needles, flamboyant teapots, platoons of faded lead soldiers, Victorian etchings mounted upon warped, stained boards, a scattering of Nazi regalia, paste jewels . . . Martin, whose confidence had returned, began to feel excited about the forthcoming dinner at Le Beaujolais.

'Now, I've booked a cab for half-past seven; but we'll have to sneak you past Old Tom,' he said, stroking Francesca's hand.

'Who's Old Tom?' Francesca eyed her young man with mock

suspicion, and then, humorously, assumed the countenance of a coquette.

'Tom's the porter, but it's perfectly all right . . .'

'We're not going to be disturbed in the night are we?'

'No! It'll be fine.' Martin's heart began to pound again. Francesca's chestnut-coloured hair was damp, and looked dark against the collar of her white raincoat. Her long eyelashes appeared black, and glistening; her mouth was pale. The scent of lily of the valley mingled with the smell of cigarette smoke and wet clothes.

'I love you,' said Martin, again, uselessly.

Francesca squeezed his hand. On their way out of the shop, the young man bought his girlfriend a white imitation-silk scarf, patterned with large black triangles.

At a quarter-past seven that evening, the couple waited for their taxi in the entrance hall of the student hostel. Francesca, beneath her unbuttoned white raincoat, was wearing a short black dress. She looked out of place in the shabby, echoing hall, with its torn and dog-eared posters advertising student events and popular political groups. Secretly, she was thanking heaven that she would never be a student. A trio of high-spirited young men walked past her on their way to the pub, and whistled as they caught her eye. Francesca turned away, but smiled despite herself. Martin, almost elegant in his grey suit, did not deign to comment. Old Tom was not on duty yet.

At Le Beaujolais the young lovers were served by a silver-haired, continental gentleman who was wearing a dinner suit, and by his tall, awkward assistant, who was extremely nervous. The restaurant was fairly quiet, and the other diners were two middle-aged couples who ate in silence, and a party of four – two husbands and their wives. The husbands (who must have been in their late thirties) were wearing brown suits, and the wives, who bore themselves rather stiffly, were dressed in extravagant sequinned blouses and long narrow skirts. They looked at Francesca, in her simple, expensive black dress, as though she was an urchin. Drink was flowing freely at that table, and the two young husbands were beginning to laugh loudly, and to conclude one another's anecdotes in loud voices, thickened with wheezing laughter.

'So she says,' bawled one, '"Me bum's all sweaty." I said, "So's mine – but I don't go telling people!"' Martin and Francesca tried to look as though this raucous conversation was a quaint entertainment being provided by low mechanicals for their amusement; a sort of tribute to their love.

Francesca began with the *Stilton Soup*. Martin had pâté. For some reason, now that they were actually at the restaurant, they found conversation difficult. The nervous young waiter brought Martin the bottle of 'house red' and seemed amazed when the young man instructed him to pour it without a prior tasting. The waiter's hand was shaking as he filled Francesca's glass. The couple began to think of nice things to say about the food and the restaurant, in order to fill the silences. Desperately, in search of high emotion, Martin considered proposing to Francesca. This event was cancelled by the arrival of the main course: *Duck Flamed in Cherry Brandy* for Martin, the *Medallions of Beef* for Francesca. Vegetables were served from a silver-plated side-dish by the young waiter. A roast potato rolled into the centre of the table and nestled, steaming, beside the cruets. Some of the *Creamed Celery* was spilt. Martin, wrestling with his duck, was rather dismayed that Le Beaujolais had not, in his opinion, lived up the suggestion of sophistication that had caused it to catch his eye. He wondered whether there was another, more expensive restaurant to which he could have taken his girlfriend. He was horrified by the thought that the real shrine of taste and beauty lay elsewhere, and that he was merely fumbling upon the distant edges of high living. Such a fear would stay with him for all of his life.

During dessert (they both had the *Banana Mousse*, as recommended by the continental gentleman) a sudden commotion took place beside the door. An old man, with long white hair and a nicotine-stained beard, quite soaked by the rain, was attempting to enter the restaurant. Martin, at first, did not realise that this man was a vagrant. Looking more closely he could see that the intruder was wearing an ancient, blackened coat, and had plastic bags from the supermarket fastened over his shoes. It was as though, prior to being shooed away by the head waiter flapping a linen napkin in his direction, the old drunk had assumed that he could slip into the warmth undetected. Turning to go back out into the rain, the vagrant's face was quite expressionless, but standing in the door he suddenly shouted: 'Fucking fucking bastard cunts; fuck y'all cunts . . .' The diners all looked up, and for a second there was silence. The head waiter had swiftly closed the door on the unwanted visitor and was now attempting, with a sigh, to explain the difficulties of dealing with such events to one of the middle-aged couples, who were nodding understandingly. The party of husbands and wives, now quite drunk themselves, were laughing uproariously.

'He'll be the cook's dad!' said one of the men, winking, 'come in for a sit by the stove . . .'

Martin had found the intrusion disturbing. Francesca spoke at length about what a shame such things were. But the event had reunited the young couple, who, for two and a half hours, had been feeling estranged. Now the night was ahead of them: a novelty, and a delight. It was the first time that they had spent a whole night together.

Martin paid the bill, which came to just over £20, and then (due to the excessive tip) the couple were bowed towards the door. As they passed by the quartet of young couples, one of the husbands said: 'It's cold out, love; hope you've got your knickers on . . .' His laughter pursued them into the street.

*

Martin and Francesca decided to walk back to the student hostel. This was Francesca's idea, and Martin surveyed the wet, dark side streets nervously. Loitering on corners and standing on the pavements outside pubs and clubs, groups of noisy young people made the area around the centre of the city appear as though there was a drunken carnival going on, only this carnival was neither light-hearted nor welcoming. Shouts and screams filled the air, and the sound of breaking glass. Parties of red-faced, aggressive young men, none of whom were wearing jackets or coats over their thin trousers and short-sleeved shirts, seemed to be making their way towards some kind of gathering, the location and purpose of which was not clear. In their turn, squads of lightly dressed girls, as drunk and as loud as their men, were clattering across the street in high-heeled shoes, pausing occasionally to shout into the open windows of passing cars. Four policemen stood at the top of a precinct beside their van, watching the crowd. The rain had stopped and the night was now cold. Clouds were blowing across the sky, grey against the moon. The city clocks began to strike eleven.

Old Tom did not look up when Martin and Francesca entered the hostel. He was sitting behind his desk engrossed in a magazine. Beside him, a small transistor radio was playing. Beyond the hall, in the student bar, some people were singing. The hostel smelt of beer and damp carpets. Hurrying through this scene, the young lovers made their way to Martin's little room on the second floor. They only met one other person coming down the white corridor – a thin, shrunken-faced boy who wore a childish expression and a brown jumper tucked into his corduroy trousers. He looked unutterably lonely. Once inside Martin's study-bedroom, with the desk lamp mended now and turned against the curtains to create a low orange light, the couple locked their door and sat down with exaggerated sighs of relief, as though they had just escaped from some danger. They lit cigarettes, and talked in low voices, and began to relax. Francesca hung her raincoat up in Martin's cupboard, and placed her black, low-heeled shoes beside the bed. Martin made coffee from a kettle on the floor, and made Francesca laugh by slipping out to 'steal some milk'. Soon the couple were giggling, and overcome with a sense of excitement at being alone together in that strange place. Snatches of conversation and laughter sounded loudly as people passed by the door; somewhere above them music was being played. And then Martin and Francesca's sexual dialogue resumed – it was inevitable that it should.

Shortly after half-past two that morning, when the hostel was quiet, Martin turned off the desk lamp and pulled the curtains open. The room, pitch-black for a second, began to reshape itself in the grey half-light that flooded in through the window. Leaning over the desk (which he always kept clear of papers and books), Martin nudged open the window, and felt a sudden gust of cold air. The smoke in the room began to clear. For more than an hour the couple had been lying together; kissing, running their hands across one another's bodies, loosening articles of clothing and then holding back, as though trapped upon a plateau of erotic hesitation. In Martin's case, this hesitation was due to fear. Still a virgin, he was afraid of the act which was so obviously about to take place. Francesca, on the other hand, was more certain of herself; and she had, moreover, 'taken the necessary precautions'. She was held back simply by Martin's timidity – but now she had decided to act. Regarding her boyfriend in the darkness, she found him to be both lovable and desirable; her love (or her infatuation, for these two qualities were indistin-guishable at that moment) was guiding her. The moment had now come – with the turning-off of the lamp and the opening of the curtains – for the couple to undress and go to bed; but both of them knew, even as they stood on opposite sides of the darkened room, that this pause was simply a brief, intoxicating gap between two gradations of physical love.

Martin, having lit another cigarette, returned from the

window (which he had been facing) to lie semi-clothed upon the bed. His eyes had adjusted to the darkness now, as he watched Francesca crossing the room towards him, thrillingly complicit with his mounting desire. She looked, to him, like a fashion plate from a 1920s lingerie catalogue. There was a seductive, archaic quality about her appearance, the gentle formality of which served only to heighten the sexual potency of her presence. She was wearing a pale cotton nightdress, cut square with lace just above her breasts, and fastened at the front with two thin satin ribbons. The nightdress was gathered at the waist, like a loose white petticoat, before falling in soft, broad pleats to a point just above her knees. This garment hung lightly upon Francesca's body, and Martin realised, as she lay down beside him, that the fine, scented material appeared to have no weight, and at the slightest touch would rise up over her nakedness.

The act of love was over – in the crudest sense – before it had even begun. Too quickly, Martin had lost control of himself; and his ambitious desire had become subordinate to mere clumsy lust. In less than a minute, it seemed, his psychology and his emotions were jolted from ecstasy to a deep, irrational depression, and thence to an overbearing sense of weakness and self-disgust. He lay beside Francesca, curled up in the darkness like a little boy, with his eyes closed. Francesca, kindly, stroked his hair. Her instinct caused her to show no surprise at the fragility of the male sexual ego; and she thought of other things. Thus, stoically, she buried her disappointment.

Later, when he reflected upon his love for Francesca, Martin Knight would blame what he regarded as his sexual incompetence on that Sunday morning in November 1978 for all the sadness which subsequently followed. In this he was wrong. Francesca would have been patient with her lover, and would have continued with their physical liaison had it not been for a draining degree of intensity that the young man had proceeded to inflict upon her. The glimpse of sexual theatre that she had offered to her boyfriend was coupled with the fact that certain images (her kneeling over him in Richmond; her slowly removing her dress in Liverpool) had locked themselves in the young man's mind as though to madden him, and become signifiers of something vast and poetic. Thus Martin craved, and adored – and thus he became unattractive.

This happened almost immediately. Between the weekend of Francesca's visit in November and the beginning of the Christmas holidays in December, Martin plagued his girlfriend with cards and letters and telephone calls. At the slightest hint of weariness or short temper in his beloved's responses to these communications, Martin would fret and brood and devise all manner of ways to make further contact. This simply made matters worse. He even began to send – at vast expense – flowers to Francesca's home and workplace. These embarrassed her.

'Oh God,' she said to Jane one day, as yet another extravagant construction of cellophane and carnations was delivered to Originale. Jane tried to mingle, in the same mute expression, sympathy and admiration. Francesca, exasperated, simply put the flowers in the sink in the little staff kitchen, and then got on with her work in silence. An hour later, the telephone rang. Jane, covering the mouthpiece, said, 'It's Martin . . .'

'Tell him I'm out.'

So quickly, Martin's romanticism had converted into a fawning, sentimental and ultimately boring single-mindedness. His sole desire was to lie down with Francesca, and 'be in love'. Francesca, who made decisions quickly, began to welcome her departure for the Soviet Union. Her appointment had now been confirmed, and she was due to leave on the 12th of January 1979. Martin, of course, was aware of this situation, but, somehow, he denied its reality. Francesca, in her turn, seldom spoke of it, and when the subject was raised between them she became evasive. She didn't want a scene; Martin was too frightened to start one.

When Martin came home (two days early) for the Christmas holidays, he felt as though all his worst, lonely fears were being realised. The short, dark days turned into long, freezing nights, and, whilst Francesca was brisk, and cheerfully practical in her attitude towards her boyfriend, Martin yearned for a seasonal romance, with long walks across the frosty, colourless Heath beneath leaden skies the colour of gunmetal. As Christmas approached, and as Francesca made it clear that she was obliged to pass the three official days of holiday with her family, the anxious young man began to consider what manner of meaningful gift he could present to his goddess. He wanted this present to combine good taste with a romantic message, the result of which, ideally, would be a dramatic return to the passion of September. He settled upon a gift in two halves: an exquisite kimono for Francesca to take to Russia with her; and a box at the opera to serve as a matchless (in his opinion) setting in which to present it. In order to pay for this extravagance he asked for all of his Christmas money to be advanced to him. His mother, believing this request to be provoked by a need to buy suitable presents for Anne, her husband and sundry other relations, handed over the money.

On the 19th of December, Martin set off to London in order to arrange the magnificent presentation. He was like a man possessed, in many ways; he gave no thought to the ramifications or the logic of his enterprise, and concentrated merely upon the short-term chances of its success. He was both blind to sense and driven: the beautiful (he thought) must surely succeed. And yet in his heart he knew, quite surely, that the romance was over. Even in purely practical terms the relationship had run its course. Sitting upon the suburban train and watching a burst of wintry sunshine passing across the distant, copper-coloured windows of a big new office block whose foundations were deep in the soil of Vauxhall, Martin was reminded of his earlier visit, to buy perfume for Fenella. Some lines of Brooke (who was Martin's favourite poet) passed into the young man's mind, and their metre fell in time with the rhythm of the train as it clattered across the cold, grey delta of tracks beyond Battersea:

> The boy's woe was as keen and clear,
>   The boy's love just as true,
> And the One Before the Last, my dear,
>   Hurt quite as much as you.

Martin wished that he had written those lines. As the train drew to a halt, he considered writing them in his card for Francesca, but then dismissed the idea as being brutal.

In a shop which he had once walked past with Fenella, near South Kensington tube station, Martin chose a white kimono. This was not of the genuine silk variety (those cost several hundred pounds) but a pretty, fine-cotton substitute. It was white, and had some black lettering upon its back, and a branch of budding cherry blossom embroidered to one side of that. Martin, aware of the aesthetic debt to the oriental, was pleased with his purchase. The young Japanese girl who served him was eager for Francesca to be pleased; Martin spared the assistant no detail of his girlfriend's tastes, so desperate was he to maintain the illusion that Francesca was still in love with him, and would be awaiting this gift with loving impatience. The garment was wrapped in white tissue paper, and Martin was bowed out with the comment 'I hope she likes it, sir.'

He then went on to the London Coliseum, in St Martin's Lane, to see about the opera tickets. He had calculated his expenses well, and realised, as he studied the ticket prices, that he could – if he so chose – purchase a box. He determined to do so. What the young couple would actually attend, however, was problematical. On the night when Francesca had 'arranged to be free', the work being performed was *Dalibor*, by Smetna – a dull, brooding piece of immense length. Naturally, there was a box free; naturally, Martin took it. Returning home with his parcel and his

63

tickets (he had paused only to buy Anne and Tim a box of coloured table candles and a card), Martin envisaged himself sitting beside Francesca in their box. In his imagination, the scene that he created was one of *fin de siècle* sophistication: poised, elegant and deeply in love, the couple would gaze down from their dark, velvet-lined private chamber, and, secretly clasping hands with a pressure which betrayed much deeper emotions than those that a mere opera could satisfy, follow the drama beneath them with a detachment born of the fact that a far greater drama – they both knew – was playing in their hearts.

'We'll get the twenty to six,' said Martin, telephoning Francesca on the evening of 28th December. They were going to the opera the following day. Martin had not seen Francesca since the 23rd of December, when she gave him his Christmas present: an art deco tie-clip and a book about the Pre-Raphaelite Brotherhood. In the card she had written, *With Loads of Love*. On that evening, half-heartedly, the couple had sat in Francesca's room once more, only this time there were no candles, and Francesca had kept on getting up to 'see if her mother needed any help'. Martin, attempting to kindle passion, had received a chastening kiss on the nose. He had been too frightened of upsetting the girl to further his embraces. How, he asked himself desperately, could Francesca have changed towards him so suddenly? And why would she not admit it? Inwardly, he cursed and accused; then he was overcome with nostalgia and sentimentality, and felt sorry for himself. Francesca's defences were both amorphous and robust. She had done her grieving for the romance much earlier, when Martin had become too intense. She, too, had been nostalgic for the early days of their relationship, but, unlike Martin, she knew that the period of grace had gone, and that no future for them lay ahead. Having first been concerned by Martin's devotion, she had then become bored with it; now, beneath the practicality which would get her to Moscow, she was becoming angry.

In the early hours of the morning of 29th December, it began to snow heavily. Silently, while the suburbs slept, the streets and parks and dual carriageways became white and mysterious. The bleak, empty week between Christmas and New Year suddenly became a topic of conversation: those who were working came home early; those at home surveyed their gardens and saw strange new landscapes – the lilac tree bending beneath a weight of snow, the rockery lost in a drift; transport became difficult . . . Martin, whilst loving the snow, was worried for the future of his plan. Francesca, however, told him not to worry, and met him in the cold, damp ticket hall of the station, where sheets of thick cardboard were disintegrating upon the floor between puddles of black water.

She seemed infuriatingly cheerful. There was not one shred of sentiment, or even personality, to be found in her countenance or conversation. Martin was clutching the parcel which contained Francesca's kimono; she affected an impatience to receive it. Ungraciously, but desperate to inject the evening with some emotion, Martin gave her the parcel as they passed through Balham.

'Oh, it's lovely!' she said, peering into the opened wrapping; 'but I won't take it out now because it'll get dirty . . .' Martin began a speech about how he wanted her to think of him when she wore it (if she wore it) in bed etc.

'Oh, that's lovely,' she said – and squeezed his hand. 'Look!' she continued, 'we're here!' She was behaving as though they were mere comrades.

Sullen and awkward, Martin trailed behind Francesca as they made their way from Embankment tube station across the Strand and up St Martin's Lane. He kept on saying, 'I'm all right,' to Francesca's repeated questions regarding his silence. He was tongue-tied. Francesca, on the other hand, knew exactly what was wrong, and simply wanted to get through the evening with the minimum of melodrama and fuss. The London Coliseum was only half filled; the box smelt musty. The attendant who took them to it seemed surprised that anyone would have booked a box for that performance, and, on finding it locked, had to go and fetch the key. Francesca tried to look happy; Martin became increasingly gloomy. He bought them both programmes, and wrote *I Love You*, and the date, in the one he gave to Francesca. She was supposed to cherish this. She put it in her handbag. Studying her profile as she sat beside him in the ludicrous, high-ceilinged box (the couple looked completely exposed to the other members of the audience, who gave them curious glances), Martin felt as though he was looking at a face in a bad dream: it was Francesca's lovely face, with the soft lips and blue eyes and slender neck; but there was a hardness across it, as though some mask was being worn to keep him out, and this new face would not open itself to the poignancy of his stare. The monumental masonry above the empty stage boxes looked dusty and foreboding as the house-lights were dimmed; the air in the opera house appeared still and foetid, as though it was absorbing all attempts at gaiety or romance. The crimson curtains looked melancholy and forlorn; the audience seemed ill-tempered.

By the end of the first scene, Martin was accusing Francesca in a furious whisper of not caring about him. At first she simply said, 'Don't be silly,' and then she began to shush him. When he renewed his accusations, during a woodwind intermezzo, she became seriously cross: 'Shut up —' At this, Martin got up, looked neither right nor left, and, grabbing his coat, pulled open the heavy door of the box. Fumbling in the dark corridor outside, where the attendant began to walk towards him enquiringly, he struggled into his coat and lit a cigarette.

'My friend isn't well,' he said to the attendant, without looking at her.

'I'm sorry sir, but it's strictly no smoking in the auditorium . . .'

Francesca, furious, was now following. In a few minutes they had clattered down the long flights of concrete steps which led to the side exist and opened onto an alley. Martin lit another cigarette, and felt the hot smoke and the cold, damp air mixing in his throat. The alley was filled with grey slush and the smell of urine. Francesca would not speak. She had her bag and her parcel clutched beside her, and she was striding ahead with the air of one who has lost all patience with a silly game. Martin tried to hold her hand. She pulled it away. In a confusion of traffic and pedestrians they regained the tube station.

'Please,' said Martin, 'Francesca – I'm sorry. It's just that you wouldn't talk to me . . .' Francesca continued to not talk to him. She sat on the train and stared at the black window, turning away from her imploring ex-boyfriend. Martin was afraid of attracting attention, and lapsed into silence. He was shocked at the manner in which Francesca smiled, and moved her knees, in order to allow a young man to sit opposite them. How could she possibly smile at a stranger?

And so it went on – all the way home. Francesca would not speak. She had decided to be silent and, cruelly (whilst quite aware of her cruelty), kept to this decision. Reaching her station, which was where Martin had to change trains in order to finish his journey, she stood for a moment on the platform and regarded her former lover coldly. Martin began new explanations, and said, 'I love you' – again. The girl, in her familiar white raincoat, seemed like a stranger. Then, when Martin attempted, as his train was drawing in, to hold her, Francesca simply said, 'Goodbye,' curtly, and left him. Later, at home, she surprised herself by weeping bitterly.

Martin completed his journey in a daze. He felt warm, and withdrawn, as though he wasn't actually present in his own body. He cursed himself for his fit of temper; he recalled Francesca's hardened expression and anger; he remembered her white nightdress. Some other man, now, would possess all that, and possess her smile, and her ways, and her personality. Another man, somewhere, would have rights to the lily-of-the-valley-scented room in Wimbledon, high up above the garden. Such a hell was too vast to contemplate.

Leaving the station, half a mile from Thornby Avenue, Martin trudged home through the freezing snow. It was thicker, and less disturbed, in his quiet neighbourhood. The gardens appeared luminous and ghostly; the roofs on the houses seemed to be reflecting the moon. The air was still, and bitterly cold. A little way from Martin's house there was a short lane with a wooden trellis, like an arch, across its entrance. In spring, the verges of this lane were a mass of bluebells, and in summer the trellis was heavy with roses. The lane simply led to someone's garage, but it seemed to promise more, and it was the nearest that Thornby Avenue possessed to rural prettiness. Now the lane was snowed over, and pitch-black at its end. A drift had spread down one side of it. Martin took his opera programme out of his coat pocket, and hurled it with all his strength down the dark tunnel. For a second, the fluttering pages were caught in the subdued street-light, and the glossy booklet looked like a shot dove, falling to earth. As it hit the bushes which overhung the fence, the programme brought down a flurry of loose snow, and then it fell noiselessly into the drift. Martin, weary with misery, walked on.

The opera programme remained in the drift, undisturbed. Ten days later, when the snow melted, its pages were blue and rotting. Still it was not picked up or swept away. By spring the booklet's cover was black, and the words upon it illegible. By the time that Martin received a letter from Francesca, with a Russian stamp upon it, to enquire after him and to tell him that she was in love with an American marine engineer called Sam, long wet grass and the thick green shoots of budding bluebells had all but buried the mildewed remains of his romantic plan.

Francesca's departure, Martin would later believe, marked the end of what he fancifully called his First Pastoral Period. His notion of aesthetics and romance, up until the first months of 1979, had been derived from a sense of archaic, rural beauty, which (he thought) combined the spirit of French impressionism with the sentiments of Keats. In that emotional landscape, with its 'windy hills' and 'pensive valleys', all aspirations towards a happiness born of (and fuelled by) love were both meditative and serene. Martin's earlier aesthetic education, at Tiles, had equipped him to think in these terms; but now, as loneliness, frustration, bitterness and jealousy became the prominent emotions under which he lived, he began to search through his new environment for spiritual stimulants that would both protect him and serve him. Thus, for the remainder of 1979, Martin Knight performed an audit upon his life, and the results of this investigation set him off on a whole new course.

In the first place, he was already in debt. During his relationship with Francesca he had made an 'arrangement' with his bank, and, with travel and presents and meals, he had swiftly proceeded to exhaust his credit facilities. A job for two months in the summer of 1979, which involved sitting alone in the basement of an insurance office in Croydon, sorting out old files, just enabled him to avoid getting into serious trouble with his bank manager. The basement in which he worked was stuffy and dark. The old files, thousands of them, had been stored away in random order over a period of twelve years. Some were rotten at the spine, and had spilt their precious contents into the narrow gap behind the metal shelves upon which they were stacked. Others, marked with a complicated code which entitled them to special treatment, and which Martin was to be sure to look out for, had nothing in them at all or, worse, had burst open once at some earlier date and were now filled with sets of papers which were not, necessarily, correct. Thus, for two months, while Croydon sweltered, Martin began to pay for the extravagances of the previous autumn. This wretched job, however, determined the Business Studies student never, in the future, to be employed in a similar capacity. It offended his sense of pride, and his notion of self-worth. It ran contrary to everything that he found engaging, or inspiring. He found the staff dull and the management stupid: they dressed badly – they had no taste; their minds were small, suspicious and pedantic. Filled with hatred, and unable to afford other distractions, Martin spent his free time catching up on college work. Indeed, this became an obsession with him. It also, sometimes, blocked out memories of Francesca, whom he still thought about, and missed horribly, and during the short, hot nights fantasised about in a manner which kept the infatuation alive. That July, during a fortnight of humid, thundery weather, Martin had a series of dreams which centred upon an English gazebo located in a sub-tropical landscape. Francesca was with him in these dreams, alternately loving and obscene. Her face was filled with a sweetness which made Martin waken with his love renewed; on those mornings he half expected to hear from her, saying: 'I've come home. I still love you just as much as I used to.' By lunchtime, however, still clinging to the shreds of this feeling even as he ate his tuna-fish sandwich or as he walked, hot and bored, through the sunny precincts and dark tunnels of Croydon's Whitgift Centre, the sky so blue behind the featureless tower-blocks, Martin would sadly admit that Russia was a long way away, and that Francesca was 'loving every minute' of her life there. Sam was taking her to the Black Sea for a fortnight in September. Martin continued filing.

In the autumn of 1979, his spirit having been oppressed by what he called 'the basement summer', Martin Knight returned to the cooler air of Liverpool and discovered that he had exchanged the 'beautiful' for the 'interesting', and the 'pastoral' for the 'urban'. The city itself, as much as anything, was the catalyst in this process. For Martin, now, had memories of Liverpool, and the streets and buildings were thus empowered with an emotional topography which required dealing with, in aesthetic terms, in order to maintain the drip of impressions to the senses. This manner of reasoning, for the second-year student, was wholly in keeping with his fondness for chemical and zoological analogies. It was vague reasoning, but it appeased him. More directly, Martin began to socialise. His academic work, as ever, won him favour with the authorities – he was even pointed out in a tense tutorial as an example of excellence.

He made the acquaintance of other 'interesting' people, several of whom were studying either Art or Design: Phil, Nora, Brian, Gareth, Robert, Anthony, Graham, Andy . . . These names, a decade later, were scarcely capable of evoking even a face; they existed as cues for reproach or curiosity, and they demanded, strangely, a sense of guilt on behalf of Martin. The attitudes which bonded these contemporaries had, at one time, appeared inviolable, and yet, with the passing of the years, so little – save embarrassment – remained of that immature anarchy. They were united mostly by their interest in punk rock. Martin, in 1986, was to attempt to write a lament for these lost friends, and the work commenced:

> When I am older and more embarrassing,
> And your girlfriend is rouged and hideous,
> When attitudes have become platitudes . . .

He didn't finish the poem, but placed it, along with Fenella's blades of grass, the snapshot and Francesca's letters, in the drawer in his old room at Thornby Avenue.

'Why on earth are you doing Business Studies?' asked Gareth one afternoon in July 1980. Gareth was studying Fine Art.

'So that I can make a lot of money.' Martin lit a cigarette, and smiled at his friend.

'Do you really think that money matters?' said Gareth. 'I think money is just a pain in the arse – spend it if you've got it; if you haven't got it, steal it. Rob a building society or something . . .' Gareth's voice was a drawl; he emphasised certain words in a manner which gave an edge of sarcasm, or deep irony, to his pronouncements. Above all, he affected boredom. The boys were sitting in Martin's study-bedroom. Fastened to the baize notice-board, to Martin's right, there was a single item: the centrefold of a new fashion magazine, printed on large sheets of thick, lustrous white paper. A single black bar occupied the centre of the sheet; above this, printed in tall scarlet capitals: POST-PUNK.

'It's all over,' said Gareth, pointing at the poster.

'What's going to replace it?' said Martin.

'Who knows – disco, synthesisers, noise. Old men.'

'Everything's going to be about money; money's going to be so important. People are tired of pretending to be urchins – they're going to start pretending to be aristocrats.'

'Well that's an improvement.' The sun had inched around the rooftops, and was now shining directly into Gareth's eyes. He put on a pair of reflective glasses. Martin continued, 'I think about the people here: they've all got their nice girlfriends, and their nice posters, and their nice nights out at the weekend. They're so depressing. They'll all end up teaching in dull colleges, or working for the water board . . .'

'So what makes you so different?'

'I'm going to be rich. I have to be rich . . .'

'What about imagination? Or inventiveness?'

'Nothing without money. It's easier to think beautiful thoughts in an ugly place if you can afford to get away from it. Anyway, I like expensive things.'

Gareth shrugged, and lit another cigarette.

Martin noticed, when Gareth had gone, that his little room was scented with the heavy smell of cigarettes, and a perfume that seemed to be sandalwood. This scent delighted him; he returned to his books with redoubled determination: columns of figures, graphs, charts, hypotheses and statistics absorbed him. Some quirk in his nature made this information easy to understand; theory lent itself willingly to practice; the student, aspiring to some cloudless, pure zone, convinced himself that

72

business could be beautiful. He wanted to master the subject, as a great painter might work upon a still life. Deep down, Martin knew that this determination was born of fear, and envy. If he failed his exams, or became mediocre, he thought, he would die amidst ugliness.

The college years were passing swiftly by.

That summer, it had been agreed between Martin and his mother that he would not take a job, but rather work at home for his final exams. He had been set large quantities of holiday work: essays, reading and a short dissertation which would count towards the eventual grade of his qualification. Martin was particularly strong in two different areas of his course work: retail marketing and corporate accountancy. He was expected to do well — as he had been at Tiles.

Towards the end of August, when Martin was pleasantly sleepy with the undisturbed routine of the vacation and about to leave for a week in Suffolk with his mother, he heard from Francesca. Two lines, written upon a postcard, announced that she was at home in Wimbledon: 'Please call if you can.' Curious, Martin telephoned his former lover.

From the moment when Francesca answered the telephone, Martin thought that her voice sounded odd: she sounded much older, and less at ease, as though many secret pressures upon her had conspired to make life continually tiring. Laughter was token, and offered merely as good form.

'So I'll see you here, at two, next Tuesday.' In this manner Francesca concluded the call. Martin made the journey back to Francesca's house with the attitude of a sentimental pilgrim. The day was overcast, and humid. The leafy road, however, still tugged at his heart, and he hoped that time had empowered him (in Francesca's eyes) with a fresh dignity. He was determined to appear aloof. Secretly, Martin hoped that Francesca would fall in love with him again. This desire for a reconciliation began to grow in his heart, and by the time that he reached Francesca's front door he felt nervous and confused. He had brought a bunch of white roses for his friend.

The change in Francesca's appearance hit Martin like a physical blow. She seemed like a different person. Her hair was long and unkempt; her face seemed drawn and sallow; her eyes had no life in them. She seemed to walk with a slight stoop, and she was wearing an old grey pullover and a pair of shapeless brown trousers. Her smile of welcome was a dutiful smile. Martin's heart sank. He was curious, but disappointed.

'Thank you so much for the flowers,' she said; 'they're lovely. How are you?' This question seemed not to require a response. 'Would you like some Russian tea; I've got used to drinking black tea all the time . . .' Martin felt helpless, as though he was acting in a play without knowing his lines. Slowly and silently, the couple made their way – with some tea upon a tray – to Francesca's room. The high room appeared unlived-in and joyless. The bed looked like a hospital bed; all the books and ornaments had been put away. On the dressing table there was a dirty quilted make-up bag and a bottle of whisky. Martin was amazed. There was no youthfulness, and no romance. Francesca sat down slowly upon the bed, as though she was in pain.

'I ought to tell you straight away,' she said, 'that I had an abortion last week.'

As Francesca told the story of her time in Russia, her voice was low and weary. She seemed to be reciting a rehearsed speech. For the first two months she had been homesick (she admitted, too lightly in Martin's opinion, that she had treated him badly: 'What a bitch I was,' she said), and then she had met Sam, and fallen in love.

'Sam swept me off my feet' (Martin's lip curled at this). 'He was in the Marines, an engineer, and he was from Chicago . . .'

'How old was he?'

74

'Thirty. He was divorced. He had a little boy back home in the States.' (The phrase 'back home in the States' hardened Martin's heart.) 'Anyway, I met him at a party the Andersons were having' (these were the family for whom Francesca had worked), 'and he seemed so completely different to anyone I'd ever met . . .' (Martin, throughout this speech, attempted to look detached, and philosophical.) Francesca continued: 'Sam knew Moscow well, and Leningrad, and he knew loads of people – Russians as well as Brits and Yanks. He took me to the ballet, and away for the weekends . . .' As Francesca reminisced, she stared at a point just above Martin's shoulder. Then her tone hardened: 'We talked about getting married; I was going to go to Chicago with him, next month in fact; and then I found out I was pregnant, and he . . .'

'What about the baby?' asked Martin. The words seemed strange to him.

'I decided I didn't want it; so I came home – but I did want it, so much . . .'

'But why did Sam leave? What happened?'

'When he heard about the baby he was furious. He said he had a child already, and that it was all my fault. He said that the Navy would be annoyed – the bloody Navy!'

Martin shook his head. He couldn't think of anything to say. He was horrified to discover that, in some ways, he was pleased Francesca had suffered for her love.

'So, my parents were furious – 'cos I had to tell them. I had to do something; they said that after all the freedom they'd given me I'd been ignorant, and behaved stupidly. They just sent me a ticket home. And then I had the abortion.' Francesca paused.

'So what have you been up to?' she said, suddenly, wiping her nose. Martin shook his head. 'Nothing much . . .' There was nothing he could possibly say. 'Will you see Sam again?' he asked.

'No. I don't want to see him . . . He wrote –'

'And?'

'He said he was sorry; he's being posted back to America . . .'

Again, there seemed to be nothing to say. Francesca, to Martin, had aged a decade in one year. Her beauty, also, was hidden; or rather, her beauty had been put away, like a toy that a child has outgrown. Martin felt uncomfortable, and wanted to leave. He was a bit bored.

'What are you going to do?' he asked.

'I want to train to be a nurse.'

And Martin knew that Francesca had made up her mind. Their respective lives, which hitherto Martin had liked to think of as still running parallel, were now diverging. There was nothing left between them. Martin noticed the kimono which he had given to Francesca, hanging up behind the door. He didn't say anything.

'What about you?' asked Francesca. She seemed a little brighter. Martin realised the futility of saying 'I'm going to be rich,' and so he said:

'I'll see what happens after the exams; I know I want to work in London . . .'

Francesca smiled. 'You always liked London; I'm sure you'll do well.'

Walking back to the station, Martin realised two things: firstly, the leafy, tranquil road in which Francesca lived no longer seemed sacred; secondly, he knew that he could become a millionaire and live like his heroes Gatsby, or Lord Henry Wotton, and still Francesca – or a girl like her – would regard him as boring. Her way, after all, was not his way. He walked on, and Francesca's tragedy ceased to hold his interest.

At Walberswick, on the Suffolk coast, Martin Knight enjoyed – or experienced – a moment of such intensity that he would refer back to it for some years, never failing, as he recalled its potency, to believe that he had glimpsed, unexpectedly, a sudden harmony between all the abstract components of time, place, memory, desire and anticipation that constitute happiness. That he should witness such a strange constellation struck the young man as rare. And yet, on the surface, the moment was quite bland. He had been walking, one Sunday evening, along the saltgrass-covered dunes which ran down to the sea. The August afternoon had been hot and bright, but dusk had brought grey clouds, and a shifting light on the placid waves. To Martin's left, a long, low wooden pier – barely wide enough to allow a single person to walk down it – stretched out into the water. A pale, pink lamp was burning at its end. Beyond this, on the horizon, a sheet of evening sunlight was falling through a gap in the clouds. The breeze had picked up, and the air smelt fresh and invigorating. As he mused upon the beauty of the seascape and the mesmeric quiet of the lonely pier, Martin suddenly turned and looked inland. There, behind the dunes, on a broad, grassy expanse where trippers parked their cars, a last solitary couple were preparing to leave. The light above this place appeared violet; further inland, on the edges of the fields, there was green shadow beneath the overhanging trees. The evening was still save for the muted booming of the sea. The couple seemed quite young: they were putting their coats in the boot of their new grey car. The car had green windows which reflected the evening sky. Martin had always said that he hated young married couples; but at that moment he wanted to live as he believed that couple to live.

Martin's final academic year passed by very quickly. He travelled home every other weekend, and spent his free time with his few casual friends. He displayed utter contempt towards those of his contemporaries who would later regard college as 'the happiest years of their lives'. He surprised himself by studying the 'job market', and going to 'open days' at various large corporations and businesses. He wanted to work in the City of London.

So quickly, the final exams had been taken. Martin did well – coming close to the top of his year – and was invited out for dinner by his tutor. They went to Le Beaujolais. Martin, who was always aware of himself as the glamorous protagonist in his own drama, spent much of his final fortnight at college attempting to feel nostalgic. The 'interesting people' had melted away, some leaving trails which seemed exotic; others simply disappearing, into vague relationships and unformed plans. There was no sense of a generation having passed. On the final day, as the departing students packed away their belongings and prepared to leave, there was merely an atmosphere of embarrassment and confusion.

Martin and Gareth faced one another in the white corridor. They were both carrying suitcases, but walking in opposite directions. They knew that it was unlikely they would ever meet again; they had always sneered at the notion of students exchanging fond farewells. Approaching one another, they each slackened their pace, then, without stopping, they both glanced up.

'See you.'

'Bye.'

Neither of them looked back. They both just carried on walking.

Martin's first thought as he stood on Lime Street Station and waited to board the London train was a quotation from Eliot:

'Well now that's done: and I'm glad it's over.'

He approached London in a burst of July sunshine; the afternoon was warm and golden. As he was due to be collected by his sister's husband an hour later, he stowed his luggage away at Euston Station and went to walk down the Tottenham Court Road. Putting on his dark glasses, he strolled into the crowds of hot pedestrians and was refreshed by what he perceived as being the urban vigour of their lives. He drank in the hot, exhaust-filled air as though it was a tonic. The traffic was heavy; the tarmac on the roads was soft in the heat. Behind him, as he passed Warren

Street tube station, a vast edifice of blue and silver reflective glass made a mountain of mirrors. In front of him, the long street, stretching south, appeared like a baking white chasm. The sky above the tall buildings was blue.

Martin walked on with the sensation that he was already master of all that he surveyed. He window-shopped, and studied displays of Italian crockery. He thought about his imminent job interview, at a large modern office near the Monument. He had been flattered by the tone of the letter that the corporation had sent him; he was amazed at the size of the 'graduate trainee' salary which was being offered. London, he thought, was money in action. The names of the shops and the offices were like poetry to him. He glanced down the shadowed side streets as though he was walking in the country and had just discovered a long, secret avenue that promised some mysterious beauty.

Three: *Love's Young Dream*

On that same hot afternoon in July 1981, a girl was accompanying her mother to the London Library, in St James's Square. The girl was called Marilyn Fuller, and she was nineteen years old. Marilyn and her mother were the same height: five feet and three inches; they could not, however, have been more dissimilar in appearance. Marilyn's mother (whose name was Josephine Fuller, née Josephine Emily Buck) was portly, with thick golden hair which came down to her shoulders and blue, peaceful eyes. She wore tinted glasses most of the time, and this touch of glamour – hinting at neurosis – appeared somewhat incongruous when placed beside the maternal tranquillity of the rest of her features. That afternoon, to combat the heat, Josephine Fuller was wearing a loose, cement-coloured cotton dress. A white canvas shoulder-bag, laden with fabric-covered volumes, hung heavily by her side. She was forty-three years old, and she always seemed rather breathless. She walked at a leisurely pace, and tried to find something interesting in all that she saw. Like a stately galleon, in fact, she appeared to drift through the sunny streets; and as she passed by the garden in the centre of St James's Square, where lemon-yellow butterflies were bobbing in and out of the warm shadows, her mouth was quite fixed in a serene, appreciative smile.

Beside her mother, Marilyn Fuller seemed like an urbane

nymph. Where Josephine was all openness, and seemed willingly to absorb every detail and stimulus that she encountered, Marilyn was restrained and demure. Marilyn (to her relief) had been born tanned, and her skin was prone to looking even darker during the summer months. Whilst not being tall, her body was perfectly proportioned, and thus she escaped from appearing 'petite' – an adjective that she detested. Her hair was brown, with a hint of red, and extremely long and straight. She wore it tied up at the back in an extravagant bow of black silk. Her eyebrows were dark and angular – which made her look serious – and beneath them a pair of vivid green eyes gazed out with a certain gravity of expression. She had soft cheeks and high cheekbones, and her mouth was neither too thin nor too full. She was rather flat-chested (she felt), but her waist was narrow and her slender brown legs made her appear athletic. She was wearing, that July afternoon, a pair of beige shorts which reached down to her knees, and a snowy white T-shirt. Despite these casual clothes, her bearing seemed formal. The only problem with Marilyn was that, with her delicate gestures and her refined, confident expression, she gave the impression that she was looking down upon all that she saw. And, in some ways, this was quite true. Were Marilyn to be asked what, precisely, she was doing with her young life, she would answer (having sought for the right phrase) that she was 'reserving herself'. She was reserving herself for something that even she was uncertain about: a great love, a breathtaking view, a mission – a combination, perhaps, of all three of these things. So far, this great vague something had not stepped forward to announce itself. And as a consequence of this, Marilyn was still reserved. She existed in a cool cocoon of her own making, surrounded by habits which pleased her and comforted her; and she only gazed out at the sordid world occasionally – like a cat, sunning itself upon the lawn, will look up from time to time to see whether or not the shade is advancing, and will seem wholly indifferent to either caresses or commands.

But Marilyn was perceptive; she took everything in, and considered her impressions from every angle, holding up her findings like cut glass to the light of her intelligence. She was not, however, a girl of many words. It was as though she had decided at an early age that most personal embarrassment is derived from a desire to communicate one's feelings too fully. That summer, in 1981, it seemed to Marilyn that the world was going mad. Perusing the morning papers at home in Greenwich, she had read that day of three hikers struck by lightning in Brecon; further on, she had come across a small item which concerned the torching, by irate commuters, of a remote branch-line station in Somerset. And then there were the riots. Those – outbursts it seemed, of irrational barbarism and stupidity – disturbed Marilyn greatly.

'You might not think that way if you were on the dole and living in a derelict council block,' her father had reprimanded her. 'Don't sit in judgement, Marilyn – go out and find the facts.' At this, Marilyn had simply looked resigned. She knew that there was no pointed in arguing with her clever, forceful father. Instead, she had drifted into the low-ceilinged, sunny kitchen, where her mother was shelling peas.

'Mummy,' she had said, 'do you think there'll be riots in Greenwich?'

Her mother had laughed. 'What are they going to do? Loot the delicatessen?' she said. Marilyn hated to be laughed at, and so she withdrew. She often wished, as she dreamt in her cocoon, that she did not have such clever parents. Her father was famous for his documentary films; her mother wrote about opera. Carmen (who was Marilyn's sister, and her elder by two years) was little help either. Carmen was always off somewhere: trekking in Europe, or working on an archaeological dig, or staying with friends in a secluded Devonian cottage . . . Carmen was quick-witted and robust. Boys would ring up for her when she was away, and sound distraught when Marilyn – who usually took their calls – could not, precisely, say when her sister would be back.

'Tell her it's Tim,' they would conclude; or: 'But she told me to ring this morning – she was quite specific . . .' Whilst, in some ways, Marilyn felt sorry for these suitors, she could not help being slightly annoyed by them. If they knew Carmen like she knew Carmen, they would know that her sister was more than capable of losing all interest in a person, place, or thing the moment a 'more interesting' alternative had arisen. In this much, Carmen and Marilyn could not have been more different. Whilst Marilyn was reserving herself for the one great experience, Carmen seemed quite determined to try out every new sensation. And yet still she was never satisfied. For Carmen, it seemed, the necessity to keep on the move quite outweighed her enjoyment of individual pursuits. This gave her a semblance of tremendous enthusiasm, and made her extremely popular. Three years ago, when Carmen had held an eighteenth-birthday party, nearly two hundred people had arrived in various states of inebriation at the Fullers' home. The real joke (as Mr Fuller – or Bill Fuller, as he preferred to be known – had said) was that Carmen herself had gone somewhere else at the last minute. Surrounded by the powerful personalities of her mother, sister and father, it was not surprising that Marilyn Fuller had simply remained in her cocoon. So far, at least, she was a loner and a dreamer, toying with philosophies of her own. But she knew (even as she accompanied her mother, aimlessly, to the London Library) that once she had found her specific desire she would astonish them all with her determination to achieve it.

Marilyn Fuller was born in the Quirinale district of Rome on 4th May 1962. At that time her parents and baby Carmen were living in an apartment near the Via Nazionale. This was close to the

Opera House (for Josephine, who was writing a book about Verdi), and conveniently central for Bill – who was researching and writing what would later become a five-part television series. Bill was a socialist film director who tackled 'issues' in a manner which the televison companies had found to be hugely popular. This was because Bill always filmed from the point of view of the underdog. His politics were not explicit, but rather implied, and as a consequence of this his work reflected the 'real drama of real lives'. Visually, Bill preferred his realism neat. He thrived on filming confrontations in 'real time', and the narration to his documentaries was sparse and factual. By 1970, when the family returned to London, via West Germany, Bill Fuller was the cynical recipient of several prestigious awards. He was also quite rich, and thus felt less intimidated by the inherited wealth into which he had married.

Young Marilyn was first attended by a Roman nanny, and then sent off to the British School in Rome, where she played with Plasticine surrounded by the confused children of ex-patriate American and British families. She had only the vaguest of memories with regard to the first eight years of her life: a vast white courtyard, the glare of which made the cool schoolroom appear quite dark; a regular walk through the Forum at weekends to visit the Farnese Gardens, which her mother loved, with their scent of broom and lemon trees. All she could recall of Germany was the grey weather, and a particularly thick soup which had made her sick. Academically, she was years behind her age. She could speak a little Italian, but she only read in her own language slowly. Her parents, it seemed, found young children to be poor companions. Carmen, however, found playmates wherever she went, and had begged to be allowed to spend the Fullers' last European summer on a campsite in the south of France, with a Belgian family her parents found too dull to contemplate. In the mean time there was the move to consider: a new house, and the girls' neglected education.

Returned to England, in the autumn of 1970, the Fullers moved into a large house in Greenwich. This house was called the Captain's House, and it was only a short walk from the Thames. The Captain's House had been built in 1812, not far (so local history had it) from a mass grave for plague victims. It was typical of Bill's macabre sense of humour that the first picture he hung in the dark hallway of the new family home was an eighteenth-century print, entitled 'Silent Death', which depicted a robed and hooded skeleton sculling a low canoe across still, eerie waters. This picture terrified Marilyn, and she always ran past it on her way to bed.

A tiny courtyard, paved with ancient flagstones, black iron railings and an ornate wrought-iron gate, made the Captain's House appear secluded and grand. The house itself was built of sand-coloured brick. It was square, tall and low-roofed. On either side of the heavy front door there were stone greyhounds. A large plaster oyster-shell added a maritime note to the decoration of the façade. Two large windows, each frame of which contained eight panes of thick, greenish glass, flanked the imposing entrance of the house. Above these, on the first floor, four identical windows looked out over the iron railings and the narrow street beyond, where an old fitter's workshop offered its blank back wall as a view. An Edwardian lamppost, its lamp encased in an iron-framed glass box, shed a ghostly light after dusk. If one leant out of an upstairs window and craned one's neck, one could just see a bend in the river and glimpse, in the distance, the City of London.

Bill and Josephine Fuller regarded Greenwich as a village. They wanted, very much, to become 'locals'. They spoke of 'the butcher's' and 'the baker's' and 'the dairy' with as much confidence as if they had been living in the depths of the country and were wholly dependent upon a small market town to service all their needs. The neighbouring chasms and dreary wastes of

Deptford, New Cross and Lewisham might just as well have been a hundred miles away. They entertained frequently, were entertained by their talented and interesting acquaintances all over London, and immersed themselves whole-heartedly in the creation of a household in which Art and Politics held equal sway as presiding spirits. Carmen – being slightly older – was sent to a local comprehensive school much favoured by the forward-thinking patrician families of the area. Marilyn – neat, quiet and pretty – became a pupil at Blackheath High School. In this manner, the two girls, already different in temperament, became socially and educationally separated as well. And yet both were to benefit from their respective paths: Carmen made friends with a great many boys, and became the centre of a particular local clique; Marilyn, reserved by nature, set to work on cultivating her sense of good taste, and trotted to and from school every day, alone and self-sufficient and pleased to be undisturbed.

By 1977, when Marilyn was fifteen years old, there were few outward signs of the true nature of her personality. At school, she excelled at no one subject or pastime in particular; in all areas of activity her progress was 'fair'. Her desk and locker, however, were always kept neat. She did not join in with the excitements and crises that befell her classmates, and she could always be found on the extreme edge of any group, her attention only partially caught by whatever issue was under discussion. Those dramas, in fact, that comprised the secret and social life of the school seemed never to touch either Marilyn's heart or her enthusiasms. She was (as one astute teacher put it) 'always looking on'. She was also said to be lacking in humour, and had a slight reputation for meanness.

Marilyn did have one special friend, however, who was called Catherine Clarke. Catherine was tall and slender, and almost as quiet as Marilyn. Together, the two girls went for walks in the park, or sat in Marilyn's bedroom, wholly absorbed in some seemingly abstract task that would cause Carmen (if she was at a loose end) to lose all patience. 'God!' she would exclaim. 'You're so . . . boring!'

Such outbursts did not affect Marilyn in the slightest. She would simply reply, quietly, 'No I'm not,' and then continue with whatever she was doing. This was because, in her heart of hearts, Marilyn knew that she was not boring. In time, this attitude (which was also a manner of defence) became a habit; the habit, in its turn, became an impression of superiority. With her green eyes forever fixed, it seemed, on some point that only she could see, Marilyn was like a moment's silence. As she progressed though her early teens, she began to develop – from this position of reticence – an air of gravity which combined with her maturing prettiness to make her, somehow, 'special'. Throughout her adult life, Marilyn would be regarded as 'special'.

One Sunday in February 1978, Bill Fuller took his younger daughter on a long walk through the City of London. Carmen was in bed with tonsillitis, and Josephine was dividing her time between studying the atonality of Alban Berg and attending to the demands of the invalid. The day, for some reason, appeared unusual. Marilyn was aware of this from the moment when she walked out of London Bridge Station beside her father. The vast terminus, which was being rebuilt, seemed as grey and solemn as a church. Directly above the glass roof which partially covered the concourse, a new office block, constructed of two wings of differing heights, soared up into the pale winter sky. Feeble white sunshine was pushing through the ivory-coloured clouds. The air was bitterly cold.

Bill had decided that this was going to be an educational trip for Marilyn. He had already prepared a route that took in many of the City's best-known landmarks, and he was looking forward to testing Marilyn's reactions to urban heritage. Added to this, he was proud of his pretty, well-dressed daughter. She did not drag her feet, or look long-suffering or bored, as Carmen might have done. Rather, in her navy-blue overcoat, with a crimson and white silk scarf providing an elegant cravat and her long brown hair tied up in its customary extravagant ribbon (crimson, on this occasion), Marilyn had all the appearance of a serious-minded young woman. She only wore a touch of make-up (pale, flesh-tone lipstick, a trace of mascara and eyebrow pencil), and her gloves (a Christmas present), which reached up above her wrists and were made of dark blue leather, gave an added note of maturity. All in all, it was a highly presentable fifteen-year-old (soon to be sixteen) who stepped out with her famous father across London Bridge. Bill was wearing a French pullover, a pair of jeans and a long Burberry raincoat. He was becoming stout in middle age, and this suited his silvering hair and his trimmed, square-cut beard.

They paused on the bridge to gaze downstream towards Tower Bridge. On either bank, old warehouses, their façades lined with small windows and broken loading bays, were brown and silent. The sun, with a final effort, burst through the wintry sky. Marilyn could see frost, hardly melted, glinting upon the piers and the towpaths.

'All this is changing,' her father began, rather self-consciously. It was a long time since he had spoken directly to Marilyn in an instructive manner. 'London,' he continued, 'used to be one of the busiest ports in the world. It was servicing, after all, what the British had the nerve to call their empire . . .' Marilyn thought about this. Bill went on: 'But now the City needs space, and it's got the money to pay for it. In ten years' time, Marilyn, you won't be able to recognise this view. It's already beginning. Look over there – and there –' Marilyn looked. Enormous skeletons of fabric-covered scaffolding, their bases fenced off with hoardings, indicated the construction of new offices. She preferred, secretly, these new buildings, with their strange shapes, dark windows and clean, confident lines, to the ramshackle prison-like structures which stared blindly out at the river. Old things, she realised, did not interest her that much. Marilyn liked nice things. Her imagination was not caught by mere antiquity.

The couple pressed on, walking towards St Paul's. The streets were empty, and filled with a bronze-coloured half-light which created an atmosphere of slumber. Fabric blinds were pulled down in the windows of the cafés; the goods for sale in the Cannon Street shops were scarcely visible on their unlit displays; the vast entrance halls of the offices were dim and deserted. Bill pointed out various examples of architectural interest: here the Victorian 'monumental' – favoured by generations of capitalists – there a remnant of the Regency, or even the Caroline. He then referred to the works and world of Charles Dickens. 'Dickens was quite remarkable: a spokesman for the people who has been appropriated by the middle classes. When we get home I'll lend you my copy of *Bleak House*. It's very long, but I think you'd enjoy it. Just read the first few chapters, about Chancery. That's the area behind us, beyond Blackfriars. The Temple, and Lincoln's Inn – the law courts. Dickens really gets the atmosphere of Victorian London: fog, tiny streets, a dreadful sense of stagnation . . .' Marilyn had planned to spend the evening sorting out her wardrobe; there were too many garments within it that depressed her, and that she wanted to throw away.

'Thanks,' she said, smiling, 'I will . . .'

Bill regarded his daughter's smile. It was a lovely smile – warm and affectionate. He was vague as to Marilyn's emotional condition. He knew that she didn't have a boyfriend (unlike Carmen, who appeared to have several) and he was slightly perturbed by this. Not that a boyfriend mattered; but he wanted so much for Marilyn to be happy, and admired. For some reason, as the early dusk began to fall, he felt as though he had not been a good father. He was always busy, often away. He recognised the self-pity in this feeling, and reminded himself of Marilyn's youth.

To mark the limit of their walk, Bill and Marilyn sat down

upon the steps of the cathedral. There were two other visitors, gazing up at the famous dome with expressions of polite interest. Bill lit one of his rare cigars.

'We'll get a taxi back,' he said. 'Would you like that?'

'It is rather cold. But I've enjoyed our walk . . .'

Bill nodded, and exhaled a cloud of cigar smoke which drifted, like a white, ragged ghost, away from the steps and down the twilit street, where silver lights were gleaming.

'How are you getting on with the dreaded O levels?' he asked, in the same tone of voice as though he, too, were about to sit those exams.

'Well . . .' Marilyn looked up at him, and wrinkled her nose. 'All right . . .'

'Mrs Hennessy said that you were doing well; a bit down in English though . . .'

'I hate English. I never know what you're meant to say.'

'How do you mean?'

'Well, they ask why something's a metaphor, or an image; and then they ask you to give examples of it . . .' Marilyn's voice was slightly husky, and she spoke in measured tones.

'Yes?'

'And it just seems obvious. I mean, things just are, aren't they?' Marilyn pressed her knees together, and studied her feet. Bill tried to work out his daughter's reasoning.

'Give me an example,' he said.

'That's just it. I can't. I mean, there isn't a right answer – like there is in Maths, or Biology. I can never think of anything to write.'

Now it was Bill's turn to feel hard-pressed for words. From an early age, he had always felt that everything could be described in a manner that commented upon its being. At length he spoke. 'It seems a silly question,' he said, 'but how do you see the world around you?'

'Well . . .' said Marilyn, slowly; and then she looked up, and stared down the hill towards Blackfriars. 'Things just happen,' she said, 'that's all . . .'

Bill was pleased by this. 'We'll make a philosopher of you yet!' he said. He then laughed, and his laugh was so infectious that even Marilyn smiled. She was not troubled by her inability to 'think creatively'; she knew, as ever, that she was not an empty vessel, or a mere slave to her age and class. She was waiting for something to rouse her into life; when that happened, everything else would fall into its place or, more likely, cease to matter. Sometimes, as Marilyn sat in her neat, pretty bedroom (which Josephine said looked Belgian) or as she walked by the river and looked downstream towards the old shipyard cranes towering like great orange insects above the still water, she felt like a loaded gun.

In the summer of 1978, Marilyn surprised her teachers by passing all of her O levels. Her parents were delighted. Carmen said, 'Jammy sod.' In the wake of this early and unexpected success, the Fullers' younger daughter was urged to return to school in the autumn and study for two A levels – French and Sociology. As Catherine, too, would be taking French as an A level, Marilyn agreed to what was, in fact, a smiled command from the authorities. After a pleasantly idle holiday, which included a visit to Florence, Marilyn returned to school.

The first year of sixth form passed by, comfortable and uneventful. Marilyn began to socialise more, but only in a rather formal manner which was the exact opposite of Carmen's boisterous 'groups'. She attracted the attention of one of Carmen's friends. He was nineteen, and called Lee. He came from Blackheath and he had two brothers, who were called Craig and Dean. Three times Lee tried to detain Marilyn in conversation, and three times he was rebuffed. He felt that the enterprise was Sisyphean, and gave up. Marilyn, secretly, was flattered by his approaches. Had she not found him ugly, she would have responded to his cheerful persistence. As it was, she endured Carmen's teasing, and then buried the occurrence in a deep grave.

For the remainder of her school career, Marilyn worked diligently but without enthusiasm, staved off boredom, and continued to wait. Her greatest joy was her new car, a blue hatchback which Bill bought for her in January 1980. Now mobile, Marilyn began to explore the shops of London.

Bill was becoming a household name. His face, stern or smiling, was often depicted in the Sunday newspapers and magazines. He wrote a book, called *Hard Times?*, about the state of the northern industrial cities. This was published with great success. Marilyn, whilst proud of her father, was not particularly interested in either his political or his artistic reputation. The new decade brought with it new opulence and new controversy. Bill was seldom at home. Josephine remained remote. Carmen, as ever, pursued her own demanding and exclusive life-style. Marilyn, by the time that she passed one of her A levels (French) in the summer of 1980, had discovered a clue to her vocation: she wanted to go shopping.

Marilyn Fuller was now eighteen. Within two years, she was to feel as though the 1980s had welcomed her as a privileged customer to the vast and complex department store which – for some people – that decade represented. Shopping, for Marilyn, was a way of life. As an activity, spending money in different ways was capable of satisfying an entire spectrum of her emotional needs. Marilyn confirmed herself through her purchases. She shopped to give shape to her life, composing her requirements and her aspirations in much the same way that a painter might mix the colours upon his palette, engaging in a dialogue with the canvas which hopefully would one day be a masterpiece. Upon leaving school, however, Marilyn had to find a job (she loathed the idea of continuing her education) and this, at first, proved difficult. For the remainder of 1980 and for the first eight months of 1981, Marilyn 'looked around'. Her parents gave her an allowance which covered her weekly expenses, but they were not prepared to finance their daughter's addiction to shopping. Carmen had always been prepared to 'do anything', from serving in restaurants to temping in large offices. Marilyn disdained such a casual attitude, and moreover she did not possess her sister's carefree, independent spirit.

'You're just an airhead,' said Carmen to Marilyn one day in April 1981.

'Well you're just a hippy. At least, you look like a hippy. And your friends smell.' The two girls glared at one another, and Bill, passing by the scene, was reminded of their rare childhood squabbles. Marilyn did not usually rise to the bait.

'Why not try to help one another?' he suggested.

'Because she'll just say: "But I can't possibly work in a shop,"' said Carmen, affecting a 'posh' accent. Marilyn left the room, and slammed the door behind her.

'What did you do that for?' said Bill, exasperated.

'Oh, she just makes me tired. She never *does* anything. The quicker she marries some rich ponce the better . . .'

'Just because she isn't like you —'

'I know,' said Carmen.

In her bedroom, Marilyn was pulling stacks of old magazines out of her wardrobe and throwing them into a corner. She seldom felt violent but, bored with having nothing to do and desperate to be in a position where she could indulge her tastes, Carmen's taunting had angered her. Hearing the noise coming out of Marilyn's room, Bill went upstairs to see what was going on. He found Marilyn sitting on her bed, with her face in her hands, crying. There were magazines scattered all over the floor; the chair in front of the dressing table had been knocked over.

'Can I come in?'

Marilyn nodded, but continued crying.

The famous political film director sat down upon his daughter's neat little bed. He wished that he could think of something useful to say. All too easily, Marilyn could become a spoilt young woman of the sort who have neither self-awareness nor sympathy for others. Bill, who lived through his work, could not bear the thought of Marilyn simply drifting, unhappily, into an empty marriage. On the other hand, he had no idea of what Marilyn wanted to do. Lamely, he simply wanted her to be happy.

'It's all right for her,' said Marilyn, eventually. She wiped her eyes, and brushed her hair out of her face. 'She's got loads of friends, and they're all really confident, and fun . . .' She spat out this last word. Bill sighed, and looked at the floor. The girl continued: 'She says that I don't do anything, and calls me an airhead; but I do do things, and I do look for jobs . . .'

'I know.'

'It's not my fault that I haven't got secretarial skills. I haven't even been offered an interview from any of the jobs in the paper. And I don't want to go to college and get a degree, and I wouldn't get in anyway. She thinks that I don't care, but I do – I'm really worried. Just because I don't go into town every night and see loads of boys . . .' And so it went on. Bill was deeply concerned. He reflected upon some recent statistics concerning graduate recruitment; computerate service industries and multi-national corporate training schemes were the place to be. He looked at Marilyn. How could he possibly tell her that she must 'do the best she can' until 'something better came along'? However he looked at the situation, he was met by a paradox. An hour later, when he discussed the incident with Josephine (who was now researching Wagner, and dwelt amidst heroes and struggle), Bill was to think once more of the conundrum which Marilyn embodied. She had been born of affluent, successful parents; the home had been filled with books; pocket money had been controlled. Why, then, was it impossible to imagine his daughter impressing a potential employer? Amongst their friends, Bill and Josephine knew of many 'creative' couples whose offspring had slipped without effort into publishers' offices or the BBC. Carmen, certainly, would make her own way. She was already planning a trip to Canada, and would work at a summer camp to add to her allowance from home. 'Special' Marilyn seemed somehow to defy all the usual routes to a career. Josephine suggested speaking to someone at the Arts Council, where there might be a 'little something'. Bill shook his head. 'There's a queue of people with PhDs who'd work at the Arts Council doing anything . . .'

'Well, she's got to do something – other young people do . . .'

Bill's political pessimism, combined with Josephine's vagueness, did nothing to solve the question of Marilyn's career. Those two interesting people, who were talented and even brilliant, could not see into their daughter's world.

That evening before she went to bed, Marilyn walked down to the river with all of her old school files in an elegant carrier bag. The bag was dark blue, and had two crimson cords – velvet to the touch – which served as a handle. Reaching the Royal Naval College, with its classical, dignified halls expressing centuries of preparation for duty, Marilyn sat down upon the ancient stone landing-stage and stared out across the water, her bag of files beside her. The towpath was quiet in the spring evening; the sun had just set, but a blue light seemed to hang above the river. She could hear, just beneath her, the tide lapping against the steps. Directly opposite, on the far bank, new flats were being built. Their half-finished shapes were dotted with tiny silver lights, denoting the extremities of scaffolding. Beyond those, to the west, a peach-coloured glow defined central London where the urban illuminations reflected off the sky. Marilyn went over the dreadful day in her mind: she hated to lose her calm, or to be seen to show distress; she knew that if she so chose, she could go to work in an office, or train to enter some business. This sense of guilt mingled with her dissatisfaction. Such courses of action, it seemed, were an admission that her early ambition – to reserve herself for a great experience – had failed. Sitting beside the quiet river, she fantasised about living in one of the new flats which were being built just across the dark stretch of water. In her imagination, she decorated the bathroom, and filled the kitchen with all the necessities of a perfect life. She recalled, from the shelves of the great department stores, all manner of products and utensils which, to her, created happiness. For Marilyn, secretly, property and products were an obscure, yet potent, route to the erotic. As it was, a great emptiness confounded her aspirations. Was this, she wondered, the void which love was meant to fill? So far, she had not met one boy whom she would ever consider knowing intimately. She had watched Catherine, who was conscientiously applying herself to a promising position in sea container transport and becoming more and more cynical with regard to relationships. And Catherine, she mused, was only six months older than herself.

A small boat, scarcely visible in the darkness, caused a sudden slight swell. Marilyn watched its progress as it sailed wide of the next bend and disappeared out of sight. It was as though the night had swallowed it. The sense of emptiness returned, stronger this time. For the first time in her young life, Marilyn experienced seventeen seconds of formless panic. The months, years – her life – stretched out ahead, with neither flesh nor spine. She thought about a glossy black paperback book which she had glimpsed upon Bill's cluttered desk. It had been filled with slips of paper which bore detailed notes in her father's neat, small handwriting. The book had been called *Nothingness*. Vaguely, Marilyn wondered whether such a book was a detailed exploration of her own condition. The night was becoming darker, and cold. The smell of the river – a combination of mud, petrol and salt – was strong. Standing, Marilyn picked up the blue bag and let it dangle beside her. She wanted to underline the dreadful day. The bag bumped against her bare leg, and the cover of a file dug into her. She winced, and was filled with mounting anger. Suddenly, she took a pace backwards, measured the limit of her swing and then, with a glorious circling gesture – like a discus thrower – hurled the bag of files as far as she could. They landed in the river, somewhere out of sight, with a noisy, satisfying splash.

Thus expressed, and feeling somewhat comforted, Marilyn returned to the Captain's House.

The catharsis which attended Marilyn's destruction of her school chattels was short-lived. From May to August 1981 she did little save help with the weekly shopping and occasionally accompany her mother to London on various erudite errands. Each Saturday she worked in a small bookshop (whose owner knew Josephine) in Blackheath. When Marilyn went into London with her mother, she felt as though she was a child again, slowly walking through the hot streets of Rome towards the Forum. This time, however, there was no magnificent view to be admired on gaining the terrace of the Farnese Gardens. There were instead the hot, crowded streets and the baking buses – their seats smelling of scorched wool – upon which Josephine liked to travel, in order to smile peacefully at her surroundings. Window-shopping, Marilyn followed. The summer became hot, and the sky a deeper shade of blue. Twice, Marilyn went for interviews at design showrooms. She hoped to obtain the advertised position, at each, of Receptionist. On both occasions, the interviewers were kind, but said that they required a young person who either knew about design, or was a trained switchboard operator. Most of all, they required a young person who, miraculously, combined both of these qualifications with an indifference towards salary. Five years later, Marilyn would smile at the abundance of such jobs. In 1981, the boom in retail was still at the planning stage. After the second of these interviews, in

August, Marilyn had travelled from Fulham Broadway to Charing Cross on a hot, rancid-smelling underground train. She had 'wanted to learn the route', but now, having failed to win the position, she simply felt trapped, and ill-tempered. She studied the sweating faces on either side of her: young men with their coats across their knees were reading newspapers; tourists with copious luggage were squeezed into corners; those commuters who were trying to catch connecting trains looked anxious and fierce. Some kicked the panels of the sliding doors when the train had to wait outside a station. Above their heads, illuminated advertisements seemed to gloat over their captive audience. All of these carefully worded texts appeared to take the misery of their readers for granted: cheerful secretaries extolled the liberty of temping; grave-faced businessmen acknowledged the benefits of decentralisation. Here and there, honey-thighed models displayed waxed legs, or leant to one side in order to show off their lustrous, 'healthy' hair. To Marilyn, unused to this environment, the presence of the sweating crowd merely determined her to never become a part of it. In fact, she was almost pleased that she hadn't got the job. Just then, a woman gave a little scream, and some of the passengers looked up. A large brown moth, with dark wings and a body which resembled a block lozenge, was fluttering about her face. Marilyn, too, detested moths, and tried to move away. This was impossible. The moth regained the ceiling of the carriage, and fluttered with exhausted wings about the light. It appeared stifled, and weary. Suddenly, as though an invisible string that held it had been cut, it fell to the floor beside Marilyn's foot. The girl looked at it; it stirred feebly. Calm returned to the carriage. Marilyn, untypically, was filled with irrational sympathy for the worn-out, hated creature. It had died, she felt, in prison.

One day the following month, Marilyn bumped into an old acquaintance from school. Pru Williams had left Blackheath High

School in 1978 and had returned, quite happily, to her family home at Fitton Place, in West Sussex. Pru had only been in London while a team of builders and restorers were returning Fitton to its former, mid-eighteenth-century glory. Pru Williams had been one of the richest girls in the school. Her country home had been built in 1758 by an English admiral who had returned victorious from the South Seas. The admiral had commenced a connection between Pru's family and Greenwich. They still owned a small mansion not far from the Captain's House. Whilst many of the girls at Marilyn's old school had been well off, Pru was the only representative of landed wealth. She was one year older than Marilyn: a voluptuous girl whose thick eyebrows, plump cheeks and blue, sparkling eyes seemed to speak of crossbreeding within the upper classes. Those girls who disliked her had called her 'a pig'. Pru, however, was loud and domineering, and had little regard for the sensibilities of those whom she had failed, quite simply, to notice. This group included not only her critics but most of the staff and pupils. She had always liked Marilyn, however, for her confident bearing and reticence, and when they met again in Blackheath High Street she was eager to know what her former acquaintance had been 'up to'. Dressed in jeans and a white hand-tailored man's shirt, Pru's enthusiasm was loudly expressed.

'God!' she bawled, 'it's really great to see you! I wondered whether or not I'd bump into any of the old gang. How are you! You look fabulous — as always . . .'

'Pru! Is that you? Under all that hair?'

Within minutes, an intimacy that had been waiting for some years to declare itself had found freedom of expression. With all the restrictions of school lifted, and all the comments that had attended sudden friendships removed, the two girls regarded one another with pleasure. The upshot of their meeting was an arrangement to have dinner together, the following weekend, in Greenwich.

'I'm back here now,' said Pru, 'but I'll tell you all about it when we meet. Incidentally,' she added, with the self-assurance of a woman twice her age, 'it'll be my treat, so don't disembowel the piggy bank.'

Marilyn, as she walked home, felt as though a heavy, suffocating curtain had been lifted. Good old Pru! she thought, with exaggerated fondness. Pru would know what to do.

That Saturday, at eight o'clock in the evening, the two girls met for dinner in a Pekingese restaurant which stood not far from Greenwich Pier. The restaurant was called '63'. Marilyn had been to 63 once before, on her seventeenth birthday. Then, she had been overawed by the luxurious combination of the modern and the oriental from which the restaurant derived its reputation for exclusivity. Now, as she took her place – five minutes early – beneath the glass roof of 63's upstairs dining room, she felt as though she was coming home. Drifting, Marilyn had become open to influence. The restaurant was constructed, it seemed, of glass and greenery. As an example of commercial minimalism, it was years ahead of its time. The tables were set wide apart, and each one was lit from above by a single, finely-focused spotlight. Thus, the space between the tables appeared blue, and increased the sense of intimacy. Thick white tablecloths absorbed the light; in the centre of each table there stood an orchid in a plain glass vase. The chairs were high-backed, and made of bamboo. Waiters moved discreetly through the blue darkness. Marilyn ordered a glass of mineral water. It arrived containing a tiny cube of lime. Looking up, Marilyn could see verdant creepers extending across the metal frame of the glass roof. Above those, the ash-grey evening sky. It was still light, and banks of dark cloud were visible. The scarlet lights on the wing-tips of an aeroplane passed smoothly overhead, precise despite their altitude. Marilyn felt happy, and relaxed. The other diners, talking quietly, seemed miles away. And then Pru arrived. She had parked her car at forty-five degrees to the kerb, quite regardless of what accidents might befall it or what obstruction it might cause. Throwing her keys and a packet of imported American cigarettes onto the table, she greeted Marilyn warmly.

'This is nice,' she said. 'Have they done it up? What a gorgeous dress . . .'

'Oh, thank you.' Marilyn was wearing a simple cream-coloured dress that resembled a tunic, low-necked and buttoned up the front. Sleeveless, this garment revealed her slender tanned arms. Upon her bare feet were gold raffia-work shoes. Her hair was tied up with a gold ribbon. Several male diners had already glanced more than once in her direction. Pru, who was taller than Marilyn and larger-boned, was wearing a pleated black skirt and a lilac V-necked pullover. Her hair, too, was worn up, with a tortoise-shell clasp. Around her throat her pearls hung in a single elegant rope. Pru's hair was golden and thick, beneath her blue eyes, her mouth was wide and her lipstick pink and old-fashioned. She spoke in a loud voice, and annotated her conversation with brisk hand gestures, often laughing at her own enthusiasm. The fondness which the two girls had felt for one another seemed to increase with each course of their meal. As Pru devoured *Sesame Prawn Toast*, and Marilyn sipped a *Consommé of Spring Vegetables*, they exchanged accounts of recent years. There was a willingness on either side to please, and to show sympathy.

'When I was at home – bored out of my mind – one of the workmen took a bit of a shine to me. He was really nice actually, but nothing happened. He said that our garden was "Arcadian" – which seemed odd. I had to tell him that living in Arcady was pretty bloody dull. He gave up after that. Great eyes though. Have you got a boyfriend?'

'No –'

'You surprise me – a girl like you. I thought that you'd be married, or fighting them off . . .'

'Hardly.'

Pru ordered a bottle of champagne, and the more Marilyn drank the more eager she felt to talk.

'I'm not doing anything much,' continued Marilyn. 'Actually, it's all pretty desperate. I just seem to have fallen into a bit of a black hole . . .'

'Oh! We can't have that –' (*Beef with Ginger*, *King Prawns* and a bowl of *Saffron Rice* were delivered to the table.)

'I can't bear the thought of winding up in some office, like poor old Catherine,' said Marilyn, 'but I can't keep killing time for ever. There's money, for one thing . . .' For Marilyn, who was usually so reserved, to offer so much information about herself was rare. Pru, however, seemed to give her confidence. Conversation, for once, came easily. With the arrival of dessert (*Sizzling Toffee Apples*) Pru became confidential.

'Actually, you could be just the person I'm looking for.' Pru leant back in her chair, and exhaled cigarette smoke across the table. 'I'm thinking of starting a small business; that's why I'm here in fact – to start the ball rolling. Have you got time to come back for coffee and I'll tell you about it? Margot' (this was Pru's elder sister) 'is at the Courtauld now, did you know? So we're camping out at the other place. It's really nice.' The 'other place' was Pru's Greenwich house. Marilyn happily followed her friend. She was aware that Pru was from a different class to herself, and this, somehow, seemed to increase the novelty of being with her. Also, it suggested that whatever plan Pru might be working upon would be bound to succeed. 'Money breeds money,' her father had said. Indifferent to the ideological implications of this platitude, Marilyn was already enjoying the warmth of secure wealth.

The 'other place' was similar to the Captain's House in both age and size. The furnishings at Pru's house, however, were sparse. Various extravagant chairs, removed from Fitton Place, and a quantity of large damaged paintings were all that the reception rooms contained. Two tea-chests, half unpacked, revealed boxes of cutlery and crockery amidst swathes of black tissue paper. A crate of red wine stood beside the large stone fireplace; fashionable magazines and a few records were propped up beside a cupboard. Everywhere, there were indications of considerable affluence. A Chanel carrier bag, bigger than any carrier that Marilyn had ever seen, was standing in the hall. 'Margot bought a coat,' said Pru, in a surprised tone of voice, when Marilyn commented upon it. The hub of Margot and Pru's domestic existence lay in the large kitchen, where a long scrubbed-pine table stood before the window. It was cluttered with papers and glasses. A display of dying flowers served as a centrepiece. A jar of Fortnum & Mason ginger preserve stood opened beside the flowers, with a sticky spoon inside it. Margot was out. Marilyn could not help noticing a strong smell of rotting vegetables, as though someone had forgotten to empty a dustbin. Pru made coffee in a slapdash manner, pouring the milk without taking her cigarette out of her mouth. All the time, she continued talking.

'Margot's frightfully trendy. Well, you might not think so. She's going out with some wasted youth who wears black all the time and looks like a drug addict. In fact,' she added, conspiratorially, 'his parents farm the land not far from us, and it's all a big act. But anyway, Margot's all right except when she's being "arty" – then she's awful. She's got these two Italian friends staying here at the moment. They've gone out for dinner . . .' Then, as Marilyn slipped off her shoes and curled up in a large, comfortable chair (spoil of some demolished cottage parlour, and darkened by centuries of proximity to an open fire), Pru explained her plan.

For some years Pru had been aware that she would inherit a certain amount of money on her eighteenth birthday. She was now nearly twenty. This sum, whilst not being enough to retire upon and lead a life of 'mindless extravagance', was sufficient to invest in various ways. Half of it, already, had been reserved; the other half, Pru's father had suggested, could be made to work more directly. Having studied the market for small businesses, Pru and her father had agreed that catering, in the City, was a much required service.

'What sort of catering?' asked Marilyn, imagining a canteen.

'Like sandwich shops, only "high-class". There's so much rebuilding and expansion going on in the City, and Daddy says that it's going to increase. What a lot of the young execs. require is a half-way house between old-style boozy lunches and something more trendy, faster, and cheap. That's where we come in . . .' She stressed the 'we' with a smile. Marilyn smiled back encouragingly.

'I'm buying – well, Daddy's buying – an old shop premises in Carter Lane; that's just behind St Paul's. It's really small but it's fine for what we want. The plan is to sell really good sandwiches – which are incredibly cheap to make – and salads, but with a continental twist. As opposed to mouldy old cheese and tomato, or corned beef, we'll do more exotic things – I've nicked loads of ideas from the café in Harrods, and Mummy's been a mine of information. The great thing is not to be too ambitious, and to make sure that everything is fresh, and sold or thrown away on the day. That way we don't need loads of extra fridge space. If the place looks nice, and up-market, then the people'll come. They'll come even more,' she added, 'when they realise that far from being a Greasy Joe's we're serving really nice food. There's so many new things coming on to the market as well – fruits, and salad things, and soft drinks. It's the big new thing.' Pru's enthusiasm was quite infectious. To Marilyn, the idea of running such an establishment seemed too good to be true. No sooner had she pondered on the joys of assisting with such an enterprise than Pru said: 'The thing is I need an assistant. Will you think about it? Even if it's only to help out for a few months. We can work out a wage so that nobody's embarrassed . . .'

Marilyn accepted this offer immediately. Here, she felt, was something that she would both enjoy and succeed at.

'It's just take-aways?' she said, 'no waiting at tables . . .'

'My dear,' said Pru, reproachfully, 'the very idea! Gels from Blackheath High, waiting at tables! What would Mrs Hennessy say?'

Thus, amidst laughter and reminiscences about school, Marilyn became Pru's assistant.

Time, for Marilyn Fuller, began to accelerate. After some years of idleness, Pru's personality had an invigorating effect upon the girl. The next three years passed swiftly by. The café, which Pru christened 'Truffles', was a tremendous success. The girls officially opened their business in April 1982, and were amazed at the number of people who queued daily for 'High-Class and Continental Provisions'. Pru was a calm and efficient entrepreneur. The demand for sandwich lunches in the City was such that any take-away restaurant, let alone the more exotic and flattering version which Truffles presented, was bound to succeed. Carter Lane, in those days, was a narrow street of high, old buildings. Away from the main road, it had all the allure of a pedestrian thoroughfare, and this was good for business. Other small shops were opening along the street. Carter Lane, whilst not pretty, became 'up-market'. The sandwich shop itself was small but, with white paint, large mirrors and a daily changing supply of fresh flowers, it took on a cheerful and sophisticated air. Pru hired two 'lunchtime assistants' (pretty, quiet, young girls) and between them the four members of staff could offer a brisk service. The girls were extremely popular with the (largely male) customers. Pru was adept at remembering regulars – who were flattered by her attention. After six months, telephone orders were being taken. Pru's father, it seemed, had identified a lucrative gap in the market. Marilyn enjoyed her work. She was excellent at buying in groceries; she was always finding new, enticing ingredients. She dealt with tradesmen deftly, exacting discounts by whatever means appeared dignified. She developed a streak of charm which had hitherto been hidden, and which was capable of turning most men into weak, foolish victims. Her smile came more easily. Profits soared. By the spring of 1983, Truffles had been featured in stylish magazines and the national newspapers. A collage of these articles, most of which included a photograph of Pru and Marilyn beaming in French aprons as they held out trays of *Pasta Salad* or *Sticky Ginger Pudding*, was displayed above the shining sink. From ten in the morning until four in the afternoon, the girls were rushed off their feet. These hours, to Marilyn, did not seem too strenuous. Her confidence increased by the month. But her relationship with Pru, centred around work, never became more or less friendly than during their first dinner together. The girls did not meet socially.

Between 1982 and 1984, the city which surrounded Carter Lane began to change. Marilyn began to notice this more and more. Everywhere she looked, on her way to work, there were new buildings, new services and new businesses. The financial centre was being reinvented as a display case for the latest designs and the newest trends. The black metal, chrome, tinted glass, unfinished brickwork and Italian marble which eight years later would appear so bland and stale were beginning to set the tone of commercial activity. To Marilyn, who liked 'nice things', this was the triumph of good taste over dullness. She thrilled to the subtle comfort of it all; and she was always eager to try out a new brand, or a new range, of almost any domestic product. She lived, happily, in the landscape of the latest television advertisements. Her new cocoon, in fact, was a post-modern palace.

Marilyn also noticed that people were spending their money more freely; extravagance, amongst her customers, was a much-loved, rather comic activity. The girls began to stock champagne in their fridge. They quickly sold out. They put up their prices.

Nobody noticed. The City, it seemed, was going on a gaudy spending spree. From time to time, however, Marilyn would serve customers from the junior clerical level of the large offices. These, she supposed, were the pale young people from the outer suburbs, the filing clerks, the 'Leg/Aud Secs' for whom the trivial free magazines were distributed by strange creatures outside the tube stations. Briskly, she would talk fearful secretaries of 'the wrong sort' through the selection of 'High-Class and Continental' sandwich fillings. Equally briskly, she would take their money, reluctantly offered five-pound notes and handfuls of carefully counted change.

'Four bloody quid!' she heard one girl exclaim to her companion. Truffles did not cater for their sort. For the most part, Pru and Marilyn served a seemingly endless stream of confident young men who arrived in their shirtsleeves and who boomed their orders in loud voices. A trick of class, or an inflection in the social language, ensured that Pru and Marilyn remained 'superior' to their customers. The customers, in fact, aspired to the ambience of Truffles; a tiny transaction between vanity and self-worth made the formula irresistible. All over London, at that time, similar transactions were being carried out, on a greater scale or a lesser. The social climate, for the new middle classes of that period, was deceptively balmy. Seldom straying from that part of London which endorsed this illusion of opulence, Marilyn detected no fluctuation upon the barometer of her sense of comfort. England, she felt, was hers. She might just as well have been living in a tiny village seventy years earlier, dispensing tea and cakes to the local gentry.

Still she had no boyfriend, and seldom thought of love.

In September 1983, Truffles closed its doors for a month. The staff needed a holiday; the café required decorating. Pru was having the white interior changed for the autumn: the palest russet shades were going to be introduced. Also, there would be a heavy hat-stand, made of dark wood. The business was flourishing. Marilyn was surprised, however, when Pru invited her down to Fitton Place for a party. Accordingly, she set off for Sussex during the second week of September. Despite herself, Marilyn was flattered by the invitation.

She had seldom been out of London. She made the journey on a hot afternoon; first, laboriously, she drove through the suburbs of south London, frequently being caught in traffic jams. These endless high streets, to Marilyn, appeared as tawdry shanty-towns, where poorly dressed people struggled with shopping and children. For the most part she ignored the scenery, and tapped her fingers on the steering wheel in time to the music on her cassette player. Then, gaining the motorway, she watched the wealds of Surrey open up before her beneath a vast, cloudless sky. On the low escarpments of the downs, the trees were still in full leaf. The long lines of speeding cars seemed to disappear into a hot, pale mist, each one with a golden triangle of light glinting upon its roof. Marilyn had recently bought a new car. Secure behind tinted glass, and comfortable on her 'scientifically designed' seat, Marilyn began to drive faster. She loved cars. Her new one was black, with blue windows, and had lavender-coloured upholstery. Beneath the long bonnet a powerful engine purred efficiently; inside, from four concealed speakers, a mesmeric and sinister pop song boomed out its hypnotic beat. This song, which was the longest track on a record that Marilyn had heard by chance and then grown to love, was to conjure up, in later years, all of her memories of the forthcoming visit. For Marilyn, who cared nothing for pop music, her loyalty to certain songs was a simple matter of sensual enjoyment. She had no interest in the status of different musical factions. On the seats behind her, Marilyn's luggage was strewn in a stylish muddle. Her best dress, sheathed into the polythene cover so thoughtfully provided by Lilliman & Cox, was hanging from a white hook above the rear side window. Glancing at Pru's hastily scrawled directions, which lay on the seat beside her, Marilyn identified the motorway turn-off, and then swept down a minor road which led swiftly to a lane.

The lane was lined, like an avenue, with poplar trees. The sun, in the mid-afternoon, appeared to lie just beneath the treetops; as Marilyn drove along — more slowly now — bars of shadow flicked over her car. Beyond the trees were wide, open fields. Marilyn had no idea what grew in them. Through her dark green glasses, they appeared to be yellow. The countryside was deserted. The lane, according to Pru's directions, should have been quite short. Fearing that she was lost, and wanting to stretch her legs, Marilyn pulled over to the side of the road in order to consult a larger map. Getting out of her car, she was buffeted by the heat. The air seemed thick with it, and filled with the rich scent of mown grass overlaid with the odour of manure. Marilyn leant against the side of her car and enjoyed the warmth. She was wearing a short, rust-coloured skirt and a white T-shirt. She listened to the low hum of the car engine cooling, and then walked over to the edge of the fields. The empty view, tranquil and golden, began to absorb her, and her mind wandered. After the hectic pace of life which she had invented for herself in London, there was something quite bewildering about the hot, desolate countryside. Fitton Place could not be very far away; gradually, Marilyn began to feel rather shy. She wondered what the house would be like; moreover she reflected that she had never liked large parties. The little visit, quietly, began to seem like a chore. Returning to her car, Marilyn felt quite suddenly as though she wanted to go home.

Fitton Place was a country house as opposed to a stately home. It was, in fact, less grand than Marilyn had expected it to be. The house itself was large and square and built of red brick. Many long windows, set in white frames, stared out across the small park, the gravelled forecourt and the neat, yellowing lawns. The 'home farm', a mile from the house, had been converted into a home-made-yoghurt factory. Beyond the lawns (where croquet was played) there was a 'dell'. Here, surrounded by aromatic shrubs, stood a neo-classical temple. It ought to have been idyllic. Marilyn, upon arriving, was shown to a little attic bedroom. Directly beneath the scorched roof, this room was hot and airless. The bed was narrow, and heaped with too many blankets and sheets. Pru apologised for this on the strength of the number of overnight guests who were expected. But there was something different about her tone of voice; she appeared to be almost offhand with Marilyn, as though that girl had no real place in the build-up to the festivities. Marilyn developed a headache. The party was due to start at ten o'clock that evening.

No sooner had Marilyn installed herself in her little room than Pru seemed to sense her discomfort. She was quite blunt about it, and this made matters worse.

'Are you pining for London already? I mean, just say if you've had enough.'

'No, of course not. It's all fabulous . . .'

Marilyn felt as though she had been deposited in the middle of some drama, and was now supposed to perform. A chasm, somehow, had opened up between the two girls. Working together in Carter Lane had provided some bond between them; now, everything seemed wrong. A terrible darkness began to settle in Marilyn's mind during the early evening.

'Off to join the landed gentry?' Bill had said that morning. 'Be sure to dress for dinner,' he had added, with a perceptible sneer. Marilyn, remembering her father's words, set out to try and find Pru. In the enormous hall, she bumped into Margot and three young men. Margot's lack of interest in Marilyn verged upon the offensive.

'Oh, hello,' she said, briefly, and then turned back to her

friends, and spoke to them in Italian, with exaggerated gestures. Marilyn did not know what she was supposed to do. Pru, seeing the little group, bounded up to Margot. Ignoring Marilyn, the two sisters began to talk at great length about unknown young men who were 'bloody funny' and 'a real laugh'. At first, Marilyn asked questions, and tried to smile at the brief anecdotes that were offered to illustrate the irresistible appeal of these various characters. Soon she gave up.

More young people began to arrive, some already in dinner suits or long dresses, others with suitcases. Absurd, loud and utterly at ease, these new arrivals awoke an irrational fear in Marilyn which was heavily laced with hatred. She thought about going to change, and then she simply wandered from room to room, alone and unquestioned. A club was congregating, and she was not a member. Nobody, however, would have been so offensive as to ask her, directly, to leave. A long bar and a buffet were being installed in the ballroom. Outside, on the lawn, loud and boisterous games were being played. Two young men, shouting 'Tea! Tea! Where's our bloody tea?', came roaring down the corridor. 'Oh, Sabrina!' wailed a high-pitched nasal voice from the lawn, 'you're perfectly bloody hopeless!' And then further screeches of laughter. To Marilyn, this was like the worst teenage nightmare. She could not understand why Pru had invited her in the first place. Desperately, she sought out her business colleague. Pru was playing croquet, and barely acknowledged her assistant's approach. 'Shot!' boomed a young man who was wearing dark glasses and a panama hat. Feeling as though she was being watched and criticised from all sides, Marilyn breathlessly told Pru a made-up story about a telephone call, and the need for her to return to London at once.

'Oh, I'm sorry,' said Pru, still watching the game as she spoke. 'Well, do what you think is best. Toby!' This last word was roared, as a sandy-haired boy tried to cheat. Feeling rude and crushed, Marilyn withdrew. She knew that she had to get away from Fitton Place, and from the dreadful, braying guests that it contained. Their self-assurance and their loud voices and laughter seemed to mingle into one awful yell for pleasure. Marilyn knew that she had strayed outside her class.

In minutes, her bag was packed and she was driving swiftly through the park. It was now growing dark, and at the main gates she nearly hit a Land Rover. Two girls with plump faces and sweaters tied around their shoulders gazed down at her superciliously.

'Cunts,' said Marilyn. She was amazed at herself for using that word. She had never spoken it before, and she had always felt that she never would.

Reaching Greenwich shortly before midnight, Marilyn was overjoyed to discover her father, sitting at the kitchen table, eating Greek cheese and grapes. A glass of pale yellow wine stood beside his plate. Before him there was a typescript.

'Hello,' he said, 'back so soon?'

'Yes,' Marilyn sighed, and then smiled. 'It was awful.' She was so happy to be at home again. She realised that she was one of those people whose greatest joy is to stay in. 'What are you reading?' she asked. Bill raised his eyebrows in surprise, and then popped a grape into his mouth.

'Landed gentry not all they're cracked up to be, eh?' he said.

Pru Williams had been wondering how to get rid of Marilyn for some months. Now that the café was a success, she wanted to run it on her own, with a staff whom she could pay a 'junior' wage, and who would have little say in the day-to-day planning of the business. Also, now that Marilyn was more confident, she was beginning to irritate her self-assured friend. Pru had seldom spent much time considering the feelings of those who were not from her own little set; at first, she had felt that she could fire Marilyn 'nicely' – sweetening the pill by inviting her to Fitton

Place. Then, faced with her assistant in the flesh, she had found that she was not equal to the task, and this had simply increased her anger.

'It's so difficult,' she had said to a young officer from Sandhurst as they lay, at dawn, in a drunken and unresolved embrace on the ballroom floor after the party. The officer, who was trying to caress her breasts, had murmured agreement, unsure of what she was talking about. Pru's voice grew louder. 'I'll just have to tell her to go.' She frowned. Then, the matter dealt with, she pushed the officer away. 'Oh, stop it . . .' The officer, nearly asleep, stopped.

Thus, towards the end of October 1983, Pru 'had a chat' with Marilyn. This took place on the pavement outside Truffles. It seemed best to get it over with. It was half-past nine in the morning, and Pru was feeling short-tempered. Marilyn had already realised that something was wrong. For the previous two weeks, Pru had been displaying a cool, distant attitude. She had been hoping that Marilyn would simply leave.

'Listen,' Pru began, 'I've got some bad news for you, darling. I'm afraid that our little partnership will have to end . . .' Marilyn felt a cold sensation in her stomach. This was followed, almost immediately, by a sense of relief. Far stronger than she had been two years ago, she decided to let Pru suffer the difficulty of getting rid of her. 'It's like this,' Pru continued, talking very quickly, 'I'm probably going to sell this shop at Christmas; I'll get a fortune for it at the moment. It just doesn't make sense to hang on. We're doing well, but property is worth more than sandwiches . . .' She gave a little laugh. She was, in fact, going to buy the first floor of the premises, and open a wine bar. 'So anyway, I'm beginning to wind things down and there's really no need . . .'

'It's all right,' said Marilyn coldly, 'I was bored anyway.' She had not meant, in fact, for this to sound as rude as it did.

Inwardly, she was still recalling the hatred that she had felt at Fitton Place. In her mind, that brief visit represented a humiliation which seemed akin to poison. To her, in fact, it had been an absolute.

'Oh,' said Pru, pleased that Marilyn's abrupt comment could be put down to ill-breeding. She became patronising. 'I don't want you to think that I'm not grateful, or anything like that, so I'd love you to take this . . .' She handed Marilyn a long, pale green envelope which was made of thick, expensive parchment.

'What's this? There's really no need . . .'

'Well I want you to take it – and thanks . . .'

'Is that it?' said Marilyn.

Pru, standing in the doorway, looked at the pavement. 'Yes. I think so. But do keep in touch . . .'

'Oh. Well. Bye then . . .'

No kiss was exchanged. Suddenly, both of the girls were embarrassed. They had, after all, worked together for nearly three years. Later, Pru was to congratulate herself on handling the situation so well. Marilyn, with some money in the bank, went home to Greenwich to consider her situation. In the envelope, she discovered, there was a cheque for £250.

Marilyn Fuller was now twenty-one years old. She felt much older. In the weeks that followed her dismissal from Truffles she performed an audit upon her life and, much to her surprise, she did not find herself wanting. In the first place, physically she felt more defined. She was now five feet and six inches tall, a respectable height in her opinion; she had lost the childish quality that her face had once revealed and now, in its place, there was a gravity about her features which touched, subtly, upon beauty. She had had her long hair cut, into a sleek bob; and she began to wear darker, more tailored clothes. As ever, she wore little make-up. Her eyes, too, appeared to be a deeper shade; there was a softness about her expression which, when she smiled, made the recipient of her affection feel singled out for particular attention and warmth. Regarding herself naked, she knew that her slender body was capable of pleasing both herself and her admirers.

Marilyn also discovered that she was tired. Her ambitions, although present, were temporarily exhausted. Thus, throughout the autumn and winter of 1983, with money in the bank and few demands upon her time, she pursued a quiet life – returning, in fact, to a pleasant cocoon. Now that she had forged links with a particular life-style, she had the confidence to navigate a considered course through the demands of her aspirations. It did not, to Marilyn, seem like a time for pessimism. Rather, she became an epicurean consumer, always residing one step ahead of her needs. Also, most importantly, she began to think of love.

In January 1984, Marilyn was invited to her friend Catherine's flat, in Chiswick. She had not seen Catherine for nearly a year, and accepted the invitation happily. Catherine's boyfriend, Stewart, would also be present. Stewart worked in Catherine's office.

'Will you be bringing anyone?' Catherine asked when the meeting was arranged by telephone, just after the New Year holiday.

'Oh no,' Marilyn laughed. 'Does that matter?'

'Don't be silly. I'll see you on Friday, at eight . . .'

The evening was freezing when Marilyn drove to Chiswick. Greenwich, beside the still, black river, appeared to crackle with frost. The coloured lights upon the mast of the dry-docked *Cutty Sark* looked distant and forlorn. Marilyn had not been aware that Chiswick was so far away. She drove through the outer city, glancing up from time to time at the empty offices, which were filled with blue or ivory-coloured light. London had just returned to work. An air of resignation seemed to mingle with the cold and emptiness. Marilyn loved to drive at night. Passing through Battersea, with its colourless tower-blocks and long rows of ornate, red-brick Victorian apartments, she wished that she had someone with her to share the enjoyment which she felt, and to turn the evening into a pleasant extension of a contained domestic happiness.

Catherine's flat was on the first floor of a new, small block. It stood in a quiet street, both sides of which were lined with new small cars. In all the house windows, some with elegant blinds and others with extravagant flounced curtains that looked out of place in such modest-sized dwellings, there were soft lights, and evidence of a quiet evening being spent at home. At the end of the street, there was a short parade of shops. Many of these were newly refurbished, and filled with luxury goods: a florist's; two small restaurants, already quite full; an antiques shop; a large delicatessen, still open. The window of the delicatessen was quite filled – ornamentally – with bottles of mineral water. All of this, to Marilyn, was quite in order. She felt relaxed, and happy. She smiled to think of her nervousness, the previous year, on approaching Fitton Place. Catherine, she knew, was from her own, moderately well-off, background. And she had seemed happier since meeting Stewart. Marilyn wondered what this young man would be like.

'Hi!' said Catherine's voice, cheerfully, but made strangely small through the entry-phone.

Marilyn climbed the smart wooden staircase. Everywhere was neatness and order. At the top of the stairs there was a black plastic tub which contained a small palm tree, the splayed leaves of which were buffed to a lustrous shine. Instinctively, Marilyn checked that the plant had been watered. The earth was moist, and warm.

'Hi!' Louder now, Catherine greeted her friend with a wide smile. A narrow hall, lit with a pale blue light, extended into the flat behind her.

'Hi!' There followed a moment's confusion and laughter whilst Marilyn took off her leather jacket and handed it to Catherine to be thrown onto the spare bed. Marilyn was wearing a long black pleated skirt of a fine material which held its creases; with this, black tights and a pair of low-heeled shoes which were black patent on one side and black suede on the other. A loose pullover, made of dark blue wool interwoven with a silvered, lilac-coloured thread like tinsel completed this ensemble. Marilyn was congratulated upon her clothes. Catherine, who was wearing a white shirt and a black, narrow skirt, had just got changed out of her work clothes. She was still very pretty, with dark hair, a pale face and kind, brown eyes. She looked tired, however, and she seemed rather harassed.

'I'm cooking,' she explained with a smile. 'Go through . . .'

Marilyn went into the long main room of the flat, which served as both a lounge and a dining room. She entered with humorous caution, aware that she had heard two male voices, conversing quietly. At her entrance, the two young men both rose to their feet. One of them, who was slightly taller, buttoned his suit jacket as he stood. Catherine made the introductions.

'This is Stewart,' she said, patting the arm of the fair-haired, slightly plump young man who was closest to her, 'and this is Martin.' The taller of the two strangers smiled, and held out his hand. Smiling back, Marilyn shook hands. Then, as Catherine presented her with a glass of red wine and then returned to the kitchen 'to finish burning dinner', Marilyn sat down in a wide, low, leather armchair, and surveyed the room and its occupants.

Behind the leather sofa upon which Martin and Stewart were seated (the former leaning back, with his legs crossed, and smoking – almost daintily, Marilyn thought – a cigarette; the latter leaning forward, with his elbows resting upon his knees and explaining how he and Catherine had met), there was a long window. This was covered by a grey venetian blind. In one corner there was a thin black metal stand which held two spotlights. These were turned towards the cream-coloured wall. On the wall closest to Marilyn, there was a framed poster: a 'fine art' edition of a photograph by Norman Parkinson which depicted a young woman, with hat and veil, standing in a New York street. The rest of the wall was bare. Behind Marilyn, in the far corner, there stood a small television and a large cassette player. A wicker chest stood against that wall. The other half of the room was occupied by the small dining table with its four matching chairs; new cutlery, a wooden pepper-mill and bottles of wine and water stood ready for use. The carpet was grey. Everything, it seemed, was brand-new. To Marilyn these furnishings appeared bland and lifeless.

'I love your flat,' she said, when Catherine reappeared.

'Oh, thanks. I'm just getting used to paying the mortgage, so I haven't been able to do very much with it . . .' The two young men smiled politely.

'I think the pasta's almost dissolved,' said Catherine, getting to her feet again.

'Do you want a hand?' said Stewart, loyally, rising to follow her.

'Thanks.'

The couple left the room. Marilyn smiled at Martin again, and asked him how he knew Catherine. She thought that he had beautiful eyes. The rest of his features looked, to her, as though he was 'growing into them'. There was a leanness, and a handsome gravity, but he seemed ill at ease. In three years, thought Marilyn, he'll be gorgeous . . . Before she had time to catch what Martin was saying, Catherine and Stewart returned bearing food and plates. The little company sat down to dinner. Marilyn was opposite Martin. Talking to the table at large, he seemed more relaxed, and became (Marilyn thought) quite funny.

The meal, typically, was comprised of spaghetti, tomato and pesto sauce, and salad. Fruit and cheese followed. The cassette player murmured quiet, 'jazz-influenced' pop music; a saxophone and piano accompanied a white girl's husky voice. Naming the group whose tape was playing, Stewart said enthusiastically:

119

'They're doing a concert at the Albert Hall. Would you like to go?'

'I'd sooner go to a hanging,' said Martin, smiling. Marilyn laughed.

'Well you still like all that weird arty stuff – that's like being at a hanging . . .'

Catherine explained to Marilyn that Martin and Stewart had worked together before Stewart joined her company. Now Martin was still in the City, and doing 'rather well'. Marilyn looked at Martin more closely. He had taken off his black suit jacket, and was wearing underneath a crisp white shirt and a silver and green tie. The tie, thought Marilyn, displayed good taste. His dark hair was cut short, and seemed to be gelled at the sides; a shadow of stubble had formed upon his chin. His appearance seemed to mingle convention with a certain irreverence. Marilyn had noticed that, instead of traditional black brogues, Martin was wearing black Chelsea boots, with pointed toes. His belt, too, was of black leather with a delicately carved silver buckle. His cuff-links were silver skull and crossbones. Those, thought Marilyn, were rather vulgar. He smoked a great deal, and drank freely. His accent was that of a public schoolboy, touched with a City twang. Socially, Marilyn could not place him. As the evening progressed, she glanced at him from time to time. Neither of them, it seemed, could find a way of entering into a natural conversation.

Stewart did most of the talking. He was demonstratively affectionate towards Catherine, and spoke a great deal about 'our boss' and 'our office'. Catherine, too, seemed happier than Marilyn could recall having seen her. In the little bright kitchen, so white as to almost dazzle the two girls, Marilyn helped Catherine make coffee, and asked her how she was.

'Things are really good,' said Catherine, extracting cups and saucers from the white cupboard; 'we're incredibly busy at work, but I enjoy it . . .'

'Stewart's nice.'

'Yes, he's really great. We've been going out together for nearly a year. It's a bit difficult at the office though; people make stupid comments and there's the danger of seeing too much of one another, but other than that it's fine. What do you think of Martin?'

Marilyn smiled. 'I haven't made up my mind yet. But he's terribly good-looking . . .' The girls laughed.

'Does he have a boyfriend? Not that I'm fishing or anything . . .' Marilyn laughed.

'He's just split up with someone. I never met her. But Martin's great.' Marilyn got the impression that her friend was simply saying these things in order to attempt some pleasant matchmaking that would conclude the evening nicely. She changed the subject, and the conversation turned to Greenwich, and Pru Williams. United by their different reasons for resenting that girl, Marilyn and Catherine returned to the sitting room clutching coffee, crockery and milk.

A little after midnight, as Catherine was falling asleep against Stewart's shoulder, the party broke up.

'Can I call a cab?' said Martin. 'I'm going to Vauxhall . . .' Glancing out of the window he said: 'Look! Snow . . .' The street was covered in a fine layer of thick, trembling flakes. 'I'd better make a move,' he added, 'you know what it's like the moment the English weather deviates from rain.'

'I'll take you,' said Marilyn, suddenly. 'It's on my way and my car's just – there . . .' She pointed.

'Heavens! Is that yours?' said Martin. 'I love black cars.'

'Well there you are,' said Marilyn, smiling, 'my car's black.'

The four young people exchanged farewells and thanks. Stewart and Catherine did not 'come downstairs' because 'they'd just get cold'. Martin hunched his shoulders into a long black overcoat. Marilyn fastened her leather jacket.

An hour later, Stewart and Catherine were lying in bed. Stewart, pleasantly drunk, had taken off Catherine's short nightshirt. Their love-making followed a precise pattern, and caused both of them nothing more than fleeting satisfaction. Afterwards, as Stewart lay his head on Catherine's breast, she would call him 'her baby' and stroke his hair. She could never make love without imagining her insides, and these gynaecological images, passing through her mind during the moments of passion, made her hate herself and wish, briefly, that Stewart would go.

Marilyn and Martin drove back through streets made soft and quiet with snow. Martin glanced at Marilyn's profile as she was driving; she drove, he thought, like a man. Close beside her, he could see her fine profile and dark eyelashes; as she changed gear with a single, steady push upon the clutch and a deft pulling-back of the gear-stick, he could see her long leg, stretching elegantly beneath her skirt. He allowed himself a few moments' fantasy. In the cold car he could smell her leather jacket and her perfume. He wondered whether or not she liked him. Approaching Vauxhall he offered directions to the quiet street of tall houses where he lived.

'This is really kind of you,' he said, 'I hope I haven't taken you miles out of your way – just here is fine . . .'

Pulling in, Marilyn parked her car beside a house which seemed bigger than the rest. The porch had a pillar on either side, and large bay windows looked out over the street.

'I live in the attic, actually,' said Martin, looking up. They smiled at one another.

'It's lovely to have met you,' said Martin. 'Please call me somtime, if you've got nothing better to do . . .' He gave Marilyn his business card, and quickly wrote his home telephone number on it.

'Thank you; I will,' said Marilyn. Shaking hands once more, they parted. As Martin was unlocking the front door, he watched the red lights on the back of Marilyn's car disappearing down the dark street. The road seemed grey with fallen snow.

The following week, Catherine rang Marilyn. Curiosity had got the better of her.

'Did anything happen?' she asked, feigning roguishness.

Marilyn laughed. 'What do you mean, "Did anything happen?"?'

'I just had this feeling – I hope you don't mind me saying . . .'

'Of course not; but I didn't know that anything was meant to "happen".'

Catherine blushed. She was glad that Marilyn couldn't see her. To cover the embarrassing moment she invited her friend out for a shopping trip.

'Thanks again for a lovely evening,' said Marilyn, as the call concluded. She had not said that she had put the business card upon her dressing table, and turned it over each night, wondering whether or not to call the person whose name it bore:

MR M. G. C. KNIGHT: SYSTEMS ANALYST.

Four: *Things Happen*

When, in January 1984, Catherine Clarke told Marilyn Fuller that Martin Knight was 'doing rather well in the City', her phrase seemed to hint at something more than the moderately successful career that that young man was pursuing. Martin was not destined to become a tycoon, or a financial genius. At the time when he met Marilyn, he was working in a City office which provided a service to the greater apparatus of the Square Mile. On his business card he was described as a systems analyst. This position had its place within a company that supplied information technology – as opposed to skill at arbitration or creative economic thinking – to the banks and the brokerage houses which did the real work on the home and foreign exchanges. In short, as the City existed as a great and complex institution with a defined hierarchy, Martin's role within it appeared to be, subtly, 'below stairs'. He was acutely aware of this fact.

Work, for Martin, began with his interview at the office near the Monument. The day was hot and humid – the last Thursday in July 1981. As he walked across London Bridge, at a little after two o'clock in the afternoon (his appointment was at three), he felt uncomfortable and conspicuous in his new 'office' suit. The suit was grey, and flecked minutely with blue. It was made of some deceptively coarse material. The jacket, which was double-breasted and had thin lapels, pinched him under the arms; the trousers – neither too wide nor too narrow, and thus shapeless – appeared to sag at the front, and cause the belt supplied with the garment to rise up ridiculously and press into Martin's stomach. The young man had to keep on stopping in order to readjust his clothes. A new white shirt, one cuff of which had been stained with oil from the handle of the train door, and the Tiles Old Boys' tie completed this outfit. On the verge of joining society as a working adult, Martin felt resentful, and mediocre. In order to compensate for this, he brooded upon angry, violent thoughts as he walked along. Believing himself to be exceptional, he did not want to conform to the demands of graduate traineeship. On the other hand, he could detect the brittle bravado of a schoolboy in his attitude: the pupil who, summoned by his teacher for punishment, drags his feet and ruffles his hair as he makes his way to the masters' common room. The City, meanwhile, drew closer: an edifice of high, white buildings, separated by dark entrances to chasm-like streets. Martin had already worked out his route to the office: it wasn't very far from London Bridge. But he was aware of an emptiness behind him; this seemed to stretch back all the way to Thornby Avenue, and a pastoral notion of the past. Suppose this is the very last of freedom? he thought. To Martin's right, the river looked cool and green, widening beyond Tower Bridge; to his left, many-windowed buildings, old and new, glinted in a white haze. Directly ahead, an imposing financial headquarters, adorned with an elaborate clock, stared impassively towards the approaching interviewee. This, Martin guessed, was the clock which T. S. Eliot had made famous:

With a dead sound on the final stroke of nine.

Eliot, not Brooke, now seemed to be the young man's spiritual companion.

Reaching the north bank of the river, and finding himself literally in the shadow of the City, Martin's bearings scattered, and his bravado drained away. He felt like a new boy. He was forty minutes early, but he wanted to locate the office in advance, in order to approach it with confidence and on time. He knew that he had to turn right when he reached Monument tube station, but the station was already in front of him, and had several entrances. Martin paused, and leant against some low railings that lined the busy junction. Men and women, dressed in neat but rather shabby clothes, were hurrying by. Here and there, small groups of prosperous businessmen drifted past, for all the world, thought Martin, like prefects at a public school. Shops and cafés had their doors open to the hot street; they seemed out of place amidst the vast offices and colourless thoroughfares. An atmosphere of formality and antiquity seemed to mingle with the brand-new and the archaic. Here, Martin recognised, there was a labyrinth, crossed with major roads and fragmented by tiny alleys and courtyards. As he had been in his first year at Tiles, Martin felt overawed by a sense of power and the suggestion of hidden, serene heights. He also realised that there was an invisible code at work, informed by traditions and know-how, of which he knew nothing. Essentially a snob, Martin wanted to dominate the City, and to be amongst those who enjoyed its privileges. He contemplated the banking district romantically: from the pale-faced clerks hurrying back to their desks and their telephones at the end of a late lunch through to the potent glimpses of authority that were implied by grand, high windows, Martin saw a structured universe in miniature, complete with horrors and wonders.

Just then, a girl walked by. She looked sullen. Her hair was dyed black and held off her face with a leopard-print headband. Her short skirt and old shirt were black, as were her stiletto-heeled shoes. By her side there was a green plastic bag, with the handle of a collapsible umbrella protruding out of it. Martin recognised her lapel-badge: it said EVERYONE HAS THEIR PRICE. Here was an ally, thought the young man. The girl was talking to herself as she walked along. Her muttered words were audible as she passed: 'Fuck fuck fuck fuck fuck . . .' Martin wondered what this girl did, and why she was swearing so violently. For a moment their eyes met. Beneath heavy powder, the girl's face appeared to be the colour of lavender. Her heavy-lidded eyes were filled with hostility. A diamanté stud gleamed upon her left nostril. Martin, in his ill-fitting suit, suddenly felt ridiculous. He began to look for Fish Street Hill, where his interview was due to take place.

Fish Street Hill, in those days, was a slippery cobbled road which ran down to Billingsgate fish market. Early in the morning, particularly during hot weather, a stench of rotting fish overhung the greasy cobbles, and the gutters were choked with market debris: broken wooden boxes, bloodstained sheets of paper and even heads and tails of fish. Closer to the market itself, mounds of dirty ice would be melting beside the drains. Office workers, still in an early-morning daze, would skirt along the top of the hill on their way to work – deafened by the drills and cement mixers in the neighbouring building sites, dazzled by the bright sun and sickened by the odour of putrefaction which seemed to hang, fermenting, in the still, hot air. This foetid atmosphere appeared to wash like a warm, consuming wave against the lower sealed windows of those offices that were built closest to that section of the Thames. Later, the fish market was moved, and a prestigious new building took over the site; when Martin started work, however, he had to face the smell and litter of the old market every day. Richmond Data Services, where the young man was initially employed, was housed in office premises which stood between the Monument and Fish Street Hill.

On the afternoon of his interview, Martin entered the offices of Richmond Data Services with a mind quite emptied of thought, ambition, or curiosity. He had noticed, as he approached the two sets of glass wing-doors with a steady tread, a little coffee shop, called Rossos, which stood – impudently it seemed – on the other side of the street to the grey, featureless building where his fate would be decided. He could just glimpse, beyond the large handwritten menu which filled the café window, three dark-haired young men who were busily injecting polystyrene cups of coffee with steam, and deftly making sandwiches. Rossos, it seemed, did good business. Briefly, as he ascended the three broad steps which marked the portal of a new life, Martin imagined himself having breakfast in the little café. This imagining of a rounded urban lifestyle gave him hope.

The reception area of Richmond Data Services was as featureless as its exterior; the office had been designed and built in the 1960s, on the 'block principle' of modernism. As a consequence, perhaps, of this, nearly every room and corridor within the premises was either too big, too small, too long, or too short. The lobby was the size of a school hall, with a high ceiling, a long black desk and a further set of swing-doors which led to two lifts. The floor was made of grey marble, but this was scuffed and unpolished. The street-facing windows, tall and wide, were covered with dusty net curtains. Shafts of afternoon sunlight, like stretched golden shadows, pushed through the curtains and fell in elongated oblongs onto the grey floor. Four tubs of artificial plants stood at regular intervals along the length of the windows. Opposite the reception desk, where a constant flow of visitors, members of staff and internal telephone calls kept the two white-shirted security men busily engaged in rhythmic activity, there was a green-carpeted area occupied by four aluminium seats, upholstered in bright green fabric. Each of these low-backed seats offered space for three people. Several of the cushions were stained with coffee from the vending machine which stood in the corner. Upon the vending machine, fastened beside one of the buttons, a small, handwritten note declaimed: *White with sugar is malfunctioning: Maintenance please correct.* In front of the seats there was a glass-topped table, upon which were strewn a scattering of dog-eared magazines and two brown ashtrays. The magazines were called *Information Planning* and *Communications Management*. That day's copy of the *Financial Times*, with a white 'circulation' label stapled to its front page, lay crumpled upon one of the seats. Two other people were waiting: a tall, nervous young man, clad in a hairy tweed suit and a pair of country brogues; and a short, plump girl with brown curly hair, who was sitting with her handbag on her knees. She looked as though she was trying to memorise something. The air was heavy and dry. In the background, two female switchboard operators could be heard connecting calls. Their voices rose up at the end of each statement: 'Putting you through,' or 'That line's still busy.' As Martin approached the reception desk, the tall young man was asked to 'make his way to the third floor'. Martin felt a cold sensation in his stomach.

The two security men were obviously 'characters' within the building. Every member of staff who passed by them seemed to exchange a greeting, platitude, or quip. Office dramas, whose complexity was a mystery to Martin, were hinted at in a fragment:

'Still there then, that package?'

'Yes, he never came back.'

'Typical!'

Martin stood before the older and shorter of the two guards. Just as he was about to speak, a cheerful girl hurried by, her high heels clattering on the floor.

'All right, Joe?'

'You'll wear yourself out, you will!'

Martin smiled, as though entertained.

Joe looked up at Martin. 'Yes sir, can I help you?' He assessed the visitor with a single glance. Boredom and suspicion appeared to register in his eyes.

'I've got an interview with Mr Spiller, at three o'clock. My name's Martin Knight.' He offered his letter of invitation in order to substantiate this statement. The guard took it, read it carefully and then said: 'Take a seat please. They'll call you when they're ready.'

Martin sat down not far from the plump girl. She seemed not to notice him. She was wearing a blue-and-white-patterned blouse and a navy-blue skirt. Her legs were bare. On her feet were black high-heeled shoes, only the toes of which were polished. When she suddenly raised her hand, to nervously push back a strand of loose hair, Martin noticed a large damp stain beneath her arm. It seemed pointless to attempt conversation. His mind was still quite empty. He felt as though he was not present in the scene, but merely watching it from a distance, like a spirit. His timidity had gone, and he almost felt amused. A porter approached the reception desk, pushing a comical little trolley. There were three cardboard boxes on this, inscribed in black felt-tip pen: S–Z, GENERAL AND SAMPLE DESPATCH and OLD FILES. The porter was a young man, and he was wearing a green overall. The girl beside Martin was summoned: 'Make your way to the third floor please; someone'll meet you at the lift . . .' Straightening her skirt and walking, like a condemned prisoner, with lowered head, towards the lifts, the girl departed.

If that's the competition! thought Martin.

His mind, now, was beginning to rouse itself. He leant back, and lit a cigarette. Having seen nothing that particularly impressed him, he no longer cared whether he got the job or not. He seemed to be waiting for a long time. He daydreamed, partially forgetting that he was about to attend an interview. He knew that he was lucky to have any job prospects at all. Many of his contemporaries at college had not even bothered to apply for jobs. He fiddled with a safety pin that he had fastened, like a secret badge, inside his suit jacket. His thoughts were interrupted by a burst of laughter from the reception desk: 'Well, where there's life there's hope!' the older guard exclaimed. And then:

'Mr Knight? Make your way to the third floor please; someone'll meet you at the lift . . .'

Striding forward like a distinguished guest, as opposed to a potential trainee, Martin made his way to the third floor. The young porter, watching him pass, looked down at the floor and sniffed.

Later, Martin would recall his interview with Mr Spiller as being an exercise in the learning of confidence. Perversely, it was his innate sense of superiority which earned him a position as one of Richmond Data Services' three new graduate recruits. Also, Martin had often shone in the eyes of authority. He appeared to know, instinctively, when to listen carefully, when to question intelligently and when to display a trace of arrogance which did not go unnoticed by his superiors, and which raised him in their opinion above the rest of the timid herd. As a student primarily of atmosphere, Martin was adept at playing out certain roles that were required of him; it was in the expression of his honest feelings that he encountered difficulties.

At the interview, Mr Spiller had shown Martin an 'organagram' of the company's corporate structure. The organisation was not as big as Martin had assumed it would be. In essence, RDS was divided into 'Systems' and 'DATEC'. Both of these departments were concerned with the planning and sale of office-technology systems.

'In fact,' said Mr Spiller impressively, 'you could say that we buy and sell information. Now what do you think of that?' He tapped the diary upon his desk with his pen. Martin looked interested. The interviewer continued: 'Most business these days is controlled by two factors: the market – we can't influence that directly – and communications. The firm that communicates efficiently will be the winning firm. New technology, and the correct implementation of that technology, can increase a company's business one-hundred-fold – or even more. Time, as they say, costs money . . .' Martin wondered whether Mr Spiller had been repeating this speech all day.

'It sounds very interesting,' he said.

'As a graduate recruit we'd get you involved in most aspects of Systems work; then we'd assign you to a particular department, working on one of the current projects. Where do you see yourself fitting in?' This last question came unexpectedly, and was designed to catch out the inattentive interviewee. Martin had anticipated it.

'Marketing and Development,' he said, firmly.

The older man looked pleased. 'A good choice,' he said. 'Did you just pick it out of the air, or do you have a special interest in that area?'

At this point, as he leant forward to answer, Martin recalled both a lecture he had enjoyed at college, and the fact that Plato accords Socrates a 'divine voice', which spoke to him from time to time. He launched into a brief speech, impressively pitched and persuasively worded, which dwelt upon the importance of innovation and marketing in an increasingly competitive business world. The phrases seemed to form ready-made in his mouth, with neither awkwardness nor ambiguity to impede their eloquence. Mr Spiller, for the first time that afternoon, listened to a candidate without growing bored. Martin, aware that he must not overplay his hand, widened his little thesis to incorporate some thoughts of his own upon the future of high-street retail and then, disarmingly, apologised if he had shown naïvety. It was a masterful performance. Finally, Mr Spiller spoke, and this time his voice was lower, and confidential, as though he was talking to a potential equal.

'What's your computer experience, Martin?' he asked. 'I say this because we have another, unadvertised opening, down in a section called DogFox. We weren't going to consider a trainee, but . . .'

'Could you tell me a little about the section?'

'Gladly. DogFox is on the communications and marketing side; it's a new systems-implementation section, headed by Dave

Runner. Dave and his team, briefly, are working on systems which can override specific internal information problems. It's highly computerate though . . .' He paused, and tapped his diary once more. Martin nodded. 'Let me speak to Dave; if he's agreeable to taking on a trainee, and seeing how it works out, then we might be able to fix you up. Can I ask – are you waiting to hear from any other interviews?'

Cleverly, Martin said, 'Only one; but I wanted to explore all the possibilities before making a decision . . .'

'Can you hold off for a week? And we'll be in touch shortly . . .'

'Of course . . .'

Buoyed up by this interest, Martin began to consider the reality of working at RDS. The office, the streets which surrounded it and the routine that would be inaugurated should he gain a position all began to assume a new air: this environment, and these stimuli, would take control of his life. As yet, inwardly, he was too bewildered to assess what bearing these new qualities would have on the delicate tissue of his moods. Mr Spiller's pen, lying now to one side of his company blotter, would begin to have an influence which extended all the way to Thornby Avenue and the romantic, pastoral past. For Martin, who was concerned mostly with the pursuit of happiness, this new turn in his career would advance his exploration of himself. He would have to measure himself against his aspirations, and try to advance hopefully.

A month later, at the beginning of September 1981, Martin began work at Richmond Data Services. He was a privileged trainee within the élite of DogFox. His salary, large for those days, was £8,300 per annum.

That September was misty and humid. A brilliant Indian summer, however, appeared to be blazing behind the low haze, and this broke through from time to time, revealing a deep blue sky and flooding the City streets with rich, amber-coloured sunshine. The start of the new season, compounding a sense of change, coloured Martin's moods. He felt as though a new era was beginning, and he detected the poetic within it. He was intoxicated by London – although he only knew one small part of the city – and he immersed himself throughout the mellow days, so filled with new impressions, in both memories and anticipation. The City appeared like a cathedral to him, surrounded by redevelopments that made the landscape seem alive. He loved the theatre of the buildings, and the drama of light and weather to which they responded. Wandering cautiously through this vastness, Martin discovered new aesthetic ambitions and new types of beauty to conquer. With his first wages he bought a new suit: it was black and well cut, and cost more than he could really afford. He also bought a record player, and reached the end of his first salaried month with no money.

At first, Martin commuted daily to the City. His local station, which had been built in the 1930s, of red brick with a gabled slate roof, had glass-canopied platforms and sombre, damp waiting rooms. As the tracks stretched back into the autumn haze, away from London, Martin could just see the bend – overhung by tall trees – around which his train would arrive. In the mornings, shafts of sunlight fell through these trees, and the train would emerge through the mist with glinting windows – an insubstantial outline, swiftly drawing closer. The platform was usually crowded: Martin's station, on the edge of the countryside, was the first stop at which the train took on many passengers. The commuters seemed to exist as a tiny society of their own. The older men, who had been travelling to London for many years, stood in small groups, or waited alone, looking stoical and formal. They appeared like the weary officers of a hard-driven battalion. Martin, ambivalently, regarded himself as a subaltern. The younger commuters, whilst being more casually dressed, were less patient with the deficiencies of the service. After three months, Martin determined to free himself from the bondage and humiliation of commuting. He no longer wanted to appear suburban. In the mean time, he had no choice but to join the travelling army. On bad days, when the train service was disrupted, he felt as though he was participating in a situation comedy, as one of the 'little men', too mediocre and too insignificant to lift himself above the low farce of cancellations and delays. Aspiring to surroundings and routines that flattered his notion of himself, Martin began to regard the suburbs – with the exception, sentimentally, of his home – as being petty, shallow-minded and ugly. London appeared to mock its outlying settlements, and to treat the inhabitants of those areas with disdain. Later, Martin would alter this belief.

The journey to London Bridge took nearly an hour. The many stations on its route became familiar to Martin, and each one appeared to have a separate personality. Having reached the vast terminus and spilt out of the train as one of the hurrying throng, Martin then walked over the bridge and on towards the Monument. Daily, as a reflex action, he thought of Eliot's 'Waste Land' as he strode towards the City. He was one of many young people who had reacted against the principle of office life by reciting that poet's moving description of days spent in clerical purgatory. To Martin, the City was 'unreal'; at times he did wonder, self-consciously and with a tinge of self-pity, how many death had undone. And then he would buy his cup of coffee. The City was enriched, for Martin, by the great poetry which it had produced. Thus his despondency was, in those early days, superficial. Walking across the bridge, he was fascinated by some of the workers who walked beside him. The oddities were mostly male. One man, for instance, with hair as white as his shabby raincoat, would always be talking to himself as he walked along, as though rehearsing his justification for some felonious activity. Another man crossed the bridge with a small transistor radio pressed to his ear. Most, however, enacted Eliot's line:

And each man fixed his eyes before his feet.

All in all, initially, Martin was wholly bewildered by his new life. On the one hand, his emotions responded passionately to the new impressions which were beginning to inform him; on the other hand, deep down, Martin had the sense that he was walking on ice, and that there was some terrible chasm beneath him. He was terrified of this fragility, and of discovering that his pursuit of beauty had been curtailed. He feared for the safety of the 'fourth dimension' which love, previously, had enabled him to perceive. Silently and invisibly – like a colourless, odourless gas – boredom began to seep into his days at the office called DogFox.

Martin began to suffer from a form of emotional vertigo. His moods would rise or plunge with alarming rapidity. Each day, as he walked past the tube station, he would see an 'old soldier' who sat on a box, playing an accordion. This elderly entertainer was short and heavily built, with red, sagging cheeks covered with purple broken veins. He wore a black eye-patch and a black beret. His good eye stared ferociously ahead. His white moustache was stained with nicotine. As he played – extremely loudly – boisterous, infectious tunes, he would add to his performance by shouting to the passing workers as though they were embarking troops: 'Off you go, lads!' and 'Up and at 'em!' This character filled Martin with hatred and horror. He felt as though the old man was gloating over the captive workforce, and mocking their position by treating them like foot-soldiers. Passing this grotesque busker was the worst part of Martin's day.

Sometimes, if Martin's train was cancelled, he would travel to one of the other big southern stations and then complete his journey by underground train. On one occasion, ridiculously, he felt his throat tighten and his eyes prick with tears as he heard another busker – this time playing the violin – who was performing Fauré's 'Pavane'. The music filled the crowded

137

subway with its gentle melancholy and its anguished crescendo. Martin stopped to listen. He suddenly imagined all the buskers in London playing a fragmented symphony, with each member of the orchestra playing in isolation and the whole city, like an antiquated, monumental squeeze-box, pushing forth a majestic requiem from the entrances and halls of its underground railway stations. As the last note of the Pavane died away, ignored by the hurrying crowds, Martin gave the violinist a five-pound note. Inwardly he rejoiced in his role as a moved, anonymous patron.

During these autumn months, Martin's office routine began to define itself. He grew used to the early-morning stench of Fish Street Hill, and could equate a partial reluctance to go to work with the smell of rotting fish with which his working day commenced. DogFox section was located on the lower ground floor of Richmond Data Services. Thus its windows looked out into an 'area', beneath the level of the pavement. Martin was amused, as opposed to impressed, by the military-sounding title of his department. But he was pleased to be working with a small team as opposed to in a larger, less prestigious section. It was an open-plan office, sectioned with baize-covered partitions, and it housed fifteen members of staff. A further row of partitions screened the department from the corridor which ran down one side of it. Four long windows, covered by net curtains, ran the length of the other wall. At one end of the office there was a kitchen area, with fridge, water-cooler and vending machine. DogFox was privileged to have its own vending machine. A notice, written in biro, demanded that staff from other sections did not use the DogFox vending machine. Two stained trays, one of which was cracked, were propped up beside the dirtied wastepaper bin in which used plastic cups were to be deposited. A second notice insisted that DogFox staff must always dispose of their cups in the 'kitchen' bin. At the other end of the office, Dave Runner and Paul Fines had their own special enclosure.

This area contained two large desks (or 'work-stations'), some chairs for meetings and three five-drawer filing cabinets. Charts, 'planners' and the RDS official calendar covered the wall behind them.

Dave was in his middle thirties; he was short, dark-haired, bearded and enthusiastic. Born in Durham, he had graduated from London University before taking up a teaching and research post at an American college. From there, he had returned to the 'real world', but something of the informality of campus and faculty attitudes was still reflected in his bearing and countenance. Outwardly he was cheerful, and he always called his staff by abbreviations of their Christian names, if this was possible. His northern accent made him appear friendly and down-to-earth. He was devoted to information technology, but he was also a liberal, and a family man. This made him more popular than many of the other managers. Martin liked Dave Runner.

Paul Fines, on the other hand, was terse, reticent and sarcastic. He was friends only with those people who didn't like Dave, because secretly he wanted his superior's job. Paul was from Oxford, and took a seemingly instant dislike to Martin. 'I really can't see why they've put you here,' he said to the new recruit; 'we're half-way through an assessment of the project and, to be honest, we haven't got the time to brief you . . .' Paul spoke of DogFox as though it were a secret mission. He then gave Martin four large folders bound in white plastic, which explained in great technical detail the development of the project. It was Martin's first job to read these folders, and to write a brief report on them. 'We won't expect you to get anything right,' said Paul, 'it's just that he,' he jerked a thumb towards the manager, 'wants you to get some background.' Martin set to this task assiduously. Paul was pale and had short fair hair. His eyes seemed colourless. He wore expensive, charcoal-grey suits, and he walked with a swagger. To his favourites, he would always lean extremely close as he whispered some joke or comment. He had a trick of staring directly into the eyes of whoever he was talking to, and then feasting upon their embarrassment. This trick worked particularly well when he was trying to be likable or amusing.

Most of the staff in DogFox were male, and in their late twenties or early thirties. The atmosphere was one of academic quiet mingled with vocational determination. It was, in this respect, like working in a laboratory. From time to time, however, staff meetings were called, and then the workers displayed a sense of humour, laden with departmental and technical references, which Martin was surprised to find himself aspiring towards. Half of the young man's nature – but no more – was attracted to the efficiency and seriousness of the office. The other half was bored, and sought relief in daydreams.

Three women worked in DogFox (Hilary, Gillian and Carole) but only one of them was friendly towards Martin. Gillian, who was tall and pretty, would occasionally join the new recruit for a cigarette in the kitchen area. She did not question Martin about his background, but was prepared to offer advice and explanations with regard to the politics and work in the office. Martin, believing he had made a friend (and being desperate to do so), presumed too quickly that Gillian would always mother him, and pass on sympathy and guidance. 'Well, you'll just have to read it again!' she snapped one afternoon when Martin asked – in a mock-wheedling manner – for yet further elucidation of a complex paragraph in his folder. Humiliated, the young trainee crept back to his empty, conspicuous desk.

It was unfortunate for Martin that, initially, he found himself to be a victim of office politics: as Paul Fines was his direct line-manager, and as Paul did not like Dave Runner, he was frequently being put in positions where the section manager was questioning his activities. If Martin did something right for Paul Fines, it irritated the otherwise cheerful Dave Runner; if he followed Dave's counter-instruction directly – seeking to win back approval – it got him into trouble with Paul. Either way he irked somebody, and thus lost the autonomy so vital for gaining confidence. In the end it was Stewart Richards, a quiet, portly young man, who took Martin to one side and explained the situation to him. Stewart was a loner within the office, and considered to be rather feeble by the DogFox élite. The two young men struck up a friendship, and went out to buy their sandwiches together at lunchtime. In a few sentences, Stewart outlined the purpose of DogFox to Martin:

'It's an Information Technology "package",' he said, rather timidly. 'Basically that means a set of systems which cover electronic filing, word-processing, advanced telecommunications, micro-computing, electronic mail distribution –' he drew breath here, humorously, 'forms-processing and computer ergonomics . . .'

'Eh?' Martin laughed.

The two friends were sitting in the smoky public bar of The Clarence, an old pub which stood not far from Billingsgate. On the little table before them were pints of beer and long, crusty rolls filled with cheese and tomato. Secretly, Martin preferred less noisy surroundings, but he did not want his new friend to think him a snob. He was touched by Stewart's attention and, moreover, was starved of conversation. Stewart, in his turn, was rather overawed by Martin. He had seldom enjoyed the role of experienced superior, and thus he offered Martin much advice.

'Don't worry about it; you'll soon get the hang of programming. And Dave's all right, he knows what Paul's like. He'll put you on Systems Training soon, and then Returns, I should think. That's what happened to me. Actually, it's quite interesting. You begin to work out what it's all for, and how the different bits fit together . . .' Martin wondered whether he ought to make the comparison between DogFox and the universe that had just slipped into his mind. He decided that it would be rude, and so he smiled and nodded. 'Right,' he said.

After this conversation, Martin began to feel less lonely. He now had Stewart to talk to at the office, and thus he felt less conspicuous. As the first three months passed by, and as he began to relax, Martin rediscovered that part of himself which was naturally romantic, and inclined towards subversive attitudes. With this, concurrently, he regained his confidence, and began to do well at the office. It was as though the two halves of his nature fuelled one another. Later, Martin was to wonder how he survived for so long without one aspect of his personality unbalancing the other; in the mean time, held stable by a hesitancy which he mistook for inner strength, Martin maintained his successful balancing act.

Christmas passed, and the new year began its slow, dreary advance into spring. Martin, sometimes accompanied by Stewart, began to discover the strange, nervous world of 'after-work' socialising: the waits beside cold damp tube stations, the breathless walks through clearing streets to pubs and bars, the empty darkness of the City after nine in the evening, the quick drunkenness which followed meagre, hastily eaten suppers. Martin was beginning to need a social life, and with the fulfilment of this need came an exploration of central London. It was a typical enough path for a young person such as himself, but he was not, by nature, a hedonist. He wanted to belong to a 'set', and thus enjoy company in surroundings and a manner that would make him feel in harmony with the great city. Very quickly, Martin became the dominant partner in his friendship with Stewart; he played Holmes to Stewart's Dr Watson. He also pursued fashion, and had his hair cut fashionably short at a Chelsea hairdressing salon. He introduced slightly foppish elements into his work clothes; he put up a little poster beside his desk at work; it said FINAL ACADEMY: INDUSTRIAL PUNK ROCK.

'I thought punk was "out",' said Gillian.

In time, Martin was put on 'Returns'; this was a form of technical proof-reading, the results of which were delivered

142

directly to Dave. He also began to work on specific computer programs, and to learn the basis of systems analysis. He became something of a 'character' in the office, but was generally liked. He made a point, however, of not joking with the security men when he passed by their desk and showed them his pass.

Often, on Friday evenings, Martin would get the last train home. The station, cold and brightly lit, would contain various groups of drunk workers and nervous, solitary travellers. Often slightly drunk himself on these occasions, Martin would buy a cup of coffee from the one little buffet that was still open, and then stand close to the shuttered concourse newsagents, sipping the boiling, bitter liquid and studying his surroundings. Here and there, locked in hopeless embraces, lovers would be parting. Martin, poetically, found something strange about the contrast between their passion and the work clothes which these people had been wearing all day. He wondered how many of these couples were pursuing doomed illicit romances and were going home with prepared stories and feigned expressions of despair at having to 'work' so late. Young women, some little more than girls, would be travelling alone, wrapped in shabby overcoats and sitting with their bags close beside them and their heads drooping with sleep. Other strangers could be seen staring out of the black train windows and chewing tepid, savoury-smelling hamburgers. Occasionally, someone would be sick. It was a curious, after-work world, partially volatile and partially despairing; it seemed to exist beyond normality, and create an atmosphere in which anything could happen, but nothing ever did. Humanity, so hideous to the individual when crowded together in the depression and discomfort of morning, began towards midnight to seem lonely and vulnerable, failing in its attempts to enjoy itself as much as it had failed in the acquisition of a pleasant, healthy working routine. This, Martin knew, was the fate of some of the travelling workers who existed between the city and the suburbs. Despite his own internal contradictions,

143

the thought of such a compromise filled him with despair. The joyless poetry of the last train home, in some ways, was a vital lesson in his aesthetic education, and he studied it carefully.

In February 1982 the City appeared to freeze over. The grey buildings looked as lifeless as stones; the excavations in the building sites were filled with ice. At dusk, the sky seemed bronze. The streets, for some reason, appeared quieter. Martin found this seasonal change intoxicating. He wished that he could immerse himself in the cold atmosphere, and feel that he was inhabiting the frozen heart of the City. He wanted to visit every quiet corner of the half-lit labyrinth, and to study the play of wintry light upon the river. One evening, instead of seeing Stewart or going home, he went for a long walk around the clearing streets. By nine o'clock he had reached Whitechapel. The subways of the underground station were deserted. Still the need to explore drove him on. It had seemed, on his walk, that the real essence of the eerie beauty that he was trying to locate was always one step ahead of him. Like a ghost, the spirit of the cold night had drawn him deeper and deeper into the network of alleys, unfrequented courtyards and brilliantly illuminated thoroughfares. Sometimes, he would find himself beside massive pillared mansion blocks with high, small, dingy windows; then he would walk into a paved piazza, where violet and pink lights were wound around the heights of scaffolding and cranes that flanked the rise of a new tower. Often timid, Martin now walked the streets quite fearlessly. All that he saw seemed to touch his emotions too acutely; and he was reminded of the moment, some years earlier, when he had stood upon the dunes at Suffolk and watched the departing couple. Now, the most dismal building or dark street corner filled him with inexplicable longing. Finally, at ten o'clock, he sat down upon a cold bench. He was at a road junction, where the many streets converged and widened; heavy traffic, heading towards the Commercial Road, had broken the mood of the evening. Banality returned. The moment had passed.

'It's hopeless,' said Martin.

The urban, for Martin, had now usurped the pastoral. His aspirations, enthusiasms and sense of aesthetics were all linked to the city. In the back of his mind, like an idyllic dream, images of sun-drenched countryside and stylised, serene gardens lay undisturbed and uncalled-upon. By August 1982 the desire to live in London had driven him to explore the possibilities of obtaining a mortgage. He was delighted by the seriousness and courtesy with which the building society treated him. He learnt that if he could pay a small deposit, his borrowing potential was enough to purchase a small apartment. His initial desire, to live in the Barbican Centre flats, was, however, impracticable. But the urge to own property drove him on. His mother, who had monitored this enthusiasm, finally offered him £2,000 to put towards the deposit. 'It's what your sister got,' she said. Martin, disastrously, began to feel like a rich man, and spent his money freely. He had met up with various old acquaintances from Tiles, and through them been introduced to a wider social circle. His friendship with the kindly Stewart began to dwindle. Stewart, in any case, was about to change jobs. Martin tried to introduce his office colleague to his other friends, but this experiment failed. The Tiles contingent found Stewart dull; Stewart regarded the public schoolboys as pretentious and loud. Cursed with a kind heart, Martin tried to divide his time equally between these two different kinds of friendship. He found the set from Tiles more sympathetic to his notion of himself, and so he was secretly pleased when Stewart handed in his resignation.

On Stewart's last day there were cakes, and a 'drink-up' after work. Dave Runner, like a tutor on a class outing, talked about DogFox to whichever of the tipsy workers were prepared to listen. Some, seeking advancement and approval, did not leave the manager's side for a moment. It was suggested that Paul Fines and Hilary were having an affair. Obscene jokes and uproarious laughter attended this speculation. Martin, who was working on 'being interesting', talked about himself, and art, to Caroline and a quiet young man called Richard Hayter. Stewart got drunk.

Richard Hayter, the most mysterious man in DogFox, was to demonstrate to Martin, by example, a rule quite vital to surviving within an office. Richard could sometimes be seen having 'little chats' with Dave Runner. On these occasions, Paul Fines would absent himself from the enclosure which he shared with the section manager, and go to talk to one of his favourites – raising his eyes to heaven and pointing towards Richard. Richard, it seemed, was having personal problems. He was often late, and on more than one occasion had left the office early, with the expression of a man possessed. Finally, in October 1982, he was dismissed. This unpleasantness was the talk of the office. One afternoon, Dave Runner's usually moderate voice was heard to shout: 'I'm sorry Richard, but it's final; I can't keep . . .' The rest of the staff bent quietly over their desks, listening intently. A few sniggers and exchanged glances acknowledged that everyone in DogFox was monitoring Richard's confrontation. Martin, inwardly, felt sorry for him.

When Richard left the section manager's desk, the office was embarrassed to see that he was crying. Grotesque with misery and nervousness, the dismissed worker picked up his coat and case. 'Going home,' he snuffled. Elsewhere in the office, people had now lost interest in the drama, and were talking in their usual voices. Looking neither right nor left, Richard strode out of the office. To Martin, this all appeared quite sudden. He had no idea what Richard's crime might be. For the rest of the afternoon, the other staff were all on their best behaviour. They saw in the humiliation of their colleague an attempt to shine. Steve Clary, who worked with Martin, peered into the latter's enclosure and said: 'Never, ever, show your feelings at work. You'll always end up looking a prat – like Richard.' Martin nodded, and registered this piece of advice. He wondered why Steve had made a point of offering it to him. A little while later, Hilary sauntered over, eager to discuss the event.

'He had that coming,' she said.

'Why?'

'Well, he really was becoming boring. His girlfriend's left him. You'd have thought she'd died the way he's been carrying on. And he does bugger-all work, which puts his files on our desks . . . We've all got problems. He was just sorry for himself.'

'But he seemed really nice,' said Martin, cautiously. Hilary regarded him with a smouldering eye.

'Do you know what he spent his time doing?' she said. 'Come here, I'll show you.' She led Martin to Richard's abandoned desk. Martin felt ghoulish, hovering above the scene of the upset. Hilary was undeterred. 'There!' she said, flinging a paperback book onto the desk, 'that's what he was doing.' The book was a copy of *The Oxford Dictionary of Quotations*. Martin looked puzzled.

'I don't get it,' he said.

'You're not the only one!' Hilary paused impressively and then said: 'He was memorising it! Richard was memorising that book! That's what he did all day. He said it kept his mind "off things".'

'He was memorising *The Oxford Dictionary of Quotations*?'

'In one.'

'How far had he got?'

Hilary laughed. 'I don't think our Richard was quite all there,' she said, returning the book to its drawer. 'But can you blame Dave for getting pissed off?'

Martin went back to his desk, and got on with that afternoon's returns. Frequently bored himself, he felt that there was something romantic and worthwhile in Richard's strange – if selfish – activities. He was afraid that he, too, would have behaved in such a manner. And then he remembered the complete absence of dignity in Richard's departure, and shuddered. Often, when he could not sleep, Martin had found himself recalling those occasions in his life when he had publicly displayed self-pitying emotions. These memories caused him acute embarrassment. They reminded him of drunks who, believing that they are displaying fine insights or noble sentiments, are simply causing onlookers to feel bored or disgusted. For Martin, who frequently sought an audience, and who often believed that his emotional responses were romantically poised and therefore interesting, it was vital that he remember the advice that Steve had given him.

In November 1982, Martin received a substantial increase in salary. No longer a trainee, he now earned £10,300 per annum. He spent less time at Thornby Avenue, and often preferred to stay at a friend's flat, rather than curtail his evening to catch the last train home. When he did this, he would wake up in the morning extremely early and, negotiating his way around a strange apartment, take great delight in showering and preparing coffee before his host was up. He would sample different aftershave lotions, depending on where he was staying, and all of the following day he would be able to scent the interruption of his usual routine.

Martin's friends, for the most part, were young men with similar backgrounds to his own. They were young lawyers or accountants or bankers – all enjoying the first freedom which their professional incomes were bestowing upon them. They practised a form of conservative hedonism, couching their little indulgences in a cradle of common sense. This gave their revels a controlled, self-satisfied tone. Their confidence was boundless. With these young men was a quantity of young women; most of these girls worked in big offices and were pursuing their own careers with a determination which rivalled – and outstripped – that of their male counterparts. Couples formed and dissolved, aspiring towards a brief, halcyon period of domesticity which never seemed to flower. Their playground, at first, was the wine bars, pubs and moderately priced restaurants of the City, West End and Holborn. It was easy to forget that many of these young people had only been out of college for two years. They would arrive in ones and twos at whatever venue had been decided upon, proudly bringing the problems of the working day with them. Self-importance could be derived from displaying impatience and dissatisfaction with whatever purely local crisis had occurred in one's office. To arrive in a bad temper, and to say, 'Oh, it's just work,' had the effect of making one seem in some manner indispensable to one's employer. These were young people who, three years later, would arrive and say, 'I'm gasping for a glass of champagne . . .'

As these evenings progressed, with jokes, confessions, manifestos and alcohol, this self-importance would be replaced by a certain flirtatiousness, or boisterousness, which, undetected by the participants, recast them as little more than spoilt teenagers. Martin, who liked to appear unconventional, was drawn to both the solid respectability of his male companions and the demands to be 'interesting' or absurd, which were usually voiced by the girls. For the most part, however, he got on better with the girls. Generally, he was liked. As ever, he was flattered by attention, and the slightest compliment would redouble his confidence. Sometimes, however, he would be filled with hatred at the sight of his generation enjoying themselves, and then he would become withdrawn, and brood darkly on those areas that, in his own mind, came within the boundaries of 'art'. Nobody, on these occasions, took much notice.

In the spring of 1983, Martin was seized by two contradictory impulses. The first of these, which was amplifying as opposed to declaring itself, was a thirst for cultural knowledge. The young man was overcome by a sense of ignorance, and a gnawing passion to get to grips with those subjects that he felt would increase his understanding of himself and his ability to impress others. Having always spent a lot of money on clothes and records, he began to buy books: philosophy, history, poetry, biography and the history of art. He would go to the large bookshop at London University, and there spend hours browsing the shelves in search of those volumes that seemed, cosmetically, to satisfy his needs. Thus, on one occasion, he emerged with a life of Voltaire, a history of the Counter-Reformation and a curious, expensive paperback which was called *Discussions in Contemporary Culture: Structuralism and Beyond*. It was this latter purchase which caused him the greatest satisfaction. Discarding Voltaire and the problems of religious persecution, he immersed himself in a vague understanding that nothing was quite as it seemed, and that a phenomenon, in fragment, could be made to mean anything. This idea excited him. It appeared to sit comfortably with his own romantic sense of never quite getting to the point. Also, he admired the scientific language in which the book was written: as cities were described as 'texts', and as texts themselves were sometimes referred to as 'architecture', so too did Martin, in search of a new aesthetic language with which to describe the poetry that he had detected in the contemporary and the urban, begin to absorb these phrases, and to save them for future use. In this he was quite sincere. He would study the sunset – for instance – reflecting off the windows of one of the new, audacious, mirrored buildings beside the Thames, and think of that structure as a 'signifier' to be 'decoded'. He could 'read' in the design of shops and the shape of the city's street furniture an explanation, he thought, of contemporary society. As the unexpected, the ironic and the dramatic began to shape the appearance of new developments, so Martin began to feel in harmony with the mixture of fashionability and profundity that he believed they expressed. In short, by searching for an instant, aesthetic understanding of his surroundings, Martin had located an intellectual climbing frame upon which he could clamber to his heart's content – quite unaware of what, precisely, he was trying to achieve. By finding this short cut Martin appeased his vanity, but not his mind. He used this new erudition to make himself feel more interesting than his friends.

The second desire that began to assail Martin during the spring of 1983 was more easily described. As the air became softer, and as the trees beyond the station began to bud, lust, tireless and remorseless, commenced an assault upon the young romantic. Thus Martin's life, as the weather grew warmer, became dominated by the desire to be wholly, clinically artistic, and by the desire for flesh. Between them, these two intoxicating concerns gave him no peace. He would alternate an ascetic passion for cultural understanding with fantasies of physical love. Having sought relief for the latter in the crude habits of adolescence, he would then be seized with self-disgust, and a longing for passionless isolation. Despite this vivid reaction, he became, briefly, addicted to pornography. Having no girlfriend, and discovering his hidden desires to be subtly perceptible and capable of making him unattractive, he was drawn to the brightly coloured photographs and facile texts of readily available sex magazines. Nervously, he would make detours in his route about the City in order to buy these humiliating periodicals. Reaching up, his desire overcoming his embarrassment, to take down a particular magazine, he would glimpse the orange flesh and theatrical underwear of the models depicted on its cover. This moment, he swiftly realised, was the only erotic aspect of a transaction with pornography. Once the purchase was made, he would resume the mask of respectability and hurry off home. These magazines brought him little pleasure. Instead, he retreated into memory, and turned over the worn-out and stylised images that he retained of Francesca, extending, in his imagination, the real scope of these scenes to incorporate his need for the obscene. Eventually, weary and bored, Martin abandoned these fantasies and ceased to buy pornography.

The spring months, however, directed his glance towards the bodies and profiles of unknown girls whom he saw on the street or in the train. Sometimes, his desire for these anonymous beauties masqueraded as a form of love, and he imagined true happiness, spent with some girl whose soft mouth, brown arms, or dark eyes had inspired his longing. A beautiful girl, he believed, would focus his senses completely, and make the whole of his existence romantic. By June 1983, Martin had started to read American novels, developed a passion for the works and philosophy of Andy Warhol, and was seeking to consolidate his life-style by finding a lover and buying a flat. To him, these ordinary activities and ambitions were directly attached to the subtle workings of what he liked to call his soul. The common-place, for Martin, was painted over with his sense of the vital and the extraordinary. 'This is my time,' he would say to himself, sometimes.

Unexpectedly, in July 1983, the DogFox office received a postcard from Richard Hayter. It depicted 'The Angel Standing In The Sun', by Turner. On its reverse was written:

'If I should die,' said I to myself, 'I have left no immortal work behind me, nothing to make my friends proud of my memory; but I have loved the principle of beauty in all things, and if I had had time, I would have made myself remembered.'

John Keats, February 1820

'He probably memorised it,' said Paul, nastily.

Caroline tried to find fault with the grammar, pedantically.

But Martin mulled over this strange message, and felt as though a valuable ally had slipped through his fingers. He wondered how his colleagues could fail to be impressed by such a touching communication. Sadly, there was no one to ask about this. In the context of the office, the flaunting of poetry and sentimentality merely seemed ridiculous. And yet the staff of DogFox were not stupid; they discussed books and the cinema; one or two were 'theatre buffs', whilst others discussed the Sunday papers seriously. To Martin, such methods of responding to art and ideas were banal and conventional. He was irritated by debates about well-known authors or controversial films. Sometimes, he would try to subvert the office discussions by referring to structuralism, or deconstruction. But his arguments were vague, and he quickly got shouted down. In short, Martin believed that people like himself and Richard Hayter had the monopoly on acute sensibility. He did not fully realise that it was absurd to seek recognition, and even praise, for attitudes that – unknown to him – were considered immature and self-indulgent when relied upon to stand for an exceptional or heightened personality. He was still blundering, seeking to reconcile the poetry which he felt within him with the equal urge to enjoy a flippant, comfortable life.

With summer, when the hot City, at lunchtime, seemed to shimmer amidst brightness and shadows, Martin began to feel restless and weary. He contracted a sore throat, which he blamed upon the DogFox air-conditioning unit, and spent a week at home. Sitting in the garden in the shade of a small lilac tree, he spent his time ruminating upon his future and comparing his career with that of the authors and artists whom he admired. He was depressed to discover that Balzac, Gide, Keats, Rimbaud, Brooke and Flaubert had all served their apprenticeship to greatness (or had even achieved greatness) by the time that they were thirty. Martin was now twenty-three. Was there a chance (he wondered) that he would suddenly pick up the pen or the brush, and clamber towards immortality in the seven years which separated him from the slopes of genius? He no longer wrote poetry, he had never been able to draw, and his piano days were long since past. In his heart, Martin knew that he desired instant-gratification – in all things. Dimly, as he analysed his tastes and his sensibilities, he began to perceive that products and money were the tools of his art. He tried to console himself for the poverty of this notion by recalling the aphorisms of Wilde and Warhol. Could genius not be lived? – as a sublime paradox, wholly suited to the times? The fashionable magazines all seemed to suggest that luxury, disposability and 'selective consuming' were new art forms. Fashion itself had become as witty as it was political – but politics bored Martin. They were always discussed by the dullest and most humourless members of any company, and they simply seemed to spoil the fun. The same could be said for religion – only religion was even more vague, and more complicated, than politics. But both of these subjects contained useful words which could be applied, glibly, to art. It was one of Martin's greatest joys to locate political or religious metaphors that he felt described a book, record, film, or painting. Such definitions, particularly when they crowned the trivial with ironic overstatement, appeared to Martin as the highest achievements in sophistication. They implied both wit and knowledge, and they granted one – through repetition – citizenship to the land of contemporary culture and fashionable polemic. This land appeared to multiply its wonders daily, fed by opulence and new technology. It was a breathless race, however, to keep abreast of the latest developments. But still Martin felt himself to be on the outside: he could absorb, but he could not find his own path. In order to compensate for this sense of frustration, he told himself that all the clever ideas of the fashionable commentators were merely an illusion – sophisms invented by people who were not brave enough, or rare enough, to be like the lonely, isolated artists of days gone by. These thoughts, however, only occupied a fragment of Martin's time. For the rest, his attention dwelt upon work, money and love.

In September, having saved up his deposit, Martin began to search for property. For six weeks, this process took him all over

London. The city, he realised, was divided into zones; not simply geographical zones, which indicated historic or economic status, but also emotional zones, each one quite distinct, and each one quite capable of working upon the mind, as surely as the weather. Martin's favourite areas, needless to say, had previously been identified as desirable, and thus were far too expensive for him to live in. With a sigh, he abandoned the idea of purchasing a quiet studio in the Royal Borough of Kensington and Chelsea. His attention was then drawn to the riverside developments that were just beginning to rise up beyond the City. Having visited the area and found it desolate and barren, he dismissed the notion of living in what would be called 'Docklands'. Also, he was scared of being lonely. Very quickly he set to work on exploring the inner suburbs of south London: Battersea, Putney, Clapham and Vauxhall. Here, where old houses, ruined during the 1960s by avaricious landlords, were now being restored, he found a mixture of the suburban and the genteel which virtually satisfied his aesthetic needs. After several false starts and one missed opportunity, Martin was finally shown a top-floor apartment in Vauxhall.

'It's rather unusual,' said Brian Champion, the estate agent. Martin had noticed that many of the new estate agencies now looked like wine bars; Reeves, in Battersea, with whom he was registered as a buyer, had large Chesterfield sofas, and a girl who gave you freshly brewed coffee served in dark green china cups.

Brian and Martin visited the apartment early one evening. It was the third week of September, and Martin had come to the viewing straight from work. The late afternoon had concluded with a light shower, and the streets smelt fresh and damp. Brian, respectfully awaiting his client, was wearing a grey double-breasted suit. He spoke with an accent similar to Martin's, and he understood the art of subtle flattery. 'Come from the City?' he asked, as he unlocked the front door of the house; his tone seemed to mingle understanding with sympathy, as though to

say, 'We're equals you and I – always busy, always on the move.'
Martin was charmed by this.

The house had just been restored. It contained five self-contained apartments. The communal hall and stairway were softened by a pearl-grey carpet; the walls were painted pale blue. Discreet lights, glowing dully behind stylish, frosted shades, created a warm, private atmosphere. The sash windows on the two landings were freshly painted, and had shining brass locks.

'Excellent security,' said Brian, as they mounted the stairs, 'but the whole area's coming up. Never can be too safe though. Got a car?'

'Not at the moment,' said Martin, vaguely.

'More trouble than they're worth,' replied Brian, quickly; 'nowhere to park – some wretched warden on your tail all the time.' Both the young men chuckled.

They had now reached the top landing. 'Have to pack the fags in,' said Brian, unlocking the front door of the top flat.

'Actually, is it all right to smoke?' asked Martin.

'Oh, go ahead – I do all the time . . .' With a gentle push against the rich pile of the carpet, Brian allowed Martin to pass before him into the flat. 'You're going to like this one,' he said confidently.

An expert in his field, Brian turned on the 'dimmer' lights to create a stylish ambience. He knew – like a seducer – the importance of first impressions. Beyond the little hall (the whole apartment smelt of fresh paint) Martin could see a long, wide room. To the north, the roof sloped down to head height, with a large, modern skylight. On the other side of the room a further long window allowed in the evening light.

'This is the main room of the property,' said Brian, ushering Martin into a space which, unfurnished, appeared quite vast. 'You could do anything with this room,' continued the young estate agent; 'all newly fitted – excellent builders and architect on this job – and for the price . . .'

Martin glanced around the large room; he found it quite irresistible. The skylight, particularly, entranced him. He had seen such rooms in television adverts: sparse, modern, remote – and yet comforting.

'Show you the rest of the property,' said Brian, striding purposefully towards a second door; 'fully fitted kitchen – fridge, dishwasher, washing-machine – not large, but highly compact; they're connecting the cooker next week . . .' The little kitchen was white, with a tiled floor. A low window, forced to an eccentric position by the rebuilding, enabled one to study the street below. Track-lighting gave the room a bright, slightly clinical air.

From the kitchen, one went into a small bathroom. This too was white, tiled from floor to ceiling, and had no window. 'Power-shower,' said Brian, nodding. The bedroom, which was reached from the other side of the main room, was equally attractive in Martin's eyes. It was only moderate in size, but it had a low ceiling and a long window which ran the length of the far wall. A fitted wardrobe, with sliding doors and a set of white shelves, completed the furnishings in this room. The window looked out over an obscure garden, which had two tall trees at its end. Martin thought of Francesca's room in Wimbledon. The whole property was quite delightful; in such a setting, he believed, he could live most happily. Informed by such a dwelling, his confidence and his attitudes would find new strength. And yet it was quite an ordinary flat, and little more than typical of its period.

'I love it,' said Martin, returning to the main room.

'Thought you might,' said Brian, standing with his slim document file pressed against his chest.

'Remind me of the price . . .' Martin knew the price perfectly well, and it was more than he could comfortably afford. The figure, when Brian repeated it, had ceased to be real. If Martin cut back on his daily and social expenses, he could just afford the small apartment.

'Believe me,' said Brian, 'in two years' time you'll be able to sell this place for twice the present asking price. In fact,' he continued, with an anxious yet resigned tightening of his lips, 'you'll be lucky if this is still on the market by the weekend; there's a queue of people ready to view, and I slipped you in first . . .'

'Done!'

And so, by the end of September 1983, Martin Knight had become a home owner. This, for him, was a spiritual advance. Property and possessions were now the stage upon which the aesthete could perform. He could create a drama, he believed, that would lead to the elusive heart of happiness and beauty.

Home ownership increased Martin's opinion of himself. More directly, it severely depleted his income. His bank, however, was more than happy to extend him 'every possible facility'. They made the process of borrowing appear flattering to the customer. Thus, at a time when Great Britain was beginning to be spoken of as 'two nations' – one poor, the other extremely wealthy – Martin Knight could exist in a small world which enjoyed the benefits of credit. Every aspect of daily life, from travelling to shopping, appeared to be reinventing itself, as a process, for those people who did not have to consider the cost. A new class of Briton, neither 'upper' nor 'lower' in background, was busily extending the scope of his territory. And it was a curious world which this new class inhabited; there was a prevalent attitude, comprised of a myriad impressions, amongst its young members, that some comforting spree was getting under way. Whilst, occasionally, the politics of that era were vehemently criticised by those who were enjoying the illusion of opulence that was being created, the illusion itself was so strong and so persuasive that its boundaries could not be perceived. For this particular class, participating in a self-assured, cosmetic renaissance, all things appeared possible. Their tastes and their ambition flattered, a generation of young consumers was taking up residence in an urban wonderland. Later, Martin would say that they were led like lambs to the slaughter. In the mean time, he found a lover.

Recalling his brief relationship with Andrea Twine, Martin would sometimes say, with a knowing, world-weary smile, that a young man will listen to the problems – however dull – of any young woman whom he finds attractive. Indeed, Martin's dalliance with the dark-haired Andrea began with a sharing of confidences: Andrea, the friend of a girl who went out with an Old Boy from Tiles, was one of the more perspicacious members of the little set with which Martin socialised. She worked for a Fulham antiques dealer, and she was half Canadian on her mother's side. She was rather short (for Martin's type), but her oval-shaped, lightly tanned face was pretty – the more so, thought her admirers, because of her fashionable, heavy-framed glasses, which gave her the air of a serious businesswoman. She wore severe dark suits, and her brown hair was held off her forehead with a velvet headband. Her earrings and her watch displayed a refinement of modern taste; she wore a lipstick that was a shade between burgundy and purple. When she smiled, she revealed small, extremely white teeth. She did not smile often. It was this gravity of bearing which attracted Martin to her. Andrea was usually distraught about something – her flat, her job, or her health – but she spoke with confidence about *objets d'art*. To Martin, bored with the cheerfulness and quick wit with which many of the girls he encountered could dispel any hint of 'intensity', Andrea's humourless insularity appeared both clever and sophist-icated. They began to seek one another out at group gatherings, and moved to sit next to one another at supper parties. Martin played the part of an understanding confidant – this was a role that he had perfected during his early friendship with Christine. He also affected an effeminate love of gossip, passing comment on people and trends in a way that reinforced the notion of a local, fashionable society. In this manner – a simulation of what the young romantic assumed to be the conduct of London's *cognoscenti* – Martin seduced Andrea by presenting himself as 'different'. Thus, his pursuit of the girl was primarily an act of extended seduction. In a matter of weeks, he had become a Don Juan with regard to this discontented young woman. He could watch himself drawing her nearer; he began to gauge, with mounting interest and pleasure, the effect of his words and his presence upon his prey. Alone, he would think how boring Andrea's litany of complaints and problems could become; but then he dwelt upon her physical charms (which were increased in his imagination) and determined to enjoy them in reality. Watching Andrea cross her legs, or slide along a sofa to sit next to him, he was intrigued by the graceful movement of her body beneath her clothes. Her glasses, too, seduced him; behind their polished lenses her dark eyes appeared to shine. And then he gave deeper thought to his plan, and widened his exploration of himself: could a seducer have a conscience? Was there an unassailable right and wrong, morally, in his planned intentions towards this girl, who attracted him even as she bored him? Or was Andrea, too, quite aware of the sexual algebra at work? The problem seemed to sit like an unsolved matrix, gradually and pleasingly finding its way into a greater equation.

A supper was planned. Martin filled his new flat with freshly cut flowers: blue chrysanthemums emerged luxuriously in a pale mist of gentle ferns; 'ambient' music, sweetly minimal, chimed drowsily from black-cased speakers. The low, uncovered modern sofa, which Martin had bought quite cheaply, was strewn with powder-blue cushions. This formed the central furnishing of the large, flawless room. A *Salad Niçoise* and a bottle of chilled amber-coloured wine (chosen by price, and the unusual typography upon its label) stood invitingly upon the black, circular dining table beneath the skylight. The two chairs, which appeared to be made out of the wire meshing employed in the construction of supermarket trolleys, stood neatly awaiting their occupants. In the moments before Andrea's arrival, Martin experienced a surge of happiness – but it was a fragile joy, as though derived from a prize too easily won.

Andrea was impressed by Martin's apartment, but she was too proud, or too polite, to express her enthusiasm at length. She was wearing a smart ivy-green suit, the jacket of which had slashed silk collars; her skirt, perfectly pressed, showed off her legs to good effect. She was carrying a slim briefcase. She was perfectly aware that the young friendship was about to become physical. She had brought, in her briefcase, a second pair of tights and a toothbrush.

Within seven weeks – by the end of November 1983 – Martin felt burdened by a time-consuming and unnecessary relationship. His hypocrisy with regard to this issue was boundless. Having contrived to seduce Andrea, he now found himself resenting her – as though it was she who had instigated the affair, and had expanded its scope to permit the physical. The sexual element of the liaison had swiftly bored him. Now, between bouts of routine and unimaginative passion, the couple simply squabbled. Andrea, it seemed, was permanently consumed with discontent and melancholy. Also, she insisted upon hearing Martin's precise views on every aspect of her dissatisfaction.

'I don't bloody care,' he snapped, early one morning – causing Andrea to cry. At the end of the previous month, Martin had received his annual 'assessment' at DogFox, the result of which was a minor promotion and a further increase in salary. Now usefully computerate, Martin was contributing to the project in full. This had the effect of increasing his sense of responsibility. Little by little, the side of his nature which desired the respectability and security of 'doing well at work' was defining itself more clearly within his personality. In short, he was becoming rather pompous. Andrea, on the other hand, was losing the sympathy of her employers. The only thing that held Martin back from making an early break with his partner was the cowardice which his kind heart inspired: he did not want to see Andrea suffer because he was afraid of the guilt he would feel. Instead, they argued.

The crisis came to a head on 30th November 1983. Martin had arranged to meet Andrea at the National Film Theatre, beneath Waterloo Bridge. They were going to see *Whatever Happened to Baby Jane?* Martin did not want to see the film; Andrea was late. The cross young man paced up and down beneath the dark bridge which spans the river at the point where the Film Theatre stands. It was raining. The river appeared black, and greasy; reflected silver and orange lights seemed to slip across its surface. Martin disliked that area of London: he found the various arts venues to be vulgar, unfashionable and shabby. The blank façades of the National Theatre, with their flawless surfaces, were the only architectural features of the district that he could tolerate. Despite the rain, the evening felt warm and airless. The film had already begun. With mounting fury, Martin lit a cigarette, and then continued his pacing. He had left the office early in order to arrive on time.

Just then, a young, bearded vagrant (one of the many who would later throng that particular network of subways and precincts) approached the young aesthete and asked for a cigarette. This redoubled Martin's anger, and he offered the cigarette at arm's length, between his fingertips. A few seconds later the beggar returned.

'Could you spare some change?' he said. Shrunken-cheeked, long-haired and wearing an insipid smile, the beggar stood for everything that Martin despised. Filled with hatred, he handed the shuffling damp youth a coin. This provoked a confession. The beggar's voice was slurred — a grotesque attempt at polite conversation.

'I'm a philosopher y'know.' Martin recoiled at the smell of his assailant's breath. The beggar continued, 'What do you do?'

Martin had not anticipated this question; like a monster, he rounded upon the beggar.

'I'm a systems analyst,' he snapped.

'What's that?'

'It's a person who earns a great deal of money; now go away.' Thus expressed, and already feeling ashamed, Martin strode off towards the cinema, in order to wait for Andrea in the little bar. Inwardly, he blamed his partner for the depression and anger that the beggar had inspired in him. As he was walking away, he heard the beggar say, 'What a wanker.' For a moment, Martin agreed with this verdict upon himself. Under different circumstances, he was sympathetic towards beggars. Philanthrophy made him feel noble.

When Andrea finally arrived, breathless and chattering excuses and accusations towards those who had detained her, Martin said nothing. He sat, tight-lipped, in the little bar, with his overcoat wrapped closely about him, and stared directly ahead. Andrea had been caught in the rain. Her wet hair (Martin thought) made her look ugly.

'Well, let's go in then,' she said, eventually.

'There's no point — it's started.'

'But we can't just waste the tickets . . .'

'And we certainly can't disturb everyone. You know what this place is like: sour film buffs and their hideous girlfriends . . .'

Andrea flared up. 'What's the matter with you? I couldn't help being late; and it was your idea to come here. You're the one who said we ought to "do things" . . .'

Martin did not speak. He was watching the raindrops, orange on the dark windows, glistening in the street-light. He wished he was alone.

'So what are we going to do?' he said.

'I've got a headache – it's from the screen of that bloody computer . . .' Andrea rubbed her forehead. She would not look at Martin. This infuriated him.

'Are you hungry?' asked Martin.

'Not particularly . . .'

'Well, we might as well leave then. I'll call you tomorrow . . .' He stood up.

'But I thought that I was staying with you. I've brought all my stuff . . .'

It was true: Martin had hoped that sex would enliven the tedious relationship. Now, as he was congratulating himself on feeling celibate and aloof, he wanted to go home, relax in an aromatically scented bath and continue reading Italo Svevo – whom he was enjoying. The thought of Andrea wearing his dressing gown and sitting on his sofa to dry her hair – a habit of hers which he disliked – depressed him.

'This is hopeless,' he sighed. Andrea looked up.

'What do you mean?'

'This feels like the end . . .'

With no warning, Andrea burst into tears. Now it was Martin who could not look at his partner. Already, at the sight and sound of her weeping, he felt sorry and ashamed.

'I'm sorry,' he began, stretching out his hand.

'Oh, go to hell.' The girl got up, threw her embroidered shawl across her shoulder and walked quickly away from the bar. Her head was held high, but her eyes were shining. Her problems, locked deep within her as though in the maw of an iron vice, remained unsolved. Martin's unkindness was added to the list.

Ten minutes later, and feeling light-hearted (as well as pleasantly philosophical), Martin began to walk towards Waterloo Station. Were he to encounter a beggar now, he felt sure that he would err towards generosity. In his heart, he knew that he had behaved carelessly. But he was prepared to excuse himself.

'What were the alternatives?' he said, out loud. His overcoat was open, and his footsteps rang upon the paved walkway. He was walking behind the Festival Hall, and gazing up at the flagpoles on the Shell Building. He could hear wire ropes slapping against the high masts in the humid wind. The sky was clearing. The light around the half-moon appeared pale blue. As he approached the entrance to the railway station, which looked cavernous and monumental, Martin suddenly recalled his thoughts at Lime Street Station, when he had just left college. He supposed that the architecture of the termini lay behind this recollection, triggering a pattern of thought:

'Well now that's done: and I'm glad it's over.'

The grey ghost of T. S. Eliot seemed to watch the young aesthete with bored, cynical eyes. 'An answer for everything,' said Martin, as he ascended the illuminated steps with a light tread.

Six weeks later, temporarily removed from the little circle which both he and Andrea Twine frequented, Martin Knight met Marilyn Fuller at Catherine Clarke's little dinner party.

For Martin Knight, the year 1984 – as a legendary date – had always possessed a romantic quality. A signifier of futuristic despair, the year which was just commencing, as cold, short days, made him think about mythologies and 'fictions'. As the City began to grow in power and fashionability, and as those media that commented upon popular, or 'meta'-culture became more entrenched in their own vision of urban society, so too did Martin, as a willing consumer of these infatuations, begin to find something invigorating about living in a year that had been marked for oppression and despair. This bleak, almost operatic backdrop, which bore no resemblance to the temper of daily life, appeared to grant a vitality and a poetic force to the gathering momentum of the self-conscious decade. In short, all things, in Martin's little world, had taken on an ability to be 'infinitely transferable'. This was pleasing. It enabled one to play with concepts of irony, and thus to accept a received idea of 'phenomena' (this word was now in common usage) on a level which recreated reality as a seemingly malleable substance. Or so Martin liked to think. By this, in essence, he meant that the slightest of observations could infer the greatest of statements. As various strands of culture began to converge and comment upon one another, so too did it seem that rules no longer applied. A grand liberation had taken place. As Martin rarely referred, with any real interest, to those people or opinions that were not sympathetic to this view of the *Zeitgeist*, he had little to measure the worth of his opaque enthusiasms against. Even if he had, he would simply have thought that those who were not interested in his particular concerns were living in the Dark Ages. Above all, Martin's excitement at this time was born of the fact that he felt as though an era was just beginning; this – like a glimpse of a forthcoming season that, as an essence, achieves potency – compounded the notion of change.

Martin's salary, by this time, was a little under £14,000 per annum. This was considerably more than many young people of his age earned. As ever, he was extravagant; he paid his mortgage, lived well and had no savings. Information technology, and the various aspects of this technology that DogFox was researching, was now beginning to define itself within the bullish atmosphere of business. Martin's work was wholly technocentric, and he thrived upon the modernity of this occupation. He was swift to raise an eyebrow, and utter a few terse words, when computers were described as 'boring'. But, often, he was bored; and he looked back at the arts with envious eyes. He sometimes wished, as he walked through the City at lunchtime, that he was more directly involved with banking. The snob in him demanded this. He admired the ritual and the hierarchy of the banking world. His pride was wounded when, on one occasion, an Oxford-educated member of his social circle referred to systems analysts as 'skivvies'. His ambition, however, did not extend to seeking a job with a bank. The suburbanite in Martin 'knew when he was well off'. Moderately content, and well paid, he plodded on.

One day, at Vauxhall Station, Martin met Christine. He scarcely recognised her at first, nor she him. She was standing beside the steep flight of stairs which connects the subway to the platforms. She was struggling with a push-chair, and two small children were tugging at the seams of her trousers. Her figure, which had once seemed so lithe, now appeared coarse and shapeless. Her gestures were ill-tempered and awkward. She was shouting to one of the children as Martin approached. 'I said no!'

'Can I help?' Martin was aware of the satin lining of his overcoat as he said this.

'Thanks, it's all right . . . Martin!' Christine finally recognised him. She stood up straight, and pulled down the front of her short suede jacket. She was still pretty (thought Martin) but there were bags of tiredness under her eyes, and her features seemed to be pinched with weariness.

'It's so long since we've met,' said Martin, 'how are you?' The platitude seemed to hang in mid-air, denying conversation.

'Oh, I'm fine . . .'

'Are these yours?' said Martin, gesturing towards the staring children with a smile.

'One of them is – Sophie,' said Christine. 'The other's – I'm looking after . . .'

'Oh – that's great.' Martin didn't know what to say. 'Are you still in New Cross?'

Christine hoisted her little girl onto her hip, and said, 'No. Jon's decided to move; we're married now. We're going down to Dorking . . .' Martin, suddenly, imagined a desolate tin hut, surrounded by weed-choked fields. He smiled.

'What about you?' said Christine. Her eyes appeared to narrow slightly.

'Oh, I live just round the corner –'

'That's nice.'

'Yes, it's good for work . . .'

'D'you go home often?'

'Now and then. What about you?'

'Oh, not for a while now. It's so difficult with the children . . .'

The conversation, it seemed, would not become real. Martin helped Christine with the push-chair, and then decided to leave.

'It's good to see you,' he said, again. 'We must catch up one of these days . . .'

'Yeah . . .' Christine smiled, 'see you . . .' And thus the former friends parted. As Martin was leaving, Christine watched his tall, affluent figure disappearing down the steps. For a moment, she detested him. She had not said, nor would have dreamt of mentioning, that her marriage was a farce, her husband violent and boorish and that her doctor, that morning, had told her she was pregnant again. Frequently, Christine could barely get out of bed, so deep was her depression.

'Mummy . . .' said the little girl, impatiently.

'All right,' said Christine, 'come on . . .'

The sky was white over Vauxhall Station.

That evening, just as Martin was entering his flat, he heard his telephone stop ringing. Wondering who might have been trying to contact him, he poured himself a drink, threw his overcoat onto the bed, and began to run a deep bath. As usual, he scrutinised his face in the mirror as he passed through the bathroom. He was satisfied with his features; his left eyelid, however, was becoming slightly inflamed. Whenever he blinked, a pricking sensation caused his eye to water. Just then, the phone began to ring once more. Turning off his bath and lighting a cigarette, Martin hurried across the room to answer it.

'Hello?'

There was a slight pause, and then a woman's voice: 'Hello – is that Martin?' The voice seemed familiar; it was rather low, and hesitant. 'Yes,' said Martin, trying to sound friendly. He dabbed his eye.

'It's Marilyn Fuller – we met at Catherine's . . .' Martin's heart leapt; he had given considerable thought to Marilyn, and even cursed himself for not obtaining her telephone number. He retained a vivid memory of the girl: her profile in the dark car, and her elegant gravity. In the manner of young men who expect a swift development of any friendship, he had almost given up hope of hearing from Marilyn. Sitting on the floor with his back against the high, bare wall, he cradled the telephone receiver between his chin and shoulder. He was still aware of his eye pricking, and of a soreness beginning to spread across the tender skin of his lower lid. He had to keep on blinking.

'How nice to hear from you,' he said, 'how are you?'

'I'm fine. How are you?'

'My eye,' he said, in tones of mock solemnity, 'is causing me serious trouble . . .'

Marilyn laughed. 'Why is that?'

'I don't know . . .'

'You're probably tired. Or is it a stye?' Marilyn was sitting in a high-backed antique chair, made of wood which was almost black, in the dark hall of the Captain's House. Above her, 'Silent Death' sculled eerily over still waters. Her mother was working in her study; her father was out. Having decided to call Martin, Marilyn was now feeling pleased that she had responded to her impulse. There was something reassuring about Martin's eye being inflamed.

'Am I disturbing you?' she said. 'I can call another time . . .'

Did this mean, wondered Martin, that the call was merely casual? To him, the conversation was already laden with significance. He wanted to ask, 'What are you wearing?' in a flirtatious, jocular manner. Instead, he said, 'No. I've just got in. Other than distracting me from my pain, you are not disturbing me . . .'

Marilyn tried to laugh again. 'Good,' she said. 'The thing is, I was wondering whether you're going to be free next Friday evening?'

'I think so. Yes . . .' Martin glanced across his big living room; he had not turned the lights on, and the orange street-lights were throwing vast shadows across the floor. Marilyn's low voice entranced him; he felt as though he could hear her smiling. Marilyn, in the dark hall, raised a strand of her fringe away from her face with one finger; she was wearing jeans, and a navy-blue V-necked pullover; her legs were crossed, and she was leaning forward. 'The thing is,' she said again, 'my father's giving a lecture at the Royal College of Art, next Friday evening, and I was wondering if you'd like to come? It might be really boring, but Catherine said that you were interested in art and things . . .'

The invitation could not have been better pitched to capture Martin's enthusiasm.

'I'd love to,' he said. 'It's kind of you to think of me . . .'

Marilyn found this gratitude a little sickly. She wondered whether she was making a mistake. 'Well,' she went on, rather more formally, 'it's at eight o'clock, in the main lecture hall – wherever that is. It'll be really difficult to park, so I'm coming to Charing Cross and then getting the tube to South Kensington; why don't we meet somewhere around there?'

'I could meet you at . . .' Martin thought hard; meeting-places, he knew by experience, were vital to creating a good impression. 'What about the steps of the Albert Memorial?'

'A little cold if it's raining,' said Marilyn, quickly. 'Why don't we meet in the arcade, by South Kensington tube?'

'Fine. What time?'

'About seven-thirty – if that's all right?'

'That's fine . . .'

'I'm sorry not to be able to pick you up. You liked my car so much . . . Can you drive?'

Martin was delighted by this obscure turn in the conversation: 'No,' he said, 'sadly, no . . .'

'You ought to learn,' said Marilyn. 'It's great to be able to drive . . .'

The conversation appeared to be over. Martin could not work out, precisely, whether Marilyn was being serious or fashionably vague. He decided to excuse himself before the pleasant call had a chance to become ambiguous.

'My eye's killing me,' he said; 'I'd better go and do something about it.'

'Bathe it with salt water,' said Marilyn firmly, 'that'll be the best thing . . .'

And thus the call concluded.

For the remainder of that week and for the first four days of the week that followed, Martin could not think of Marilyn without experiencing a warm sensation. At night, as he lay down, he dwelt in his imagination upon the potential of the friendship. An overwhelming gentleness attended his recollection of Marilyn's voice and features. He also bought a copy of Bill Fuller's book, but found it hard going. He did not know that the socialist documentary film-maker was now researching applications of critical theory to a vision of contemporary Great Britain. He did know, however, that Bill was rumoured to be making a feature film about the General Strike. In the mean time, it was the daughter of this celebrated thinker who occupied Martin's thoughts.

The weather remained cold and grey. The leafless trees in Greenwich Park looked black against the dark blue skies of late afternoon. Beyond the river, the City was dotted with silver lights. Marilyn – who was technically unemployed – began to question her motives for calling Martin, and thus creating a 'situation'. She was both apprehensive and lonely. She had

171

detected in Martin, however, a strand of infectious energy which drew her to him. She wanted to be in love.

Day and night, surrounded by books and papers, Bill Fuller prepared his lecture.

Five: *An Attractive Couple*

'What to wear? What to wear?'

Marilyn Fuller spoke these words out loud as she stood, alone in her room, at the Captain's House. She was preparing to meet Martin Knight. The doors of her white wardrobe were open; behind her, on the bed with its pale green duvet, there was a small pile of clothes – shirts, jumpers, suits and skirts – a soft pyramid of textures, shapes and patterns which seemed to merge into a single shade of dark burgundy. These had already been rejected as being unsuitable for the evening's appointment. It seemed as though the spoil of a thousand shopping trips – carefully chosen and moderately expensive garments – was declaring itself to be quite incapable of providing an outfit that would serve for both a 'date' and an evening function at the Royal College of Art. And yet, despite this dilemma, Marilyn felt light-hearted. Leaning forward, she took down from its hanger a prune-coloured skirt which she had never worn. She held this garment at arm's length for a moment and then, turning to face the mirror, pressed it against herself. 'Vile,' she said. That skirt, too, was tossed onto the bed.

It was half-past five; outside, the freezing afternoon was turning into dusk. Marilyn glanced out of the window; with half of her mind she was considering her appearance, selecting and rejecting a succession of 'looks'; the other half of her mind wandered. She could just see, beyond the black railings which separated the old house from the secluded street, the stern form of the antique lamppost. A pallid light clung about its lamp, illuminating a small area of pavement and causing the growing darkness to appear more mysterious. By association, Marilyn thought of ghosts. When she was younger, she had often imagined a mournful spirit, of the type which is cowled and which trails behind it diaphanous rags of mildewed shroud, gliding silently – but with great purpose – down the narrow street overlooked by her bedroom window. Now the ghost seemed distant. For Marilyn, ghosts had made the dismal Sunday evenings of winter their time. But now it was a Friday, and the weekend – as a sodium-lit metropolis – seemed to urge life, and the living pursuit of happiness, and novelty.

In the end, Marilyn decided upon a short skirt which was high-waisted, thickly belted and made of dark blue tweed. With this she wore a black polo-necked pullover, black tights and black suede court shoes. Thus attired, she felt as though she had struck the right balance between the formal and the casual. She would wear her long black overcoat to keep out the cold. Then, a little late, she tended to her make-up. She prided herself upon the fact that this process would not take very long. In keeping with the fashion of the times, Marilyn first powdered her face to a pale translucence; next, she defined her eyes and eyebrows with effective traces of black kohl; after this, deft upward brush-strokes of mascara. Now, green, gentle and pretty, her eyes gazed softly back at her from the mirror. 'Well, that's all right,' she said. Marilyn then put on her lipstick; this was a time when fashionable girls painted their mouths a vivid scarlet. The result of this, against pale skin and dark eyes, was dramatic. Finally, the girl ran a brush through her lustrous bobbed hair. She was not vain, and therefore did not linger in front of the mirror. Standing and slipping on her overcoat, Marilyn looked tall, sleek and opulent. She tugged briefly at the short seams of her skirt, wriggled once – in order to 'straighten herself' – and then picked up her gloves. The reticent, modern girl was ready to go out. Suddenly, an afterthought: picking up a phial of dulled glass, Marilyn atomised two small clouds of expensive, musk-scented perfume about either side of her neck. After she had left the room, ribbons of this fragrance remained floating in the air.

Descending to the dark hall, Marilyn called out: 'I'm going! Bye!' – but no one answered her. She could hear the sound of running water; Josephine, she assumed, was having a bath. Checking that she had her keys, Marilyn let herself out of the heavy front door and then, bracing herself against the cold, set off towards the station. She was just passing by the dry-docked *Cutty Sark*, its black masts appearing to rush up into the darkness, when she saw her father. He was leaning against the balustrade beside Greenwich Pier and smoking a cigar as he stared out at the river. He had gone for a stroll in order to collect his thoughts prior to delivering his lecture. He was wearing shabby corduroy trousers and a pair of scuffed brown brogues. Around his neck there was a thick woollen scarf, and the big collars of his coat were turned up. He looked (thought Marilyn) both old and young. He could have been, to judge from his appearance, either a millionaire or an off-duty janitor. He was deep in thought.

Hurrying towards him, the heels of her expensive shoes clattering upon the iron-hard cobbles, Marilyn waved cheerfully. Her father turned, and smiled.

'Are you off then?' he said.

'Yes – I'll see you there. Is everything all right?'

'You really ought to think before you ask that question.'

For a moment, Marilyn thought that something was wrong, and then she saw that her father was joking. 'You're bringing a friend, aren't you?' he asked.

'That's right.' Marilyn was pleased by the manner in which her father could ask sensitive questions without embarrassing her.

'Well, I hope you won't be bored. I don't want to wreck your evening.'

'Don't be silly; I'm really looking forward to it – and he'd better like it or I'll ditch him.' Bill laughed at this.

'Your only vice is loyalty,' he said. 'You'd better be off; we've got a dinner with the great and the good directly afterwards, so I don't know when we'll be back.'

'That'll be nice . . .'

'I loathe dinners.'

'Well, good luck.' Marilyn kissed her father.

'I'm getting too old to give lectures,' said Bill, smiling.

Waving once more, Marilyn began to walk briskly towards Greenwich Station.

By the time that she reached South Kensington, Marilyn was thinking far more about her father's lecture than she was about Martin Knight. This, had he known it, would have depressed the young egoist. The meeting that was about to take place had occupied his thoughts almost constantly; that afternoon, in the office, he had not been able to concentrate upon his work. The computer screen before him had been filled with dull figures – none of which could indulge his interest in Marilyn; the corridors of RDS had been used by complacent, work-wearied people – none of whom knew Marilyn, or could share in his excitement. For Martin, the thought of Marilyn had risen like a single, glittering star, touching the cold world with its radiance and making all that did not bow down before it seem lifeless and insignificant. There was a mystery about Marilyn, and a novelty, which appeared to make all other notions of romance appear adolescent and insubstantial. Martin was even disloyal to his past, and he recalled his passion for Francesca with a pitying smile. Andrea Twine seemed like an event from another life.

Finally, at half-past six, Martin got up from his desk (which had been cleared and tidied for the previous hour) and prepared to leave the office. The empty desks (he was the last to leave that evening) and the filled wastepaper baskets seemed to create a potent stillness; the overhead lights, encased in hollow planks of bevelled plastic, and the concealed air-conditioning units, were still humming. The secret, eerie atmosphere that fills a deserted office was just beginning. Now that the activities, crises, boredom and routine of the working day were over, the open-plan office appeared unknowable. And yet, there was something intimate about the silence and the emptiness. I want to remember this moment, thought Martin; and then, putting on his overcoat and locking his briefcase inside a cupboard (he did not want to have to carry anything), he left the deserted precincts of DogFox to the unreal existence which they pursued after the departure of the last worker.

Making his way to Monument underground station and then descending from the blue cold into the push of dark backs bathed in yellow light, and the hurrying white faces surrounded by breathless chatter, Martin decided that he must, that evening, keep watch over his natural tendency to try to create an impression. He had given much thought to the notion of affectation and, finding himself guilty of acting and speaking for effect, he now determined to err on the side of reticence. But what (he thought, as the crowded train rattled westwards) do I do if that simply makes me boring? It was better to be boring, he concluded, than to seem like a fool in Marilyn's eyes. By the time that he reached the arcade at South Kensington tube station, Martin had fully rehearsed his new role: he would be polite, and attentive, and ask more questions than he answered. In this manner, he thought, he would retain Marilyn's interest.

Martin would recall his second meeting with Marilyn, and his first impressions of her at that meeting, as being a process of 'crystallisation', such as he had read of in Stendhal. As with all great events that can befall a young person, there was both a major assault upon his senses and a lesser; the first blow – a warm, sweet wave – was created by Marilyn's appearance: it was as though a benign deity, cognisant of Martin's aesthetic aspirations, had conjured up a woman who answered, physically, his subtle desires point for point. And more: in Marilyn there was, to Martin, a gentle refinement of his tastes; she animated those qualities for which he had yearned, and made them both adult and sensual. She appeared, as it were, ready-made; she would not be a toy of fantasy but, rather, she eclipsed fantasy and replaced that banal cartoon with a gracious reality which demanded respect. In a moment, the young man realised that he would have to grow up if he intended to court the young woman before him. Thus received, Marilyn's presence then began to consume Martin; as a droplet of strong dye will colour a basin of clear water, so too did Marilyn inform Martin's existence and remain with him, as a shaping influence, for the rest of his life.

Marilyn was thinking of the time as she watched Martin approach. She did not want to be late for the lecture. She thought that Martin looked well dressed and pleasing to the eye, but he was slightly shorter than she had remembered him. She wished that she could concentrate properly on their meeting.

'Hi!' she said, resting her modest weight upon one foot. The couple did not know whether to kiss or not. They shook hands.

'Hello, I'm not late am I?'

'No, not at all. But do you mind if we start walking now? Apparently it's going to be quite packed, and I don't want us to get lost, or anything . . .'

Martin found this reception a little brusque. He would have liked to settle down for half an hour in a quiet café, and put the meeting on a more personal footing. As it was, he felt incidental to Marilyn's concerns. But he feigned cheerfulness, and began to follow her out of the arcade and across the busy junction which leads to Exhibition Road. The great museums towered above the couple; ahead, a dome of blue sky scattered with stars hung above the railings of Kensington Gardens.

'I'm sorry to rush us,' said Marilyn. 'Have you come straight from the office?'

'Yes. It was easy though. I'm looking forward to the lecture. Has it got a title?'

'Probably – but I doubt if I'd be able to pronounce it, even if I knew it . . .'

Martin glanced down at Marilyn's ankles as she walked; her slender legs, hidden within her overcoat, moved to the rhythm of a swift, confident tread. Her perfume came to him as invisible crescents of aromatic scent, warming the cold air. As yet, she did not seem to have looked at him directly. He began to grow discouraged.

'It's left at the top, isn't it?' he said.

'That's right – and then straight on, past the Albert Hall . . .'

'I never liked the Albert Hall,' said Martin, 'I prefer . . .' and then he checked himself; he was afraid of seeming pretentious. Surprisingly, however, Marilyn replied:

'Yes. I know what you mean. It's that kind of old-fashioned ugliness which is really depressing.' Had her parents overheard this remark they would have known, instantly, that Marilyn liked Martin, and was keen – beneath her anxiety – to appear interesting. Less self-conscious than Martin, Marilyn too had given much thought to their meeting. She did want to interest him (her choice of clothes had not been disinterested) but she also wished to monitor that interest; she was far too reticent, and too cautious, to create any sense of intimacy without being certain of how to proceed. Also, she would have liked to look at Martin and study his features, but now, to her surprise, she felt shy. Thus, swathed in contradictions and silent conditions, the couple reached the steps of the Royal College of Art.

*

The entrance hall of the grey, modern college was crowded; waiters were circulating with trays of white wine and mineral water.

'Who on earth are all these people?' said Marilyn, politely declining to 'leave her coat'. Martin, who felt hot and clumsy, left his overcoat with the attendant.

'They must be the audience,' he said. He was extremely impressed. He knew that Bill Fuller was a well-known figure, for he had seen him on television, but this serious congregation, which was comprised of the young and the old, the fashionable and the ferociously unfashionable, made him understand that his companion's father was an important man. This raised Marilyn even further in his eyes.

'I wonder where Daddy is?' Marilyn glanced around the chattering throng. 'Or Mummy, come to that.'

'Can I get you a drink? And then we could look for your parents, if you'd like to?'

Marilyn smiled at him; 'Thanks,' she said. 'And, you know, I think that I will leave my coat after all . . .' She slipped off her long coat; its satin lining seemed to glide off her shoulders in a single, elegant movement. Blue tweed, black polo-neck and long, slender legs were thus revealed.

'Allow me,' said Martin. He was pleased, so far, with the manner in which he was behaving. His confidence returned. He knew, as he moved quickly towards the attendant who was taking coats, that he must not make one error in his handling of the occasion. The treasure which he was holding, so precariously, could not be allowed to slip, fall and shatter. As he handed over Marilyn's coat – a warm, soft, scented bundle – he recalled a line from *Death In Venice*: 'How dare you smile like that! No one is allowed to smile like that!'

These coy sentences warmed him like a secret, sentimental indulgence. Approaching a waiter, he suddenly realised that he did not know whether Marilyn preferred wine or water. He retraced his steps, half afraid that he would find the young woman in conversation with another man. This thought terrified him. Already, he was jealous. Marilyn, however, was alone. Equally, this fact amazed Martin. She's so beautiful, he thought, surely, everyone can see that?

'I'm sorry,' he said, 'but would you prefer wine or mineral water?'

'Oh, just water, thanks . . .'

And Martin hurried off again.

When he returned with the drinks (wine for himself), Marilyn slipped her arm through his; she did this with formal elegance. Martin knew immediately what was meant by the gesture: a polite statement was being made, in which he was declared to be Marilyn's chosen escort. Far from implying some potential intimacy, this gentle act (Martin could feel Marilyn's slender arm resting lightly upon his own) deepened the young woman's air of gravity; Martin felt the touch of a class and a disposition which were not suburban. He rose to this impression with discreet alacrity. This did not go unnoticed by Marilyn as they walked, handsome and modern, through the crowded hall.

'There's Mummy,' said Marilyn.

'Ought we to go over?'

Josephine, who was wearing a long midnight-blue dress and her tinted glasses, was talking with great animation to a gentleman whose silver hair was as distinguished as his immaculate dinner suit and green velvet bow-tie. He appeared to be listening with great attention, and obvious respect. He was stooping down to catch Josephine's words above the noise of neighbouring conversations, and he nodded from time to time with sudden firmness.

'I don't think we ought to disturb them,' said Marilyn. 'It'll be time to go in soon, anyway. Do you mind all this? You're not bored, and wishing you hadn't come?'

'Not at all; it's great.' Martin wished that he could have found a better adjective. 'What does your mother do?' he added.

'She writes about opera . . .'

'Quite an artistic family!'

'You haven't met my sister . . .'

'I didn't know you had any brothers or sisters . . .'

'I've only got one sister – Carmen – but that's quite enough.'

'Don't you get on?'

'Let's just say that between them, my parents and my sister, it's quite difficult being "normal".' And then Marilyn squeezed Martin's arm, gently. Delighted, the young man allowed himself to pat Marilyn's hand. He tried to do this as though it was the most natural thing in the world, and his pleasure increased when Marilyn neither flinched nor withdrew her arm. Never before had he studied, with such rapt attention, a person who spoke of being 'normal'. Hitherto, such a word had been an anathema to him. 'Normal' people, at college, had been 'stiffs'.

'They're going in,' he said, as the impressive, self-assured crowd began to make their way towards the open doors of the stage-lit lecture hall. 'Shall we join them?'

'Let's,' said Marilyn.

Martin would recall the evening of Bill Fuller's lecture as being a turning point in his life; he would think that his being, as Marilyn began to influence his existence, had finally been affirmed. This belief, for Martin, was both an intellectual and an emotional decision. What was remarkable to him was the fact that the suggestions which Marilyn embodied should all coincide, and respond to one another, and create a growing network of associated hopes and impressions. It was as though a new life had been offered; he felt as though he had been waiting outside a particular house in the dark and the cold, and had finally been permitted entry. The spirit of beauty – which was happiness, to Martin – was now within reach. Aware of Marilyn sitting beside him, her grave profile cut by the hang of her shining hair, Martin followed Bill's lecture with close attention. He felt as though a truth was being offered to him personally, and that the confirmation of this truth was embodied in the girl whose warmth he could feel just a hand-span away.

Bill Fuller had been invited to speak at the Royal College of Art to a distinguished invited audience, as part of a series of lectures which were intended to comment upon the cultural significance of 1984. To be asked to lecture was an honour; and the speakers were granted full permission to follow whatever manner of argument they believed to be relevant. Of the five lecturers who spoke in the series, three of them offered speeches which were wholly autobiographical. Bill, however, came across as a prophet.

'I am not a socialist,' he began, 'or a communist; I am a post-modernist . . .' The term 'post-modernism' was one which was just becoming controversial, and Martin found himself thrilling to this pronouncement in much the same way as he had done when he first heard the expression 'punk rock'. There was something glamorous about Bill's considered use of this difficult, contemporary label. Martin, too, wanted to say: 'I am not a romantic, nor an aesthete; I am a post-modernist . . .' The glamour which the words conjured up was reflected onto Marilyn. Bill continued by reading an extract from 'Letter to Lord Byron' by W. H. Auden. He cited these lines as being representative of his early career.

We all grow up the same way, more or less;
    Life is not known to give away her presents;
She only swops. The unself-consciousness
    That children share with animals and peasants
    Sinks in the Sturm und Drang of Adolescence.
Like other boys I lost my taste for sweets,
Discovered sunsets, passion, God and Keats . . .

Bill's voice was filled with authority and humour. He's really performing, thought Martin, and he's doing it so well. Having lured the audience into a good-natured, attentive mood – as though they were listening to a light radio programme – the lecturer then began to undermine their contentment, by offering uncomfortably bleak predictions about the political course that he believed the country to be following. Statistics about cuts in arts funding and arts education were read out; the rise of consumerism was charted; the two nations were described. And yet Bill Fuller's tone remained affable. He laced his speech with quotations from advertising campaigns, and then described the manipulation of 'signifiers' that he felt to be placing Great Britain under a spell. Martin glanced at Marilyn, wanting to say, 'He's so right – I've noticed that . . .' but was held back by the fear of disturbing the girl, who was watching her father so closely.

'. . . grim, hawk-faced yuppies, living in warehouse conversions and learning how to walk through walls.' A burst of knowing laughter greeted this description. The fact that Martin had aspired to becoming one of the same young people whom Bill was describing increased his pleasure as opposed to weakening it. Then, adjusting his half-moon spectacles, Bill explained that he had become a post-modernist against his will: 'My arrival at post-modern conclusions,' he said, 'could be termed as an apostasy. What could be more decadent, or more self-centred, than the post-modern credo?' Somewhere in the darkness a man's voice said, 'Quite,' loudly. At this point, Martin was aware of a rustling sound beside him. He turned to look at Marilyn, and saw that she was crossing her legs and glancing at her watch.

'Are you OK?' she whispered. 'You're not bored?' Martin shook his head, and smiled.

'At present rates,' Bill was saying, 'a person currently earning twenty-five thousand pounds per year will be worth six and a half times that sum, in terms of credit-worthiness, by 1987.

There are statistics to prove this . . .' Martin dwelt on this fact for a moment, and felt pleased. He had the sensation, as he glanced about the audience, that he was a member of the *cognoscenti*; finally, it seemed, he was hearing the secrets to which only the cultural aristocracy were party. This gave him confidence, and added to the joy of sitting beside Marilyn. 'I'm dating a film director's daughter,' he thought, with great satisfaction.

The film director concluded his lecture by speaking of 'civil disobedience, and the rise of motiveless anarchy'. During this part of the speech, many of the people in the audience cupped their chins in their hands, and nodded gravely.

'We have faith in the notion that property is sacred,' said Bill, 'and we see ourselves as a nation of moderates. But what happens if, in 1994 for instance, we wake up one day to discover that post-modern society has blurred the rules so much, and so effectively, that humanism has become eccentric? Shatter meaning, and you shatter, inevitably, ethics . . .' Someone behind Martin said in a low voice, 'That's old Bill Fuller and his left-wing journalese again . . .'

By now, however, Martin's legs were beginning to ache. He was aware that he had missed a vital twist in Bill's lecture and was applying his understanding of its introduction, wrongly, to its conclusion. Giving up, he wondered whether Marilyn would go straight home. Wildly, he considered inviting her back to Vauxhall. Bill, acknowledging applause, was thinking nothing at all.

After the lecture, Martin took Marilyn to a small, dark café, not far from the tube station. The intellectual stimulus which he had received from the oration (in retrospect it had the aura of a sermon) immediately took second place to the sight of Marilyn slipping off her coat and sitting with her elbows upon the little table, facing him. On the wall behind her, glowing dully within a brace of crimson, tasselled shades, two low-burning lamps cast dust-coloured shadows across her face. Martin lit a cigarette and smiled at his companion.

'Well,' he said, 'what did you think of it?'

Marilyn looked down at the table, and seemed to be studying the backs of her hands. 'Oh, I thought it was really good.'

'Do you think your father means what he says? I mean, do you think that he's right? About everything?'

Coffee was brought to the table, pale and scalding, in glass cups. Marilyn sipped through the steamed milk, cautiously.

'I suppose that I just see it as Dad's work,' she said. Her eyes were lowered. 'I mean, I'm not arty, or an intellectual, or any-thing . . .' She appeared to be nervous about saying this. Martin wanted to reassure her; he wanted to say that he didn't care what she was, providing she would grant him another meeting.

'Well, I thought it was really interesting,' he said. 'It's funny, I never think of our generation as having intellectual parents . . .'

Marilyn smiled, but said nothing.

A few minutes later, she began to tell Martin about Truffles, and about her daily routine in Greenwich. Then she asked him what he did, and how he came to know Stewart.

Post-modernism was forgotten; but Martin, later that evening, told Marilyn that her new, expensive, 'designer' watch was, in fact, post-modern.

Martin Knight had always been afraid of mediocrity and of ridicule. When he feared that he could be seen as possessing either of these qualities, his depression was enough to slacken his pace on the most bracing and cheerful of mornings. The beginnings of his love for Marilyn Fuller, however, appeared to banish these anxieties quite utterly. In addition to her prettiness and her style – for these were the two features that Martin first adored in his new friend – Marilyn brought with her, from her background and her family, a secure packet of undoubted glamour. This glamour was comprised of a myriad details, some of which were so small, yet so vital, that they seemed like those props which can be found in great paintings: simple informants, and banal, initially, to the point of invisibility, yet once noticed wholly indispensable to the genius of the finished work. Martin, as an aesthete, was sensitive to these details. In short, during the weeks which inaugurated his friendship with Marilyn, he deconstructed the young woman, and rejoiced in what he found to be her romantic perfection. Marilyn, meanwhile, remained cautious.

'She's so . . .' Martin sought to find the right words, one afternoon at the beginning of March 1984, that would render Marilyn's beauty articulate to Steve Clary.

'Well stacked?' suggested Steve, coarsely.

Martin did not even smile.

A fortnight after their meeting at her father's lecture, Marilyn granted Martin a second date, this time to visit an art exhibition. They would then return home to Greenwich, for tea. It was important to Marilyn that Martin visited her home. The meeting was arranged for the first Saturday in March. The weather that day seemed to Martin to be registering an advance in the season: the biting wind had dropped, the monotonous white skies had cleared and a 'greenness' (he could think of no better term to describe it) appeared to be scenting the air and colouring the gentle afternoon. He was to meet Marilyn at two o'clock, at the entrance to Bond Street tube station. Thus, at five minutes to two, he was waiting at the rendezvous, smoking a cigarette and watching the passage of the Oxford Street crowds. Every shop appeared to be thronged with people; in the wide, illuminated entrances to the department stores, people were leaning heavily upon the glass doors and pushing their way with determination towards the glittering displays of the perfume departments. Then there were the new, tastefully designed shops, which carried only their own brand of goods; these shops appeared to mingle efficiency with style: they had been conceived for shoppers who required a small, homoeopathic dash of luxury with their hitherto merely 'high-street' purchases. Restful greys, dynamic stripes and rich, refreshing leaf-greens were used to create the seductive ambience of these new shops. Through colour-co-ordinated packaging and presentation, these latest additions to the retail repertoire seemed to affirm quiet self-confidence. 'We may be functional,' they seemed to suggest, 'but we can make you feel pampered and successful.' Identical products, gathered together in careful patterns, created their own magic. Martin thought that this was extremely clever. Studying the busy street, he felt as though each shop represented a particular mood; and, as a whole, the shops became a state of mind.

To Martin's left, just beyond the junction of Davies Street, South Molton Street and Oxford Street – where three rivers of atmosphere appeared to converge in a kind of dizzying white water – he could see a girls' clothes shop. It was large, bright and modern. Its wide windows were filled with female mannequins which were dressed in the spring fashions and arranged in languid poses. Behind the mannequins, tacked to high white screens, there were three identical photographs, each one of which was the size of a door. This multiplied image depicted a tall, blonde girl, whose hair was 'scrunched' and whose skin was tanned to the colour of liquid honey. She was standing upon her toes, with her legs pressed close together, and she was staring at the passing shoppers with bright blue eyes and a wide, winning smile. She was wearing nothing but a turquoise pullover with a high, rolled collar. Saucily, she was pulling the sides of the garment down, in order to cover her upper thighs. These images directed gusts of uneasy eroticism across the crowded pavement. Martin, out of respect for Marilyn, did not allow his gaze to dwell upon them. Thus he became more aware of the photographs, and their power was intensified.

That afternoon, Martin was wearing blue jeans, black boots, a white shirt and a long dark overcoat. His neat hair had just been cut. His neck and cheeks were finely scented with an 'old-fashioned gentlemen's aftershave'. Clad in this uniform, he felt physically self-assured. He had hoped that the sun would come out, so that he could wear his dark glasses. When Marilyn arrived, pausing momentarily upon the tube-station steps in order to get her bearings, Martin thought that she looked lovelier than ever. She was dressed in black, with a short skirt and a leather jacket, the sleeves of which were pushed up to reveal her slender forearms. She was wearing black suede gloves and carrying a black satchel which was inset with rubberised panels. This time, upon meeting, the couple kissed. Feeling Marilyn's soft mouth, and tasting the fragrance of her scarlet lipstick, Martin experienced a longing and a tenderness far greater than anything that he had known before. This passion, poetically, appeared to drive deep into his heart.

Strolling – closer together now – the couple turned their backs upon the shops of Oxford Street, and began to make their way towards a small gallery. They were going to look at an exhibition of the works of Joseph Beuys.

It was Martin who had suggested that they visit the exhibition; since Art – a subject which was usefully interesting – had provided the occasion for his second meeting with Marilyn, he now relied upon it to give tone to the third. Marilyn, who was still gauging her interest in Martin, was content to fall in with this plan. She regarded the tea at Greenwich to be her contribution to the afternoon. When her father had asked her that morning how she was going to spend the day, he had been surprised to hear that his younger daughter was visiting an art exhibition.

'Is that with Martin?' he asked, casually.

'Yes. And then we're coming here for tea.'

'Oh, good.' The film-maker studied his daughter as she delicately ate her yoghurt.

'Is Martin an artist?' he asked, after a brief pause. His voice revealed a faint trace of boredom.

'Oh, no; he works in the City – with computers . . .'

Bill stood up, and scratched the back of his head. 'Oh well,' he said, 'at least your friend can probably afford to buy art. That's a much better thing than making it,' he added.

'I know,' said Marilyn. It was impossible to tell whether she was being ironic or serious. Making his way to his study, Bill thought for a moment about Marilyn's day. He was pleased that she seemed to have found a boyfriend; in many ways he was doubly pleased that the boy in question appeared to be from sturdy professional stock. He had always dreaded the thought of Marilyn taking up with a Bohemian. He could not help wondering, however, what his daughter would make of Joseph Beuys.

Marilyn, that afternoon, made little of Joseph Beuys. The exhibition was quite small, but it contained, along with some photo-etchings and 'blackboard' pieces, various objects which the German artist had made to express his political and artistic theories: cans of film, audio tapes encased in felt squares, 'wooden postcards', a record, an iron shovel, and twelve bottles of red wine, their labels printed with the large black initials F.I.U. There was also an old tape recorder, the leather case of which was daubed with a red cross.

'It's really very beautiful,' said Martin, at length. 'In fact, it's like being in a shop.'

Marilyn looked at the bottles of wine respectfully. 'How much would those cost?' she whispered.

'God knows. Considerably more than your average plonk . . .'

'But why? I mean, it's probably gone off by now, anyway . . .'

For the second time that day, Marilyn was in danger of being misunderstood. Martin was hoping that his interest in the works was not making him appear boring, or affected. Still, he could not answer Marilyn's reasonable question from any position of knowledge. To Martin, the works on display were romantically industrial and militaristic; but he could not explain why they were 'art', or why they should cost so much. The two young people, therefore, were equally sincere in their responses to the exhibition. Marilyn, who had a very strong sense of what she liked, felt the objects to be ugly and deliberately obscure; Martin, whose self-conscious aestheticism in fact amounted to a similar notion of taste, was drawn to the mystery of what he did not understand.

'I don't know,' he said, finally; 'but I'm glad we came. Would your father know about this sort of stuff?'

'Probably. He's got loads of books on art and things – What's that?'

Martin looked at a label. 'Fat and human hair,' he said. Marilyn pulled a face.

As they were leaving the gallery, Martin inhaled its scent. The smell of varnish and fresh paint, cooled by the air-conditioning, seemed to mix into a clean atmosphere of modernity and affluence. He found this scent both comforting and inspiring.

Once they were outside, Marilyn slipped her arm through his.

'Would you like to come to tea now?' she said.

The couple travelled from Charing Cross to Greenwich by train. The elderly carriages appeared to haul themselves sluggishly across the blackened brick viaducts which carried the tracks through Waterloo East and London Bridge. On either side of the line, their uppermost windows looking empty and dirty, unrestored offices and small factory-like warehouses appeared derelict and forlorn. There were rusted iron walkways, and fire escapes with peeling paint; beyond them, closer to the southern bank of the river, new pale office blocks looked clean and dignified.

'I counted thirteen cranes from here the other day,' said Marilyn. 'Thirteen . . .'

191

'I work just over there,' said Martin, pointing to a gap between the buildings.

On the northern side of the river, there was a rising geometrical clutter of blue glass and white façades. The emptiness of the City, echoing glamour, gave Martin confidence. As the train gathered speed, rattling towards New Cross, he looked at Marilyn and said, 'Are we going out together now?'

'I don't know. Maybe . . .'

This answer satisfied Martin, and he changed the subject. 'Do you come into London often?' he said.

'I live in London . . .'

'I mean, central London?'

'I come in to go shopping – vast expeditions, I'm afraid . . .'

Martin leant back in his seat, and crossed his legs. The carriage was virtually empty. Shabby housing estates and tall blocks of council flats dating from the 1960s were slipping dimly past in the middle distance. Martin glanced at them, and then turned to Marilyn once more.

'Oh, I'm probably as bad,' he said, 'I spend far too much – on things I don't need, really. I'm worst at lunchtime: it's so easy just to break up the day by going to buy something . . .'

Marilyn smiled; she was beginning to like Martin. To a friend, now, she would say that she 'really liked' Martin. At the exhibition, and after her father's lecture, she had not been sure; but watching the handsome young man admitting to a simple weakness that she shared made her feel more relaxed.

'It's nice to buy nice things,' she said.

'What do you like buying most? I mean, really like buying?' said Martin. This question sounded flirtatious. Marilyn looked at her knees. Martin was afraid, for a moment, that she was laughing at him.

'Well,' she said, cautiously, 'I really like buying things for the bathroom, actually; and I love buying make-up, and clothes; and things for the kitchen. There's this really nice shop in Ebury Street –'

'I know it! You mean the place with the awning?'

'Probably, yes. With all those weird things for taking stones out of plums, and fabulous terracotta bowls, which are incredibly cheap in fact . . .'

Martin nodded enthusiastically. 'There's another place,' he said, 'on the corner of Sloane Street and Sloane Square, where they've got these beautiful bunches of dried flowers; I mean, I know that dried flowers can look really twee and tacky, but these are really unusual. And they do those big blocks of soap, with old-fashioned lettering stamped on them . . .'

While they were talking, Marilyn considered her new friend. She had never heard a boy speak so fervently about soap and dried flowers. It was funny, and not quite right, but now she was enjoying herself.

'I hate all that black and chrome stuff though,' she said; 'it's so easy, and boring . . .'

'For people who drive cheap sports cars . . .'

'And girls who drink cocktails . . .'

'And think that they're being sophisticated.'

'Particularly if it's got a sparkler in it!'

Revelling in snobbery, the couple alighted at Greenwich.

Martin had never been to Greenwich before. Walking with Marilyn away from the station with its hanging baskets of moss and geraniums, and on towards the elegant grey jumble of small shops and sash-windowed town houses, he felt once more the breath of a class which was not his own – however successfully he might dissemble to the contrary. He was reminded, as they passed by the imposing church with its pillars, urns and evergreen graveyard, of a town in a children's picture book: antiquity and oddness – a pattern of unique picturesque features – seemed to raise the place, like a miniature, domestic Venice, above the tug of the ordinary and the ugly. It seemed to him that there was novelty on every corner. The presence of the river, too, made the atmosphere exotic: on the muddy flats at low tide, tugs and barges would lean to one side, moored by taut roopes the width of a man's arm; downstream, the alien apparatus of industry and engineering towered above its own forlorn precincts of metal, concrete and deep, sinister channels. Rusted skeletons of scaffolding, and broad yards quite crammed with twisted debris, existed just beyond the historic residential scope of the borough – and thus saved the place from mere prettiness. And yet Greenwich was already becoming complicit with the good-taste industry. The Fullers, however, withdrawn from gift shoppes, lived beyond the maw of that gentle exploitation.

Reaching the pier, where in summer pleasure boats disgorged their cargo of tourists, Marilyn led Martin along the railinged river walk, past the lawns of the Naval College and then, by way of two short, cobbled streets, to the front door of the Captain's House. Martin, needless to say, was enchanted by all that he saw: the glimpse of the river, with blocks of new apartments rising up on the opposite bank; the impressive counterpoint to this that was created by the classical bulk of the Naval College; the dark, trailing branches of the trees overhanging the railings . . . All of these details were made relevant to Martin by Marilyn's presence. Marilyn and her surroundings appeared to inform one another, quite naturally. As she was searching for her keys, she pointed to the lichen-covered greyhound which stood beside the porch.

'Daddy hates that,' she said.

Martin nodded; feeling self-conscious and nervous, he patted the greyhound's head. It was rough to the touch, and cold. He was suddenly afraid of entering Marilyn's house: he felt overawed by the need to appear acceptable.

Once inside the dark hall, Marilyn threw her leather jacket across an antique chair, and then, as though she had rehearsed the words, called out a greeting. In the distance, a typewriter could be heard, tapping erratically. 'That'll be Mummy,' she said. To the couple's left a closed white door, inlaid with six uneven panels, denoted Bill's study. He was out. Uncertainly, as though he was undressing for a medical examination, Martin took off his coat. He put it down gently, on the chair where Marilyn had thrown her own. Then, without looking at him, Marilyn took Martin by the hand and led him into the big, bright kitchen. The first thing Martin noticed in that room was a large bowl, filled with overripe grapes and pears. Beside the bowl, in a tube of grey marbled cardboard, there were some sticks of incense. A brilliant pink twig and a heap of fragrant ash gave evidence that the incense was regularly burnt. CASSIE, VETIVERI AND FRANJIPANI BURNING STICKS, stated the label on the tube. A Mayfair address was printed down the side of the label. A sweet, musky smell seemed to hang in the kitchen.

'Please, sit down,' said Marilyn, busying herself with teacups and filling the kettle. 'I bought some lemon cakes,' she added. Martin watched the elegant girl as she moved deftly around the kitchen, opening drawers and extracting plates whilst closing the fridge door with her foot. There was something delightful about studying the young woman in her own home, and Martin secretly felt the pleasure of a voyeur as he watched her. Marilyn, meanwhile, was worrying that Martin would be bored. She wanted to recapture the mood which had united them, briefly, on the train. It was the first time that she had 'invited a boy home', and now she was filled with a vague sense of panic. She was glad that Carmen was not present to see her fluster and to gloat over her discomfort.

'This is very kind of you,' said Martin, uselessly; then, in the doorway, Josephine appeared. The young man stood up, and smiled.

'This is Martin,' said Marilyn.

Josephine smiled weakly, and extended a limp hand.

'How do you do,' she said.

'Hello,' said Martin, aware for a moment of a slight pressure upon his palm as they shook hands.

'Have you had a good afternoon?' asked Josephine, advancing with a serene smile to sit down; 'it's been such a lovely day,' she added. From her study, the strains of *Parsifal* could be heard.

'I hope that we're not disturbing you?' said Martin, suddenly. This question sounded eccentric.

'Me?' said Josephine. 'Oh no, not in the least . . .' She looked at her daughter, with a concerned expression. 'Marilyn, I hope that you're not giving Martin one of those awful old cups . . .'

'I was going to use the yellow ones . . .' Marilyn paused obediently.

'How could you!'

Martin could not work out what manner of relationship existed between mother and daughter. He remained standing, and smiled foolishly.

'Marilyn tells me that you're writing about Wagner?' he said, boldly. Josephine turned, impressive in her long skirt and embroidered shawl.

'That's right,' she said, sweetly; 'are you interested in Wagner?'

Rashly, seeking to shine, Martin expressed an opinion upon the castles which Ludwig of Bavaria – 'the Dream King' – had constructed, and their relevance to the Wagnerian aesthetic.

'But the poor man was quite mad!' said Josephine, 'a tyrant, in many ways – don't you think?'

'I'm afraid that I don't know much about it . . .'

'I see, well . . .' And then Josephine appeared to relent; for a moment she had come alive, and for a second the polite, suburban young man had caught her interest. She now accepted the truth of the situation, and withdrew those antennae with which she detected new acquaintances who might, possibly, hold her attention. Martin, instinctively, knew that he had failed the small test that might have admitted him into that class of beings whom Josephine took seriously. And yet, he had set this test for himself; he had wanted to shine – had shown off, just slightly – and now his ignorance had found him out. The process had required no help from Josephine. A more experienced person would have kept to light conversation.

Marilyn was now pouring tea – extremely weak for herself. 'Do smoke,' she said to Martin, 'I know you're dying to . . .' A pretty ashtray, made of cream-coloured china in the shape of an ivy leaf, was produced from an untidy drawer. Marilyn poured tea for her mother, dropped in a slice of lemon and then, carrying her own cup extremely carefully, sat down beside Martin at the broad stripped-pine kitchen table. Josephine regarded the young people. 'Lovers' approach,' she murmured. Marilyn winced.

'You've been to the Beuys,' she said, at length. 'Did you enjoy it?'

'We were a bit mystified,' said Marilyn, 'but it was very interesting.'

'Don't let your father hear you saying that; he met Beuys when you were just a little girl – they argued.'

'What about?' asked Marilyn, suddenly interested.

'I'm not quite sure . . . You work in the City, don't you, Martin?'

By now, Martin had lost his bearings completely. He wished that he was alone with Marilyn. 'That's right,' he said. 'It's pretty boring I'm afraid . . .'

'No it isn't!' said Marilyn, loyally, 'it's really complicated. I think it sounds interesting.' Martin gathered that his friend was trying to build up his fallen image. He tried to catch Marilyn's eye and smile, but only succeeded in spilling his tea.

'Oh! Disaster!' said Josephine, not stirring. 'Marilyn, get Martin some more tea; has he had a cake?' Martin began to feel like a puppy. Just then, to make matters worse, Bill could be heard coming down the hall. Marilyn, Martin and Josephine all looked towards the door, expectantly. Bill's bearded face peered around it.

'Hello!' he said. 'You must be Martin . . .' There appeared to be genuine friendliness in his voice. Marilyn smiled, and looked pleased. Once more, Martin got to his feet and shook hands.

'Hello,' he said.

'You're getting some tea? Good. Marilyn, are those lemon cakes?'

'Yes.'

'From the place that I like?'

'Yes.'

'You anticipate my every whim. They're such a great colour – that yellow . . .'

Martin smiled. He could not help wondering at the marked contrast between the kindly man who was accepting cakes with the enthusiasm of a schoolboy and the stern, bleak prophet who had lectured at the Royal College of Art. Bill had put down a pile of books; Martin glanced at the cover of the topmost volume. It was called *The Sickness Unto Death: A Christian Psychological Exposition for Upbuilding and Awakening*. The author's name was Søren Kierkegaard.

'*Giant*'s on the box tonight,' said Bill. 'Now there's a film,' he added, turning to Martin.

'I've never seen it, I'm afraid . . .'

'What! Jimmy Dean's finest – you must watch *Giant*!'

Martin liked Bill as much as he feared Josephine. 'I'll certainly watch it,' he said.

'Good. Make Marilyn watch it as well . . .' Bill winked at his daughter.

'They've been to the Beuys,' said Josephine; 'they found it mystifying . . .'

'My feelings entirely. Beuys is like Joyce – they'll be arguing about him for centuries . . .' Bill poured himself some more tea.

'Beuys and Joyce: that's funny,' said Marilyn. Martin smiled.

'Beuys will be Beuys,' answered Bill. Josephine stood up, and then extended a hand to Martin once more. 'I do hope that we'll meet again soon,' she said; 'I'd love to know that you'll be popping in and out . . .'

'Thank you – it's nice to meet you . . .' There was a moment of confusion. Martin wondered whether or not Josephine had created it deliberately. Bill, realising that the young people were feeling uncomfortable, said, 'See you later,' and then pursued his wife out of the room. Once they were alone, Martin let out a long sigh.

'Oh, heavens!' he said, quietly.

'It's over with now,' said Marilyn. She turned on her chair to face the pale young man. 'I hope it wasn't too awful?' she added.

'No. Not at all – I just feel I made such a fool of myself.'

'Why? I think they liked you . . .'

'Anyone would think that we'd just got engaged – I don't mean that unkindly . . .'

Marilyn laughed. 'I know. Did you like the cakes?'

'I lost my appetite rather; I liked your father though.'

'He's sweet. Mum's more like Carmen. But she can be all right too . . .'

It was half-past five. The kitchen was now filled with the low light from two china-shaded lamps. Outside, beyond the little paved courtyard, the street appeared blue. Martin, in that house which he would have been so happy to own, felt like a tourist in a palace. Even the kitchen cabinets, with their mottled blue doors, delighted him. At the far end of the room, leaning against the wall, there was a large framed print of a glaring bewigged gentleman. On the window sill there was a luxurious quantity of partially melted, thick wax candles, such as one might find in a church. Everywhere, it seemed, there was cultural and aesthetic treasure. Martin yearned to be included within this atmosphere as much as he yearned for Marilyn.

'It's a beautiful house,' he said. 'Is it old?'

'Yes – very. Mummy used to say that she couldn't move for ghosts. You can imagine what that did for my beauty sleep.'

Martin bit back an easy compliment. Marilyn's feet were now resting upon the side of his chair; she was hugging her knees, and from time to time brushed her hair back over her ears, revealing delicate silver earrings. Her legs appeared slender and sleek; she had kicked off her shoes. She was thinking of how timid, in many ways, Martin seemed. Marilyn as a rule did not like timid men. She had always imagined that her love would be given to someone more relaxed and dominant than Martin. 'What do I really think of him?' she wondered, as the young man asked her questions about her school and about Rome, which 'he had always wanted to visit'. Above all, Martin appeared to be independent of her family; his enthusiasms and sense of humour were not their enthusiasms or their sense of humour – however much he might aspire to their society. Also, there was an attempt at roguishness in Martin's personality, and a stylish modernity. His affectations, she decided, were superficial. In short, Marilyn was making a conscious decision to love Martin. For Martin, the decision to love Marilyn had been taken of its own accord. He was powerless to prevent it. He could not, in his own mind, find adequate superlatives to describe the young woman.

'I say,' he said, finally, 'would you like to come over to my flat this evening, and watch *Giant*? We could pick up some food on the way; when does it start?'

Marilyn looked in the newspaper. 'Oh – not until half-past ten . . . But I could take my car. That would be lovely . . .'

The couple were happy now. They had a plan.

Outside, beyond the empty street and the dark, deserted workshops, the river flowed on towards Dartford.

That evening, in Martin's flawless apartment, the lives of the two young people meshed. They dined upon French cheese, olive bread, a packet of smoked salmon, 'Italian-style' salad and toffee ice-cream; the film enthralled them. Inwardly, as Martin watched James Dean, he hoped that he too could find an occasion to collapse in the ballroom of a large hotel, wearing a crumpled dinner suit and a pair of dark glasses. Such a demise appeared breathlessly romantic. Towards midnight, Marilyn lay down upon the low, uncovered sofa with her head resting against Martin's chest. She could hear his heart beating. A few minutes later, she could feel him stroking the nape of her neck, and did not find the sensation unpleasant. But she hoped, on this occasion, that 'things' would not go 'too far'. At a little after one o'clock in the morning she stretched, kissed Martin's neck and said, 'When can I next see you?'

In this manner, Martin Knight and Marilyn Fuller became a couple; or, in the jargon of their generation, a 'unit'.

To be loved in spring was a process which burnt deep into Martin's personality. Each day, and each new stage of intimacy, left its mark upon his mind. The 'fourth dimension', which he perceived to be love's creation, appeared to envelop him. All things, now, had a new meaning – because of Marilyn. As the weeks began to pass and as the relationship proceeded through all the usual gradations of fondness and sharing, the young couple rejoiced in their discovery of one another, and set about celebrating this discovery in the traditional way: dinners, shopping trips, the cinema, Kew, attending a party 'together' – the bond growing stronger now – long weekends, the spontaneous, trivial gifts that endorse great passion, the sentimentality that follows superficial quarrels . . . Summer drew closer, like a low, golden wave. Martin, filled with confidence, enjoyed his work far more because each day ended with Marilyn.

From time to time, the couple discussed, earnestly, what Marilyn ought to 'do'. Usually, these conversations took place in the early evening, with Martin detecting a sadness, or a seemingly irrational ill-temper, sullying his lover's mood. Marilyn spent her days – cheerfully at first – looking after the Captain's House and running errands for her busy parents. But she missed the spine which Truffles had put into her weeks. She was toying with the idea of starting a business of her own.

'But it's so expensive in London! If you've got Pru's sort of money, then it's OK, but for ordinary mortals . . .' She tossed back her hair, and stared at the new table (made out of cement blocks and reinforced glass) which Martin had bought from a well-bred designer in Pimlico.

'Well,' said Martin, with tremendous determination, as though a solution was easily within reach, 'have you got any capital?'

'I've got Aunt Jennie's money . . .'

'What's "Aunt Jennie's money"?'

'Oh . . .' and Marilyn looked doubtful. 'It's something that I'm not supposed to talk about until I get married. In fact, I'm not supposed to even think about it until I get married . . .'

Martin's interest was immediately aroused. The sombre conversation appeared to be growing brighter.

'Aunt Jennie,' said Marilyn, 'was Mummy's aunt – but we called her Aunt Jennie. She was quite rich, and had this big house in Shropshire . . .'

'It sounds like a children's story . . .'

'Yes. Well, Aunt Jennie died, and after the house was sold and everything was totted up –'

'"Totted up"!'

'"Totted up"' (here Marilyn patted Martin's knee, fondly). 'Carmen and I – I was about ten – each got some money. And that was "Aunt Jennie's money". If I'm not married by the time I'm twenty-five, Daddy says I can have it anyway. He says that it's earning interest . . . Did I tell you that Daddy called me a fascist the other day?'

'No! Really?'

'I said that I wanted a new car – a German one. One of those big ones with thick wheels. I love German cars, particularly the black ones . . .'

It was early evening – the second week of July 1984. Marilyn and Martin were sitting side by side upon Martin's sofa. The windows and skylight were open; the sounds of the street – traffic, a radio, children playing in a garden – reached the high apartment as though from a great distance. Martin knew that Marilyn's ill-temper and dissatisfaction would evaporate now. He studied her profile as she talked; her face was turned slightly to one side, and her bobbed hair appeared to be streaked with gold and copper where it was touched by the setting sun. She was wearing a white cotton dress, which was gathered at the waist and which then came down to her knees in stiff folds. This was fastened with buttons of mother-of-pearl. Her skin looked dark against the crisp fabric. Her golden sandals were placed neatly (both Martin and Marilyn could be extremely tidy) beneath the glass-topped table. Martin, once more, luxuriated in Marilyn's loveliness. Often, when he dwelt upon her beauty, he felt insecure – however reassuring the young woman might be. This both frightened him and increased his desire. He believed his love for Marilyn to be infinite, and was afraid that she could never love him as much as he loved her. It was an old formula, and he never discussed his anxiety, for fear of seeming weak. Later, he would regard the early months of their relationship as being occupied by two strangers. His mind returned, urgently, to Aunt Jennie's money.

'If you don't mind me asking, how much were you left?'

'I've never told anyone – except Catherine; I don't know why. It's not as though it was a fortune . . .'

'You don't have to tell me if you don't want to . . .'

Marilyn regarded her lover. Having changed out of his work clothes, he was now wearing a pair of grey trousers and a black T-shirt.

'It was about thirty thousand pounds. But it's in a building society, so it's probably more by now . . .'

Once more, Martin was aware of the wealth that, since he was a teenager, he had always believed the urban middle classes effortlessly to possess. At home, in Thornby Avenue, such sums were only whispered about. But he made no pretence of his surprise.

'Marry me!' he exclaimed, roguishly. A look of sadness came into Marilyn's eyes.

'Ask me again sometime – properly,' she said.

At this, the mood of the conversation changed. Martin, both remorseful for his outburst and flattered by the apparent seriousness with which it was greeted, became tender and apologetic. All discussion of what Marilyn ought to do was forgotten now; love had replaced pragmatism. So easily, the young couple tumbled into the welcoming territory of caresses. As yet, habit had not spoilt the pattern of their desire.

By September 1984, Martin Knight and Marilyn Fuller had entered into the 'second phase' of their relationship. A routine had been established; a form of diluted domesticity had engulfed them. From these ingredients, the couple created an adequate happiness which, in the manner of couples, they believed to be unique. Also, they began to socialise; a little at first, and then a great deal. When they gave gifts or sent birthday cards, they now signed their names together: 'With much love from'. Marilyn attended occasional classes in 'So You Want To Run Your Own Business?' at a local college of further education (where she drew amorous glances from ambitious young entrepreneurs) and Martin, secure at DogFox, began to yearn for swifter promotion and increased responsibility. RDS's rival, Resol UK, were beginning a recruitment drive, but all the new positions that were being advertised were going to be based near Bristol, as part of Resol's long-term relocation plan. Thus, there was a new joke at RDS: when a member of staff was late, or could not be found, the comment was made: 'He's gone to work for Resol!' Dave Runner, an academic at heart, referred to Resol as 'cowboys'.

The phase of after-work revels, for Martin, was now over. Martin and Marilyn's new friends were mostly couples of their own age: Jamie and Kim, Robert and Gill, Simon and Sabrina, Graham and Emma, Hugo and Henrietta, 'Oats' and Vicky, Tim and Karen. And then there were individuals who pursued their single lives in a manner which appeared to be slightly remote, or even eccentric: Lily, Mark, 'the other Martin', Sasha and Jeremy. All of these names, however, collectively represented a way of life. Wherever these young people gathered, in comfortable surroundings which never seemed to vary, they appeared to embody stability and affluence. As the months passed by, the salaries of these friends increased. In their middle or late twenties, most of these young men and women displayed the security and confidence of solid middle age. They were united by certain reference points, which engendered a particular language and a single, shared vision. Childless as yet, the nucleus of this little society worked and played within a privileged urban routine. Most were buying their first substantial properties – the era of shared houses was over – and marriage (hitherto little more than a will-o'-the-wisp) was swiftly becoming a steady beam to pull towards. Engagements and 'plans' were on the increase. That autumn, which was filled with mist in the early evenings, could be regarded for Martin and Marilyn's 'crowd' as the beginnings of the giddy ascent to the zenith of disposable income. It was a time when the principal London railway termini could boast booths that sold nothing but smoked salmon and squat jars of Dijon mustard; and it was approaching a time, so the curators of apocrypha would later say, when a man's ambition could be measured by the colour of his braces.

Martin, however, still believed himself to be intellectually superior to most of his companions. His aesthetic enquiries were now channelled through his love for Marilyn, but he remained determined to find, colonise and absorb 'the interesting'. From his college days, he maintained the desire to appear subversive; this manifested itself as a propensity for dreaming and a fluency in fashionable polemic. During his journeys to the office, he read demanding books which hinted towards romantic bleakness or sophisticated, ironic despair. In short, he espoused all of those art forms that endorsed dissatisfaction. Such were the props with which he shored up his comfort. He assumed that this was a reversal of the usual position.

Marilyn continued to entrance him. Her figure, voice, clothes and mannerisms all delighted him equally. Sometimes, as they lay in bed, he would run his finger down the length of her naked body, and believe that he had never seen such perfection of form. When he looked at other girls, he pitied their lovers. Marilyn, for her part, clung to Martin in the belief that the happiness which she felt would somehow become wholly real. For beneath her happiness and her sense of contentment there remained a doubt: when she looked at her lover, or when she paused to think about him in his absence, she would feel as though she was still trying to make a decision. Try as she might, she could not merely drift – as Martin did – across the surface of an unsullied contentment. This doubt, however, remained in the wings of her mind; its shadow was too pale to darken the stage upon which her happier thoughts were performing. Thus, hand in hand, the lovers proceeded on their way.

In February 1985, Martin obtained his first credit card. Up until that time, he had forgone the temptation of immediate access to considerable credit facilities. Now, finding himself 'a little hard up', he submitted his details to a credit-card company, and quickly received his card in return. He thought that the card was extremely beautiful: it was moss-green, with raised silver numbers running across it. When he first held the credit card, and weighed it in his palm, he had the illusion that he was holding something heavy – like a loaded gun, or a full packet of cigarettes. He was astonished at the amount he was allowed to borrow. With the gleaming card tucked inside his wallet he felt confident, secure and carefree. He determined to be sensible, and only to use it 'if he had to'.

'I don't know how you've survived for so long without one,' said Simon. 'What do you do about telephone bookings and hotel reservations?' Hitherto, Martin had always paid by cash or cheque. A whole new world of convenience was opened up; he christened the card by taking Marilyn out for dinner, to a new restaurant in Endell Street, WC2. The restaurant was on the first floor of an old office building; it was dark and intimate, and cunningly designed to look as though it was decaying.

'Would you care for a drink before you order?' beamed the bright young waitress. 'The house champagne is really nice . . .'

Two glasses of champagne were ordered.

The couple were seated upon old kitchen chairs, which had been splashed with emulsion paint and then varnished. Above their heads, tacked to the ceiling, a length of fine fabric embroidered with silver thread created the sense of dining within a pavilion. Concealed spotlights illuminated displays of gold-painted twigs and bullrushes; a stuffed owl, glaring from within a Victorian glass case, was placed upon a shelf between the two uncurtained, street-facing windows. A large colour photograph of a decapitated snake hung upon the dark green wall beside the staircase.

'Jumble-sale chic,' commented Martin.

'I'm going to change places with you,' said Marilyn, rising.

'Why?'

'So that I don't have to look at that revolting photograph.'

'It does seem rather unnecessary . . .'

The restaurant was beginning to fill with couples, and small groups from neighbouring offices. Soon, every seat was taken. There was a sense that, for many of the diners, the restaurant was merely an extension of the office. The cooking, which was advanced for those days, was minimal. Everything was described as a 'packet' or a 'bundle'. The sauces were ingenious. Later, when Martin recalled the hundreds of dinners and lunches that he had eaten since the christening of his first credit card, he wondered at how exciting and inspiring his 'restaurant years' had initially seemed. It had all seemed new and significant, during his first years with Marilyn. Dining had endorsed them as an affluent urban couple. Within their little society, at that time, the mere names of different restaurants had spoken volumes about the people who dined at them. Later, Martin would think of the 'food of love':

> that, surfeiting,
> the appetite may sicken and so die.

To Martin Knight, in 1985, love and food had been inextricably linked.

The bill, at the restaurant in Endell Street, had come to £56.00. Offering his card, and signing the slim, discreet slip which was passed to him, Martin congratulated himself – wrongly – on the fact that he still had enough ready cash in his wallet to take Marilyn home in a taxi.

Thus the couple began to spend – seriously.

Martin would sometimes say, with great assurance: 'Affluence isolates.' By this he meant that wealth – or the illusion of wealth – can enable a person to avoid those aspects of life that they do not wish to encounter. In this manner, a world within a world is created – the inner world being a reflection and a reversal of the corresponding isolation created by poverty. Fancifully, but with no small amount of initial self-satisfaction, Martin would then extend his reasoning to calculate the effect of opulence upon the imagination. In this, he emphasised his inability either to hold a firm opinion or to reach a definite conclusion. On the one hand, he believed that deprivation could force a person to yearn – and therefore strengthen the analytical faculties and the apparatus of aspirational romance; on the other hand, he supposed that wealth begat self-confidence and autonomy, and thus liberated the individual from humdrum drudgery and granted them freedom to explore experience as they chose and thus see the world, as it were, 'from above'. But what if riches simply dulled the mind, and created boredom? When faced with the maxim 'Know thyself,' Martin Knight was plunged into confusion and contradiction. Inspired by Marilyn's father, he bought himself a small collection of the writings of Søren Kierkegaard. One entry, in particular, touched him deeply:

> I feel the way a chessman must, when the opponent
> says of it: That piece cannot be moved.

In the mean time, all of those products and services that more prudent, or less extravagant, people would refer to as luxuries, Martin regarded as necessities. With Marilyn to love, and money to spend, he immersed himself in the pleasant routine.

The most satisfying aspect of this routine, for Martin, was to feel that he was keeping in step with the latest developments that comprised the urban life-style. With Marilyn, he absorbed all that which was new and interesting: films, shops, exhibitions, adverts, concerts, magazines, restaurants, books, clothes – even shaving creams, aftershave lotions and shower gels had their place on the list of significant phenomena. In short, any product, service, or event that offered itself for consumption was fuel for the business of living. These items were discussed at length by the couple, and formed the basis of the language which was used within their little society. Indeed, these discussions and this language were the basis of Martin and Marilyn's relationship. To

Martin, who mingled his own philosophy with a liking for élitism, all the interesting aspects of his small, modern world were capable of commenting upon one another.

'We're approaching an age of inverted commas,' he pronounced one evening in July 1985, after dinner at Graham and Emma's new flat in Dulwich.

'But we're living in an age of grey carpets,' replied Hugo.

'I don't think that it's grey carpets, necessarily,' said Emma. 'What about burgundy carpets? Everyone at work seems to have a burgundy carpet.'

'This is silly,' said Sasha; 'who cares what colour the carpet is? I'm sorry, but it's true . . .' Sasha's habit of closing all her statements with the phrase 'I'm sorry, but it's true . . .' irritated Marilyn.

'I'd like to see you live with a brown one,' she said; 'I mean, every morning, imagine – a brown carpet. Anyway, lino's making a comeback.'

'Really?' said Emma. 'That reminds me of my primary school –'

'And people being sick.'

'Did you have a matron who smelt of Dettol?'

'We used to have lunches which smelt of Dettol,' said Hugo.

The evening had been typical, and quietly enjoyable. Graham and Emma, without admitting it, had planned the informal dinner quite carefully. That morning, however, as they passed between the bedroom and the bathroom, each preparing for work, they had told one another that they would 'simply throw something together'. At lunchtime – it being a Friday, and therefore relaxed – Emma had visited the large new 'food hall' near her West End office; and Graham had spent an enjoyable twenty minutes in the wine merchant's in Pudding Court, not far from Threadneedle Street. Thus, when they both reached home in the evening (both slightly, but not terribly, late) they had feigned slight panic and a partial, weary annoyance at the prospect of their guests. Their shopping formed a collection of bags upon the kitchen table. Emma, still wearing her work clothes, had immediately commenced to wash salad, whip cream and place poached salmon in the fridge. Graham, 'in his department', had unwrapped bottles of wine from their sturdy brown paper and got in his partner's way by putting them in the fridge to chill.

'Do you want to use the bathroom now?' he enquired.

'Why? What are you going to do?'

'I thought that if I have a shower now, then you could have a bath afterwards?'

'What about the table? Someone has to lay the table.'

'Well, I can do that while you're having a bath . . .'

Emma looked vexed, and made the colander clatter. 'Put those in some water,' she said, passing two large bunches of irises and lilies to her sheepish husband.

'What time are people arriving?'

'About eight –'

'It's almost warm enough to eat in the garden . . .'

'Oh, Graham – no . . .'

'Well, we could leave the french windows open . . .'

Graham retired, laden with flowers, to see to the windows; then he slipped into the bathroom. Fifteen minutes later, invigorated by the cool water and his grapefruit-and-aloe 'splash', he returned to the kitchen. 'How are you coping?' he said.

'Everything's under control,' said Emma, 'but now I must have a bath . . .'

Thus harmony was restored. By eight o'clock, the dining room was illuminated against the pale summer evening by white candles; the flowers stood in a magnificent display upon the broad 'original' mantelpiece; and *Gazpacho* was ready to serve. Six guests were expected: two couples and two 'singles'.

Graham worked in shipping and Emma was an information officer. They had moved in together earlier that year. Both were

211

doing well. They were in their late twenties and, as such, amongst the more senior members of Martin and Marilyn's acquaintances. The oldest members of the group (and regarded, thus, as a kind of Oberon and Titania) were Hugo and Henrietta, who ran their own business. Hugo and Henrietta were fondly thought of as hedonists of the old school; they drank heavily, were loud and outspoken, fought in public and were quite inseparable. People always smiled when Hugo and Henrietta entered the room; their presence seemed to raise the company's spirits, and suggest that there was a state of ideal partnership to aspire towards. They were always called 'good old Hugo and Henrietta'.

'We're not the bloody cabaret!' Henrietta would roar sometimes, as she threw her hat to one side, and took her place beside her husband.

Shortly before eight, as they sat in their drawing room awaiting their guests, Graham had said: 'It would be nice just to watch television,' and Emma had agreed. Martin and Marilyn, too, had frequently asserted to one another: 'It's nice just to stay in and watch TV.'

Going out was nice, but staying in was nicer.

Towards the end of September 1985 there was a 'shake-up' at DogFox. For Martin, who was now responsible for 'Systems Implementation', this reorganisation of the office structure had immediate, and unfortunate, consequences. To begin with, Dave Runner had 'gone upstairs'; Paul Fines – to the general relief of the other staff – was transferred to DATEC.

'So who's going to replace Dave?' asked Hilary, addressing those six members of staff who were still working, early one evening, shortly after Dave's departure had been announced.

'It might be someone from Finance,' suggested Steve.

'An internal promotion? I don't think so,' said Luke Caldwell, leaning back on his chair to stretch.

'What about that bloke who's been hanging around with Spiller? He looks keen,' said Hilary.

'He's a spy,' said Martin, mysteriously; 'in fact, I'll bet that he's from Audit.'

'Hasn't Audit been moved to Baker Street?' said Hilary. 'I thought something went horribly wrong, when they had to audit themselves, and half of them lost their jobs . . .'

A chuckle ran around the office. It was pleasant to sit at the end of the day and discuss those subjects that guaranteed the opportunity both to gossip and to criticise.

'Has anyone noticed how slack Mailing are getting?' said Phil. 'I was having some discs delivered the other afternoon, and I had to ring Mailing twice to find out where they were . . .'

'Where were they?'

'Somewhere on the third floor. Some bloody secretary could have wiped the lot.'

'Sexist pig,' said Hilary.

'I think you'll find that your assumption that I meant a *female* secretary makes you more sexist than me – whose phone is that?'

The office was silent for a moment.

'It's next door,' said Martin, eventually. 'It just sounds as though it's in here.'

It was a Wednesday. Martin was in the middle of a complex and time-consuming project. He was more than a little bored. Marilyn was on holiday with her mother, in Austria. At first, Martin had welcomed the chance to spend some time alone; indeed, during a mature conversation the previous week, the couple had congratulated themselves on their mutual need for independence. Now, Martin was afraid that Marilyn would be enjoying herself too much without him. Since that time he had become rather irritable, and prone to waves of despondency. On the Sunday after Marilyn departed, he had visited the Hayward Gallery, and found himself cursing the other visitors. He regarded their interest in the works on display as being mere affectation. That same evening, as he sat in his flat and ate a meagre supper of sandwiches and soup, he had calculated that his overdraft was about to reach its new limit. Added to this, he now had two credit cards to support, as well as his mortgage to pay. For this state of affairs, he blamed other people, and felt sorry for himself. Work had become tedious. Promotion and a higher salary seemed distant.

'So who's it going to be?' he said finally to his assembled colleagues. 'I've got an awful feeling that it's going to be the Spy . . .'

That Friday, Mr Spiller introduced the staff at DogFox to Christopher Glencross, their new Manager.

'It is the Spy!' hissed Martin to Steve. Steve raised his eyebrows, and studied the new arrival closely. Mr Glencross was a 'company man'. He had worked in several sections of RDS over many years; he was neither an academic nor a liberal. He believed that DogFox had existed as an experimental department, a law unto itself, for too long. He thought that the staff within DogFox were too removed from the wider workings and policies of the firm as a whole; and he thought that office discipline was lax. Within a week, he had instigated major changes in the daily routine:

a signing-in book was placed beside the photocopier, in which members of staff had to sign themselves in and out of the office, with date, time and initials;

lunch breaks were not to exceed their one-hour duration, and had to be taken at an agreed time between twelve and two-thirty. 'Unoffical flexi-time' was not on;

coffee breaks were stopped: 'Staff may take coffee to their desks, but must not congregate informally in the kitchen area';

files were not to be borrowed – Martin was appointed to be DogFox Information Officer;

no personal material was to be kept in the office – it could constitute a fire hazard.

In short, the bubble which DogFox had represented to the company was burst. The resentment which the 'élite team' had rather enjoyed was now turned against them directly. Mr Glencross had no favourites. His manner, when dealing with his staff, was to criticise them in the style of a bad prep-school master.

'Train late?' he would enquire, mildly, when someone arrived after their 'usual time'.

Or (loudly): 'Of course, you were just about to give me the returns . . .' when the person on that week's returns had not yet moved them from their in-tray.

It was Hilary who left first. One morning, having attended a hospital appointment in Soho, she arrived at the office late, soaked by the rain and in a dreadful temper. She had forgotten to inform Mr Glencross of her absence, and had merely rung in late. She was just shaking out her umbrella and attempting to dry her hair when the new Section Manager strode up to her desk.

'The Spec 2 file,' he snapped. 'I've looked on your desk, I need it, and I can't find it.'

'Oh,' said Hilary, 'if you'll just give me a moment . . .'

'I want it now, Hilary, please.'

Red-faced, Hilary flung down her umbrella and then, still wearing her dripping raincoat, rummaged with considerable fury through her in tray.

'There!' she shouted. 'All right?'

'Five minutes please, Hilary.'

Hilary followed the Manager into his enclosure. 'I don't know what he bloody wants,' she said loudly as she passed by Martin's desk. Martin nodded sympathetically.

Hilary resigned that very day. Martin longed to follow her example. He, too, had been 'bollocked' by Mr Glencross. Mr Glencross embodied all of those qualities of life which Martin most despised.

*

By the end of November 1985, the situation had become intolerable. The once-pleasant routine of work now filled Martin with despair; he felt as though his every movement was being monitored, and he spent his days in the office quite certain that a storm was brewing. An invisible weight of disapproval appeared to have been placed upon his shoulders; this, in turn, reduced the young man's confidence and made him make mistakes. As a result of these mistakes, and the angry comments with which Mr Glencross greeted all errors, Martin became demoralised. It was only a short distance from this state of affairs to a series of confrontations between the aesthete and the new Section Manager. Martin, recalling the advice which Steve Clary had offered him, refused to be drawn into a round of little chats with his superior. He had no desire to be placed upon unofficial 'probation' by Mr Glencross; similarly, his pride and his sense of good taste were affronted by the thought of becoming an office invalid – a person like Richard Hayter who, entrenched in problems at work, was forced to decay, as it were, in public. To combat these sour thoughts, Martin began to take driving lessons and to ponder upon means of escape.

Once more, it was Martin's innate sense of superiority which was due to save him. The relative merits and disadvantages of Richmond Data Services and their rival, the decentralising Resol UK, were a frequent topic of conversation amongst the staff at DogFox. Indeed, in many ways, employees at RDS regarded Resol as an old friend. They were used to studying the progress and development of their competitor and, on occasion, had come across their counterparts from the rival firm. Resol, whilst being smaller than RDS, was a much younger, more progressive company. It was owned and personally managed by Dick Alryn, an energetic, middle-aged tycoon who had made and lost his first million by 1973. The areas of information technology which DogFox researched and marketed were the sole concern of the 'slimmer, fitter' Resol. Now, as Mr Glencross had cast a shadow across the atmosphere in Martin's office, he was inclined to make a move.

'It's time that you left, anyway,' said Marilyn.

'But how?'

'Why not simply write to Resol direct, and offer yourself as a package?'

'I could do . . .' Martin cheered up a little bit at the thought of this. 'On the other hand they're still advertising . . .'

'Then go for it.'

'But what if I didn't get the job? And Glencross found out? Which he would.'

Marilyn sighed. The discussion about Martin's job had now eclipsed their earlier conversations about her own lack of employment. She did not want to see Martin suffering, but at the same time she was losing patience with his bad moods. The couple were dining, unwisely, at a small, chic restaurant in Soho. The chef at this restaurant – young, fashionable and bearded – was already a personality. But the exotic dishes which were served to the young couple might just as well have been porridge. The mere sight of the extravagant, expensive menu had made Martin feel weary. The meal had been supposed to be a treat, as well as a chance to discuss things. The fact that the couple dined out nearly every other night had detracted from the novelty of the occasion. Marilyn pushed away her *Honey-Glazed John Dory*; Martin stared dully at his *Warm Salad of Mixed Leaves and Chicken Livers.*

'The trouble with Resol,' he said, 'is that they're moving to Bristol.'

'So?'

'So, yes: they are recruiting; but all the jobs are at their new office, in bloody Bristol. Would you want me to move to Bristol?'

'I just want you to be happy –'

At this, Martin became even more depressed. He assumed that Marilyn was cooling towards him and that, had she loved him as much as he loved her, then she could never have suggested such a thing.

'Oh, well, if you don't care!' he said. He looked away from his partner, and lit a cigarette. A waitress appeared, dressed in black.

'Was everything all right?' she said, taking their large white plates away.

'Yes – it was fine, thank you,' said Martin. The couple had scarcely touched their main courses.

'What a waste of money,' said Marilyn. Martin shrugged. He was brooding upon his girlfriend's comments about Bristol. 'Do you want any coffee?' he said.

'Not particularly.' Marilyn sounded prim as she said this.

Martin surveyed the restaurant. A party of four, two men and two women, were conversing loudly at a neighbouring table. Their accents were like a caricature of the English upper classes at play; they appeared to be totally at ease, and were wholly oblivious to the noise they were making. At another table, two young women, dressed in the height of fashion, were gazing superciliously about the room. They seemed to be too bored to even speak. The waitress brought Martin his bill: it came to nearly £80.00. This was due to the bottle of champagne that Martin had ordered and that was still standing, only half empty, in the ice bucket. Once more, the young man experienced a sense of nausea, as though he was being force-fed as a punishment for gluttony. The sparse, 'minimal' interior of the restaurant was brightly lit. Two large paintings, of dark, abstract composition, seemed to shout from the wall. The ceiling was painted the colour of dried blood. 'Let's go,' said Martin. Silently, Marilyn put on her coat. The fear that he had angered his girlfriend was now added to Martin's list of anxieties.

Outside, the narrow pavement was crowded with young people who were noisily making their way towards a night club. They shoved and jostled the other pedestrians, quite unintentionally but without any form of apology. Screams and howls seemed to fill the air. Walking towards Shaftesbury Avenue, Martin counted three vagrants, the last of whom was propped up beside a pile of boxes and urinating upon his bare feet.

'Oh God . . .' muttered Martin, as he looked away.

The traffic was heavy, and the streets appeared to be filled with drunken, hostile people. When the couple reached Marilyn's car, which was parked near Long Acre, they discovered that the driver's window had been smashed. The seats were covered with broken glass. 'And they didn't even take anything!' wailed Marilyn, later. Tired and irritable, Martin and Marilyn returned to their respective homes. They knew too well that they would only argue if they spent the night together.

Martin travelled home by taxi. He sat back in a corner of the seat and studied the streets. Lavender-coloured shop-lights and dark doorways gave way to the inner hinterland; it all appeared dismal and worn out. Passing by a large pizza restaurant and seeing the customers eating from heaped plates, Martin was filled with despair. How could they? he thought. What's the point in pretending?

The taxi driver pulled back the glass partition which separated him from his fare.

'This is a crap job,' he said, by way of conversation. 'Twenty-two years – wasted.' Martin wondered whether or not his downcast features had attracted this confession. 'So what do you do?' the taxi driver asked.

'I'm an art critic,' lied Martin.

The dreary autumn dragged on towards winter, filled with dissatisfaction. The low grey sky, to Martin, looked stupid and sullen. Gusts and cold drizzle made the City streets slippery, and heavy rain caused the overcrowded tube trains to smell of damp wool and wet hair. While the situation in DogFox continued to deteriorate, so too did the various entertainments that London had to offer appear, quite suddenly, to lack atmosphere. The capital, to Martin and Marilyn, now resembled a shabby carousel upon which the public rode round and round; vertigo and boredom were the twin sensations which the veterans of this ride experienced. To keep in step with urban society and attitudes now struck the young couple as being *passé* and boring. The truth of the matter, however, was that Martin and Marilyn had gone out so much, and had been so eager to socialise and consume, that they had exhausted that part of themselves which could respond to novelty or find enjoyment in their earlier distractions. In short, they felt stale; but between themselves they referred to their boredom as 'cynicism'.

'London's becoming old-fashioned,' said Martin, one wet afternoon at the beginning of December 1985. The couple were making their way through Leicester Square. They had just walked out of a film that neither of them, in truth, had wanted to see. The streets were crowded with shoppers. Scarlet tinsel was blowing in the wind from the roof of a news-vendor's hut. A poster was glued to a builder's hoarding; it said: DEATH BY EXTREME BUGGERY.

'I just hate it,' said Marilyn. She was tired and cold, and the linings of her suede shoes were becoming damp. She was thinking about her diet. In keeping with their latest routine, the couple were going to buy some food, return to Martin's apartment, have hot baths and then watch television. Martin refused to dine out on Saturdays: he said that it was vulgar. Increasingly, Marilyn preferred to stay in with her boyfriend; she no longer felt the need to go out. This, sometimes, caused arguments, but Martin was too apathetic to get worked up. Added to this, Marilyn was getting tired of their friends, and Martin was worried about money.

'There's nothing so dull as other people's babies,' she said, 'and they're all getting terribly broody. Babies and careers; careers and babies. I wouldn't mind, but I end up having nothing to say. Nobody ever asks me what I've been doing . . .' Thus, resenting her contemporaries, Marilyn devoted herself to Martin. She no longer questioned her feelings, she merely accepted them.

At the beginning of January 1986, Martin passed his driving test. Filled with new confidence, he determined to 'sort things out'. He applied for a position with Resol – now he would be able to drive home to see Marilyn whenever he liked – and was successful. The position with Resol represented a promotion: he would be Assistant Marketing Manager.

'You're right to get out of London,' Dick Alryn had said, passing the interviewee a cup of coffee. 'The big boys are weighed down by overheads; we want to work towards the '90s. And Bristol's a beautiful city – terrific standard of living – and the house prices are so reasonable . . .'

The notion of Bristol as 'a beautiful city' began to obsess Martin and Marilyn. Far from being a burden, the thought of the move began to excite them. Their spirits lifted, as they talked about spending 'really nice' weekends together, and 'getting to know the area'. Martin would be working at Rutbridge Business Park, and the relocation incentives were considerable. Happily, he began to work his notice at DogFox. I'll be in Bristol in the spring, he thought poetically. The thought of how well he would be able to live, and how improved his routine would seem, dispelled any fears he might have had. His mother, too, was pleased.

'I'll be able to come down, once you're settled,' she said.

New life was breathed into Martin and Marilyn's relationship. Seeing her partner so happy and restored to his former humour made Marilyn wish that she was going with him.

'And think about your business idea,' said Martin. 'It would be so much cheaper to get started in Bristol, and there's such a good market – for almost anything. Who knows,' he continued, waggishly, 'if it was a success we'd be rich . . .'

Three minutes later, Martin proposed to Marilyn, and Marilyn – with tears in her eyes – accepted.

'Well, now we will be rich!' joked Martin.

The engagement was greeted fondly by both families. It seemed like a long-awaited piece of good news.

'But we're going to get settled first,' Martin and Marilyn kept on saying: they were going to find a 'really lovely' house, Marilyn was going to start a business (she would decide what sort later on) – in short, they were going to decentralise.

Their friends, secretly, thought that this was both fashionable and shrewd.

Six: *Being Pilgrims*

Some twenty miles south-west of Bristol, occupying an area of
land which had been drained, flattened, re-surfaced and land-
scaped, stood Rutbridge Business Park. Completed in October
1985, it was the largest development of its kind in that part of the
county, and it had been constructed to the mutual satisfaction of
nearly all the parties involved. Politicians had spoken of 'vision', a
member of royalty had referred to 'enterprise and initiative', and
even the environmentalists (whose advice and support had been
sought from the start) had published a loose-leaf report in which
the Rutbridge Development Corporation was described as both
'far-sighted' and 'aware'.

The Park was approached by a smooth, sienna-coloured road,
the surface of which seemed to purr with pleasure as one drove
along it. On either side, lush fields spread out, peppered in spring
with delicate poppies; and here and there, to vary the perspect-
ive, small groves of young deciduous trees fluttered their gently
unfolding leaves in the breeze. Beyond the fields, in the north-
eastern corner of the development, there was a shallow lake. At
the top of the lake a broad expanse of brown rushes created an
atmosphere of stillness. There were also water-fowl: mallards
and swans.

The anchor-structure of the Park's business premises was
known simply as Unit 5. This was a long brown building which

had been built out of the mellow local stone, adorned with primary-coloured pediments and ornamental railings and roofed with a resilient hybrid of perspex and glass. It looked rather like a tent. Thick steel wires stretched taut from each angle in the external cornice (thus creating an architectural pun upon the use of the flying buttress) and these were embedded, at ground level, in small concrete blocks. The differing lengths of these wires, and the according expanses of their surfaces left open to the elements, were capable of creating a bizarre musical effect. In high winds, or when Unit 5 adjusted (as it was designed to do) to various settlings in the ground upon which it stood, a low-toned hum would begin to fill the air. This provoked, amongst the cultural élite of Rutbridge, much use of the word 'Aeolian'.

In the rest of its features, Unit 5 was rather plain. Beside the primary-coloured witticisms of the façade's adornments, large single-pane windows, set in frames of pale wood, were carefully tinted to naturalise the incoming light. Whilst the architects had forgone the use of an atrium to create the sense of airy space, the massive transparent roof appropriated this function, and so Unit 5 still possessed the feel of being open to the sky. Thus workers could watch the changes in the weather, and the progress of cloud formations could alter the mood of the offices in a moment. When the sun began to set and long shadows began to push their way like grey barges across the sparkling surface of the brand-new lake, there was a feeling in the air, and a resonance from the land and water, which seemed to suggest that one was living at the end of the world.

Orbiting Unit 5, and connected to it by further sienna-coloured roads, there were six satellite business premises, each of which was a smaller version of the anchor-structure. Added to these was the sports and conference centre, with its coolly terraced dining room and its kidney-shaped swimming pool, which was floored with an aquamarine mosaic. A small ornamental garden stood between Units 3 and 4, and this was based upon an eighteenth-century design which had been unearthed in the muniments room of nearby Drilling Hall. An intricate box-hedge maze would hopefully release its aromatic scent throughout the summer months, whilst, planted at regular intervals and neatly encircled by fragile timber frames, the rose bushes of Rutbridge's first summer might one day make pleasing bursts of colour above the dusty gravel paths. Far away, across the length of the horizon, a low range of hills could be seen as an ash-blue shadow; and over to the west, just audible, the distant motorway kept up its constant roar. The development had attracted six businesses in all, and with the exception of the two majors (Intafreight and Resol UK), who had been encouraged by the generous relocation grants, they were locally evolved concerns.

The relocation of Resol UK to the Rutbridge Business Park was touched with the pioneer spirit. To Martin, who feasted upon manifestations of the contemporary, there was an unreal quality to the brand-new premises, and a potent juxtaposition between their modernity and the countryside which surrounded them. This effect was beyond the quantifying grasp of fashionability, and thus, to the young aesthete, both pure and desirable.

While Resol's warehousing facilities were still based in Essex, a time had come (just twelve months prior to Martin's appointment) when the cost of maintaining a London-based head office had made it financial sense to decentralise the bulk of the Sales and Administration departments to a location devoid of the capital's rising high costs. A committee had duly set about assessing the various alternatives, and very quickly the Rutbridge Business Park had emerged as the best-favoured option. There were inevitable redundancies, but few of the London staff had shown the slightest interest in moving to the West Country, and so individual settlements were made for the sudden loss of jobs. This (unknown to the ex-employees) was precisely what the upper management at Resol had hoped would happen. A whole new staff was recruited for Resol's Rutbridge operation, and this included the post of Assistant Marketing Manager.

The already flourishing business took new strength from its relocation; and one of the direct results of this upward profile was to increase the passage of work which ran through the Marketing department – known as COM. COM (the initials referred to procedural shorthand) was the central section in which Resol contracts were broken down into BR1s, BR3s and MISC. These different groupings described not only the technical specifications of individual contracts, but also denoted the financial value of each order. Once analysed, these data were vital to forward-planning. Thus, COM performed a double function, and (like Martin) studied itself relentlessly. The importance of this work determined that COM employed over twenty members of staff (divided into COM (Home) and COM (Resale)) and the department was overseen personally by Dick Alryn. A skeleton staff had been operating at Rutbridge since the late autumn of 1985. By April 1986, when Martin commenced work with Resol, a full team had been gathered.

Dick (or 'Dicky') Alryn liked to communicate with his staff, and he did this by playing tennis with them, whatever their rank. He was a few years short of fifty, unmarried, physically strong, and handsome. He was also immensely popular. In a manner which was the envy of textbook-trained managers, Dick Alryn appeared to have a natural rapport with his employees. He broke down timidity and embarrassment, he understood precisely the meaning of the word 'delegation' and – most of all – he got results. Whilst his eccentricities (wearing a tracksuit to the office for instance) would sometimes prompt jocular comments, not once was there a whisper of disloyalty. Eschewing both Western and Japanese management techniques, Dicky had a way of making his staff believe in the strength of the team. To this end, he liked to be thought of as a Pirate King, sailing the seas of information technology in search of new markets to plunder. Martin found this notion of strength incredibly attractive. Also, Dick Alryn paid his staff well.

Initially, Martin had sometimes feared that his move to the West Country would fill him with sentimental longing for the distant capital and for the top-floor apartment in Vauxhall which had been the scene of the early, heady months of his love for Marilyn. Now, when he reached the city of Bristol and began his new routine of work, the change was so swift and so complete that a new aesthetic mood inspired him. Certain of Marilyn's love, and flattered by the attention which Dick Alryn paid him as a junior executive of Resol, Martin felt that he had recentralised as opposed to decentralised, and that a whole new life was beginning. Bristol, throughout the pungent spring of 1986, appeared to be blue and grey; it seemed to be a tranquil, dignified place, yet large enough, and touched by new development and modernity, to retain an urban quality. Bristol was both ancient and modern: a city of neat precincts and colourful hanging baskets of geraniums; in Bristol, heritage mingled with contemporary affluence. This mixture of moods – the pastoral and the urban, the old and the new – was Martin's ideal. He could not have lived in a purely rural community, and his wariness with London had disinclined him to seek further for glamour within the inner cities. The vast old houses of Bristol's richer suburbs seemed to hint at the opulent calm and prosperous solidity of provincial mercantile comfort. Considering these mansions, with their serene gardens and their monumental features, Martin felt the tug of history. He pictured a notion of middle-class life that was wholly consecrated to good taste and wealthy formality. The human scale of Bristol, when compared to the vastness and hierarchical zoning of London, made him dream of a harmonious existence. What he meant by this was a sense of security held in place by aesthetics.

Also, to Martin, there was an obscurity about Bristol which he found deeply romantic. Away from the self-consciousness of London, it seemed to him as though the contemporary and the confrontational became more interesting. In London, where all things were given their place on the cultural scale as soon as they announced themselves, there was a tendency to create a premature staleness; in London, an exhibition had no sooner opened or a record been released than the *cognoscenti*, terrified of being seen to be ill-informed, had added it to the list of significant events and pronounced sentence upon it. In Bristol, Martin revelled in the joy of having removed himself from this process. It seemed to be the most fashionable thing to do. He felt no sense of inferiority; rather he looked upon those who remained in London, paying exorbitant prices for their tiny slice of self-satisfaction, with pity. In cheaper Bristol, which was reinventing itself as a contemporary city, he believed that he could place his aspirations within his means.

All that spring, as Martin familiarised himself with his new duties, Marilyn became more loving. The couple existed in a blissful state which their approaching marriage renewed daily. Every little job and each small term of separation increased their happiness and their optimism. All things were new, and in every discovery they found an advantage. Bristol, as the sun became warmer and the breeze softer, seemed to live up to their sense of good fortune. For the first three months, however, Martin had to rent four nondescript rooms in a featureless district not far from Bristol Parkway Station. Ordinarily, he would have found this plain, post-war dwelling quite unacceptable. As it was, he was seldom at home in the little flat, with its metal-framed windows and coarse brown carpet, and hence it was treated as a fond joke by the young couple. They called it 'Mon Repos'.

'But there's no point in shelling out for something nicer,' said Martin; and Marilyn agreed.

The search for a 'really nice' property was already under way.

Also, the couple appeared to have more money than they knew what to do with: Martin's new salary was just under £20,000 per annum, plus a contribution towards his moving expenses; in addition to this, he had sold his apartment in Vauxhall for a considerable profit to an energetic young woman who worked for an oil company. As Brian Champion had hinted, the rapid escalation of property prices in London at that time had almost doubled Martin's money.

Marilyn had now come into possession of her legacy from Aunt Jennie.

'Here you are,' said Bill, showing his wide-eyed daughter a cheque for nearly £50,000; 'you can join the idle rich now.' He did not add, even as a joke, that Marilyn had been both idle and rich for nearly all of her life. Marilyn thanked her father, and then put the cheque on her dressing table, next to a bottle of moisturiser.

Once they had banked these various sums, Martin and Marilyn were extremely gratified by the manner in which their new bank manager not only treated them with courtesy and respect but also invited them into the branch 'to join him for drinks with other Gold Card customers'. Attending this soirée, half facetiously, the couple were offered credit and overdraft facilities of such proportions that they scarcely dared to consider them. Bob Crimner, their personal financial adviser, spoke at great length about 'high yield from high investment'; and Sally Miggins, one of the junior cashiers, circulated nervously with bottles of white wine. Secretly, Martin delighted in his role as a prosperous young citizen. He felt comfortable in his well-cut dark suit, and Marilyn attracted envious glances from other men in the room. She was wearing a plain, pale green suit, with a white silk shirt and pearls. She appeared glamorous as opposed to 'smart', and she leant with lazy self-assurance upon her fiancé's arm.

'What we're really after is the right house,' said Martin, with the air of a man with money to spend.

'Simon Fowler, in our Property Services department, would be more than happy to advise you on that one,' replied Mr Crimner. 'Whereabouts are you looking? In Bristol itself?'

'Yes,' said Marilyn, with a lovely smile, 'in Clifton . . .'

'Oh, there are some beautiful places up there, you're quite right. And you'd be surprised at the prices. A lot of those older properties are very big, even when they're turned into flats. How much were you thinking of spending?'

And so the conversation continued, pleasant and reassuring.

As they were leaving the bank, Martin and Marilyn felt as though they owned the world. Walking down the quiet street, where the architecture of four centuries blended into a single vista of gracious antiquity, the couple were aware of silver lamps twinkling beneath the evening sky and of a pale blue amphi-theatre on the heights of which was Clifton, encircling the dignified, elegant city. There seemed to be no darkness, only a soft grey light.

Martin and Marilyn were determined to 'get settled' before they got married. By this, they meant that they wanted to have made their home before they entered into the time-consuming administration of a wedding. Also, Martin did not want to irk his new employers by taking time off so soon after his arrival. In the mean time, their search for a home was accelerated by their growing dislike for the four little rooms which Martin was renting. As they regarded their life in Bristol to be laden with opportunities for comfort, the couple were eager to shake off the last vestiges of 'living out of a suitcase'. Usually, Marilyn would drive down to Bristol on each Thursday evening; then the couple would house-hunt throughout the weekend – punctuating this search with dinner at Marwicks, a grand restaurant in the new, sophisticated style. Finally, somewhat tired and depressed, Marilyn would return to London on the Monday morning.

'I hate leaving you,' she would say, as the weekday routine

recommenced. Sometimes, she would leave little notes for Martin in his suit pockets: *Counting the days*, or *Missing you madly*. Soon, Martin had quite a collection of these small slips of paper. He treasured these messages, not least because he was in love with Marilyn's neat, firm handwriting. She always wrote with a fountain pen, and she was conscientious about her grammar and spelling. In some ways, her secretly delivered billets-doux were her most intimate form of communication. Sitting in his small office at Resol with its black furniture and grey venetian blind, Martin would sometimes pause in his work and marvel at the good fortune that had brought him to his love. Even Dick Alryn had said, 'Your young woman friend is extremely attractive.'

At the end of July 1986, Martin and Marilyn bought and moved into their dream home. They were overjoyed with their purchase. It was the largest (occupying the entire first floor) of the three apartments in Ash House, a beautiful listed building which stood behind a row of protective cherry trees in a peaceful backwater of Clifton.

Ash House, like the terraces and mansions that surrounded it, was built of sandstone, and dated from the Georgian period. It was separated from its neighbours by an avenue of tall chestnut trees; and in summer, when the breeze came to lift the leaves and the blossom of these flowering giants, the fact that the house stood upon a hill was combined with a sense of leafy tranquillity, and this created an Olympian feel to the place as a whole. Ash House was built in the Classical style. Twelve large sash windows looked down from its mellow façade, and the low pediment that crowned its upper storey was given further character by a small circular niche. The enormous front door, as black as a gondola, was inlaid with six sunken panels, and there was an elegant fanlight of clear glass above it which neatly reflected the box-shaped lamp hanging above the chessboard tiles of the porch. A polished brass knocker, as heavy as it was antique, seemed to defy the uninvited to lift it.

Behind the house there was a well-kept lawn, and this was flanked on either side by a high wall which from May to September was ablaze with flowers of the climbing and creeping variety: coy, fragrant honeysuckle, spinning white garlands of gentle clematis and tumbling cascades of old-fashioned roses – their petals a shade of the palest of pinks and their thorns the colour of claret. A warm wave of scent washed over this lovely garden, which commanded a view of the whole city centre and was just a short stroll from the Avon Gorge.

Once inside Ash House, visitors were struck by the splendour of the hall. A buffed marble floor provided an elegant setting for a long mahogany table upon which stood a bust of Pericles. Behind Pericles, and glaring slightly from the gloom of a nigrescent background, the figure of William III, dressed in a scarlet costume and with his hand upon the hilt of his sword, could be seen within its frame of dulled gilt. It was as though, many people had commented, the stylish monarch was adjudicating the passage of those who walked before him. From the hall, there were three alternative routes: two through stout polished doors that led to the ground-floor flats and a third, more impressive still, up the broad, heavily banistered staircase to where Martin and Marilyn's property officially began. Halfway up this staircase there hung a huge painting in the style of Stubbs which depicted a sleek thoroughbred standing patiently beside its groom. It was an early joke between Martin and Marilyn to refer to this horse as 'Dobbin'. Two large windows let squares of sunshine onto the point where the staircase turned, and then, from the wide landing with its iron-bound chest and its two Japanese vases, a short corridor, carpeted in royal blue, led to the couple's front door.

Swiftly, Marilyn made the decoration of the apartment her sole concern. In this, she excelled. For nearly three months, while Martin worked late at the office, the determined young woman had a small team of decoraters working on each room in turn. This was an expensive business but, as Marilyn kept saying, 'it would be worth it in the end'. Sometimes, the upheaval was so chaotic that Martin and Marilyn preferred to stay in the Bristol Holiday Inn; and there, for two or three days at a time, they would meet in the evenings to picnic upon club sandwiches and champagne, brought to them by room service. It was, Martin would later think, an idyllic period. By the third week of September, however, the decoration of the apartment was almost complete.

One advanced through a square, compact hall, and almost at once there was a surprise in store, for this had been panelled in a pale wood, stained fresh-water green. The panelling stopped at shoulder height, and above it ivory-coloured walls took over. The spaciousness of this effect was set off to good advantage by a large potted plant with monstrous crimson leaves. Just inside the hall there was a low, oblong frame made of African hardwood, and this was an ingenious device in which umbrellas and boots could be left. The floorboards of the hall were bare and heavily varnished. They had been highly polished with lime-scented wax.

From the hall one passed in to the drawing room, and this was a triumph of Empire pastiche. Taking advantage of the high ceiling, and liberating from beneath many years of crudely applied gloss paint a delicate tracery of mouldings, Marilyn's eye for the grand had instantly recognised the potential for damson silk hangings and 'witty' gold paint. The two large windows were dressed with moss-coloured velvet curtains, which were gathered at their middle by tasselled sashes. In the evening, when the sun was setting over the city, the view from these windows was superb. During the early autumn, when Martin and Marilyn had finally taken possession of their finished home, they would sometimes sit for hours, with their fingers touching, and study this wonderful view. A burgundy-coloured carpet, with a rich, soft pile, gave off its timber-like odour of newness.

In the dining room, which was extremely large, Marilyn was

aided in her aesthetic scheme by two pre-existent features: a fireplace of pink Portuguese marble and a french window which gave access to a slender semi-circular balcony. The fireplace had required no assistance to draw attention to its grandeur, but Marilyn placed above it, with gentle conceit, a small portrait by S. J. Peploe. This painting, like Marilyn's money, had come from Aunt Jennie, and it was entitled simply 'Woman In Black Hat'. This was without question the most valuable object in the apartment. At the other end of the long room, above a graceful, satin-cushioned seat with arched back panels and slender, finely carved legs, there was a large gilt-framed mirror. The dining room was papered in 'silk-effect', with a subtle, milk-coloured stripe. The room was carpeted in pale green, and dominated by the vast rosewood table. The polish on this table was so deep as to create the illusion of a thin film of translucent liquid gently floating upon the flawless surface. The table could seat eight comfortably, and each place was marked with a matching high-backed chair. Those three guests who were facing the french windows could glance as they ate at the spectacular view. In the following months, Marilyn would sometimes say to her guests, 'You can see the church spire from . . .' (and the diner would be directed to turn slightly to the left) 'here. Isn't it lovely?' And the guests would agree that it certainly was, because Marilyn was so nice. A small chandelier hung primly above the dining-room table, and in the corners of the ceiling, eccentrically, there were small clusters of carved and painted pineapples. These, maintained Martin, were a nod to the Augustan.

Martin and Marilyn's bedroom was large and bright and airy. It was painted off-white. A wide bay window (the only such window in Ash House) looked out over the garden, and as the couple lay in bed they could see the lower branches of the chestnut trees. This reminded Martin of being on the bridge of a ship. The bedroom was furnished with a long antique dressing table which stood before the window (Marilyn's bottles of perfume and tortoise-shell vanity boxes stood upon this), and a broad, two-seated sofa upholstered in pale green and strewn with cream and gold satin-covered cushions. Upon a low, highly polished chest there stood a large blue and white china bowl, filled with fragrant pot-pourri. A tall Victorian wardrobe had its place on the other side of the room to the painted mantelpiece (a dark-wood-framed mirror above this); the wardrobe was enormous, with sliding rails for ties and glass-fronted cabinets for COLLARS. The bed, with its bank of white pillows and luxurious white duvet, was low, broad and set away slightly from the rear wall. A pile of new hardback books – biographies mostly – could usually be found beside Martin's side of the bed. At night, when the pretty, china-shaded lamps were creating a warm, low light, the atmosphere within this room was both tranquil and sensual. A bathroom, newly refurbished with an Edwardian-style bath, with brass and white-enamel fittings, was connected *en suite* to the couple's bedroom. This bathroom, which possessed a tall stained-glass window and some of its original maroon and white tiling, had been restored, in Marilyn's opinion, to the elegance of its period. A white wickerwork chair stood in one corner, a languid potted palm in the other. A large cupboard, with mirrored doors, was fastened to the wall above the wide, shallow washbasin. To either side of the basin there were grey marble sills, upon which stood a carefully selected range of fragrance- and colour-co-ordinated bathing lotions. An old-fashioned towel-rack with heated chromium pipes was hung with thick white towels. A small Victorian lamp, with a brass stand and frosted-glass shade, created a subdued glow in the evenings. This room was particularly perfumed, with a mixture of Marilyn's scents and Martin's aftershave.

Later, when visitors came to stay at Ash House, they were never invited to inspect the couple's bedroom and bathroom. This was not necessarily unusual, but it seemed to join in with other attitudes which implied that the display of Martin and Marilyn's life-style was over, and that one had received one's due, and that now one was utterly alone and unwanted – at least until breakfast time, when one's presence was required again, and the fragrance of Italian soap would drift in appealing ribbons from Marilyn's bath, mixing with the smell of Viennese coffee to fill the bright, echoing kitchen in a manner which inspired optimism. The kitchen was a triumph of artifice: high technology concealed within rustic fittings.

The remainder of the apartment was comprised of a moderately sized study – which contained many stacks of books waiting to be sorted, a writing desk, lamp and computer – and the guest bedroom and bathroom, both of which had been swiftly but tastefully wallpapered and furnished. Guests, faced with a wide double bed heaped with lace-trimmed pillows, and the bunches of dried roses standing upon the guest-room mantelpiece, and the chest of drawers lined with scented paper, and the ubiquitous bowl of pot-pourri, were instantly envious of Martin and Marilyn's comfortable home. In every room there were elegant details: ebony-framed engravings depicting local scenes or obscure eighteenth-century statesmen; carefully chosen antique chairs which had been bought inexpensively from sale rooms and then reupholstered; exotic, oriental and Indian mirrors, with heavy silver frames; and everywhere, pervading the apartment, a mixture of sweet and aromatic scents. The overall effect was that of pseudo-aristocratic sumptousness, rendered more interesting by ethnic and historic exotica. Josephine, to her daughter's fury, declared that the apartment looked like a cross between a country-house hotel and a set for a television costume drama.

'But that doesn't mean that it isn't successful,' she added, by way of apology.

Much of this success was due to the couple's supremacy at shopping. Shopping, in many ways, was the true foundation of their relationship, and as an activity it was never so much a chore or a routine to the young lovers as an expertly choreographed mining of moods. From the regular Friday-evening visits to the vast food halls or the hypermarket, where comfort – and excitement – could be found in the presence and acquisition of exquisitely packaged groceries and the magical patterns of identical products, through to the more refined pleasures of tracking down or discovering by chance individual items in one or other of the smaller shops, Martin and Marilyn knew no rivals when it came to the art of purchasing. A good day's shopping would amass both black olives in virgin olive oil and the latest records; or a terracotta bowl and a new brand of toothpaste. These purchases would then inform anew the atmosphere of the elegant apartment in Clifton; not merely as the fripperies of an affluent young couple, but as a tangible means by which Martin and Marilyn displayed and shared their love for one another.

One evening, towards the end of September 1986, Marilyn told Martin that shopping, for her, was an aphrodisiac. She said this in a playful manner, as though she was merely joking, but once she had transferred three bottles of Chilean wine into the crowded wine-rack, and placed her new burgundy-coloured suede shoes back into their wrapping of thick violet tissue paper, she underlined her comment by making love to her partner in a manner which stayed with him, as an intoxicating memory, for many years. Alone with their property, their shopping and their love, Martin and Marilyn believed that they had found true happiness, and began to plan their wedding.

As an idea, the thought of marriage had been shedding a benign, comforting light upon Martin and Marilyn's activities for nearly nine months. Now, established in their tasteful home, the couple were faced with the reality of this concept. At first, the expression 'when we're married' had served the young couple as a phrase that was capable of reflecting an entire spectrum of moods; now, as they faced one another over their flawless dining-room table and tried to arrange the practicalities of the event, they found themselves at a sudden loss. It seemed that however they tried to approach the 'big event', one or other of them felt uncomfortable with what they believed the style of the various versions of the proceedings could represent.

'How about a really big wedding,' suggested Marilyn, 'with all of our friends, and a . . .' she sought the right accompaniment to this plan, '. . . and a string quartet?'

'A string quartet?'

'Yes – in a marquee.'

'But we were thinking of doing it at Christmas. Who'd want to stand in a marquee at Christmas?' Martin chuckled at his fiancée's impetuosity.

Marilyn thought about this.

'Well, how about hiring an old church hall? Or a museum. Can't you hire a museum quite reasonably?'

'That's a good idea,' said Martin, slowly. He made a note, writing: *1): Museum* on the piece of paper before him.

'But then again,' said Marilyn, leaning forward on her elbows and resting her chin upon her fists, 'didn't Harry and Victoria have a museum?'

Martin tried to remember.

'You're right,' he said eventually, 'they did.' He crossed out *'Museum'*.

There was silence for a while, and Marilyn leant back in her chair and stared up at the ceiling. She looked as though she was in an examination, and trying to recall an elusive fact. At length she spoke.

'Doesn't the room look lovely in this light?' she said. 'I always love coming into this room, because it always looks different at different times of day.'

'We're straying from the point.' Martin smiled at Marilyn's sudden deviation from the matter in hand. She was wearing a voluminous navy-blue skirt which reached down to her knees, burgundy-coloured tights, a dark blue jumper and a pair of flat navy-blue shoes. She was also wearing a plum-coloured velvet hairband.

'You look like one of those girls you see in Fulham,' said Martin, unwisely, 'the sort who wear their boyfriends' shirts with pearls . . .'

Marilyn coloured. She hated to be ridiculed, even lightly. She snatched off the hairband and threw it across the room.

'There!' she said, with a forced smile. 'Better? Or shall I go and change completely?'

'Oh, I'm sorry; I didn't mean it like that . . .'

'Well . . .'

'Let's get on!' Martin feigned sudden energy. 'I know, let's work out the basic details first, and then worry about everything else later. Now, first thing: when do we want to get married?'

'Soon.'

'How soon?'

'What about . . . the first week of December?'

'You mean the first weekend?'

'Yes. Do you want some tea?'

'That would be lovely; hold on . . . the first weekend of December is the . . .' Martin looked in his diary. 'Yes. That would be fine. In fact, it would be more than fine . . .' There was no need for this sudden endorsement of the date; Martin was simply pleased to have sorted out the first detail. Marilyn rose from the table in order to make some tea. She paused for a moment, and looked out of the french window. It was late afternoon, and the city lights could be seen twinkling in the dusk; the garden looked bronze, and damp, and pungent. In the furthest corner, a patch of amber-coloured light from an unknown source could be seen diminishing upon the old garden wall. It was a Saturday, but Ash House was quiet.

'You can sort of feel the countryside,' said Marilyn. 'You can sort of know that it's there, like you can with the river at

239

home . . .' she checked herself; 'at my parents' home . . .' she said. 'I love the way Bristol is like a real town,' she continued; 'I mean, in London, unless you're in Knightsbridge or something, you feel as though you could get lost all the time. I know where I am in Bristol,' she finished, 'it's so nice . . .'

'I know what you mean,' agreed Martin. 'It's all on different levels – that's what I like; like the suspension bridge, and then all the different church spires; there's always a good view, wherever you are . . .' So far, neither Martin nor Marilyn had strayed beyond the city centre and the residential areas of Clifton and neighbouring Redlands. The more remote, less affluent districts of the city were unknown to them.

'Do you want: Earl Grey, Lapsang, jasmine, Green Gunpowder or ordinary?' said Marilyn.

'Oh, Earl Grey please . . .'

Marilyn departed to make the tea. Entering the kitchen, she switched on one of the concealed lights beneath a fitted cupboard, and then took out two teacups with matching saucers. These were made of fine china, and decorated with a parody of extravagant floral designs. They were printed on the inside with a detail from the head and shoulders of Michelangelo's 'David'. Having warmed the teapot and filled its matching milk jug, Marilyn then arranged the tray with her customary attention to detail. Some sweet Italian biscuits were placed upon a plate; three spoonfuls of Fortnum & Mason's Earl Grey tea were carefully dropped into the teapot. While she was waiting for the kettle to boil, Marilyn realised that she had more or less given up her idea of starting a small business. At the bank, she had obtained some relevant leaflets, but despite the friendly prose and easy-to-read graphics with which they offered advice to the would-be entrepreneur, Marilyn had quickly lost interest in them. She wished that she could simply be presented with a shop to run, in the manner that Truffles had entered her life. Marilyn liked shops; she didn't want to fiddle around with loans, and accountants, and business plans. Also, her capital was somewhat depleted.

In the dining room Martin, too, was thinking about procedures. At work he was forever coming across the word 'procedural', and trying to increase the efficiency of procedure whilst eliminating paperwork. Paperwork was one of Dick Alryn's greatest dislikes. 'Don't generate paperwork!' he would exclaim. 'It's boring and it's expensive. Our business is to make paperwork redundant!' Now, as Martin looked at the sheet of paper before him, with the word *'Museum'* crossed out upon it, he thought about the procedure of getting married. He remembered his sister's wedding, and how lacking in style he had considered it to be. Secretly, his sense of snobbery with regard to the image of an event was more acute in 1986 than it had been when he was a teenager. He wanted his wedding to be sophisticated, and flattering to his notion of himself. He even wondered, as he gazed thoughtfully at 'Woman In Black Hat', whether Marilyn's father would pay for the marriage to take place in Italy. Then, pondering his selfishness, he thought about other people's weddings: But they're just as selfish really, he thought. It's just that they're tacky and selfish . . . Who on earth invented those dreadful white wedding dresses, for instance? And who actually likes wedding cake? Quite suddenly, as though realising a threat, Martin was filled with hatred for the concept of traditional weddings. Thus, as Marilyn brought in the tea, he was complimenting himself on retaining what he considered to be a robust aesthetic sense. He crossed his legs and lit a cigarette; he felt as though he had reached a decision and, as a consequence, he was pleased with himself. He knew that he could never suggest an Italian nuptial, but the word 'sophisticated' had now allied itself in his mind with the word 'small'. Marilyn slid gracefully back onto her chair; her green eyes, thought Martin, looked bright and alluring beneath her dark eyebrows.

'Small,' he announced.

'I'm sorry?'

'Small. Wedding. That's what we'll do . . .'

Marilyn's face fell as she put down her teacup.

'I don't know that I want a small wedding,' she said; 'I think that . . .'

'No — wait a minute.' (Martin had a talent for 'selling' ideas, and he knew that his determination was infectious.) 'We want to get married at the beginning of December; most of our friends are in London, and we don't know what they'll all be doing or whether they'll be able to come down. We don't want to turn this place into a hotel for the weekend — and you *know* what it'll be like — and we can't very well ask some people but not others . . .' Martin was talking quickly now, and the vagueness of his argument was thus concealed. 'If we make it small, I mean, *very small*, with just your parents and my mother, we can avoid all that awful stuff with receptions and speeches, and people you've never heard of turning up with children, *and* you can avoid the wedding-dress syndrome . . .'

Marilyn smiled. 'What's the wedding-dress syndrome?'

'It's when you have to do lots of stuff just to please other people; don't you remember when we went to Caroline and Robert's, down in Dorset, and you said that you'd never seen Caroline looking so unhappy?'

'That was her hair! Her hair was awful!'

'Exactly.'

Marilyn laughed.

'I mean,' continued Martin, taking Marilyn's hand, 'I want you to have a lovely day, and to feel really special — if we have just a very small do, and then maybe a few of our closest friends for dinner . . . And you know perfectly well that you don't like white wedding dresses . . .' He smiled artfully at his yielding fiancée.

'We could take a private room at Marwicks . . .' she said, brightening.

'That would be great . . .'

'And I did see the most fabulous dress in . . .' Marilyn named a shop in Sloane Street.

'Buy it!'

'And then we can just leave, for the honeymoon . . .'

'And see the rest of our friends when we go up to Greenwich for New Year . . .'

Thus, by playing upon the received idea of 'small' as a token of sophistication, Martin convinced Marilyn that his plan (engendered, secretly, to avoid bad taste) was correct. Marilyn, who was thinking of clothes and shoes and her diet, was quickly won over.

'There's just one thing,' said Martin. 'We'll have to start going to church.'

'Oh yes – I suppose we will . . .' Marilyn looked doubtful for a moment. 'There's that really pretty one just down the hill,' she said. 'We could go there . . .'

A fortnight later, when the couple's plan had been received with relief by Bill, Josephine and Martin's mother, Marilyn spoke to Martin about her doubts with regard to starting a business. She didn't want to appear lazy, nor did she wish to seem beaten. Thus, she merely announced a postponement of her project.

'I think you're quite right,' said Martin. 'It would be dreadfully expensive, and if it went wrong you could lose an awful lot of money. You've really got to be able to afford to lose money, at first . . .'

'That's what I think.'

'Did you see this?' Martin passed a copy of *Business* magazine to his fiancée. On page 37 there was a photograph of Fenella, Martin's first love, clutching a silver trophy. She had just been awarded 'Young Businessperson of the Year' at a dinner in the City.

'But that's . . .' said Marilyn, reading the caption.

'Fenella – that's right; I didn't even recognise her at first . . .'

This was untrue; Martin had studied the photograph closely, and had thought that Fenella looked very attractive. To Marilyn, however, none of Martin's relationships prior to Francesca were any cause for real jealousy.

'Hasn't she got thick wrists,' said Marilyn, 'and man's hands . . .'

'Has she?'

'Yes – but she's very pretty . . .'

Martin and Marilyn were sitting up in bed, propped on pillows of luxurious depth and softness. It was just after midnight.

'The secret of being taken seriously,' said Martin, 'is to take yourself seriously. It's a trick I could never master,' he added. Martin had been proof-reading a Resol document, in bed, when this conversation began. His papers were now resting upon his bare chest whilst Marilyn studied the magazine.

'You were in love with her, weren't you?'

'I was very young . . .' Martin laughed.

'Did you sleep with her?'

'I think that in those days I considered sex to be a desecration of the beloved . . .'

'You mean she wouldn't let you,' said Marilyn, without looking at Martin. She was fascinated, however, to see this image of one of her finacé's legendary *amours*. Martin retrieved the magazine, and paused to look once more at Fenella's bright smile, frozen in black and white print.

'I can't remember why she won it, now,' he murmured.

'Cosmetics. It says so.'

'Oh . . .'

Marilyn ran her hand across Martin's chest; he slipped his arm about her.

'Am I as pretty as her?' asked Marilyn.

'Much more! You're beautiful; she's – well, she's attractive . . .' Martin hated himself for this disloyalty to his past.

Fenella had retained a brightness, over the years, which had seen the young romantic through some hateful nights of insomnia. He had not seen Fenella, he remembered, since the afternoon on the Heath when he had made his ludicrous presentation. But it wasn't ludicrous, he thought; it was probably the most generous gesture she's ever received . . . Marilyn's soft voice broke in on his thoughts; she wanted to dispel the pale spirit of Fenella.

'I love you,' she said, simply.

Martin asserted his love for her with equal conviction.

'I'll be so happy when we're married . . .' Marilyn continued, 'and I'll think about the business idea again in the New Year . . .'

'I'm sure that's right.'

They turned out the lights, and lay for a few minutes in one another's arms. The curtains were drawn back, and the low yellow moon, nearing its fullness, flooded the room with silver light. The dark shapes of the great chestnut trees could be seen against the blue night sky. As he was falling asleep, Martin returned to his memories of the sun-scorched Heath and the sight of Fenella, in her white man's shirt, disappearing out of view beneath the immense suburban sky. The following day, he attempted to write a poem, but gave up after the first three lines.

On the third Saturday of October 1986, at a little after four o'clock in the afternoon, Martin was making his way up Park Street, in the centre of Bristol, having just spent a pleasant two hours buying new books. Disliking the fashionable British novels of the period, which both he and Marilyn found boring, he had finally treated himself to the three-volume translation of *Remembrance of Things Past* by Marcel Proust. That morning, as Marilyn was discussing her plan to redecorate the study, which she felt had been passed over and looked dowdy, Martin had suddenly remembered the handsome volumes of Proust, and thought how splendid they would look stacked neatly beside the antique pen holder and paper-rack that his fiancée had recently bought. Not that his interest in the books was wholly cosmetic: as he perused the bookshop shelves, and then glanced through the first volume of the enormous novel, he had chanced upon the famous lines which conclude *Swann In Love*: 'To think that I've wasted years of my life, that I've longed to die, that I've experienced my greatest love, for a woman who didn't appeal to me, who wasn't even my type!' It was Martin's way to find most perfect and most artistic those statements in art that he believed expressed his own 'secret' story. In Proust, he hoped to find a fictional world in which he could lose himself throughout the winter months. It would be pleasant, for instance, to take Proust with him on the brief winter honeymoon – which would be spent in Vienna. In some ways, the couple's first choice of honeymoon city (Venice) would have been more Proustian; but Marilyn had been to Venice before, and said that it would probably be foggy in December. Martin, reluctantly, had agreed to Vienna as a seasonal alternative. Marilyn, who had been to Austria but not to its capital, was sure that Vienna would be pretty in winter.

In addition to Proust, Martin had bought a learned work which was published by one of the university presses and which was called *Playing The Game: The Spirit of Empire*, and a slim volume of verse by a much-discussed contemporary English poet. There was also a detective story for Marilyn, which was bound in a clever facsimile of its original dustjacket. Feeling the compact weight of these purchases as he carried them up the hill in their lustrous, claret-coloured carrier bag, Martin felt at peace with the world. Encountering a florist's shop that also sold exotic fruits, he went in and bought a large bunch of roses – so crimson as to seem almost black – and a pound of kiwifruit. The roses were wrapped in cellophane, and then again in stiff blue-and-white-striped paper.

'Can you manage the fruit in a bag?' the assistant asked.

'That's fine,' replied Martin, rearranging his parcels. His black wallet slipped smoothly down the satin lining of his overcoat, prior to resting in his inside pocket. Leaving the shop and turning up his collar, he could smell the rich perfume of his 'Frankincense and Myrrh' aftershave lotion. Then, beginning the long walk to Clifton, he inhaled the cold air with delight, and studied the effect of the autumn sunshine upon the venerable stone of the City Museum and Art Gallery. Once more, he delighted in the sense of civilised scale and order that he perceived the architecture of Bristol to express. The week had ended well at Resol, with a 'confidential talk' with Dick Alryn about the current COM project. Martin had emerged rather well from this discussion. He had identified, analysed and assessed a new competitor in Resol's field, and Dick had congratulated him.

'That's very helpful, Martin,' he had said, 'very helpful indeed. Work put in on these areas is never wasted, and I'd like you to present your report at the monthly finance meeting. Well done!'

With this success still glowing warmly in the back of his mind, Martin was now looking forward to receiving the weekend guests who would be arriving that evening. Julian and Paul, as a progressive gay couple, were always interesting, and Marilyn adored them. Julian worked in advertising, and Paul was a researcher for one of the television arts programmes. Martin was pleased to be entertaining a gay couple; it increased his sense of sophistication. Marilyn, while he had been shopping, was preparing a lavish dinner. She would have to 'pop out for some double cream', she had said, but the guests were not expected before seven o'clock. There would be time for a drink in the restfully lit, sumptuous drawing room, and then a late dinner. After that, Paul had promised to show the couple a rare film that he possessed on video, about the New York rock group The Velvet Underground. This, to Martin, was a perfect way to spend an evening. Thus, as he walked at a leisurely pace along the broad, tree-lined pavement, he was filled with a sense of good humour and well-being. His contentment, it seemed, was complete; his blessings appeared to interconnect, forming a sweep of happiness that was wholly unsullied by any anxieties or doubts. Wherever he looked in his mind, everything was in its proper place. He admired the trees and the houses and gardens as he walked along; he inhaled the smell of bonfires and damp grass; he sniffed at a cluster of three late roses which were overhanging a wall.

As he was nearing Ash House he noticed a tall, distinguished-looking young man who seemed to be vaguely familiar. The young man was wearing a green, calf-length overcoat, grey flannel trousers, an army pullover and brown brogues; his black hair was either thinning or watered back, and his fine features appeared both learned and well-bred. While he was approaching this figure, a succession of former acquaintances passed through Martin's mind, but none of them quite answered to the appearance of the young man who was strolling towards him. The stranger, too, was studying Martin, and his face was registering a similar struggle with recognition. When they were almost facing one another, however, the stranger said:

'Martin, Martin Knight?'

'Piers! I thought I recognised you!'

Pointlessly, the young men both laughed, and Martin put down his parcels in order to shake hands.

'How nice to see you,' said Martin, suddenly delighted by this chance meeting; encountering Piers seemed to add a final flourish to his mood of contentment.

'What are you doing in Bristol?' he continued. 'I thought you'd be an ambassador by now, or working for MI6 . . .' Without realising, he had slipped into the faint sarcasm which had distinguished his generation at Tiles.

'Well, I've been searching for your name in the newspapers too,' said Piers. 'Never found it though. What are you up to?'

'I asked first . . .'

'I'm working at the university – terribly dull . . .'

Martin looked interested, and lit a cigarette.

'Which bit of the university are you in?' he asked.

'Well, I'm linked to Modern Languages but lecturing in Linguistics – politically, it's rather difficult . . .' Piers, in fact, was the youngest lecturer that the university had ever employed. His teaching responsibilities were minimal; most of the time he was writing a radical story of semiotics. For Piers, post-modernism was a professional concern.

'What about you?'

Martin shrugged. 'I work in marketing,' he said, 'for an information-technology firm; I've been here about six months . . .'

As the conversation continued, Martin was aware that he wanted to make a close friend of Piers Harding; he felt as though his life lacked seriousness, and he envisaged pleasant talks with the Tiles genius in which philosophical arguments could be explored and matters of aesthetics discussed. Piers, briefly and modestly, told Martin about the three universities which he had attended since leaving school. His work appeared to be funded by a quantity of generous scholarships. Martin was not quite sure whether he envied this progress or not. Piers looked prosperous enough; and Martin dimly recalled that Harding's father was a bishop – or a judge.

They began to talk about books – prompted by Martin's shopping – and Martin, feeling unprepared, suggested to Piers that they meet for dinner the following week.

'I live up in Clifton,' said Martin, 'with my girlfriend – well, fiancée actually . . .'

'Oh, congratulations.'

'Would next Friday suit you? For dinner?'

'I think that would be fine . . .'

Addresses and telephone numbers were exchanged; the two Old Boys shook hands once more.

Pleased with this encounter, Martin hurried home. He suddenly realised that he would be needing a best man.

*

When he reached Ash House and discovered Marilyn surrounded by the debris of her cooking, Martin told her about his meeting with Piers. Marilyn was pleased that Piers would be coming for dinner the following week: she enjoyed entertaining. For that evening's meal, she had prepared *Tomato and Mint Soup*; a 'fun' dish of *Liver and Locally Cured Bacon with Sweet Onions*; and an extravagant *Raspberry Pavlova*. A *Selection of English Cheeses*, bought from the Speciality Cheese Shop, would punctuate the main course and dessert. Champagne, two bottles of Rooster Hill Cabernet Sauvignon and a bottle of Sauterne would accompany the dinner. This was a dinner in the grand style, and Marilyn had dressed her dining room accordingly, with crimson and gold place-mats, heavy silver cutlery, crystal glasses and four thick white candles, held in tall candlesticks of 'modern' twisted and distressed iron. Marilyn loved to create such displays, and to provide little touches of the unusual. This delight in the details of entertaining was shared by Martin, who knew how to thank and compliment his fiancée in a manner that made her feel all the more triumphant. In the past, when guests had roguishly asked whether 'Martin just did the washing up', the couple had exchanged fond glances. 'We have an arrangement,' Marilyn would say, mysteriously, and then people would comment, 'Oh yes?' in a laughing, suggestive tone of voice. Thus, Martin and Marilyn looked forward to their dinner parties as events which made them feel more loving, and more intimate. These functions were vital to holding their relationship in place. They went with the range of shower gels and the Old Master drawings, reproduced in lavender-coloured ink, which could be seen within black frames above the washbasin in the guest bathroom.

That evening, Paul Edge and Julian Summers arrived at Ash House shortly after seven. It was the first time that they had visited Bristol.

'Isn't it fabulous!' called Paul, as he made his way up the broad staircase towards his smiling hosts.

'We were looking for the postcard-rack in the hall; or a woman selling guidebooks,' added Julian, following him. Julian was thirty years old, tall, well-built and fair; Paul was twenty-seven, shorter than his partner, and had closely cropped black hair which emphasised his wide smile. Julian was wearing a dark green tweed suit, with a black polo-necked jumper and suede shoes; Paul, more casually, was dressed in jeans, a thick crimson pullover, black workmen's boots and a heavy navy-blue wool coat. On his head there was a forester's khaki hat, with fur-lined ear-flaps. The two guests were in high spirits, having driven at excessive speed from London.

'Getting out of Islington took us nearly as long as getting down the motorway,' groaned Julian, as he carried his small suitcase into the hall.

'God knows what was happening in the West End – it was solid, everywhere . . .'

'It's just Saturday,' said Julian, 'nightmare; traffic from hell – God, what a beautiful flat!'

Martin and Marilyn welcomed their guests, and a few moments were spent in the removal of coats and cases to the guest room.

'This is fabulous,' called Paul, 'it's enormous . . .'

'Would you like some tea?' asked Marilyn.

'Oh, that would be great.'

'We've got: Earl Grey, Lapsang, jasmine, Green Gunpowder, or ordinary . . .'

'Oh . . . Earl Grey please,' said Julian.

Marilyn disappeared into the kitchen. She was wearing a short, sleeveless black dress, black tights, low black shoes and black earrings. An expensive man's watch gleamed upon her left wrist. Martin was wearing a white shirt with cut-away collars, a pair of charcoal-grey pinstripe trousers, a thick black belt, tartan socks and black brogues.

'We haven't seen you for ages,' said Julian, dropping heavily onto the drawing-room sofa, 'but this is really nice . . .' He glanced about the room.

'Marilyn did a lot of work on it,' said Martin, 'and we're really pleased . . .'

'For a place this size you'd pay at least two hundred thousand in Holland Park,' said Julian, exaggerating the sum slightly in order to pay a subtle compliment.

'Thankfully, it wasn't that much,' said Martin, 'but we love it. The building's really quite old, and it hasn't been too mucked around. You can't see now, but there's a fabulous view.'

'Are you anywhere near that big bridge?'

'Yes, it's just over there − we'll have a look in the morning . . .'

Marilyn came in bearing tea, swiftly followed by Paul. Paul was the more boisterous of the two guests, and he teased Marilyn continually, in a way that made her cry with laughter. It was rare to see Marilyn lose her reserve and Martin, despite himself, was pleased that no heterosexual male could entertain her so thoroughly. He liked Paul and Julian tremendously, and could not be jealous of Marilyn's fondness for them. She had known Julian in Greenwich, and the friendship had survived.

Sitting back in a tall, Victorian armchair, Martin sipped his tea and studied his guests: the conversation was flowing easily, and gathering strength; no awkwardness threatened. Marilyn, kneeling beside the tiled fireplace, looked pretty as she poured her own tea. The scene, thought Martin, was both friendly and dignified. He relaxed, warmed by happiness.

Dinner, too, was a great success. Marilyn's cooking was richly complimented, and Paul and Julian proved themselves to be considerate and appreciative guests. The conversation covered mutual acquaintances, the turmoil of London in comparison to the calm of Bristol, television, offices, foreign holidays and house prices. Thus, no one was left out.

The *Raspberry Pavlova* was greeted with little gasps of joy; Marilyn offered to pass on her recipe.

'You said that you'd give me your recipe for *California Sponge*,' said Julian, wistfully, 'and you never did . . .'

'The *California Sponge* is a secret,' said Marilyn, laughing.

'Bet it's out of a packet,' said Paul.

'You can go without if you don't shut up!' replied Marilyn. 'There!' She banged a slice of *Pavlova* onto Paul's plate, and feigned a *moue* of sulky reproach.

'This is better than sex,' said Julian, as the raspberries, cream and meringue melted in his mouth.

'It's instead of sex,' said Paul.

The four white candles made a pavilion of brightness around the dinner table; at the far end of the room, glinting in the shadows, the marble fireplace created an impressive backdrop. The diners each had before them a glass of rich, golden dessert wine; contentment and good humour enveloped the four young people. From time to time, Martin would offer assistance to his fiancée in a low murmur, and then Marilyn would pat his arm, or rest her hand on his shoulder, to express her gratitude for this consideration.

'Does Martin chain you up in the kitchen, then?' asked Paul.

'Only when I let him.'

'We're becoming terribly conservative,' said Martin.

And thus the conversation turned to politics.

'I don't know who I hate the more, the Left or the Right,' said Julian; 'on the one hand I loathe *that woman* from the bottom of my soul; but then, in other ways, I'd sooner have a lot of clients who are prepared to pay for expensive campaigns, than be looking for a job . . .'

'You're just a New Reactionary,' said Paul, 'I think . . .'

'But so are you! Think how pissed off you were about the lefties in your office; you said that they were all up their own backsides . . .'

'What I said,' said Paul, 'was that they seem to think that they've got a monopoly on virtue . . .'

'And then there was that woman who said you "ought to have a voice", because you were gay . . .'

'Oh, well, that was just sickening . . .'

Martin listened to this exchange with a mixture of curiosity and amusement. His own politics were wholly vague: by temperament, he was an élitist and a snob; by nature, he was sentimentally concerned about social injustice. He despised the fashionable Left, whom he regarded as under-achievers determined to take the romance out of life and instigate a herd-like mentality of naïve self-righteousness; similarly, he found the arrogance and pomposity of some of his wealthier acquaintances equally loathsome. In short, he followed his vague aesthetic course – which he now regarded as post-modern – and this was the cult of finding meaning in surfaces. He was nervous, however, of trying to explain his position. He wondered what Marilyn's father would have said.

'Have you seen any of the new Scottish painters?' he asked.

'Not personally,' said Paul.

'They do these big paintings which often depict lost hikers, or characters becoming the victim of their own confusion; on the one hand they're terribly traditional, but on the other they're subverting the whole notion of confidence and direction. They're very romantic, I suppose, but hugely relevant . . .'

'Quite,' said Julian. 'But there's nothing new about being lost, you know; most of our clients don't really know what they want – they're just trying to shift a product, and we invent images that will make them feel more secure about it . . .'

'But don't you sometimes feel that it's all coming to an end? That "the centre cannot hold"; and that nothing matters any more, in the deepest sense?' Martin realised that this thought was poorly expressed.

'I'm not quite sure what you mean – but everything matters if it didn't, then we wouldn't be having this conversation . . .'

'It's a very easy conversation to have, when we're sitting here in the lap of luxury,' said Paul. 'There's a bit in E. M. Forster,' he continued, 'where he talks about certain people standing upon their money "as though on islands" – we don't know anything really, not with our islands of money . . .'

Marilyn sighed. 'But you work bloody hard for it,' she said.

Julian laughed. 'I don't,' he said. 'I just sit in an office in Charlotte Street and wait for the phone to ring.'

The following Friday, when Piers Harding came to dinner, Martin raised his fears that 'nothing mattered' once more. He knew that he was seeking a simple, slogan-like answer to a complex and amorphous question. Piers, who was wearing a dark blue suit and a Harvard University tie, seemed disinclined to take Martin's worries particularly seriously. On several occasions he let the issue drop, and turned to ask Marilyn questions about herself, which pleased the young woman. Martin, however, returned to matters of philosophy while Marilyn was fetching the *Toffee and Pecan Flan*.

'But where does post-modernism lead?' he asked, earnestly; 'we're bombarded with information and signals . . .'

Piers blinked at his host, and smiled. 'I'm afraid that I can only answer one massive generalisation with another,' he said. 'Try to think of post-modernism as a means, as opposed to an end. Stick to it as an aesthetic theory – romanticism in a suit, if you want; ethically, it simply dictates that an individual loses his subjective autonomy, and becomes a mere transmitter of other people's ideas. That's quite neat, but it has some far-reaching, rather serious consequences . . . Or it would have, if it held water . . .'

Marilyn returned with the dessert.

'So post-modernism doesn't matter?' said Martin, hopelessly.

'I wouldn't say that; but it's a hugely misused term. Gosh! That looks good!'

Marilyn smiled.

'There's some *Vanilla Custard* too,' she said, departing once more.

'Marilyn's extremely nice,' said Piers. 'You've picked a goodun there.'

'Yes . . .' said Martin, vaguely. He felt rather foolish.

When dinner was finished and the three young people were sitting in the drawing room drinking their coffee, Martin asked Piers about the book that he was writing.

'Oh, you don't want to know about that,' said the academic, embarrassed. 'Let's sing the old-school song or something instead . . .'

'I'd be really interested to hear about it,' said Marilyn. She liked Piers.

Thus, in a tone of voice which suggested that his work was neither interesting nor important, Piers delivered a brief synopsis of his arguments.

'Assuming the importance of Hegel,' he began. He knew these words so well, for they had been playing a tantalising rhythm in his mind for nearly four years. His hosts, however, were baffled by his thesis. Martin, not wishing to appear stupid, nodded from time to time as Piers mentioned Saussure, Foucault, Merleau-Ponty or Derrida, but he could only follow those parts of the argument that he could visualise, as a narrative. Marilyn looked at the carpet.

'You ought to meet my father,' she said, finally. 'He's into all that . . .'

'I've read his book,' Piers replied. 'Or is there a new one?'

'I'm not quite sure – probably . . .'

And the conversation, to the visible relief of the guest, turned to less exclusive subjects. Outside, an early frost was stiffening the drifted leaves; the night sky was clear over Bristol, and the air smelt of cold. As Marilyn began to tell Piers about the forthcoming wedding, Martin realised that he had encountered his intellectual ceiling. He knew that he would never be able to follow the arguments which his friend had propounded, no matter how many books he might read; and this was because his mind, he believed, was not constituted to hold opinions. Images and dramas alone could activate his imagination, and lead him down the way of the interesting towards the beautiful: Marilyn's profile and body, certain music or paintings, the play of weather upon the surroundings, an attitude embodied in a form, however abstract – these things engaged him. Thus, as he sipped his coffee, Martin felt frustrated. This slight depression caused him to interrupt the conversation. He wanted to 'acquire' Piers, or, at least, his ambience.

'I say, Piers,' he said, suddenly, 'would you mind being my best man?'

Marilyn laughed.

'Nothing like the subtle approach,' she said.

Piers looked surprised.

'I mean,' continued Martin, 'it's going to be a very small do, so you wouldn't have to do anything – but I'd be really grateful . . .'

'Well . . . I'm very flattered,' said Piers, putting down his coffee cup carefully, 'but are you sure? Isn't it meant to be someone you'd trust to look after your wife, in the event of a fatal accident or what have you?'

'Perhaps. But I'm sure you'd be terribly good at it. You won't have to make a speech or anything. You just stand next to me, and hold the ring . . .'

Piers, who was as envious of Martin's domestic comfort and happiness as Martin was of his intellectual prowess, was suddenly drawn to the smiling couple. Marilyn had moved to sit on the floor, with her back resting against Martin's knees, and she too was smiling encouragement at him. They look so vulnerable, thought Piers, and yet they seem to have so much, and each other . . . His own life was emotionally barren.

'It's very kind of you both,' he said, smiling, 'and if you really want me to, I'd be honoured.'

'That's settled then,' said Martin.

'You'll have to meet Catherine – who's looking after me,' said Marilyn.

The couple's wedding now dominated the conversation. Piers, politely, expressed an interest in all of the details. Secretly, he was rather bewildered by Martin's sudden invitation. The request had contained a slightly desperate edge, he thought, yet at the same time it had made him feel sorry for the young couple. He searched, mentally, for the right way to describe this impression to himself. It's bad form, he thought, finally. But he detected the touch of Tiles in this criticism.

Shortly before Piers departed, Marilyn showed him the brochure which depicted Sacher's Hotel, in Vienna, where the couple would be spending their honeymoon.

'Oh yes . . .' said Piers, 'it's the birthplace of *Sachertorte* – the recipe's kept in a safe, you know '

'Heavens!' said Marilyn. 'Isn't there anything you don't know?'

On the morning of his wedding day, Martin Knight received two letters from his bank. Marilyn, respecting tradition, was at her parents' house in Greenwich; her groom, having spent a restless night troubled by vivid dreams, was thus breakfasting alone as he studied the morning's mail – as though through a sheet of thick glass. The first of the bank's letters was signed personally by the manager, and it congratulated Martin and Marilyn, 'as established customers', on their marriage; the second letter, dispatched by an unfeeling computer, requested 'immediate funds' to restore the couple's current account 'to its agreed limit'. This letter, too, was signed personally by the bank manager.

'Well, of all the . . .' But Martin, who was tired and nervous, could not find the right words to express his outrage. The problem was not a serious one, but it soured the cold, grey morning. The couple had spent a great deal of money; but there was still £21,000 in Marilyn's building-society account, and the thought of this, superficially, took the edge off Martin's worry. The honeymoon, however, would be expensive: Bill and Josephine were paying for the tickets and the hotel as a wedding present, but Martin was taking £1,200 in traveller's cheques to ensure that the week would be as carefree as it was luxurious. He had sometimes felt, as he calculated their budget, that he and Marilyn were running a large, expensive machine to the limit of its powers: mortgage, credit cards, bank accounts and countless minor subscriptions to different services all added up to a considerable out-going. Of late, it seemed, the couple were always a little, but not very, hard up. In order to keep some capital in reserve, they had agreed to further borrowing and increased limits, without really counting the cost. The extra few per cent of interest which they paid for these extended facilities had never seemed to amount to very much. Despite Martin's talent for business, he was wholly incapable of monitoring his own financial affairs with anything other than a cursory glance; it was almost as though he considered prudence with regard to money to be vulgar, or an admission of failure. Extravagance, and detachment from the sobering truths of income and expenditure, were necessary to his illusion of opulence. His greatest rages were directed at those who quibbled over the division of a restaurant bill. Thus, as he looked at the two letters from the bank on the morning of his wedding day, his final pronouncement upon them was:

'What a bore . . .'

He sighed this observation, self-consciously. He would simply have to transfer some funds from one account to another upon his return from Austria. The little problem would be dealt with, but the letters had tainted Martin's mood.

*

The small wedding passed without incident. Later, Martin was surprised to discover that he could remember very little about it. Piers, dressed in a charcoal-grey suit (for the wedding was not formal), had arrived to collect the groom at a little after two o'clock in the afternoon. The couple's suitcases were standing in the hall, ready to be taken to the airport hotel after the evening's dinner party. Martin, wearing a double-breasted suit of black wool with a white shirt and crimson tie, had been watching television when his best man arrived. There seemed to be very little for Piers to do. The young men did not really know one another very well, and thus there was little chance for either confidences or sentimentality. Piers, in fact, felt rather as though he was taking a minor part in an amateur production of a dull play.

Martin, for his part, was straining to find some significance in the day. Having dressed that morning, and checked through his list of Jobs to Do on the computer, he had then attempted to review his life and find some dramatic resolution to its progress in the service that was about to take place. He was excited, but he could not feel resolved; the day, somehow, remained commonplace. He began to panic. What if I don't really love her? he thought, lighting a cigarette. And then he noticed a pair of Marilyn's shoes nestling beside the sofa, and accused himself of being ridiculous. I expect it's quite usual for people to feel strange on their wedding day, he thought. He also recalled that there was a passage in one of F. Scott Fitzgerald's novels which testified to this.

Marilyn, too, was tired. She had driven down to Bristol with Catherine and her parents feeling worn-out and irritable. She was looking forward to the evening's dinner party, when she would see some of her old friends, but her head ached and the skirt of her new suit was an inch too long.

'Are you all right?' Catherine would say, from time to time, anxiously glancing at Marilyn as Bill Fuller's large, battered estate car hurried down the motorway.

'Just so long as there isn't a traffic jam,' said Marilyn, smiling weakly.

Josephine, throughout the day, maintained a tranquil smile of vague amusement.

Martin's mother, dressed in a grey suit and wearing a new blue coat, had cheerfully insisted that she would 'make her own way' to the wedding. There was a sadness in this independence which greatly troubled her son. Since the death of her husband, Mrs Knight had vigorously applied herself to voluntary work and evening classes. To Martin she still appeared young, and she would always laugh gently at his concern for her. Busying herself with her own routine, she presented an image of constancy to her sensitive, selfish son. She was pleased that he was prospering, and she liked Marilyn – whom she had met twice – but her calm, practical temperament never seemed to vary. Thus, whilst Martin sought to explore what he considered to be extreme states of mind, his mother represented rootedness and security. Martin's sister, who now had two small children, had sent her brother a cut-glass bowl and a card which wished the newly-weds 'much happiness on their wedding day'. The bowl was placed in the study.

The mellow Anglican church, with its finely pointed spire, was pretty and prosperous. Piers Harding, in fact, could not help thinking that it seemed only to lack a blue and white bowl of pot-pourri to complete its ambience of comfortable good taste. The vicar, who was as comfortable and affable as his church, bestowed benign greetings upon the small congregation. His tone was one of cheerful informality as he proceeded through the wedding service; with a rehearsed quip, he explained to the small company that they would dispense with the traditional hymns and confine themselves, as he put it, 'to the real business of the day'. Including Martin and Marilyn, the wedding party consisted of seven people: Bill, still wearing his long raincoat, stood in the second pew with his arms folded; he appeared to be studying the service as opposed to participating in it. Josephine, by his side, held her prayer book as though she was looking after it for a friend. Mrs Knight, alone on the other side of the aisle, looked pleased, tired and respectful. Catherine, more emotional than the bride, was overcome with nervousness and had to keep on clearing her throat. Piers, politely bewildered, performed his single duty in a manner which suggested obedience to an irrational procedure. The vicar's friendly voice boomed loudly in the large, empty church, which was lit by concealed spotlights against the dark afternoon. The air was filled with the scent of flowers and musty hymnbook bindings. It was cold.

Marilyn, to Martin, looked grave and beautiful as she took her place beside him. Her father, having given her away, had then returned to his pew – a lapse in etiquette that was overlooked by the vicar. Marilyn's expensive new suit was ivory-coloured. She wore this with a thin, cream-coloured jersey with a high, simple collar and a string of pearls. Her copper-brown hair was newly cut, and her make-up was limited to a touch of colour upon her cheeks and a pale, lustrous lipstick. She could have been attending an interview for a job. But when she said 'I do,' in a low, calm voice, Martin felt his throat tighten and tears prick his eyes. For here was his companion for life: young, determined, wise and beautiful; here, apparently, was the conclusion to his restless search for happiness and beauty.

Later, Martin would think how typical of his life it was that he hardly knew his best man.

Vienna, warmed by its mildest winter in thirty years, was fog-bound and damp. Martin and Marilyn, arriving for their honeymoon, were slightly disappointed to be greeted by thin drizzle, as opposed to thick snow or clear frosty air. Their taxi drove cautiously down the dual carriageway which separated the city from the airport; in the middle of the afternoon the mist was dense, and all that could be seen were low concrete walls and the muted red and white lights of the other cars.

'I can never believe that you haven't been abroad before,' said Marilyn, squeezing her husband's hand. 'You always seem as though you've been everywhere . . .'

Martin was flattered by this. He was dazed by the rapid succession of events which had led the couple to this fog, and he felt as though he was trying to catch up with himself. The wedding night, spent at one of the vast, modern airport hotels where all the restaurants offered a twenty-four-hour range of meals – from breakfast to a four-course *à la carte* dinner – had seen the newly-weds behaving as though they had just survived a wearisome and trying day. At first, as they stood alone in their large, featureless room and stared at the shrink-wrapped bottle of presentation champagne, they had barely spoken. They were both excessively polite to one another and as they unpacked their overnight bags – sensibly kept separate from the main luggage – they squeezed past one another between the wardrobe and the bathroom saying, 'I'm sorry' and 'My fault' in forced, cheerful voices. They had arrived at this hotel at two o'clock in the morning, and were due to check in for their flight at noon that day. They were both exhausted, yet neither of them felt sleepy. Finally, after they had ordered some coffee and sandwiches – for the sake of something to do – Marilyn flopped down upon the large bed and Martin, feeling nervous, had sat beside a long, sealed window and smoked a cigarette. Neither of them wished to test the other's emotions. They talked about commonplace things; they agreed that it had been nice to see some of their old friends. Presently a waiter arrived with the coffee and sand-wiches.

'It's a shame that Hugo and Henrietta couldn't make it,' said Marilyn, rearranging her 'going away' skirt in order not to crease it.

'But their telegram was funny —'

'What did it say again?' asked Marilyn, smiling.

'"Are detained, don't wait,"' said Martin, chuckling. He loosened his tie, and poured his bride some coffee.

'The sandwiches look pretty deadly,' said Marilyn.

'They've given us a sachet of mustard though — and some Daddy's Sauce . . .'

'How attractive.'

Martin laughed. Slowly, he could feel his confidence returning. All day he had felt detached and empty-headed; now, in the modern, impersonal bedroom, he could feel the beginnings of intimacy once more. He wanted to tell Marilyn that he loved her, or to make love to her, but he was still fearful of what her reaction might be. It's silly, he thought, as he looked at the cold blue letters of the neon sign upon the hotel roof, we've lived together, and yet I feel as though we've never been alone together before . . . He wondered what Marilyn was thinking.

'Why don't you come over here?' said Marilyn. 'You seem so far away . . .'

Martin extinguished his cigarette, and the couple lay down together. Having turned off the lamps, the bedroom was immediately filled with neon illumination.

'Have you booked a wake-up call?' murmured Marilyn.

'For ten.'

Despite the sound-proofing of the hotel bedroom, the roar of departing and landing aircraft was constant. From where he was lying on the bed, Martin could see the perimeter fencing of the airport, and long lines of white, violet and orange lights, some of which were moving. All this activity seemed distant. Marilyn was lying with her head upon his chest, and one of her slender arms draped over his shoulder. Her eyes were closed, and her breathing was becoming more regular. Soon, uncomfortable in her bridal lingerie, she fell asleep.

By the time that they landed in Vienna and made their way

264

through the white fog towards their famous hotel, Martin and Marilyn felt more relaxed. They were determined to enjoy themselves, and greeted their suite with sighs of approval and childlike, irreverent giggles. The suite was vast; marble, thick blue carpets and large, gilt-framed mirrors predominated. The bed, Marilyn calculated, was nearly the size of the guest bathroom at Ash House. Three tall windows, facing a main street, were hung with heavy velvet curtains. An extravagant flower-stand contained a large bouquet. The television was hidden inside an antique cabinet, as was the mini-bar. The windowless bathroom was panelled. A sitting room, complete with heavy furniture, an oil painting of the Empress Elizabeth and a cocktail cabinet, was connected to the bedroom by a white panelled door which swung noiselessly on well-oiled brass hinges. It was a grand hotel in the old style, and the corridors, reception areas, bars and dining room all displayed undiluted luxury.

'The grander a hotel is,' said Martin, carefully, 'the smaller and more mirrored the lift.'

Respectful bell-boys, with their white gloves threaded neatly under the epaulettes of their jackets, stood to attention beside the long reception desk. Young men in tailed coats strode briskly about their business, efficiently handling the daily administration of the hotel. Martin felt at home in these luxurious surroundings and his good humour communicated itself to Marilyn. Inspired by this elegance, he courted his pretty young wife with all the romance that he could muster: on the second morning, he went for a walk on his own — solely to have a large bouquet delivered to the suite, where Marilyn was washing her hair; £400 was spent, in two minutes, on a bracelet which Martin presented to Marilyn concealed in a box of white chocolates. The bracelet was studded with amethysts.

Sexually, the couple exploited the luxury and size of their suite.

But with regard to Vienna itself the newly-weds were swiftly rather bored. The city was smaller than they had imagined, and neither of them had researched the history or the geography of the place prior to their arrival. Also, the fog remained. The couple looked at the statue of Mozart in the Stadtpark, but their visit was brief, for the morning was damp; they made their way to the Votivkirche, and passed twenty minutes exploring its dim aisles and side-chapels; they thought that they recognised locations from *The Third Man*; they took taxis to Schonbrunn, where Mozart had played for the Empress, and to the Belvedere, which was closed. The weather conspired against extended sightseeing.

They found the shops dull.

'The clothes are dreadful, as well as expensive,' said Marilyn, as she looked at a display of brightly patterned jumpers. 'I wonder what the young people do . . .'

'Visit Carnaby Street in their hordes.'

'In fact,' said Marilyn, as they resumed their afternoon's walk, 'it's a terribly middle-aged city . . .'

'I suppose so; but some of the buildings are fabulous – they're so grand . . .'

'But it all blends into one after a while – like the cakes. If I see another cake . . . My poor diet must be ruined . . .'

After a little while Martin said:

'But we don't have a café-culture like this; we've got pubs instead . . .'

'That's true. I love Sacher's though; I could happily live there . . .' said Marilyn.

'For about a thousand pounds a week you can.'

Thus, Martin and Marilyn spent most of their honeymoon luxuriating at Sacher's.

The city of Freud, Mahler and Mozart carried on its business beyond the couple's tall windows. Living off room service and watching the Music Channel on their wide-screen television, Martin and Marilyn commenced their marriage. Their relationship, as ever, was both informed by, and a reaction to, their immediate surroundings.

They returned to Bristol in time to plan for Christmas. They had spent £900 of their traveller's cheques. Returning the remaining £300 to their bank account, Martin congratulated himself on not being too extravagant.

Seven: *Everything Matters*

Christmas Day 1986 found the newly-weds encased within a cocoon of untypical solitude. They awoke late on Christmas morning, and exchanged presents while still in bed. Marilyn gave Martin an antique fountain pen and a pair of enamelled cuff-links. Martin gave Marilyn a long 'Polo' raincoat (which she had chosen herself) and a pair of pink suede gloves. They had decided not to spend too much.

In the afternoon they went for a walk. Standing upon Clifton Suspension Bridge, they gazed down at the city of Bristol. Far below them, following the course of the river, speeding cars could be seen, their headlights making tiny fans of yellow light. The buildings, old and new, appeared grey, and touched by a bluish mist; between them, orange and violet lights denoted the main streets; irregular patches of darkness completed the twilit tapestry. The sky was grey and heavy, but a low bar of ivory-coloured cloud was lying across the horizon. The suspension bridge with its towering, capped piers was now illuminated; it appeared to hang above the Avon Gorge, floating in blue darkness. Distances became difficult to gauge. From time to time a cold wind caused the couple to bury their chins in the collars of their overcoats.

'Someone was telling me at work,' said Martin, 'that when people jump off this bridge, their weight in relation to the drop makes them pile-drive into the mud on the riverbed. They suffocate as opposed to drown . . .'

Marilyn pulled a face.

'I'm getting rather cold,' she said.

The couple walked briskly back towards the lights of Clifton. The elegant streets were quiet, and the houses looked as though they were asleep. Somehow, on Christmas Day, the decorations of holly and scarlet ribbon that hung upon some of the front doors appeared desolate and redundant.

'The period between Christmas and New Year is always so strange,' said Martin. 'I remember when I was at RDS, and used to have to work just after Christmas, the City was like a vast, deserted film set. It seemed to go with the cold. I rather liked it.'

'Carmen and I always used to fight on Boxing Day,' said Marilyn. 'She had this way of finding my favourite present, and making fun of it. It didn't matter what it was – a doll, a book, a dress . . . She'd just start finding fault with it; and she wouldn't know when to stop . . . Do you know what I mean? It was really awful.'

Carmen was now living in Toronto, and the sisters seldom corresponded. Martin had never met her. But he enjoyed hearing stories about Marilyn's childhood; they seemed to make the young woman more precious, and rare.

It was dark when they reached Ash House.

'I'm going to have a long, hot bath,' said Marilyn, 'and then we can watch that film.'

In February 1987 Martin and Marilyn went to visit Martin's mother at Thornby Avenue.

The suburb, Martin noticed, was changing. Many of the larger, older houses had been demolished, releasing valuable plots of building land. On the site of an Edwardian house and garden, twelve identical town houses could be built. New crescents, closes and culs-de-sac proliferated. But certain landmarks of

Martin's childhood remained: the short lane where, years earlier, the aesthete's opera programme had decomposed was untouched; a tall sycamore tree, which overhung the entrance to the Heath, was still standing; Carew Road retained its patch of resurfaced tarmac that looked like a bearskin rug. The small parade of shops, which stood half a mile from Martin's house, had been replaced by two three-storey office buildings. Neither of these was occupied. They were like empty boxes. Their dim, pristine interiors contained neither desks nor computers; loose wires sprouted from their white walls.

'It's ridiculous,' said Martin's mother. 'They're knocking down all the old buildings, yet no one's moving into the new ones. And the price of the houses! Those little places on the other side of the road are seventy-two thousand pounds! And they're much smaller than this. I don't know where these young couples get their money . . .'

'People earn far more these days,' said Martin.

Marilyn nodded, but looked bored.

'It's the same at the top of the High Street,' continued Mrs Knight. 'Wilson's has gone, and the old music shop . . . That whole block has been taken over by a supermarket, and a multi-storey car park. No wonder the little businesses can't compete, and go to the wall. All the character goes. And they've turned the Arcade into a precinct, with all the same shops that you find everywhere – you might as well be anywhere . . .'

'I suppose people want to live close to London,' said Marilyn, 'and then commute . . .'

'But the trains have always been dreadful,' said Mrs Knight.

'I can vouch for that,' said Martin.

'Well, we're happy to be out of it,' said Marilyn. She was finding the visit depressing. The suburb, to her, was drab and ugly. The people, too, seemed poorly dressed, and petty in their movements. They looked suspicious and pleased with themselves all at the same time. Almost mad, some of them, thought

Marilyn. Then, not wanting to appear rude, and secretly wishing to make up for her bad mood, she complimented Mrs Knight upon her new kitchen.

She doesn't have to be quite so regal about it, thought Martin. He knew that Marilyn disliked Thornby Avenue, and he was sensitive to her attitude. In this manner, occasionally, Martin resented Marilyn's urban upbringing, and her apparent indifference towards those people or places that she did not find sympathetic to her tastes. Mrs Knight, modestly, explained to her daughter-in-law that the new kitchen was labour-saving as opposed to decorative.

'But the tiles are pretty,' said Marilyn.

'How are your parents?' said Mrs Knight to Marilyn, once the kitchen had been praised.

'They're very well, thank you; except that they're planning to move . . .'

'From Greenwich?'

'Yes. Daddy's been offered a job in Los Angeles, so they might be going to California.' Martin already knew about this.

Bill Fuller, disgusted by the state of film- and arts-funding in Britain, had finally accepted a long-standing offer of a teaching post at UCLA. He would be Professor of Visual Theory. Josephine, exhausted by her lengthy analysis of Wagner, was hoping to research a 'fun' book about American musical comedy. The couple would not move, however, until September. Marilyn was dreading their departure.

'You'll be able to go and visit though?' said Mrs Knight.

'Oh yes,' said Marilyn eagerly; 'we'd love to go to the States anyway . . .'

'And you sister's in Canada, isn't she?'

'That's right, yes . . .'

'Well, maybe you could do a round trip . . .'

Marilyn nodded, and gently placed her teacup on the little side table.

The room was growing dark. Martin turned on the lamp. He thought that his mother looked tired. For a moment, irrationally, it seemed to him as though all of the glamour that the Fullers enjoyed was gained at his mother's expense. He recognised the lack of logic in this impression, but still he could not dismiss it. In his heart he felt guilty, but he did not know why this should be. Suddenly, he felt a rush of sentimental loyalty towards the Heath, the sycamore tree, and the bearskin rug of tarmac.

Resol UK, driven by the infectious enthusiasm of Dick Alryn, began to expand.

'I have two rules,' said Dicky to Martin early one evening in March 1987: 'Upgrade and Rotate.'

Martin looked politely impressed. He was sitting in his employer's large office at Unit 5. The evening was mild, and the fields which surrounded Rutbridge Business Park were being combed by a gentle wind. On Dicky's desk there was a white ring-bound folder which contained a thick document. This was entitled 'Resol UK: Home and European Expansion'.

'I've got a lot of good suits,' said Dicky. 'These days, a good suit can cost five or six hundred pounds. Now, I can afford good suits; but supposing I couldn't?'

Martin nodded.

'Well, prosperity is a question of attitude, and appearance,' Dicky continued. 'So instead of buying three cheap suits, I'd buy two really good ones, and rotate them . . .'

Martin tried to understand this system. He couldn't see why the hypothetical poor man would be any better off.

'And I'll tell you another thing,' said Dicky. 'Never, ever, buy a new product or service without upgrading. If you move, get a bigger house; if you buy a new car, buy a faster one . . . Always go up; never stay on the same rung of the ladder. People notice these things. That's what this,' he tapped the folder before him, 'is all about. These are good times, Martin, for the person who takes advantage of them; you and I both know that. And that's why your wife drives a BMW . . .'

Martin found this last comment vulgar. But he did not say that Marilyn had always bought her own cars.

The manifestation of Dicky's philosophies was three new branches of Resol: the company opened offices in Manchester, Edinburgh and Brussels. This bullish expansion had been frowned upon by some of the more senior executives at Resol UK. They felt that Dicky was taking risks: heavy borrowing, secured against untested markets, could be a recipe for ruin. Dicky, however, regarded such faint-heartedness with thinly veiled contempt. All over Britain, he maintained, businesses were expanding; the enterprise economy needed Resol UK. Carried along on a mounting wave of enthusiasm that intoxicated even as it counselled, Dick Alryn was not in the mood for doubters or cynics. It was for this reason that he shared his enthusiasms with Martin. He liked to think of the young executive as an acolyte. The plans for expansion had sullied the hitherto concentrated support that Dicky had received from his staff.

To Martin, who had received a New Year bonus as well as a slight increase in salary, Dicky's plans were perfectly in order. The young man had ceased to study the broader context of Resol's operations; in many ways, now, he simply told Dicky what he wanted to hear. The affluence of the times appeared to dispel all notions of doubt. From his friends in the City, Martin was continually hearing stories of vast salaries offered over lunch, or of personal fortunes made with a single phone-call. Whilst the facts behind these legends remained obscure, Martin considered his own affluence to be an extension of their mythology. In many ways he had merely drifted into success, whilst the basis of his situation was childlike in its simplicity: he spent far more than he earned, but his character was complicit with a culture which suggested that this was perfectly normal. The actual sums of money involved now seemed abstract. Thus Martin found excuses for his extravagance. The banks encouraged him, and his employer confided in him. Poverty and inconvenience were unfortunate qualities which troubled the inhabitants of a distant, unreal community. Martin sometimes believed, wrongly, that he was now living in the fourth dimension.

Dick Alryn, as a businessman, had always been an adventurer. In June 1987 his speculative interests turned towards the lucrative property market. For Dicky, who was becoming slightly drunk on money-making schemes, this latest branch of his business affairs was a private venture, and its details were not known to the senior staff or employees at Resol UK.

But Dicky's plan, in essence, was simple: forming a partnership with an acquaintance of his own age, who was called Bob Ensall, Resol's captain created a private company. This company was called Bayswater Property Management. The two partners, in the summer of 1987, then located and purchased three large, dilapidated town houses not far from the Edgware Road. An architect was employed to renovate the acquired property and to transform the three shabby houses into desirable luxury apartments. This would be a costly process, but Bayswater Property Management had every belief that they would resell the flats, once building work was completed, for a considerable profit. To fund his share of the scheme, Dicky borrowed heavily. In the mean time, Resol UK continued with its programme of home and European expansion, the details of which took up a great deal of Martin's time in COM.

The summer of 1987 saw Martin and Marilyn prospering within their idyll. The chestnut trees were in flower; the garden at Ash House, with its mass of heavily petalled, fragrant blooms and its broad, sunny lawn, became a place where Marilyn sunbathed throughout the long afternoons. She no longer thought about her plans to start a small business. Rather, she shopped, read and tended to the flawless apartment. There was always, she said, 'some little job to do'. So that summer, for the first time since she met Martin, Marilyn thought about herself. The lazy days encouraged this process.

In the mornings, after Martin had left for work, Marilyn would enjoy a cool shower. This, in many ways, was the part of the day that she enjoyed the most. Alone in the big apartment, the young woman swiftly became absorbed in her own routine. The August days were particularly hot, and Marilyn loved to feel the soft needles of cool water in the shower; the water seemed to loosen little knots of tension, and then caress the body. A grapefruit shower-splash added an invigorating perfume to this process.

Having showered, Marilyn would then dress in the lightest of clothes: knee-length shorts and a white cotton shirt. Then she would go to prepare her breakfast, which she ate on the little balcony, facing the sun. Fresh orange juice, tea and two croissants were soon neatly arranged upon her tray. She never ate lunch. The next hour was filled with leisurely breakfasting. Marilyn would glance at a magazine article as she slowly ate her croissants and sipped her tea and orange juice. Her favourite magazines were those that dealt with domestic interiors and fashion. As she read, and felt the hot sunshine on her legs and arms, Marilyn's mind would fill with ideas: fabrics, indoor plants, wallpapers, Tunisian baskets, exotic salad ingredients, kitchenware, make-up, fitness regimes and self-tested analyses of body-consciousness. These ideas, considered daily and renewed monthly, became an accretion in Marilyn's thoughts: over the years, an obsessive consideration of life-style had presented to the young woman a single, vast concept of happiness. This concept was comprised of a myriad details from lingerie to holidays, but to Marilyn, who knew its composition and geography so intimately, it seemed like a physical thing: another home, as real and accessible as Rome or Paris. It was as though the country of life-style had its own defined place on Earth, and exported its influence to millions of people like Marilyn.

At eleven o'clock in the morning, Martin would telephone his wife.

'Hi. How are you getting on?'

'Oh, I'm just finishing my breakfast . . .' Marilyn would laugh as she said this, and carry the telephone into the drawing room with the receiver cradled beneath her chin.

'It's all right for some! Are you OK?'

'Fine. Hot though. I've got to go into town shortly, is there anything I can get you?'

The daily shopping trip was the spine of Marilyn's day.

'Have we got any grapefruit? I really like grapefruit . . .'

'I'll get some. Anything else?'

'I'm sure there is, but I can't think at the moment . . .'

And then Marilyn would ask: 'How's work? Are you busy?'

And Martin would give a brief account of his morning.

Finally, when both of the young people had reassured themselves as to the happiness of the other, they would say:

'Love you, bye . . .'

This telephone conversation would start the next phase in Marilyn's day. Having returned her tray to the kitchen and wiped over the long, tiled work surfaces, the young woman would then make a brief inspection of the apartment, gathering laundry or tidying scattered books and magazines as she went from room to room. A cleaning lady came twice a week to do the hoovering, dusting and polishing. With the exception of a few small items, Marilyn sent the laundry out. Surveying her home, Marilyn would picture redecorations in her mind's eye. More often than not, she was seeking some ambient detail that would add to her overall scheme. Usually, this detail was achieved: more natural light or less; an ornament or piece of furniture removed or changed; a mirror repositioned. And then there were the major projects: the guest bedroom, for instance, and the study. These rooms, in particular, absorbed the young wife.

That summer, in place of lunch, Marilyn drank melon juice. This was a part of her diet and skin-care programme. Then, at around one in the afternoon, she would collect her deep, narrow shopping basket, gather up her bag and car keys, and hurry down the broad staircase of Ash House (as though summoned by an urgent appointment) in order to drive into the centre of Bristol to do her daily shopping. Her black German saloon car with its blue-tinted windows would be hot and airless, and Marilyn, having opened the sun-roof, enjoyed the breeze as she drove along. She wore a pair of silver-framed sunglasses with dark blue lenses; she drove fast, and parked with elegant inaccuracy.

The city would be busy at lunchtime with workers and shoppers as Marilyn went from shop to shop. She always tried to park in the shade, so that her car would not become too warm. If she 'had time', Marilyn would call in to visit her friend Bella, who worked in a shop that sold cupboards and doors. Bella's husband Brian was a civic engineer. He had enjoyed several conversations with Martin about contemporary town-planning. Bella was dreading a possible relocation to Birmingham, and had confided in Marilyn that her marriage might be threatened by the move. Marilyn, who was level-headed, had counselled patience and compromise.

'Don't do anything drastic until you're absolutely sure . . .' she said. 'Who knows? It might not be so bad . . .'

'I know . . . But, Birmingham?'

'There are meant to be some lovely bits . . .'

'Yes, but – Birmingham . . .'

Bella and Brian had introduced Martin and Marilyn to Kathy and Simon. Marilyn liked Simon, who was a research chemist, but she found Kathy dull and sanctimonious. Kathy worked (part-time) as a social worker, and Martin had once pointed out that she seemed incapable of conversing without relating all subjects to the bleak horror of her 'cases'.

'It's so tedious,' he had said when the couple were alone once more. 'One minute Brian was talking about that play, and the next thing we know she's started in with her child-abuse anecdotes. I'm sure it's all terribly tragic, but I just don't want to know. And I bet she isn't meant to be quite so free and easy with the details . . .'

Marilyn agreed. 'Her dress was vintage British Home Stores,' she said.

Marilyn, to her own surprise, had discovered that she was greatly admired by her women friends. They came to her for advice, and seemed to attach an importance to her opinions which Marilyn sometimes feared. Never having sought to be popular, Marilyn felt like the fabled ugly duckling, which was finally pronounced to be 'a very fine swan indeed'. Martin was proud of his wife's success, and would sometimes study her while she was conversing with her friends. She always spoke rather less than her interlocutor, and thus she made her points more gracefully, and more persuasively. For Martin, who often spoke too quickly and sometimes for effect, this was a trait that he greatly admired.

Having visited the vast, air-conditioned food halls, Marilyn would then allow herself a brief navigation of the main shopping centre. She appeared to be the only cool person amidst the bustle of hot shoppers. Young men from offices, sitting outside to eat their sandwiches, would watch her as she passed. She was oblivious to their furtive attentions; if men whistled at her or called out, however, she would become seriously annoyed.

'They're just common, pathetic and ignorant,' she would say to Martin – who agreed. 'They don't seem to realise how intimidating it is, to say nothing of embarrassing. Would *you* ever behave like that? Would you?'

'Hardly.' Martin came from a class of males who studied girls in other ways, but with just as much attention. Martin's own favourite form of voyeurism was to gaze at the lingerie adverts in *Vogue*. Sexually satisfied, however, he seldom 'looked at' other women.

By three o'clock in the afternoon, Marilyn would have returned to Ash House and be arranging her deck-chair, cold drink and suntan lotion upon the lawn. Wearing a one-piece swimming costume, she would lie down with her head resting slightly to one side, and feel weightless in the fierce afternoon sun. Soon, in the quiet garden, she felt herself to be floating, and lulled by distant sounds. Clifton seemed peaceful and drowsy: a car would pass by; a hidden bird would coo in the trees.

Poised on the brink of a shallow sleep, and sensing only the light weight of her dark glasses, Marilyn's thoughts would wander. Daily concerns receded as the heat seemed to reach her with a low rhythm; her main resolve, as she felt the hot fabric beneath her, was to remember to roll over, so as not to burn . . . It seemed to Marilyn, as she sunbathed in the garden during the summer of 1987, that she was trying to rise above her life, and study its shape and course from above. She no longer had any long-term ambitions, but worried herself by seldom noticing their absence.

Am I stupid? she would think, as the sun burnt into her shoulder-blades. Am I just a little wife?

And then she would remember some major concern (such as visiting her parents before they left for America) and this would distract her. She thought about Martin, as her magazine had suggested, but failed to find any major faults in him. Their arguments, for the most part, were trivial and swiftly forgotten; neither of them had any secrets or anxieties that they felt they could not share; neither of them drank to excess, or lost their temper easily. Martin could become depressed, but he seemed to possess an instinct that distanced his problems. He used the conflicting aspects of his personality to maintain a sense of spiritual superiority and a sense of humour. This was one of the main reasons why Marilyn loved him so much: she found his self-professed 'oddness', or 'irony', comforting. So far, no major problem had presented itself to test this romantic stance. Later, Martin would wonder whether or not his wife was aware of the manner in which he had 'performed' his young life. He assumed that she must know him completely, and love him despite his self-obsession.

Finally, as Marilyn began to doze and as the sun began slowly to move westward, she would sometimes think, Are we boring?

But this question, by the time that the tanned young woman was having her evening shower and thinking about salad, was quite forgotten. Martin doubtless would have debated the niceties of the point; to Marilyn, it was of no real interest.

Sometimes, however, the thought of children crossed the young woman's mind.

For Marilyn, motherhood resembled a subject that she had not yet reached in the syllabus of life. As a teenager, she had never begged to hold babies, or dreamt of a time when she would bring a new being into the world. Similarly, she did not find young children particularly pretty, or endearing in their ways. Of late, however, Marilyn had developed a curiosity – tinged with confusion – with regard to the process of pregnancy and birth. Sometimes, as she watched young mothers struggling through the shops with their infants, she would try to picture herself with a child of her own. Above all else, she wondered what her own children would look like. Would they be fair, or dark? Would a little girl be easier to love than a baby boy? And, most troubling of all, what would one do if one discovered a complete lack of maternal instinct after the child was born?

Marilyn was physically brave. The stories that she had heard of difficult births and protracted agonising labours held no horrors for her. Her doubts and her fears were emotional. Frequently she was asked, 'Do you want to have children?' and she would normally reply, 'I'd like to sometime – but not just yet.' This answer, usually, would close down the difficult conversation. It was when other women, more certain than herself, spoke of 'body clocks' and 'getting on' that Marilyn grew concerned. But she did not know whether it was age that she feared, or the thought that she would lose the ability to have children. These questions had seldom troubled her before.

Marilyn was now twenty-five years old. In many ways, she felt much older than her years. She attributed this to the fact that she had only ever known two definite phases in her life: Greenwich and Martin. The time which she had spent at Truffles seemed distant and unreal. But Marilyn was seldom bored; she could apply herself, assiduously, to an endless succession of short-term desires. Loving her husband, and knowing only comfort, she believed herself to be luckier than most. It was the question of children that signified the future. When Marilyn looked at baby clothes, or watched a tired parent stoop down towards the tiny, reaching figure in a push-chair, she found herself thinking – more and more of late – about the years that stretched before her and what would fill them. And then she wondered whether she would lose her good figure, or change quite completely, should she ever have a baby herself. The problem was vague and enormous – an absolute. Like a pool of mercury, it seemed to shatter when she touched upon it. Martin, in the past, had merely said, 'It's up to you' – and this was no help at all. Babies, to Martin, fitted into no known aesthetic scheme. He said that he preferred films.

On 12th September 1987, Martin and Marilyn travelled to Greenwich in order to see Bill and Josephine before they left for America. The Captain's House had been sold. Boxes and packing-cases filled the low-ceilinged rooms and the dark corridors. Only a few necessities remained, and this made Marilyn sad.

'"Silent Death's" in storage,' joked Bill.

Marilyn's parents were looking forward to the move. In high spirits, they took Martin and Marilyn to an old-fashioned restaurant in Fitzrovia for a farewell dinner. Marilyn was on the verge of tears throughout the meal. This emotion had been creeping up on her throughout the visit. Finally, during dessert, she could not hold back her tears. She put down her spoon and sat with her head turned away from the table in order to conceal her brimming eyes and trembling chin. Bill, who had noticed this crisis, attempted to raise his daughter's spirits without calling attention to her crumbling self-control. This failed. Quite overcome, Marilyn buried her face in her napkin.

'Oh . . . Marilyn,' said Josephine.

'What is it? Are you feeling sick?' said Martin, confused.

Marilyn shook her head fiercely. She would not remove the napkin from her eyes. An approaching waiter, seeing the upset, discreetly withdrew. The head waiter glanced at Bill, who smiled and shook his head.

'It'll be all right,' said Josephine, not stirring.

Marilyn rose from the table, red-faced, and began to walk towards the stairs which led out of the restaurant. Bill followed her.

'Let's get some air,' he said.

Reaching the street, Marilyn stood with her head bowed while her father lit a French cigarette. Then, very slowly, they began to walk down Percy Street. Marilyn felt exhausted and foolish.

'I'm sorry,' she said. 'I've spoilt everything.'

'No you haven't. Are you feeling a little better?'

'A little, yes . . .'

Father and daughter continued their slow walk. The evening was mild. Marilyn took deep breaths. Her expensive dress looked dishevelled.

'I'll just miss you so much,' she said; 'I don't like to think of you being so far away. What if something happens?'

'We'll come back,' said Bill, simply.

Marilyn tried to smile.

'It's one of the problems of having a selfish career,' said Bill. 'They don't pay people like me to do anything in Britain, so I've got to get money from somewhere else . . .'

'What about your film?'

'Exactly. What about it . . .'

'I thought you were going to be making a film here; or in Ireland, or somewhere . . .'

'It's all fallen through. That's one of the reasons why we're moving. But it's only for a year, initially, or maybe two . . . We'll be renting a little flat in London, so you won't get rid of us entirely . . .'

They were facing the Tottenham Court Road. They turned and began to make their way back towards the restaurant.

'I'm going to look really silly now,' said Marilyn. 'My face must look awful . . .'

'Nonsense. You look lovely.'

Soon they were sitting in the restaurant again. Martin held his wife's hand. Josephine, quiet amidst the fuss, thought how different her two daughters were. She also recognised, once more, the stab of sadness which informed her that she was not a successful mother. She became, so quickly, embarrassed by such scenes.

At the end of September, in order to distract Marilyn from her sadness, Martin took his young wife to Ravello, on the Amalfi coast of Italy. Their hotel, which was expensive, clung to the steep, vine-covered hillside that overlooks the Gulf of Salerno. The town was extremely small, but the views from its terraces were spectacular.

Confronting these views, and staring down at the sparkling, languorous sea, Martin and Marilyn were restored to high spirits. Behind them, cleft by narrow valleys, the drowsy, dust-coloured hills seemed perfectly silent. In the evenings, after the day-trippers had departed, the little town was quiet. A small café which faced the simple, church-sized cathedral and one or two local restaurants were all that the place had to offer for entertainment. The hotel appeared to be empty. The couple wondered where the other guests were.

'I suppose,' said Martin, 'that there can only be twelve rooms – I mean, it's quite small . . .'

'It used to be a private house,' said Marilyn. 'I love the pillars in the hall though.'

'They're Moorish,' said Martin, eager for culture.

It became difficult to relax. On the fourth evening of their holiday, Martin and Marilyn sat in the hotel garden drinking peach juice, and gazed at the undisturbed sea. The hot days dissolved into blue, silent evenings. In the distance, a string of white lights could be seen, suggesting a busy promenade.

'That must be Salerno,' said Marilyn.

'It's miles away,' said Martin.

'I wish we had a car . . .'

'We could rent one.'

'Where from, though?'

In one of Marilyn's magazines, Ravello had been cited as the perfect setting for a 'romantic break'. But now that they had absorbed the views and visited the two principal villas (which each received three stars in Martin's guide), the couple were becoming bored. Somehow, the beauty of the place would not become articulate.

'It's a bit like Cornwall,' said Martin.

The following day, they decided to visit Amalfi.

Not knowing which of the local buses they should take, Martin and Marilyn rode down to Amalfi in a private taxi. This cost them, they later calculated, nearly £30. Marilyn was cross, and said that Martin should have argued about the fare.

'But I don't speak Italian; anyway, they're bound to rip off tourists.'

'That doesn't make it all right, you know . . .'

Amalfi, which was slightly busier than Ravello, was spoilt by gift shops and cheap restaurants. The promenade, which had promised a pleasant walk, was ruined by a sea wall of triangular man-made concrete boulders.

'I noticed some like that earlier on,' said Martin.

Marilyn shrugged. 'Well, they don't really matter.'

But Martin, who was hot and disappointed, felt that the concrete boulders did matter. This was not the Italy that he had hoped for; here, he felt, tourism mocked the sophisticated visitor. Eventually, sitting outside a café, he said:

'I really don't like this place . . .'

Marilyn rested her chin upon her hand, and looked at her husband.

'What do you want to do?' she said.

'Leave.'

'But we've paid now – and it was frightfully expensive . . .'

'Remember to add four pounds for the two lemon sodas.'

'But what will we do? It would cost us a fortune to simply go home now . . .'

'On the other hand,' said Martin, gazing at a small group of trippers, 'we've got another five nights to do in Ravello. We've seen everything that there is to see. And the hotel's so dull. I'm really sorry – I thought it would be lovely.'

Marilyn, too, was bored. There were no proper shops to look at, and they had visited all the churches twice. Secretly, Marilyn would have been much happier staying at a beach resort. But she felt rather sorry for her generous husband.

'Tell me what you'd like to do,' she said, 'and we'll do it. Do you want to leave?'

'I just feel claustrophobic . . . And there isn't anything to do. What do people do here all day? It's a mystery to me . . .'

Martin smiled as he said this.

'They had *Grease* on television last night . . .' said Marilyn.

'It's a long way to come to see a bad film.'

'I won't hear a word against *Grease*; Daddy says that it reinvented the musical . . .'

'Really? I thought that was *Saturday Night Fever?*'

'It was one or the other . . .' Marilyn rested her hand upon Martin's shoulder. 'I do love you,' she said.

Having admitted their boredom, Martin and Marilyn felt more relaxed. Seeking to gently mock their holiday, they were reunited. The following day, driven by a sense of their own autonomy, they left Ravello and flew back to London.

Arriving in London, they took a room at Durrants Hotel, and spent the remainder of their holiday seeing friends, going to the cinema and shopping. By the time that they returned to Ash House, they had spent just under £2,000.

Eventually, Martin was to realise that he preferred the idea of abroad to its actuality.

That autumn, Martin and Marilyn's married life underwent a subtle change. Their pleasant routine, which hitherto had been informed by novelty, seemed to become nothing more than a process of repetition. Shopping, entertaining, conversing, working and relaxing all took on a quality of inevitability: it was as though, now, the young couple were merely trying to replicate some previous achievement of happiness. Unfortunately, they were too close to this process to recognise fully its deadening effect. Life, it seemed, was still treating them kindly; but, little by little, their ability to look forward to various events and activities was gradually evaporating. This change resembled a quiet background noise, the source of which was impossible to locate. At the beginning of October, Martin was ill with gastric flu. Used to good health, he was frightened and depressed by the experience. He vowed to give up smoking, but discovered that he couldn't. While he was ill, he became childish and demanding. This behaviour shocked Marilyn.

Weakened, Martin had lost the self-confidence that was vital to his romantic stance; he longed, pathetically, for simplicity, and a freedom from all responsibilities. He became increasingly aware of the mountain of debts upon which his life was standing. He imagined the 'islands of money' which Paul had mentioned, and then saw his own island – like a small sandcastle standing on the edge of an approaching tide. The credit facilities which had made him feel independent were now transformed into a burden.

And yet Martin could not change his habits.

The couple had a 'serious talk', and determined to economise. Martin's most recent increase in salary was slight.

'Next year,' Dicky had said, 'we'll all be enjoying the fruits of expansion.'

Marilyn took a part-time job in Bella's shop: for two days a week (and every other Saturday) she sold expensive cupboards and doors to young women who resembled herself in nearly every way. In this manner, Martin and Marilyn made several new friends.

Thus, as the wave upon which the young couple had been riding prepared to crash down from its highest point, they felt strangely weightless. Outwardly, their lives were little altered; within, that part of themselves which registered joy and optimism was smothered. They felt like machines that hadn't been cleaned.

On Sunday, 18th October 1987, Marilyn made a trifle. The weekend had been quiet, with neither visitors nor excursions. The previous evening, Martin had tried to entertain Marilyn by playing her old punk-rock records. Marilyn had indulged this pastime. The tall black record player had boomed out the fast, witty, aggressive songs. The drawing-room floor had been strewn with brightly coloured, poorly printed record sleeves. One song had lingered in Marilyn's mind. She did not like punk rock, saw no hidden meaning within it, and was not in the least bit nostalgic for its period; it was the infectious chorus of the song – which sounded like a football chant – that she could not stop repeating in her mind. This tune was still tormenting her the following afternoon as she soaked sponge fingers in orange liqueur and began to cut up fruit:

> I am the fly, I am the fly,
> Fly in the, fly in the . . .
> Ointment . . .

Oh, that bloody tune, she thought.

Soon, however, the young woman had lined her broad, cut-glass bowl with sponge fingers and rich, thick custard. To this she added: black cherries, kiwifruit, bananas, apple slices, peach segments and raspberries. The fruit sank into the custard and was then covered with a further layer of sponge. To complete the trifle, Marilyn spread large spoonfuls of whipped cream across its glistening surface. Then she decorated the finished dessert with shavings of white chocolate and further halved cherries. The large bowl, viewed from the side, was filled with layer upon layer of fruit, sponge, custard and cream. Marilyn was pleased with this luxurious confection, and placed the bowl in the tall fridge. Such a trifle was ruinous to the young woman's diet, but she felt like indulging herself.

That evening as Martin was watching television, he heard a loud crash, swiftly followed by a furious scream. He rushed into the kitchen. Marilyn was standing next to the kitchen table, covering her eyes with one hand. The large trifle, as though dropped from a great height, was lying on the floor, mixed with shards of broken glass. Peninsulas of cream and custard spread out in all directions from the centre of the mess. It looked like something out of a cartoon. Turning to his wife, Martin noticed that a tear was running down her cheek from beneath her covered eyes.

'Just don't say anything,' she said. 'Please, just leave . . .'

Silently, Martin left the kitchen. Marilyn, for the first time in nearly two years, reached for a cigarette and slowly smoked it. She couldn't work out how the accident had happened; the bowl, it seemed, had been heavier than she thought, and slippery.

'It just slipped out of my hands,' she said, later.

'They're calling it Black Monday,' said Dick Alryn to Martin the following day. 'A complete systems overload; Stock Exchange in tatters; mucho panic in the City . . .'

Dicky was watching the small television in his office and listening to the analyses of the market crash with a fearful and bewildered expression.

'Does this affect us directly?' asked Martin.

'It'll affect everybody unless something happens . . .'

'What do we do?'

'Us? We press on; business never stops . . .'

But, as Martin was leaving the office, Dicky reflected that business had stopped. The great, sleek, international machine had choked as it gobbled. On all sides, panic and dread were seizing the minds of the fatted business community. Later, Martin recalled the apocalyptic paintings of John Martin in which cowering merchants were depicted, still clinging to their gold even as the world opened up to swallow them. Dick Alryn, on Black Monday, rang his partner Bob Ensall and sought comfort in reasoned, analytical conversation. Dicky's debts made Martin's debts look insignificant.

Throughout the following months, Martin's work at Resol did not seem to be altered in any way by the drama of Black Monday. The programme of expansion continued; COM developed its projects as though nothing had happened. By Christmas 1987, Resol UK notepaper could boast three new addresses. The offices in Manchester, Edinburgh and Brussels were small, but each had been conceived to cater for fresh catchment areas of flourishing business. Aspects of the enterprise economy appeared to be continuing under the weight of their momentum; spending and borrowing carried on as before; the illusion of opulence remained intact. To save money, however, Marilyn travelled alone to Los Angeles at the end of December. She spent a happy week with her parents and Carmen, while Martin remained in Clifton, living off ready-to-serve food from the supermarket.

1988, for Dick Alryn, commenced with a dispute between himself and Bob Ensall. As the owners and founders of Bayswater Property Management, they were concerned about the future of their project. The problems had begun in November of the previous year, when Colin Graham, of Hilary Graham Associates, New Fetter Lane, had proved himself to be an architect inadequate for Bob and Dick's demands. At considerable expense, Colin had produced a set of plans for the conversion of the Edgware properties, none of which complied with the brief that had been agreed. Colin blamed Dick, who in turn blamed Bob, and finally, amidst much ill-will, Hilary Graham Associates were simply paid off. Meanwhile, as Bob never tired of saying, the empty buildings were costing money. In February 1988 a new architect was commissioned, and this time the clients insisted upon a speedy realisation of their demands.

'You've got about two months,' said Dicky to James Menheim (the replacement architect). 'We want to get the builders in there ASAP . . .'

The result of this haste, unfortunately, was inaccurate planning with regard to the five top-floor flats. Revisions were made. Soon, Dick Alryn was wishing that he could buy his way out of the partnership. This however was impossible, for he now needed to sell the finished flats in order to cover his debts. The likelihood of making a profit was receding.

Neither Martin nor any of the other staff at Resol were aware that Dicky had secured a portion of his private borrowing against the company. Somehow the effortlessly simple reasoning of the original venture was beginning to collapse. Dicky's mood in the office began to change; there was no longer any talk of Pirate Kings or tennis. The monthly finance meetings had become deadly serious affairs, unleavened by either humour or bravado. Martin, who was working on fiscal projections from COM, was endlessly having to present his employer with discouraging news. And yet, fatally, none of this corporate turbulence appeared to be real to Martin. The aesthete was not a businessman at heart; and so long as Marilyn was waiting for him, and so long as the fridge at Ash House was filled with pleasant and plentiful food, he could not grow depressed at the thought of an office crisis. He felt insulated from such chaos. Instead, in April 1988, Martin bought a painting.

The painting resembled two hospital doors. The doors were closed to create a flat surface, and had been painted over with many coats of magnolia-coloured household emulsion. Thus, in some lights, the painting appeared quite blank; but beneath the thick surface of the paint, just visible, the outlines of the two circular windows and narrow oblong finger-plates could be discerned. Martin delighted in the understatement and purity of this remarkable painting. The young artist who had made it was highly regarded. An essay had been written about his work, in one of the fashionable art magazines. Marilyn, eventually, allowed the large painting to be hung in the dining room, where it faced the haughty expression of Peploe's 'Woman In Black Hat'.

'It doesn't go with this room, you know,' said Marilyn. 'In fact, it doesn't go with this flat. It ought to be somewhere modern, and empty.'

But Martin held firm.

'It's like it's not prepared to make the effort to be a work of art,' he said. 'It's so simple – I love it . . .'

'It's bland,' said Marilyn.

'Exactly.'

Marilyn looked at the large, empty painting and sighed.

'Actually,' she said, 'it's rather threatening – like having an unwanted guest in the room . . .' She paused. 'And it looks dated.'

'But it's only just been painted!'

'So?

All of these comments simply increased Martin's defence of his purchase. He was annoyed with Marilyn for not liking the painting. It had cost £1,500. Secretly, he was suddenly pleased that his wife found the work upsetting. He believed that Marilyn was being too conservative, and that her approach to art was becoming unromantic and weighed down with domestic caution. Hitherto, Martin's aesthetic tastes had won Marilyn's attention, if not her admiration. Now she was making him feel ridiculous – like a small boy who has bought an impracticable pet. In this reaction, Martin rediscovered his fundamental misogyny. A quarrel threatened. Divided over a matter of taste, Martin and Marilyn felt the very foundations of their relationship shudder. Marilyn, for an instant, saw deep into the heart of Martin's conceit, and she found him neither artistic nor interesting. A conspiracy of impressions whose catalyst, it seemed, was the magnolia-coloured painting, had caused the young husband to slip slightly in his wife's estimation. The grace of innocence within their relationship had departed: Martin and Marilyn, for a few hours, resented one another with the ancient stubbornness of old hands in marriage. Martin, nursing his wounded pride alone, remembered a comment that Piers had once made:

'We're all sexist, just as we're all, fundamentally, racist: it's in our nature. Men and women must regard one another from opposite sides of a deep, dark chasm; it's vital for romance, and it's vital for respect . . .'

There was little point, Martin thought, in repeating this theory to Marilyn. He was none too sure that he believed it himself. He wanted Marilyn to adore him; more than this, he wanted to remain extraordinary in her eyes. He felt that he was losing ground; he had noticed, of late, that his sexual confidence was waning.

Marilyn, for her part, disliked the magnolia-coloured painting. Its emptiness unsettled her.

During August 1988 a darkness settled upon Martin and Marilyn's life. The summer seemed stale and airless; the atmosphere at Resol was leaden and tense. Also, Martin began to notice small changes in the way that Marilyn treated him. When they first met, Marilyn's voice had seemed quiet and considered. She had always spoken carefully, and with hesitant formality. This tone, Martin thought, had suited the young woman, and had emphasised the 'special' quality that he perceived her to possess. Now, distinctly, her voice had changed. Initially, this alteration had revealed itself as a certain offhand briskness; then, in place of the epithet 'my love', or 'dear', Marilyn had begun to call Martin simply 'love'. 'Can you pass me that, love?' she would say, fixing the young man with a single glance as she reached the final syllable of her sentence, or: 'Don't do that, love,' which sounded like a shrill command. This habit began to irritate Martin, but he could think of no way in which he could comment upon it without sounding boorish or rude. Once, rashly, he mimicked his wife's tone. The result of this criticism was dramatic. Marilyn, who had been putting some crockery away, put down the cups she was holding and stared at Martin. Her face was pale with fury.

'You pig!' she said. Then, without a second glance, she rushed out of the kitchen, slammed the door and took herself to bed. After this, she did not speak to her ashamed husband for twenty-four hours. Finally she said:

'You've changed too, you know . . .'

Martin, by the autumn of 1988, was smoking thirty cigarettes a day. Marilyn, who hardly ever smoked, began to despair at the smell and discoloration that Martin's addiction inflicted upon her home.

'The curtains reek of your cigarettes,' she would say, 'and I'm tired of trying to get the smell out of my clothes – it's even in the bedroom . . .'

Martin would then apologise, sincerely, but feel cheated of his relaxation. He believed that he needed to smoke, and was dreading the instigation of a no-smoking policy at Resol. Marilyn thought that Martin was being selfish and lazy.

'At least I'm not a drunk,' he said.

Marilyn merely shrugged.

And yet, when they considered the marriages and relationships of some of their contemporaries, Martin and Marilyn were drawn together once more. So many of the couples whom they had known over the previous four years were now either divorced or separated or having secret affairs. Several of these couples had young children, and Martin and Marilyn would always say, 'It's dreadful when children are involved . . .'

Martin and Marilyn still loved one another; their love, however, had lost its pristine quality, and the couple, as ever, thrived mostly upon newness.

'Have you heard about . . .' – and Martin and Marilyn would cite some particular couple whose union was reported to be threatened. And then, with a certain degree of self-satisfaction, they would exaggerate to each other the difficulties that seemed to beset their peers. This made them feel more secure. Martin in particular would sigh, and speak as though he alone possessed the perception to diagnose the problems of his generation.

'When they bought that place in Putney, they knew they couldn't afford it: they've got a nanny – why? – and they spent a fortune on the conservatory. In London, you can add an extra nought to the price of the house; and then, of course, they don't have any real interests . . .'

It was as though he was trying to defend his own position.

Increasingly, Marilyn noticed that Martin's insecurities were given away by a certain pomposity. She had recognised this feature in other men, and she disliked it.

'Just don't go on about it,' she would say when her husband described, with lengthy digressions, his position at work, or his correspondence with the bank. Marilyn had loved Martin for his cavalier attitude towards practicalities. She had seldom paused to remember that his light-heartedness had been born of a confidence fuelled by money. So, aware of the deficiencies in their own relationship, Martin and Marilyn tried to avoid arguments by criticising other people.

As the year pulled on towards the dark tunnel of winter, Martin and Marilyn felt themselves to be skidding in their rut; their determination, and their exertions to recapture their former happiness, swiftly left them exhausted. More and more of late, Martin had caught himself using the expression 'Oh, we're trundling on . . .' In the past, Martin had always looked down upon those people who announced that they were 'trundling on'. As a result of this recognition, Martin began to yearn for subversion. To this end he began to use the word 'anarchy' in conversation, whenever he could.

In April 1989 Mrs Knight put her house at Thornby Avenue up for sale. This saddened Martin. His mother wanted to move further away from the urban sprawl, to Reigate, in order to be near her daughter and grandchildren. Thornby Avenue, once singly situated upon the boundary of a 'green wedge', was now becoming – in Mrs Knight's opinion – 'spoilt'. People dismantled cars in their front gardens and left them there to rust; little boys scribbled slogans and obscenities upon the wall by the station.

Martin discovered that he was as affected by the loss of his childhood home as Marilyn was by the departure of her parents. It was as though a light had gone out. Sentimental by nature, Martin bade a secret farewell to his old bedroom, which overlooked the Heath. The afternoon was colourless, and quiet. The little wood which surrounded the derelict asylum was leafless. The long grass stretching off towards the shallow quarry, cut by chalk-coloured paths, appeared grey and ancient – flattened by winter. The spring, it seemed, would not arrive.

Martin's room was empty. His mother had placed some of his books and papers in two cardboard boxes, 'to be sorted out'. Martin half hoped that he would find some poignant reminder of his romantically inclined youth amidst this rubbish. He found nothing: some old battered paperback books, two files filled with photocopied notes from the polytechnic, a selection of cheap rings and bracelets and an amber-coloured cigarette holder. At the bottom of a jar, however, Martin found two black badges. Upon these were printed in a small, white typeface the words WE ARE ALL PROSTITUTES and EVERYONE HAS THEIR PRICE. Martin slipped these badges into his suit pocket; and then, patting the wall beside the light switch, he hurried downstairs – for the last time, he thought later.

Bayswater Property Management, by June 1989, was in serious trouble. Builders had been contracted to carry out the conversion of the Edgware houses, but they were – to the minds of their clients – being deliberately slow and obstructive. Endless problems were reported from the site; minor accidents delayed the most simple of tasks; electricians, plumbers, or decorators failed to arrive on their allotted days; new fittings were found to be 'non-compatible' and had to be reordered. As a consequence of these mishaps, the whole project was some ten months behind schedule. In the mean time, the property market was freezing over; 'the slump' was a common topic of conversation. Dick Alryn, who had to sell the flats in order pay back his debts and defend Resol, was becoming ill with worry. His bankers were dissatisfied; their former patience and flexibility had evaporated.

Finally, one day in August, when a hand-made staircase had

been delivered seven inches too short, Dicky called a crisis meeting with Bob Ensall and the builders' manager. The afternoon was hot, and Bob Ensall's office had no air-conditioning. Two plates of sandwiches dried up in the heat as the men were arguing. It transpired, as the meeting became more irate, that Bob had refused in March to sign an agreement that would entitle the building company to a bonus payment for work completed on time.

'But that's virtually protection money!' shouted Dick. 'That's outrageous!'

Sam Petrie, the building manager, leant back in his chair. 'The details were quite clear on the contract forms,' he said. 'You'll find that we've done nothing out of order.'

'What do you mean, "out of order"?' screamed Dicky. 'It's not a question of that; you must know the state of the market. If we can't sell, we all lose out . . .'

'We're covered,' said Sam, quickly.

Dick looked aghast. Regarding Sam with unconcealed hatred, he thought that he looked like a neat, spiteful stoat. He had a small head, with a pointed chin masked by a trimmed, sandy-coloured beard; his eyes were pale, and seemed to have no lashes; his jacket was the colour of rust. Dicky also noticed that Sam had many tiny scars on the backs of his hands.

'Bob,' said Dick eventually, 'did you tell me about this?'

'I mentioned it,' replied the partner, uncomfortably.

'And so we either pay up, sue, or go bust? Is that it?'

'I think you're over-reacting,' said Sam, and then stopped. Dicky was collecting his papers and pulling on his jacket.

'I've got a responsibility to my staff,' said Dicky.

'So have I,' said Sam.

Bob sighed. He could afford to sit out the slump.

Unresolved, the meeting adjourned. Outside, there was a traffic jam of baking cars which stretched from Marble Arch to Notting Hill.

*

On the last Sunday in August 1989, Martin and Marilyn drove to Weston-super-Mare in order to go for a walk. It was extremely hot. The temperatures which were being recorded daily in the newspapers were thought to be unusually high. From early morning until sunset, it seemed, the sky was too bright to look at; and the sun was a fierce white circle blazing through a milk-coloured haze. Towards noon that Sunday, there were scarcely any people to be seen on the streets of the small town which had all the appearance of a seaside resort but which stood, in fact, upon an estuary, commanding at low tide a broad expanse of black mud. Those people who were out – some elderly residents of the town and a few subdued trippers – walked close to the buildings, the better to keep in the shade. The whole town was quiet; 'the season', it seemed, was refusing to 'take off'. And all day the dazzling whiteness continued: it seemed to reverberate in the air like a low minor chord.

The heat pressed down like an iron; the air was thick with it. At lunchtime, the seafront cafés were open, selling cheap meals of boneless and skinless cod. There were fleshy scarlet flowers on some of the little tables, but hardly any customers. Martin and Marilyn stopped for coffee. The proprietors of the café were going to close early; they were wiping down the glass fronts of the refrigerated displays and endlessly polishing the already spotless surfaces. The silent town appeared to be in a trance, mesmerised by the heat and light.

As they wandered along the broad promenade past the low bulk of the closed Winter Gardens, Martin and Marilyn were quiet. From time to time, baking draughts of hot air scooped up fine clouds of dust and sand from the beach and the pavement. Further on, where the hillside curved around the bay, it was possible to see grey-brick and sandstone gables where a few houses peeped up through the trees like mellow ruins in a dense forest. Above these partially hidden dwellings was Worlebury, with its Iron Age camp which was overgrown and covered by flinty stones. In the early afternoon, when the landscape was stupefied with heat, shafts of white sunlight pushed their way into the gloomy caverns of the tallest trees that surrounded this ancient encampment. Beyond the bay, towards Sand Point, there were deserted salt-flats and a hot little toll road.

'This place seems like the end of the world,' said Martin.

Marilyn agreed.

In the town, many of the flowers had bloomed stillborn for want of water. The lawns in front of the two, peeling, big hotels were nothing more than squares and semicircles of scorched grass, mown into stripes. The public fountain was dry. The old pier, which was broad, white and squat, baked above the low-tide mud upon its rusty iron legs. It was only later in the afternoon that the water began to creep up, advancing like a distant army glittering under the sun. Martin and Marilyn strolled onto the pier. There were very few other visitors.

At the very end of the pier, which terminated with a miniature go-kart track that was closed, Martin and Marilyn discovered a curious amusement. It was a Wild West shooting game. It was encased within a tall, glass-fronted cabinet and partially concealed beside a shuttered snacks kiosk.

'What's that?' said Marilyn, pausing to look at the game.

Inside the cabinet, but leaning slightly at a drunken angle, a life-size waxwork of a Wild West barmaid was pouting seductively through the dirty glass. The model was six feet tall, and its wig of blonde hair came tumbling over its shoulders in stiff, discoloured ringlets. Its blue glass eyes stared vacantly; it was dressed in a long, flounced scarlet frock, with a little white apron. Attached to the model at right angles there were oiled metal rods. Above its head there was a flashing target; in front of it, on the customer's side of the glass, an old pistol in a worn leather holster. Martin read the instructions on the side of the machine, and then inserted two coins.

Immediately a saucy tune began to play from a concealed

speaker, while Martin started to shoot at the flashing target. The gun made no noise, but as the firing went on, and as the target began to flash more and more frequently, vulgar bells ran out and the model started to shed its clothes. The young man began to shoot more quickly. With each 'hit', one of the metal arms would snatch away an article of clothing. The flounced dress was removed with a single, deft plucking gesture. Thus exposed, the model was wearing an embroidered corset of scarlet and black lace, and a pair of torn fishnet stockings. Once the corset had been jolted off (in the opposite direction to the frock) the model's yellowing body, with its wasp-waist and pneumatic breasts, was clad only in an under-wired black brassière and a pair of sun-faded silk knickers. The saucy music grew louder and more distorted. Marilyn watched while Martin fired away, and then she leant over the pier's balustrade and gazed down at the mud below. For miles around, it seemed, the only noise was the strip-tease tune. When the dusty brassière had been whisked to one side, the model's chest, with its scarlet-painted nipples, was brought into view. The side of one of the breasts had melted. The machine was beginning to run down, and the music, once so lively, had become a tuneless drone. With his last three shots, Martin dispatched the model's knickers. As these were dragged down into the gloom around the model's feet, the young man saw in their place a black satin heart. This was glued to the dummy. The target stopped flashing, and for a moment the stripped barmaid stood before the young couple. Then there was a noise like that of someone folding thin sheets of tin, and the little metal arms returned the clothes to their original positions.

'Happy now?' said Marilyn.

Martin tried to appear aloof, and amused. Secretly, he had found the game erotic. Marilyn had been indurate to her husband's caresses for some months. This phase had troubled Martin, but he wanted to respect his wife's moods. Thus, he buried his frustration, but found himself responsive to those diluted forms of pornography that entered into his days through advertising, magazines, films and mannequins. Also, earlier in the summer, he had caught himself studying a girl who worked in COM, and it was only his sense of good taste which had prevented him from attempting to fall into conversation with her. Marilyn, however, was Martin's erotic ideal, and he felt that he could never be unfaithful to her. This constancy was an anomaly in Martin's character.

Leaving the pier, Martin and Marilyn wandered aimlessly towards the small collection of rocks which are known as Birnbeck Island. A further pier, which was Victorian, unadorned and made of warped brown timbers, connected these rocks to the coastal road. This pier was deserted in the late afternoon. It had been built by a local landowner during the nineteenth century; both of this landowner's sons had been drowned during the pier's construction – the elder son trying to save the younger. When Martin and Marilyn reached the pier's end, they made their way down a flight of slippery concrete steps which smelt strongly of seaweed and brine. At the foot of these steps the rocks fanned out before them like a glistening axe-head; the water, gently slapping against the furthest point of the outcrop, was calm and sparkling like a million diamonds. The couple sat down and surveyed the scene before them. The heat was still intense. Martin and Marilyn stared ahead through their dark glasses.

'I don't know whether this place is really beautiful or really depressing,' said Martin eventually.

'I couldn't live here,' said Marilyn. 'I wonder why it's so quiet? I thought that Weston was really popular . . .'

'It is; but it all looks shut.'

Marilyn was silent. She picked up some loose stones and began to flick them into a still rock pool. Martin studied the movement of her brown arm against her large white T-shirt. A spiral of dust clouded the rock pool.

'I think I've hit a crab,' said Marilyn. 'Poor thing . . .'

Martin, stretching out in the heat, thought about the shallow quarry on the Heath and the old, rusted cistern which it contained. The image of a man upon an island in the middle of a lake returned to him.

'What are you doing next week?' asked Marilyn.

'I'm not looking forward to it. There's something odd going on at work . . .'

'How do you mean, "odd"?'

'Well, we're supposed to be allocating departmental budgets for next year; the COM budget hasn't even been mentioned. When I asked Dicky about it, he was so vague . . .'

'Vague in what way?'

'If I knew that, then I wouldn't be worried,' said Martin, rather sharply.

'I was only asking . . .'

Marilyn had noticed that Martin seemed to take offence extremely quickly of late.

The unseasonal stillness appeared to be growing heavier as the protracted sunset began. The white, round sun was turning to gold; the wide sky was tinged with a pinkish haze.

'I've been thinking about children again,' said Marilyn, turning to Martin. 'And I think I really would like to try . . .' The young woman had been dreading the moment when she would make this announcement. Martin looked uncomfortable and distant.

'I know what you're going to say,' said Marilyn, 'so don't start lecturing. I'm just saying: I'd really like to try . . .'

Martin sighed. In his heart, he thought of children as an unsettling symbol of responsibility. He imagined the rooms at Ash House filled with of all the paraphernalia that babies require: soft toys, push-chair, boxes of disposable nappies, bottles and blankets. He recalled friends who had spoken of sleepless nights and endless visits to clinics and doctors. The whole idea appeared ugly to him. He knew that he was too selfish to encourage such disruption. He looked at Marilyn and, finding her beautiful, tried to imagine her pregnant.

'Don't you sometimes think,' said Marilyn, leaning towards her husband, 'that you might have a little boy, with eyes like yours?' This image softened Martin's heart.

'Sometimes . . .'

Encouraged, Marilyn's voice became fonder. 'And you could play with him – or her; and learn from it . . . What are you afraid of? You love Bella's children . . .'

Martin remained silent. Two contradictory impulses were dividing his resolve. He wanted so much to kiss his wife and say, 'Yes. We'll have children,' but he could not utter the words. He mumbled something.

'What was that?' said Marilyn, smiling.

'"The pram in the hall",' said Martin, '"is the end of philosophy."'

Marilyn got up, and walked quickly towards the concrete steps.

'Marilyn . . .'

The young woman did not look back.

Rising to follow his wife, Martin glanced at the sparkling water and the low, rust-coloured rocks. The sea looked motionless, like the frozen surface of a strange copper-coloured planet. He hurried off to catch up with his tearful wife.

Why do I say such stupid things? he thought.

Piers Harding, in many ways, had always represented Martin's intellectual conscience. But since the aesthete's wedding the two young men had become genuinely fond of one another. Within this relationship, Martin assumed the role of student and seeker-after-truth; he brought his problems and his meditations to Piers, who then would offer some comment upon them which was mulled over, respected and repeated. As the 1980s drew to a close, a quantity of hopelessness began to invade the comfortable dialogue which had previously existed between the academic and the young executive. Usually, now, the only cheerful topic of conversation was Piers' completed book. Piers had shown Martin the finished typescript of his learned volume: six hundred pages of closely reasoned philosophical argument. It was due to be published the following year. Martin felt the weight of the pages, but knew himself to be incapable of understanding their content.

'It's a marvellous achievement, Piers,' he said. 'You must be very pleased . . .'

'I'll be lucky if three hundred people read it; I'm simply glad that it's over . . .'

'Are you going to write another one?'

'I'd like to, but not just yet.' Piers paused, and looked at the title page of his typescript. The book was entitled simply *Radical Discourse*.

To please Martin, Piers related the conclusion of his book to conversations which they had had together.

'It's really about "trying to get the point",' he said, 'and the difficulty of locating the moment of meaning – the pause between language and thought . . .'

Martin nodded. He assumed that the book was also concerned with those moments in which, in his own mind, all impressions – for better or worse – seemed to connect, and react to one another, and create a rare mood of insight.

'Do you ever think of being a journalist?' asked Martin.

Piers laughed. 'Why on earth would I want to do that?'

'To enable your ideas to reach a broader audience . . .'

'What makes you think that a "broader audience" want my ideas?'

'Well, there are all these new magazines, and supplements – they're all forums for debate and discussion; or so they say . . .'

'I sometimes read a Sunday paper,' said Piers, 'and it seems to me that a lot of contemporary journalism is wholly devoted to trivia. Now, I know that you think trivia is important, if you look at it in the right way, but it isn't. Some of us live in a culture where details are telling – that's all. It means nothing to the big wide world . . .'

'But you just said that you'd be lucky if three hundred people read your book. Aren't you locked up in a similar ghetto to journalists? Only your ghetto is academia?'

Piers looked at the floor, and patted his hands together. 'But I'm not in the entertainment business,' he said, 'which is what, I think, most modern journalism tries to be. There's this inane belief that all ideas are equal, and that with a little bit of smooth talking and cod philosophising any subject will lend itself to concrete theory. Consider the language of features journalism: an endless repetition of hyperbole, inaccurate history and narcissistic contrariness . . .'

'It assumes a sophisticated readership, that's all . . .'

'Wrongly. Call me an élitist, but at least the people who read my book will have to know their subject in order to understand it . . . Does that seem conceited?'

'No,' said Martin, dully, 'I think you're probably right . . .'

Piers and Martin were sitting in the drawing room at Ash House when they had this conversation. It was the second week in November 1989. Outside, the evening was cold and damp. Marilyn was visiting a friend. Martin's attention, however, was only partially focused upon the discussion. The bulk of his thoughts were occupied with worries about debt. He had not, in the past, mentioned his debts to Piers. He was ashamed of them. Lacking in his own eyes a true intellectual status, he could not bear the thought of denying the material wealth which he was perceived to enjoy. Latterly, most of Martin's monthly income was spoken for twice over by interest and loan repayments. An increasing overdraft kept in step with his life, never once falling behind. All that remained of the couple's independent wealth was £16,000 of Aunt Jennie's money. This sum, while substantial, was inadequate to finance the borrowing upon which Martin and

Marilyn's lives were based. Mortgage, credit cards, charge cards, bank loan and overdraft – they all had to be serviced. Martin's anxiety was increased by Marilyn's growing desire to have a baby. Martin had read in a magazine that it now cost £80,000 to bring up a child. He had come to believe this fact. In 'practical' discussions, Martin had outlined the scope of his fears to Marilyn, who had listened in silence.

'But where's all the money gone?' she said. 'I don't see how we've spent so much . . .'

'It's all been spent in restaurants and shops,' said Martin, 'and in living here like this . . .'

'But I thought that we were building a home . . .'

Now, as the term 'Recession' was being used more and more frequently to describe the state of the British economy, Martin felt himself to be as much a victim of debt as he had been a beneficiary of credit.

'But suppose we lived in a council flat,' said Marilyn, 'and you were out of work?'

Martin looked at his wife.

'And a baby dies once every eight minutes in Calcutta,' he said; 'it's all proportional, or relative. The banks want . . .'

'I know what the banks want. You've told me a thousand times – but it's not hopeless . . .'

'Oh, Marilyn . . .'

To Martin, it was hopeless.

At last he explained his problems to Piers. The academic, attempting to comfort with reason, ran through the financial details one by one as Martin had described them. He then offered a list of options. Wearily, Martin countered each solution with a fact.

'The truth of the matter,' he said, 'is that we're twenty thousand short . . .'

At this, the corners of Piers' mouth drooped, and he raised his eyebrows. Martin suddenly sat up.

'I say,' he said, 'I hope you don't think I'm going to ask for a loan?'

Piers smiled. 'I'm just a poor student,' he said. 'Your best bet is to keep in regular contact with your bank and all the credit-card people; bombard them with information . . .'

'I do,' said Martin, glumly.

'Being middle-class,' said Piers, 'you have an in-built need to confess . . .'

Martin sighed.

'That's true,' he said.

Dicky Alryn, too, was beset with money worries. The properties in Edgware had finally been completed, but nobody wanted to buy them.

'The market's dead,' said the estate agent, 'even for this calibre of property. And unfortunately, these are just on the wrong side of the road to long-let to an embassy. But we still get some interest in renting from overseas . . .'

Bayswater Property Management, therefore, was heavily in debt.

'It'll cost us thousands just to keep the damn things on the market,' said Bob Ensall, 'but all we can do is hope . . .'

Up and down the country, it seemed, people with business interests were hoping.

Dicky decided to sell Resol.

At that company, the fear of redundancy began to hang in the air. The business park, throughout the cold, wet early winter, seemed to crouch beneath a heavy sky. The young trees were bent by the wind; the long grass was sodden; the surface of the lake appeared to ripple angrily. The twilit afternoons seemed grim; the air smelt of iron and frozen ditches. So quickly, the Resol branch offices in Manchester, Edinburgh and Brussels had been closed down. Dicky's problem was an explosion of Martin's: too much money had been borrowed, and too little was being earned. For several weeks, the founder of Resol was engaged in lengthy meetings with his accountants. Unless the company could be sold (which seemed unlikely) receivership threatened.

On the 28th of December 1989, Martin and Marilyn were having dinner with Mrs Knight at Ash House. Before them, on large white plates, there were slices of smoked salmon garnished with halved lemons. Martin was on holiday, and the day had been spent in visiting the sales. Marilyn had bought a duvet, some bed linen, two jars of peppercorns and – from the shop in which she still worked – a packet of French tea-towels. Martin, bored by these domestic purchases, had sat for an hour in the café of the Arnolfini Gallery beside the docks, and drunk coffee. He had enjoyed watching the light upon the water and, being alone, he felt himself to be interesting once more. He liked the whiteness of the gallery; an exhibition of minimal sculptures had soothed him. He wanted silence, and a cessation of responsibility to dialogue. The plain, uncrafted works on display had seemed to embody this quality. For fifteen minutes he had gazed at a length of plastic guttering which was resting gently upon a long isthmus of pale sand. He had no idea what the sculpture was supposed to mean, but he had ceased to care. He simply enjoyed its mute presence. That morning, Martin had received a letter from Rupert Hook, a friend of his who lived in London. 'London's dead,' the letter had said, 'and no one has relationships any more. We've put the flat on the market, but even here in sunny Battersea there's no one coming to view it. We'd like to move to Europe, and Georgina's trying to find out about teaching, or translation work. I don't know what I'd do though – I just want to get away . . .' 'Getting away', Martin reflected, was all that people seemed to talk about now: 'We'd love to get away,' or 'We're trying to get away . . .' Martin's favourite record, that winter, had contained the refrain:

309

I've been getting away with it,
All my life . . .

Thus, dinner that evening was quiet. Mrs Knight was leaving the following morning, and there was a sense that the New Year holiday would be little more than a cheerless convention.

'That's the phone,' said Marilyn, without looking up.

'I'll get it,' said Martin.

He made his way to the study, and lifted the receiver before the answer-phone could intercept the call.

'Hello?'

'Martin? Dick Alryn here . . .'

'Oh, hello – have you had a good Christmas?'

'I'm afraid not; that's what I've got to speak with you about, and I don't want to drag things on . . .' The older man sounded weary, and resigned. Martin's heartbeat quickened. Dicky got straight to the point.

'I've got to let you go, Martin,' he said. His tone was apologetic, even fond. 'As you know, things haven't worked out the way that any of us would have wanted this year, and Resol, I'm afraid, will have to be wound up . . .'

Martin sat down.

'Can you hold on a minute?' he said.

'Surely.'

Martin went to light a cigarette. Marilyn looked up at him enquiringly as he was fumbling with the packet. His fingers were shaking.

'Who is it?' she said.

'I'll tell you in a minute . . .'

Returning to the study, Martin picked up the receiver once more and listened to his employer in the darkness. Dicky was brisk and practical. He explained that Martin would not be required to work his notice, and that he would be entitled to three months' pay.

'I'm extremely sorry, Martin – but business is business, and it's the same all over; you'll be getting a good reference from me, count on that, and I'm sure that you'll find something else . . .'

'What about you?' asked Martin, sentimentally loyal.

'Well – we'll see. Of course you can come in and clear your desk – any time. Now, I'm afraid that I've got several more calls to make . . .'

Hanging up the phone, Martin sat in the dark study. He felt extremely still, and quiet. Absurdly, he could only think of the prospect of unlimited holiday, and a chance to relax and pursue his own interests. In some ways, his sudden redundancy made him feel light-hearted. And then his glance fell upon a letter from his bank. Its whiteness, in the dark room, represented a demand for payment. Marilyn looked into the room and switched on the light.

'Martin? What are you doing? Who was it?'

Martin raised his head, but found that he could not speak. The edifice of his contentment had just crashed down upon him.

Eight: *Life*

Having been made redundant in December 1989, Martin Knight's misplaced sense of liberation was short-lived. Faced with mounting debts, his search for a new job was driven by a panic which made him restless and anxious. He felt as though he was staring directly into an abyss. Throughout the months of January and February 1990, he divided his time between looking for work and calculating his budget. He became obsessed by money, and would weary his wife by offering detailed analyses of their bank statements and credit-card bills. His mood would swing daily between elation and despair: a solution to the predicament would appear to present itself – and then evaporate; a conversation with the bank manager would provoke first optimism, and then rage.

'They don't care,' Martin would say. 'They're making a bloody fortune out of us . . .'

Marilyn, who busied herself with small practical jobs, would pause in her work to listen to Martin's complaints.

And then he would cite vague examples, excitedly, of companies and couples who were on the rack of debt. In this manner, Martin's years of snobbery found new expression as outrage. He was happiest when he could find some evidence to prove that the couple's situation was symptomatic of the times.

He quickly realised that he would not find a job in Bristol that would pay him an adequate salary: the larger companies were not hiring new staff; the remainder of the situations vacant in the local papers appeared to comprise of jobs in security, tele-sales and mini-cabbing. Then, turning to the national newspapers, Martin found advertisements for suitable jobs in Northampton, Luton, Birmingham and Sanderstead.

'But what about the flat?' said Marilyn. 'We'd have to sell the flat first, and that could take for ever . . .'

Despite this objection, Martin applied for three of the distant positions. He was not invited to attend an interview for any of them. These rejections increased his despair.

'I'm either too old or too young,' he said; 'I'm either over-qualified or under-qualified . . .'

Marilyn sighed.

'Don't worry,' she said. 'Something will turn up; and we're not about to find ourselves on the street!'

Martin drew no comfort from this. In his imagination, he pictured the beautiful apartment at Ash House being repossessed. Daily, he read of such cases in the newspapers.

The lowest point came at the beginning of March. The weather was cold, and the damp air was filled with freezing drizzle; in the city centre, the lights in the offices looked yellow and dismal; the heavy sky was low. Day and night, to Martin, appeared to be indistinguishable. The previous week he had attended an interview for a position in the Data Preparation department of a large company based in Croydon. The following Monday he received a brief letter which told him that he had not been successful.

'Well, that's that . . .' he said.

'I'm sorry,' said Marilyn.

Marilyn, too, had been seeking work.

'But I don't even have a curriculum vitae,' she said; 'it makes me feel so useless . . .'

She enrolled on a word-processing course and in the mean

time continued to work at Bella's shop. Bella, however, was going to close down her business. She was no longer making a profit, and her husband had been offered a job in the north, working on a project for the Canals and Waterways Preservation Scheme.

'We could sell the Peploe,' said Martin, one evening, half facetiously.

'Oh, Martin! Mummy would be furious! She'd sooner give us the money herself rather than part with that!'

Bill and Josephine were now living in Edinburgh. Bill, whose self-imposed exile had increased his cultural status, had been invited to make a new series of films for British and German television, about the history of the Communist Party in Europe. The small flat which Marilyn's parents had rented in Blackheath had been sold. Secretly, however, Martin had wondered whether or not Bill and Josephine would be able to 'help them out'. But, even if he could bring himself to suggest such a thing, it would only be a short-term solution.

'We could sell that horrible thing that you bought,' said Marilyn. 'Only we wouldn't get anything for it . . .'

'The thing is,' said Martin (frequently, throughout this period, Martin would begin his sentences with the words 'The thing is'), 'the thing is, we've got enough money to keep going like this for about nine months – if we're careful. We could put the flat on the market, but we'd probably end up losing a lot of money. That's if we could even sell it. Have you seen the number of For Sale boards down this road? It's like everyone's trying to get out. And when I think of what I got for the place in Vauxhall . . .'

Marilyn nodded. She wished that some solution could be found to their troubles, if only to put an end to the interminable discussions about their predicament. More practical than Martin, and less inclined towards self-pity, Marilyn felt as though she was constantly having to cosset an invalid. Her father, in fact, had already telephoned her and offered some money. Laughing, she had refused.

'Oh, Dad! Thank you – but it's not that bad . . .'

To Martin, the situation was that bad. But he did not know of Bill's offer.

The notion of returning to London had figured a great deal in Martin and Marilyn's conversations; but the cost of such a move, unless 'a really marvellous opportunity' presented itself, was prohibitive.

'I remember Sally saying,' said Martin, '"You can't come back once you've gone" . . .'

'That makes it sound as though we're dead or something,' said Marilyn.

'Quite.'

As Martin compared his present anxiety and constriction to his former sense of affluence and autonomy, he recalled a phrase from a pop record: 'Living too late'. It's as though, he thought, we had simply drifted out to sea one day, beyond the end of the world . . . At other times he felt as though he was living through a war. In such a manner his romantic imagination and his sentimentality began to colour the way he saw the world around him. When he mourned the loss of his former opulence, his regret was similar to that of a person remembering their first lost love.

Then, quite suddenly, he had a stroke of luck. One morning during the second week of March he came across an advertisement in one of the national newspapers: computer operatives with marketing experience were required 'immediately' by a company whose office was based near the Marylebone Road, in the West End of London. At first, Martin merely glanced at the details of the job, and mechanically drew a ring around it with his pen. A few hours later, he read the advertisement once more, and called out to Marilyn:

'I think I've found something,'

Marilyn read the job description.

'Who are Hammer & Goodwood?' she asked.

'They do some kind of massive mail-order operation – I think . . .'

'It isn't selling, is it? They sometimes word these things really deceptively . . .'

Martin studied the advertisement once more.

'No, it can't be selling; it's data-processing and systems. And the salary isn't bad, either . . .'

'But it's in London . . .' said Marilyn.

'It's a job. It's got to be worth applying, surely?'

Marilyn agreed.

Thus, with great care, Martin 'applied in writing' to Hammer & Goodwood at Mendial House, and enclosed a copy of his curriculum vitae. Three days later, he was asked to attend an interview.

Mendial House was a five-storey, glass-fronted cube which stood in a quiet street on the west side of Marylebone High Street. It had been built in 1972, for Hammer & Goodwood's American-owned parent company. By 1990, both the building and its furnishings looked shabby and worn out. An expression-less man of vague middle age called Dennis Coleman interviewed Martin in a small, plain office: a desk, two chairs and a telephone were all that the little room contained. Its window looked down into a narrow mews, where the morning sun was dissolving a light frost.

'What we're looking for, urgently,' said Mr Coleman, 'are people who'll require the absolute minimum of on-the-job training. Also, you'll have to be prepared to work some weekends. Transfer – where you'd be working – is basically a data clearing-house for five different mail-order services. I'm afraid that from your point of view the work would be pretty repetitive; and you would have to be one-hundred-per-cent accurate . . . From this' (he gestured at Martin's application), 'it looks as though you've got the relevant systems experience. In fact, you might be exactly what we're looking for . . .' Mr Coleman's features were disturbed by a brief, mirthless smile.

Martin nodded. His only desire was to earn a guaranteed salary. Having been warned in advance that his new employment would be boring, he felt like a character in mythology, being sent to endure a fantastic fate.

'I can start as soon as you want,' he said.

In this manner, Martin became a computer operative in the Transfer department of Hammer & Goodwood.

Martin and Marilyn had to come to terms with a new and complicated routine.

'You can't possibly commute from here,' said Marilyn. 'It would take hours; and think of the cost . . .'

Martin agreed. Driving to work, too, would be out of the question. He had just five days to work out what to do.

'It's a pity my mother's moved – otherwise I could have stayed with her; but even so . . . The job's flexi-time, so maybe I can work out some way of dividing my time between here and . . .'

At this point, Martin paused. Marilyn was silent, sitting at the kitchen table with her head bowed. So far, the couple had not addressed the impact that Martin's new job would have upon their relationship.

'I'll miss you so much,' said Martin.

'Drastic times call for drastic measures,' replied Marilyn with a brave smile. 'I just think,' she continued, 'that you'll be far better off working, and us having to adjust, than you would be mooching about here feeling irritable and depressed . . .'

'I suppose you're right.' Martin wondered whether Marilyn's stoical pragmatism hinted at indifference.

And then Marilyn used a particular phrase which worked upon her husband's sense of self-worth and seemed to make the new situation bearable.

'What you need is a little place in town,' she said pensively.

Immediately, Martin seized upon the notion of having a town address and a country home.

'That's it!' he said. 'Just a room perhaps – or a tiny flat – somewhere within easy reach of the West End . . .' In his mind, he pictured a small mews flat, with a window box and geraniums. Marilyn tempered this vision with common sense.

'But wouldn't it be dreadfully expensive? I mean, more expensive than staying the way we are?'

'But there are loads of rooms to rent . . .'

Martin would not be put off. That afternoon, he telephoned two south London estate agents who dealt in rented property.

'We can send you a list,' said a young woman at the second estate agency, 'or you can come into the branch. We've got rooms, bedsits and studio flats to rent right across the Tooting, Balham, Streatham, Dulwich belt . . .'

She made the process of renting a single room appear simple and affordable. An appointment was made for the following day.

But in order to make his new position worth accepting, Martin could only afford to pay £50 a week in rent. He was shown a succession of shabby, airless and expensive rooms. It was like being a student again. More than once, he thought of simply giving up. Finally, at five o'clock in the afternoon, he was shown a bed-sitting room in Streatham. He didn't know what to do. The flat was affordable but ugly. He consulted Marilyn. She told him, with a sigh, to take it.

He moved in that weekend. Marilyn gave him a small bowl of hyacinths, which was awkward to carry.

At Bristol Station, the reality of the situation overcame the young couple and made them sad.

'Shall I come with you?' said Marilyn. 'I just can't bear the thought of you travelling all the way up there alone, and then sleeping in some dismal room . . .' Her eyes were bright with tears.

Martin hugged his wife. He was reminded of films from the Second World War: the embarking soldier, the tearful wife.

'I'll be all right,' he said; 'I'll call you later – if I can find a phone!'

'Oh, you must call me; and remember, I'll come to pick you up on Friday, and we'll have a lovely weekend together . . .'

The separation was uniting Martin and Marilyn. Martin, however, as he took his seat on the quiet Sunday-evening train, felt remote and timid.

That night, as Martin and Marilyn were lying awake in different cities, the situation seemed incredible, and threatening.

Over the course of his first weeks in Streatham, Martin tried to get used to his surroundings. Reaching his little room at dusk, he would sit beside the window and stare down into the street, scarcely thinking. Initially, he had missed Marilyn dreadfully, and thought that he would never be able to persevere with the cruel manner in which he was having to earn a wage. Then his sense of isolation increased: somehow, his new routine would not connect with the sequence of events which had led up to it. He felt displaced, and bewildered; he carried himself carefully, as though he was afraid of breaking. At night, he tried to read his favourite novels, but could not lose himself in their stories. All things appeared distant and altered.

The early-spring evening would fill the street with blue light; the softening air seemed to caress the tall, melancholy houses brooding behind their ramshackle front gardens, and every now and then a cold breeze would rise up, flapping the coloured pennants which hung above the forecourt display of the garage across the road, or turning the pages of a dropped newspaper that was lying in the gutter.

It was a very long street. It ran, in fact, like a river, altering its width as it passed through the outer city, in and out of the shadows thrown across its path by tall buildings, and then pressing on into a land of compromise, where rows of suburban villas sat quietly beneath a low sky. The street changed its name, too, from district to district: where one stretch would be labelled 'High Road', the next would be called 'Lane'; where the street divided to accommodate some slender island of shabby offices, or a parade of little shops backed with cluttered yards, so too did the identity of the street divide, one half becoming 'Upper' and the other 'Lower'; and then the two halves would join up again, like tributaries flowing back into the main stream. The street went on and on, following a course which began as a delta of roads near the Elephant & Castle, gathered strength to cut a channel through the length of south London and finally petered out amidst roundabouts and dual carriageways somewhere on the borders of Surrey.

Martin's accommodation was in an old house which stood half-way down the street. It was a far cry from the mews flat of his imagination, but it was cheap, and convenient for the station. His rooms were on the first floor, with scuffed doors which opened directly onto a dark communal landing. Above and below him lodged strangers: unseen figures who would stamp up and down the stairs late at night, fumbling for their keys. Martin never seemed to see them.

The rooms were not comfortable, and Martin was loath to personalise them. Such a process would have hinted at permanency. At the front was his bedroom: tall-ceilinged, lit by a dirty bay window and sparsely furnished with a narrow bed, a tall thin wardrobe, a glass-topped table and three chromium chairs without cushions – a hotch-potch of sale-room items that the landlord had bought cheap as a single lot. The walls of the bedroom were painted pale green, the ceiling white. On either side of the mantelpiece, which framed a boarded-up fireplace, there was an alcove, and each of these contained three shelves, upon which Martin placed his cassette player and a few books. Other than this, he had inherited an assortment of oddments from the previous tenant: two candlesticks, heavily encrusted with blackened wax, two cardboard boxes filled with old magazines and a baker's plastic tray. Martin didn't like to throw these things away. There was also, pathetically, an old wine bottle which contained a single peacock feather.

The other room was the kitchen: tiny, cramped, dark and odoriferous. Day and night a small tongue of flame could be seen burning in the water heater, and there was always a feeble smell of gas. A broken cupboard, a stained breakfast bar and an ancient two-ringed cooker comprised the contents of this room. Annexed to the kitchen, in a kind of cupboard, there was a tiled shower room with lavatory and basin. During his first weeks in these rooms, Martin scrubbed and cleaned and disinfected every accessible surface. As he did so, he remembered the manner in which the apartment at Ash House had been decorated, and the lengths to which the couple had gone to find soaps that matched the frame of the mirror in the guest bathroom. We'll give it six months, thought Martin, as he stared down into the street, and then we'll put the flat on the market – unless something good happens . . .

Through the kitchen window of his little flat, Martin could look down into the yard of a disused church. The name of this church could still be made out, traced in faded gold letters upon its fallen noticeboard: St Peter's. St Peter's was a large, featureless red-brick building which dated from the 1920s. It had heavy buttresses and tall windows whose glass was smashed beneath sheets of rusted wire netting. The path was overgrown with weeds, and the grass in the yard was nearly waist-high. Used as a common dumping-ground, this tangled acre of deconsecrated land was now full of rubbish. An abandoned car formed the centrepiece, crouching in a luxuriance of burdock.

'It's pretty dreadful,' said Martin to Marilyn when he returned to the comfort of Ash House at the end of his first week. 'It's kind of studenty – without the students. But it's only temporary – let's hope. We'll just have to see how it goes . . .' He could not conceal his depression as he said this.

'I miss you,' said Marilyn, 'I miss you so much. I get terribly lonely – is it really worth all this hassle?'

Martin sighed.

'It's like the bank manager said: we've either got to pay off our debts, or service them. Obviously, if a job comes up down here I'll take it like a shot. In the mean time, we'll just have to make the best of it . . .'

Marilyn nodded sadly, and held Martin's hand without looking at him.

At nine in the morning of Thursday, 26th April 1990, Martin was sitting on a scarlet metal bench at Streatham Hill Station. His black briefcase, which contained nothing more than a packet of cigarettes and a book, was resting flat upon his knees. He was staring directly ahead with an unblinking gaze. The morning was cold, despite pale sunshine, and the station smelt dank, like a river after a heavy shower of rain. The smell of damp and mud seemed to come from the overgrown escarpment of the steep cutting which rose up behind the station buildings beyond the opposite platform. Looking up, Martin could see the back fences of the parade of small shops which lined the top of the cutting. The station was old, and had an air of neglect. Martin was dimly aware of other commuters assembling around him. His black Italian suit was nearly three years old, and in certain lights its fabric displayed a threadbare shine; the cuffs of his thick black overcoat, too, were wearing thin. The toes of his hand-made shoes were scuffed.

As he waited for his train, the young man recalled the time, six years earlier, when he had always seemed to be going to dinner parties at addresses on one or other of south London's hills: Streatham Hill, Herne Hill, Denmark Hill, Gipsy Hill, Forest Hill,

Tulse Hill . . . That was before the hosts and hostesses of such occasions had either moved up or moved out. There had been a confidence then. 'We're quite close to the grotty bit,' people used to say, referring to their first bought property, 'but there's this fabulous grocery shop which stays open till all hours; and it's really handy for the station . . .' Of course, when one arrived, one discovered a pleasant ground-floor apartment in a Victorian terrace. The couple upstairs might have left their bicycles in the narrow hall, but the warmth of money had never seemed distant. Such comfortable apartments, six years earlier, had comprised the transit-camp of the young middle classes.

And then Martin's train arrived, seven minutes late.

When Martin started work in Transfer, he was determined to offer little information about himself to his fellow workers. Silence, he felt, was both a good weapon and an adequate means of defence. There were seven other computer operatives: four men and three women. Most of them were people whose computer skills far outweighed their ability to manage staff or carry out general administrative duties. In this much, the staff in Transfer were not young; also, most of the operatives were people who, for one reason or another, were not pursuing a definite career. The joke at Hammer & Goodwood was that Transfer was like the Foreign Legion: its members had joined to forget. In terms of importance, Transfer ranked equally with Sales, who were housed on the floor above. Beneath Transfer and Sales, within the hierarchy of the office departments, were Cat. Sec. (Accounts), STAT and Waste. Waste was housed in the basement. The administrative departments were known simply as Typing, Mailing, and so forth.

The dress code in Transfer was casual. Martin, had he so chosen, could have worn jeans and a pullover to the office. As it was, he wore one or other of his old suits. Romantically, he wanted to appear anonymous. This affectation was of no interest to the other workers in Transfer. A shift system was in operation, to clear an accumulated backlog of work, and thus both flexi-time and overtime were available. The computer operatives worked out a rota between themselves, which was described and amended in scarlet-coloured felt-tip pen on a 'whiteboard' that hung just inside the door. The office, with its regularly spaced work-stations, was white, low-ceilinged and oblong in shape. The only furnishings were functional, and there was no attempt at decoration. The operatives knew that they were being paid well for their work, and were inclined to keep a steady pace rather than rushing towards the end of their task. The office estimate was that there was enough systems work to last for a year. This calculation did not take into account the generation of new 'transfers'. Martin, in fact, had little idea of what a 'transfer' was: he could function accurately within his section of the system, but he had no interest in where the data which he processed went to, or where it had come from. Len Dowlson, the office wit, had said that Transfer's computerate function was the practice of artificial stupidity.

Floor-to-ceiling windows looked down from Transfer into the street. Martin's desk was facing the window and from this position he could see the rooftops of Marylebone, which stretched away to the north side of Oxford Street. At first he felt so displaced that he could scarcely believe he was back in London, amongst buildings and streets which he knew well, and which possessed many memories for him. It was as though his new routine was separated by decades from his previous experience of the capital. He could not articulate this sensation to himself, but sometimes his 'vagueness' was so acute that it frightened him. Also, he was lonely. The staff in Transfer were polite, and would occasionally pass an afternoon in fragmented conversation between themselves, but they always looked faintly surprised when Martin asked a question. Nobody asked where he came from, or why he was working at Hammer & Goodwood.

Whilst this lack of interest corresponded with Martin's desire for anonymity, it also increased his sense of isolation and his feeling of 'living too late'. With little to distract him from this mood, Martin even began to feel remote from Marilyn. At weekends, when he returned to Ash House, he would eat well, sleep heavily and worry his wife by seeming so down-hearted. He no longer appeared to respond to his surroundings. In short, he felt as though he resembled the magnolia-coloured painting.

'You must be tired though,' Marilyn said, 'and you're bound to have lost a lot of confidence. You worked so hard at Resol, and then suddenly it wasn't there any more . . .'

Martin nodded. He felt calm, and yet there was a nameless anxiety within his calm. The weekends were always gone too quickly for him to assess this nervousness, or explain it.

As spring turned into summer, Martin began to converse with one or two of his colleagues in Transfer. There was Len, whose red-rimmed eyes and eager humour always seemed to hint at a personal sense of insecurity, and Alison Hayes, a young woman from Lancashire who worked at the desk next to Martin's. Len told Martin jokes about 'Old Stan' in Mailing; Alison tried to explain the function of Transfer. Alison smoked heavily, and the basis of her friendship with Martin was the exchange of cigarettes. Initially, Martin had paid little attention to Alison; in his mind he had described her as 'studenty' – one of those stocky girls in denims, he thought, unkindly. And yet Alison was neither 'stocky' nor 'studenty'. Her brown hair was cut short, and she wore three silver studs in her left ear. Her face was pale and her eyes were grey. Her pretty mouth was usually set in a serious expression. She wore denim jeans and a pullover or T-shirt to the office. As the weather grew warmer, she wore training shoes without socks.

In the past Alison had worked for two unhappy years in the Civil Service, and then for British Airways. She shared a flat in Kennington with a fashionably dressed girl called Charlotte

Devon, who was also from the north. Charlotte worked in 'the rag trade', for a small company called Lucy Winkworth whose offices were in Great Portland Street. When Martin first conversed with Alison, he noticed that she seldom looked at him while she was speaking. Her accent was broad, and her tone firm. She seemed rather humourless. In her speech, appearance and deportment, Alison Hayes was utterly different to any of the women whom Martin had previously known. This made her appear interesting to him.

During the early summer of 1990, while Martin was feeling so removed from his usual sense of himself, he began to be fascinated by Alison. He studied her, and found her attractive; he felt his spirits rise when she arrived at the office in the morning, and he became irrationally depressed if he realised that she was not coming in to work. He questioned himself harshly about this development in his feelings; he accused himself of 'mental infidelity' and immaturity. He determined to speak casually about Alison to Marilyn, in order to puncture his interest – but he never did. He carried his silent fascination with the northern girl around with him like a secret. In his shabby room in Streatham, he pondered on what might happen if he was not married; and then he dismissed these wild projections as being nothing more than rambling fantasies provoked by boredom. And yet he could not deny his newly focused feelings, and he began to feel terrorised by them. He told himself that he 'had had enough of women', and that he had no desire to complicate his life further. He hated the notion of pursuing a deceitful, illicit affair. Also, he hardly knew Alison. But time and time again he would soothe himself to sleep by thinking of her grey eyes, or of a romantic scenario in which Alison was offering him a new life filled with promise and optimism. He accused himself, bitterly, of letting Marilyn down, and he determined sincerely never to pursue his new emotions. He disgusted himself; and he felt sorry for himself.

*

One afternoon in August, Alison tried to explain a 'Transfer Sheet' (TRAN 1) to Martin. She was wearing white jeans and a short-sleeved shirt which was the colour of black cherries. Martin was wearing a dark green linen suit, the jacket of which was hanging on the back of his chair. The office was warm, and the desks in front of the window received the full glare of the sun. A heat haze was shimmering above the rooftops of Marylebone. Martin had spent his lunch hour wandering up and down Oxford Street, listening to the loud pop music that was being played in some of the shops, and staring at clothes that he could no longer afford.

Alison and Martin both had cans of fruit juice and mineral water before them. They felt disinclined to work, despite Mr Coleman's instructions to 'take on board' a new aspect of systems procedure. The sound of files being delivered by Mailing into the Transfer pigeonhole resembled, to Martin, the noise of a shovel being dragged through wet cement. He tried to remember which poet it was who had been forced to build his own gaol, brick by brick. It was one of those afternoons when hot weather appears to lull London to sleep: an unnatural quiet hung over the streets; the sun was like a tyrant glowering down upon the city.

'We really ought to do some work,' said Alison, eventually; she leant forward in her chair, and tapped the screen of Martin's computer with her biro. 'Right; this is the order – I mean, the sequence – probably: press "enter" . . .'

'"Enter" will give us the sequence, probably . . .' said Martin. In the corner of his eye, he was aware of Alison's bare arm, and the fabric of her shirt stretching across her shoulder. She was wearing an eau-de-cologne which seemed to slice through the air.

'Go on – do it then . . .'

'Right . . .'

The screen revealed a list.

'There,' said Alison, leaning back in her chair again.

'Is that it?'

'Yes.'

Alison read out the sequence: 'Correspondence, STAT sheet, Registry sheet, PRC 3, *Transfer*, STAT 2 sheet, Closing sheet, Dead . . .'

'You pronounce the "tran" in "transfer" as though you were saying "can",' said Martin.

'This is going to turn into the old "baff" or "barth" debate, isn't it? I've heard it before, since I was six . . .'

The feigned enmity in this brief exchange seemed to add a flirtatious undercurrent to the conversation. In the past, Martin had noticed, Alison had deftly deflected his attempts to pay her slight compliments. She knows that I'm married, he thought. It's not as though I'm hiding anything, or being duplicitous . . . Martin believed that he deserved some romantic reward as recompense for the ugliness of Streatham.

'What's a "Dead"?' he asked.

'It's what they do in Waste, poor things . . . It's the soul of a transfer – like a receipt on hard copy . . . Do you want a cigarette?'

Martin and Alison lit cigarettes. Work stopped.

'You're from Blackpool aren't you?' said Martin. As he said this, he noticed once more that Alison possessed a style which was distant from Marilyn's expensive good taste. He tried to compare the two women and, with a dull crease of unease which tugged at his conscience, he realised that he could not picture Marilyn.

'From just outside Blackpool, actually,' said Alison, 'a place called Lytham, which you won't have heard of . . .'

'I have, as it happens,' lied Martin.

'What about you?'

'Oh, I'm a product of the suburbs . . .'

'All carriage-lamps and carports?'

'Something like that . . .'

'And what about your wife?' Alison asked this question clearly, as though eager for information.

'She's from London – Greenwich . . .'

'Oh! Now, Charlotte wants to live in Greenwich. I don't mean to be rude, but that's typical of Charlotte. She's got this real thing about living the yuppie life: designer knitwear and playing Trivial Pursuit . . . But she gets it all wrong. At heart she's a clubber, and she tries so hard to be really incredibly fashionable . . .'

Martin smiled. Instinctively, he wanted to win Alison's admiration, albeit temporarily.

'It's nearly five o'clock,' said Alison.

'It can't be; what time did we start?'

'Well, I got back from lunch at three, so . . .'

'We haven't achieved very much,' said Martin. He was waiting for Alison to announce that she was going home.

'We can carry on, if you want . . .' said Alison, suddenly; 'I'm not doing anything . . .' Martin's spirits lifted.

'It's overtime, I suppose,' he said.

His resolve weakened, and he felt his being become complicit with a process of protracted seduction. As if to compensate for this sensation, and to salve his conscience, he said firmly:

'I must ring my wife, though; I said I would . . .'

This phrase sounded ugly. Alison smiled.

'Well, you do that,' she said. 'I'm going out to get another drink. Do you want one?'

'You could get me a can of mineral water, thanks . . .'

Martin watched Alison as she strode out of the office, rubbing the back of her head. She suddenly seemed taller, and she appeared to move with an easy, fluid grace. She had recently had her hair cut, with the back and sides shaved, and this new style looked simple and cool. Glancing down, Martin felt a surge of happiness as he saw Alison's bag beside his desk: it was proof that the young woman would be returning. Then, telephoning Marilyn, Martin spoke of the heat, and the boredom of work. He was particularly loving, and said that he 'couldn't wait' to see Marilyn at the weekend. Marilyn, too, was in a good mood. Catherine was coming to see her, while Stewart was away at a conference; they would be having a 'girly evening', she said. This news made Martin feel better about his excitement in the face of pursuing his friendship with Alison; an irrational and unfounded sense of virtue overcame him: his guilt dissolved. Fondly, he said:

'Now that some of the debts are under control, let's hope that we can get our lives in order. I don't want you to be a debt-widow for much longer; we didn't get married to spend so much time apart . . .'

'Well, thank God we can cope with it,' said Marilyn.

That night, Martin could not sleep. He began to invoke a fantasy from childhood in order to find comfort in his bed and gain a few hours of sleep. This exercise commenced with his imagining a distant landscape, on the far side of a tract of hostile terrain. Then he pictured the route that he would have to follow in order to reach this place: overgrown woods of spreading, wide-girthed trees, high moorlands strewn with wet rocks, and dank forests. But even as he sketched in the outlines of this fantastic geography, his doze was disturbed by images of himself: a weak, affected figure who had spent his life showing off. This jolt of awareness caused him to wake up. Pathetically, in the darkness, he called out Marilyn's name.

Then a pageant of obscene images made its way through his imagination. Disported bodies, reflecting both Alison and Marilyn, became willing participants in a vast and loveless orgy. The theatricality of their exaggerated gestures provoked first fascination and then disgust.

At dawn, fully awake, Martin sat by his dirty bay window and smoked a cigarette. Reviewing his situation, he felt himself to be trapped on all sides: worries about money, the absence of Marilyn and the boredom of Transfer all seemed to form a souring of the spirit that was reflected in everything he looked at. The West End shops, with their closing-down sales; the stupidity of newspapers and adverts; the sight of once-fashionable restaurants with their windows whitewashed over; the rampant Americanisation of young people; the ubiquitous beggars on every corner; the sense of having lived beyond one's time . . .

And then Martin accused himself of being trivial and spoilt. You just think that your own discomfort is significant, he told himself; you think that it matters . . . Why do you think that it matters so much?

Sick of himself, and sick of thinking, Martin could not answer himself. He simply wanted to go home.

The following day, Martin resigned from Hammer & Goodwood.

'Not on my account, I hope!' joked Alison.

Mr Coleman accepted Martin's resignation with the same mirthless smile that he had offered five months earlier.

'You've sorted something out a little closer to home?' he asked, politely.

'I hope so,' said Martin.

As he was leaving Mendial House for the last time, Martin felt as though he was walking into a vast whiteness. His few belongings from Streatham were packed in his suitcase; he had returned the key to the flat to the agency.

'We can't refund your deposit,' said the young woman who had co-signed the lease, 'because you didn't give us any notice . . .'

She looked angry.

'That's all right,' said Martin, 'you can keep it . . .'

'There's no need to be rude . . .'

But Martin had already left the small, brightly lit agency. His heavy suitcase banged against the door as he closed it. This was an accident.

The young woman stared at Martin's retreating figure, and for a moment she despised him.

In order to surprise Marilyn, Martin simply arrived at Ash House early that evening. He found his wife sitting in the drawing room watching television. Martin, seeing how neat and tidy the apartment was, felt tears well up in his eyes. He was clutching a large bunch of roses which he had bought at Bristol Station.

'Oh! Martin! You surprised me!' Marilyn jumped up from her chair, and hugged her husband. 'And flowers!' she said. 'Is everything all right?'

'I've resigned,' said Martin. 'I just couldn't stand it any more . . .'

Marilyn was overjoyed at this piece of news.

'Really? Really and truly you've packed it in?'

'Yes. We're paupers now . . .'

Martin put down his suitcase and the flowers, and held both of Marilyn's hands. She smiled at him, radiantly, and couldn't speak.

'You've got no idea,' she kept saying. 'You've just got no idea . . .'

'Any chance of a cup of tea?' said Martin, enjoying the sensation he had caused.

'Oh . . . Martin. I can't tell you how much I've wanted you; but I couldn't make you – you understand that, don't you? But I've been wishing and wishing that you'd come back, and I nearly phoned you, and now you're here . . .'

'You're not annoyed? You're not going to send me back?'

'Oh, never, never . . .'

'It's going to be all right,' said Martin. 'Everything's going to be all right . . .'

Marilyn took a deep breath, and then paused. She was trying to make an announcement.

'I know that everything's going to be all right,' she said, 'because you're back – and I'm pregnant!'

Martin's mind went blank.

Later, Martin tried to calculate the date when their child had been conceived. The last weekend in June 1990 was the only occasion he could think of. He had been distracted, and Marilyn had felt nervous, their bodies had come together clumsily, and their love-making had been self-conscious and brief.

'And I thought you were still on the pill!' he said, two days after Marilyn had announced her pregnancy.

'Well, that's where you were mistaken!' replied his wife, artfully.

'Who else knows?'

'My parents, and Catherine – they're so pleased . . .' Marilyn was silent for a moment. 'And you are pleased, aren't you?'

'More pleased than I ever thought I would be . . .'

'Well, thanks . . .'

'No – I didn't mean it like that. I am pleased, really. It just takes a bit of getting used to . . .'

'I know; I'm sorry . . .'

Marilyn took Martin's hand.

'I just don't know what we're going to do for money,' sighed Martin.

'There'll be other jobs,' said Marilyn; 'and we can put the flat on the market; and Daddy said that he'll help, just to see us through . . .'

'That's incredibly kind of him, but . . .'

'If it's a girl,' said Marilyn, 'I want her to be called Lucy; and if it's a boy . . .'

'But the poor child's going to be dressed in rags unless we find some money . . .'

'No child of mine,' said Marilyn, 'is going to be dressed in rags . . .'

At this, Martin determined to find a new job. The thought of this was both depressing and daunting, but a living urgency demanded that he must persevere. He did not know, however, whether he was driven by love or by his conscience.

By November 1991, Martin had managed to find a part-time job at the headquarters of a large travel company whose offices had been moved to Bristol. There was the hope that, in six months' time, this post would cease to be a job-share and be Martin's alone. He had gained this position after much searching, many dashed hopes and long periods of restless despair. His old confidence and his ability to impress authority had rescued him in the end. He was sent on training courses, and he worked hard to secure the confidence of his line-manager. He no longer questioned his dull work; he simply did it, and strove for promotion.

The flat at Ash House was on the market, but only one couple had been to visit it. Martin and Marilyn were in two minds as to whether or not they wanted to sell it. Marilyn had redecorated the study and turned it into a nursery. The walls were papered with a design of teddy bears who were wearing tutus and being carried off by large bunches of balloons. A Man In The Moon mobile hung from the curtain rail. A little white cot with lace-covered pillows and a collection of soft toys stood waiting for the baby. As the date of the baby's birth drew closer, Marilyn became increasingly cheerful.

'It's the best thing,' she would say to Martin. 'I don't think you understand, but it is . . .'

At first, Marilyn's certainty caused Martin much worry. He felt bewildered and frightened by the prospect of being responsible for a child. But he was careful to conceal these fears from his wife. He devoted himself to her needs with an excess of gallantry, and then, in the evenings or during his days off, he would sit for hours in the dining room – which had been renamed 'the smoking room' – and stare out of the window. The magnolia-coloured painting, he noticed, was beginning to show long cracks upon its surface. As the nights began to draw in, and as the couple became used to a gentle, considerate routine, a stillness seemed to settle upon the apartment that was both peaceful and profound.

One day shortly before Christmas, Marilyn spent the day in bed.

'Are you sure you're all right?' said Martin. 'Are you sure we oughtn't call the doctor?'

Marilyn looked up at her husband and smiled.

'I'm absolutely fine; don't worry,' she said, rearranging the duvet and pulling a magazine towards herself.

'You're sure?'

'You'd know all about it if I wasn't!'

Martin squeezed his wife's hand.

'If you need anything,' he said, 'just say, I'll be in the other room . . .'

'OK, I will – but don't worry. I'll get up later and have a bath . . .'

Having left the bedroom, Martin decided that he wanted to give his wife a pleasant surprise. He was overcome by the desire to comfort her, and to care for her. To this end, while Marilyn dozed Martin spent the afternoon decorating the Christmas tree in the drawing room. The previous day, Marilyn had said, 'It doesn't really feel like Christmas . . .'

Marilyn had always loved the glitter and sparkle of Christmas decorations. 'One of my favourite things,' she would say, 'is evergreen and silver . . .' Working with quiet determination, Martin installed the Christmas tree, hung it with silver glass ornaments and adorned it with small white lights. This task absorbed him, and he was pleased with his efforts as the early dusk fell. Outside, the black branches of the trees showed clearly against the evening sky. Then Martin built a log fire, and trimmed the mirrors and picture frames with holly. By the time that he heard Marilyn stirring and took her a cup of tea, the drawing room looked cosy, festive and warm. The Christmas tree sparkled in its corner; the fire threw out a rich wavering light. From time to time, the damp logs cracked and spat cinders. The smell of pine-needles and wood-smoke filled the air.

'What have you been up to?' asked Marilyn as she re-emerged from the bathroom. Her hair was tousled; she was wearing a long striped nightshirt and scarlet woollen socks.

'How do you feel?' said Martin.

'Fine; better for a sleep . . .'

'Come and have your tea . . .'

Marilyn, sensing Martin's childlike excitement, allowed herself to be led to the drawing room.

She gave a little cry when she saw the Christmas tree, the decorations and the cheerful fire.

'Oh, Martin! It's beautiful!' She hugged her husband, kissed him on the mouth, and held his shoulders as she smiled up at him.

'I'll make you some supper later,' said Martin, pleased with himself, 'and then we can watch *It's A Wonderful Life* on the video . . .'

'Have we got it? I love that film!'

'I borrowed it from someone at work . . .'

'We must put up something for the baby,' said Marilyn, still hugging her husband.

'I did.' Martin pointed towards the Man In The Moon, who was hanging in front of the window. There was a teddy bear directly beneath the mobile, with a big white ribbon tied in a bow about its neck.

'I just wish that I could make it snow for you,' said Martin. 'I do wish that . . .'

Marilyn rested her head against his shoulder.

'I know that you would if you could . . .' she said.

Martin smiled, and glanced towards the window. Then, unbidden, the thought of Alison Hayes passed through his mind and his features, for a second, became expressionless.

That night, after Marilyn had gone to bed, Martin crept into the dark smoking room once more. The room was warm and quiet. He pulled a comfortable chair to face the french windows, sat down and lit a cigarette. He didn't turn on the lights, for he found the darkness peaceful. Through the windows, in the distance, he could see the city lights. The night seemed still and cold. Not having smoked all evening, the cigarette relaxed him and focused his mind.

At first, he thought about a letter which he had received from Piers Harding, who was working at Princeton University, and which he had left unanswered. Somehow, he couldn't think of anything to write to his friend; the effort of trying to seem interesting or cheerful appeared pointless, and false. Then, as his gaze became fixed on a point of white light which was located somewhere in the middle distance, Martin ran over the pleasant evening in his mind. The couple, for the first time in many months, had relaxed and made plans. Both of them, he knew, had been aware of the struggle that lay ahead. But for once the struggle had seemed distant. The clock in the drawing room chimed one, and Martin lit another cigarette.

The baby, now, seemed quite real. Leaning back and barely moving save for the action of smoking, Martin imagined the process of bringing up the child. This direct speculation was new to him. So far, his worry had outweighed his ability to imagine parenthood. Now, in the dark, quiet room, his mind wandered. He pictured the infant, pretty but sexless, toddling between its parents in an autumnal park. It would be dressed in exquisite clothes, such as Martin had seen in the more expensive shops. Its hair would be left extravagantly long, for as long as possible, and it would wear a child's velvet hat, embroidered with sequins, which the father-to-be was sure he had seen on sale in Bristol. Martin smiled at the thought of dressing the child. He recalled the plain clothes of his own childhood.

As Martin's distant memories became bound up with imagining his own child, he saw himself as an approachable, yet slightly eccentric parent. At school, the infant would be given every opportunity to study art, or music; Martin would augment this process by taking the child to galleries and concerts. He saw himself sitting with Marilyn and their child listening to a piano recital; he imagined visits abroad, where he would explain the history of civilisation to a receptive young mind; and then there would be books: C. S. Lewis, John Masefield, Dickens, Lewis Carroll. In this child, Martin thought as he stared out of the window, he would find himself, and the opportunity to begin again on the task of getting to the point.

Above all, mused Martin, as his pleasant thoughts became vague with sleep, the child would be exposed to beauty.

MICHAEL BRACEWELL

Divine Concepts
of Physical Beauty

'Miles Harrier, well-bred, rich, good looking, but lacking energy and, on the evidence here, interesting thought or conversation, is loved from childhood, together and in turn, by three women: Kelly O'Kelly, occasional performance artist, pathologically withdrawn: Lucinda Fortune, a perky girl who does something vague in publicity; and Stella Walker-Jones, acme of female beauty, who became a model. Bracewell's subject is desire and what it means in a society in which everyone is judged by their appearance . . . What disturbs in this well turned and bleakly funny novel is the narrative voice. *Divine Concepts of Physical Beauty* is written as a fable. Character and motivation are much less important to the reader's pleasure than the plot devices, the authorial judgements, the worldly asides on adolescence and banality'
Guardian

'A wickedly funny novel'
Sunday Times

'As much a savage satire on modern English manners as it is a parable of adolescent dreams turning sour . . . Just as *The Crypto-Amnesia Club* appealed to those mysterious bits inside of us all, *Divine Concepts* seeks out the unexpected. Only this time, he goes deeper and wider. Indoor fireworks all the way'
Blitz

'What ultimately elevates Bracewell above the majority of his contemporaries is his ability to offset the bleakness of the tale by the human clarity of its telling . . . He eloquently creates a narrative gap in which the alienation of his characters may become accessible to his readers. A divine concept indeed. Embrace it well'
City Limits

ZINOVY ZINIK

The Mushroom Picker

'An extravagant farce set between the over-heated, cramped tenements of Moscow, which nourish a vigorous, uninhibited life, and the lawns of southern England, which nourish little at all. The story centres on the courtship – if seduction by pepper vodka and gherkin counts as courtship – and marriage of Kostya, a Russian for whom there is no greater good, in physical and spiritual terms, than the experience of eating, and Clea, a withering English liberal . . . Zinik's seemingly inexhaustible ability to make the metaphorical and symbolic profit from Kostya's obsession means that his novel is as inventive as it is witty'

James Campbell, *Observer*

'Zinik has both a great comic gift and an intricate critical mind . . . [he] is at his best when he allows himself to float way over the top'

Literary Review

'Zinik is well aware that national modes of humour contrast as much as anything else, and he exploits this as effectively as every other ingredient in his sexual and gastronomic farce. Seriousness and humanity are not mentioned in the recipe, but they help to season the brew; and deep down is the notion that communality survives socialism in the Soviet Union, but has not yet reached our shores'

Times Literary Supplement

ANDRÉ BRINK

A Dry White Season

Ben du Toit is an ordinary, decent, harmless man, unremarkable in every way – until his sense of justice is outraged by the death of a man he has known. His friend died at the hands of the police. In the beginning it appears a straightforward matter, an unfortunate error that can be explained and put right. But as Ben investigates further, he finds that his curiosity becomes labelled rebellion – and for a rebel there is no way back.

'The revolt of the reasonable . . . far more deadly than any amount of shouting from the housetops'
Guardian

'Impossible to recommend too highly'
Time Out

'Excellent . . . [a] harrowing and surprising story. The ultimate power of the book comes from an authoritative meditation on the traps that open up for someone who answers to himself before society'
Scotsman

'André Brink's writing is built on conviction . . . *A Dry White Season* describes the triumph of tyranny'
The Times

'Books like this one succeed . . . in drawing our emotions into politics. What will remain is the plain bravery of his characters . . . their struggle has found an honest chronicler.'
Telegraph

NICHOLAS MOSLEY

Accident

A fatal accident is the starting point of this elegantly plotted novel. The narrator is an Oxford don, whose explanation of the event induces him to interpret, via the games academics play both with their students and with themselves, in college and at home, in bed or on the river, the paradoxes of love and betrayal, marriage and infidelity. In showing how reality is not plotted but accidental, and how ethical values are necessarily created through language, Nicholas Mosley challenges the very stuff of fiction.

'A fascinating and original novel . . . Technically, *Accident* is remarkable'

Times Literary Supplement

'Nicholas Mosley's major theme is "the public face and the private helplessness". He writes particularly well the prose of shock, of the dead, small hours: and he also writes, as few can, of the pain and purpose of marriage'

Sunday Times

A Selected List of Fiction Available from Minerva

While every effort is made to keep prices low, it is sometimes necessary to increase prices at short notice. Mandarin Paperbacks reserves the right to show new retail prices on covers which may differ from those previously advertised in the text or elsewhere.

The prices shown below were correct at the time of going to press.

All these books are available at your bookshop or newsagent, or can be ordered direct from the publisher. Just tick the titles you want and fill in the form below.

Mandarin Paperbacks, Cash Sales Department, PO Box 11, Falmouth, Cornwall TR10 9EN.

Please send cheque or postal order, no currency, for purchase price quoted and allow the following for postage and packing:

UK including BFPO | £1.00 for the first book, 50p for the second and 30p for each additional book ordered to a maximum charge of £3.00.

Overseas including Eire | £2 for the first book, £1.00 for the second and 50p for each additional book thereafter.

NAME (Block letters) ....

ADDRESS ....

....

☐ I enclose my remittance for ....

☐ I wish to pay by Access/Visa Card Number

Expiry Date